Mutiny raged within . .

"Perhaps I can show you something to take your mind off your concerns," suggested Culliford, leering at her.

He turned and kicked open a heavy chest that sat at the foot of the bed. Wynn could not stifle a gasp. In the chest lay gold necklaces studded with amber and coral, pieces of Arabian and Christian gold, melted bars of silver. The other chest contained scarlet, green, sapphire, and blue Indian silks.

"Perhaps some of these things could be yours if you wished to cooperate with me."

Hatred mounted in her. "I would never lower myself to become mistress of a pirate captain," she spat at him.

He caught her wrists and pulled her to him, forcing her to face him. "A fiery little cat you are. Well, so much the better. Besides, you are already the mistress of a pirate, or didn't you know it?

"And do not think the native tribes will take any pity on you. In fact, should you cause me any trouble, I might make a gift of you to one of the Sakalava kings on the other side of the island. He is fond of white skin. . . ."

TIMBERS AND GOLD LACE

PATRICIA WERNER

PaperJacks LTD.

TORONTO   NEW YORK

AN ORIGINAL

PaperJacks

TIMBERS AND GOLD LACE

PaperJacks LTD

330 STEELCASE RD. E., MARKHAM, ONT. L3R 2M1
210 FIFTH AVE., NEW YORK, N.Y. 10010

PaperJacks edition published July 1987

This original PaperJacks edition is printed from brand-new plates made from newly set, clear, easy-to-read type. No part of this book may be reproduced or transmitted in any form or by any means, electronic or mechanical, including photography, recording, or any information storage or retrieval system, without permission in writing from the publisher.

ISBN 0-7701-0600-5
Copyright © 1987 by Patricia Werner
All rights reserved
Printed in the USA

For Iris, Katrin, Joe and Steve

Chapter One — 1696

A sailor's scream pierced the air, and Wynn froze. Clutching the shrouds that supported the foremast, she saw that a number of sailors had surrounded the captain's cabin, their pistols drawn, while on the quarterdeck above, others crouched, ready to spring, their knife blades glinting in the sun.

"By God, it's a mutiny," a voice behind her cried, and Wynn turned to see one of the ship's officers on the forecastle reaching for his firearm just as a mutineer jumped him from behind. From below deck, where most of the passengers were reclining at this time of day, Wynn heard the pummeling footsteps of sailors loyal to the captain who were rushing to his defense.

It was because Wynn preferred the open air on deck to her small stuffy cabin that she had been caught in the melee. As a shot rang out, she ducked near the railing, realizing that she was too far from the hatchway that led to the passengers' department to return. Frantically she looked about for a weapon with which to defend herself, but finding nothing that could suit the purpose she took refuge behind a barrel. She heard one of the mutineers call out his challenge.

"Come out, Captain, you're surrounded," she heard a mutineer cry, piercing through the din of fighting. For answer, a musket exploded within the great cabin, and smoke and fire belched forth, wounding two of the men standing in front of the cabin door.

"Get back you scoundrels," Wynn heard the captain yell, as he continued to blast forth fire and shot from the cabin door "I'm in command of this ship, and you'll not turn her to piracy."

So it was piracy the mutineers were bent on, Wynn thought as she worked her way along the bulkhead toward the waist of the ship in order to escape the fighting that had broken out on the forecastle deck. Noticing a hammer that had been hastily abandoned when the fighting began, she picked it up.

"Ahhgh!" The sound of a man choking made her turn around. She recognized the officer who had first shouted "mutiny." One of the mutineers was bending him backward over the railing, choking him. Wynn did not even think twice, but sprang up, her hammer raised; she brought it down as hard as she could on the mutineer's skull. There was a crunching sound of bone breaking, and the would-be mutineer sank to his knees. The officer leaned over the railing, catching his breath. Then he spied her.

"Get below," he said as soon as he could speak, but before she could move, there was a loud explosion from the deck below them. Thrown forward into the officer's arms, Wynn tumbled with him to the deck.

"Those idiots will sink us," he said, uttering an oath as they both looked up to see orange flames licking at the ship's bow.

"Look out for the mast," a sailor yelled, and from where she lay on the deck, Wynn could see that the foremast had caught fire.

Disengaging himself from her arms, the officer

barked out a command: "Lower the boats!" There was an immediate flurry of activity as the sailors rushed to the boats that lay amidships and began to lower them over the side of the ship.

It was now obvious to Wynn that the mutineers had met with far more resistance than they had expected, and due to an error in judgment had set off an explosion which was now endangering the entire ship.

"The passengers," she murmured to herself as she picked her way toward the hatch that led below. There were women and children on board who were probably frightened out of their wits. The officer saw her moving toward the hatch and called out.

"You," he yelled. "Alert the other passengers. We've got to get them off." But the first mate, a tall man in the blue and gold of the officers' uniforms, had fought his way forward, beating her to the hatch, and climbed down.

Below, all was confusion, as some of the passengers crowded the narrow steps leading to the deck, demanding to know what was going on, while others cowered in their cabins, saying their prayers. Seeing the women's white faces and the children clinging to their skirts, Wynn realized that above all she must help them to remain calm. The smoke that now began to choke them all told her the fire was spreading, and, if they were to be saved, she must help the officers to prevent hysteria from spreading. The mate already had some of the women starting up the steps, and Wynn helped them line up.

"Come now," she said, squeezing the shoulder of one very young woman with two frightened children. "Do as the officer says."

"Are we on fire, miss?" another woman asked, fanning herself with her handkerchief.

"The officers have everything under control," Wynn answered. "If we do as they say we'll be all right."

The children began to cough from the smoke that was

filtering through the compartments to them, as above them they heard feet rushing across the deck and the sound of men shouting to one another. As Wynn, who was the last woman to go up, put her foot on the bottom step, she heard someone cry, "The topgallant mast has fallen!" Her heart hammering in her chest, coughing and sputtering because of the smoke, Wynn finally managed to reach the deck. She saw that the crew had successfully unlashed the boats and were lowering the first one over the side. The passengers were grouped around the ladder, the men separated from the women, who would go first.

"A necessary precaution," the officer who had herded them to the railing was saying. Necessary indeed, thought Wynn, as she joined them. From the looks of it, the fire was spreading, and they would all have to leave the burning ship if they wanted to save their skins.

At first, Wynn thought the darkness surrounding them was a result of the drifting smoke, but as she glanced up, she saw heavy clouds gathering in what earlier had been a blue sky. One of the women pointed upward. "Look, the clouds are gathering," she said. "The Lord will send rain."

Rain. Of course. It would put out the fire. But there wasn't time to wait for the hoped-for Act of God. The passengers were beginning to climb into the boats, manned by two sailors who held the oars.

"Cast off," shouted the mate when the first boat was full. "Row as far away as you can."

"Lord have mercy," one woman prayed. "If the ship sinks, she'll pull the rowboats down with her," she said.

Although the fighting had now dissipated, the mutineers still held the quarterdeck, which had not yet been reached by the flames. From that direction came a cry, "Ship to starboard."

Looking out to sea, Wynn spotted a dark shape on

the gray horizon. But if that was a ship, it must be miles away, she thought.

"Hurry, miss. Into the boat with you," a young sailor with a cockney accent urged Wynn, helping her over the railing and down the rope ladder. When she at last stepped into the overcrowded boat, the mate cried, "Cast off," and the sailors pushed away from the hull of the ship and began rowing with all their strength.

Now cries of fright went up all around them, as the passengers, packed together so tightly in the tiny boat, saw that they were only inches away from the lapping waves while menacing black clouds gathered above them.

Two small boys, who had become separated from their mother, clung to Wynn's skirt and looked up at her with large round eyes. She tried to smile reassuringly. "Be brave now," she said. "We're going to row to that other ship that is coming to rescue us. See?"

And she pointed toward the spot on the horizon that had, indeed, grown larger. Now she could make out the white billowing sails and the rounded hulls, but the ship still seemed like a small toy — too far away to reach them before they all capsized in these big waves. Their own ship burned in earnest now. Other boats from the ship rowed nearby, climbing the mountainous waves and sliding down their backs, as the sailors did their best to maneuver the little crafts.

"Hang on," shouted the man nearest the bow.

Suddenly a drop of rain landed on Wynn's nose and she looked up. More drops followed. From the upturned faces in the boat, it was clear that others had felt the rain as well. She glanced back at their smoldering ship, but if any rain was falling on it, the flames, which were licking the sails, had yet to die.

Trying to protect themselves from the rain which was now pouring steadily down, the passengers pulled on hoods or tried to cover their heads. Wynn knelt in the bottom of the boat, hugging the two little boys with her. She had not yet had time to consider her own predicament but it suddenly flashed into her mind that she might drown.

"No," she whispered to herself. "I won't think that. We shall be saved. I must get to New York for all our sakes," and as she thought of her family in England, fear and loss tugged at her heart.

The boat rose steeply on a wave, plunging Wynn's heart into her stomach. How far were they from New York? she wondered. Too far, she knew. Though they had been at sea for nearly eight weeks, they had not expected to arrive for another two. She would have lost count of the days except for her diary.

As the waves became even higher, the shrieks of the other passengers filled her ears. Clinging to the seat of the boat, she thought of her brother, James. He would probably give anything to trade places with her right now, considering it a great adventure. In fact, he had wanted to come to New York instead of her. Maybe it would have been better if he had, for James was a much stronger swimmer than she.

The rain pelted unmercifully into their faces, and the passengers gave up all hope of keeping dry. Shivering from the dampness and chill, the women screamed as the waves washed over the side of the boat. The sailors fought as hard as they could to keep control of the boat, and no one had time to glance at the burning ship now swallowed from sight by the smoke created by the rain beating down on the sputtering flames. From across the water came the cries of passengers on the other boats. They were still near enough to the ship that, if she sank, they all might be dragged down with her.

But the sailors steered a course for the ship they had sighted, which had seen their distress and was coming to their aid. Although still some distance off and slowed down by the choppy swell, with any luck perhaps some of the passengers might be saved from drowning, Wynn hoped as she clutched the seat with her aching hands.

"Hang onto me," she cried to her two little charges. The sailors doubled their efforts to keep their small vessel afloat. Although it seemed like hours, the rescue ship grew closer. Finally shouts were heard as the ship drew up to them, and lines were tossed out. One by one the boats were pulled to the ship, and with great relief Wynn saw the passengers from the other boats begin to climb up the ladder that had been thrown down the side of the ship. Her eyes watering from sea spray or tears, Wynn read the ship's name, *Leannie*, carved elaborately on the hull.

Finally it was their boat's turn, and two sailors descended to help the shaky passengers climb toward deck, where they were helped aboard. Wynn leaned down to the little boys whose faces were buried in her skirts.

"Go ahead now, boys," she said to them as the rain continued to splash in her face. She had to pry their small hands loose before she handed them over to the sailor who reached for them.

She was as wet and chilled as if she had swum in the dark water that was hurtling itself at the small boat. And as if her thought foreshadowed her action, she stood too quickly, just as a large wave crashed toward them.

"Hang on," yelled the nearest oarsman, but it was too late. Too petrified to scream, she clutched at the air, and then, as the sailor leapt toward her, she felt herself toppling over the stern of the boat. The huge wave snatched and pulled her under, and all was darkness. She opened her mouth only to gulp in icy seawater, but with her arms and legs she stroked frantically, her skirt twisting around her legs. The wave that had pulled her down now pushed her up, and she felt for a moment as if she were flying, and then she fell back into the sea again. But in the moment she had been tossed into the air, she saw a line fly toward her.

"Woman overboard," someone cried, and then she saw a sailor from the boat dive into the waves and swim toward her.

Struggling in the foamy water, she tried to swim toward the line, but the sailor reached her first, and she felt him grasp her about the waist with one arm. She stopped struggling as he drew her forward through the water, and when she felt the line next to her hand, she grabbed it and hung on. She did not know that above her all the passengers and many of the *Leannie*'s crew had crowded to the railing to watch her rescue. She only knew that her life depended on her hold on the line and the grip of the nameless sailor who held her around the waist.

Finally they made it to the ladder, and the sailor secured it in one hand. He pulled her forward, and she wrapped her numb fingers around the wet rope.

"You're all right now, miss," said the sailor who had saved her. "Grab ahold and climb up. I'll follow you."

As she grabbed the ladder with both hands, she found that her strength had flagged, and she had to double her efforts. To make matters worse, her waterlogged clothing dragged her down, making her seem twice her normal weight. She was vaguely aware of shouts of encouragement coming from above, and she dared not look down as she reached the halfway point. It still seemed so far to the top that she was afraid her grip would not last.

"Steady, now, steady," called the sailor climbing after her.

Rung by rung, she pulled herself up, and just when she thought she could climb no farther, hands reached down to help her. She was lifted up and over, and when she felt the deck under her, the last of her strength gave way, and she crumpled into a heap.

Thankful for the feeling of oiled wood under her hands, she sat in her soaking dress, shivering uncontrollably. Someone brought a blanket, which they wrapped around her. The strong hands that had pulled her on board now supported her, and through the rain, which had lessened somewhat, she looked into the startling dark eyes of one of the *Leannie*'s officers.

He said nothing, but the serious look in his eyes, which were as dark as his wavy hair, capped by a blue and gold tri-cornered hat, penetrated through the fog in her brain. Even in this gray light she could see that there were worry lines creasing the skin around his eyes. He wrapped the blanket more firmly about her, tucking it under her chin, then he lifted her into his arms. She squirmed in his grasp, the water dripping from her hair, as he carried her across the deck.

"I can walk," she said.

But he held her resolutely and strode toward a hatch that led below. She could feel the strength and firmness of his shoulder, which she fell against. At the hatchway, he set her on her feet, and for a moment she felt dizzy.

"Get below," he ordered. "The steward will bring you something dry to put on." And he turned and left her.

The water still dripping from her, and shivering from the cold, she stood staring after him, her heart racing from both fright and exertion. The she reached for the railing at the hatchway and did what she was told. She went below.

As it was a merchant vessel that had rescued them, there were no quarters for passengers, but the unfortunate victims of the mutiny were taking refuge on the gun deck. Here it was very dark, but Wynn found her way to the gathering of women and children, some of whom had already stripped out of their wet clothes and were huddled in the blankets the steward had distributed.

"Saints be praised," said Mrs. Windebank, the matronly woman who had had a cabin next to her, as Wynn approached. "We thought you were drowned." Now, shorn of bonnet and gown, and wrapped in a blanket over her petticoats, the older woman presented a comical figure. But not half as comical as herself, Wynn imagined. No one else had received the dunking she had.

"Come now," said Mrs. Windebank. "Let's get you out of those wet things." Two other women gathered around her and held up her blanket so that she could undress in relative privacy.

"Right down to the skin now," said Mrs. Windebank, "or you'll catch pneumonia."

"We've none of us anything to wear," said a high-pitched voice, and Wynn recognized a young woman named Connie Hinton.

"That may be true, Mrs. Hinton," said the determined Mrs. Windebank. "But it's better to be naked and dry than wet and chilled. You want to reach the colonies alive, don't you?"

"Aye," said Jane Cresswell, whose husband had been in one of the boats that was towed to safety after the women and children had gotten aboard the *Leannie*. "And what if we do make it in one piece? We've all lost everything on that burning ship. What could those cutthroat mutineers have wanted with that ship anyway?"

"They wanted to turn her into a pirate vessel," said Mrs. Windebank. "Tired of the hard work and low pay on the passenger ship she was, I'd wager. But we've not lost our lives," she went on, silencing the moanings and complaints that had begun to spring up. "And our children are safe. For that we should be thankful."

"I suppose."

Connie Hinton put her hand on Wynn's arm. "How long will we be here?" she asked.

"Well, I don't know," Wynn said. "I don't think we can return to the other ship. She's too damaged. We'll just have to wait until the officers tell us."

"How do we know this ship is going to New York?" another woman asked.

"When will they tell us what they're going to do to us?"

"Ladies, hold your tongues," said Mrs. Windebank. "None of us knows the answers, and if you'll all have patience, we'll ask the officers as soon as we can. Meanwhile, keep as warm and dry as you can, and look after your children, too." Then she turned to Wynn. "None of these others has an ounce of sense about them," she whispered to her. "We'll have to speak to the officers ourselves — to find out how long we are to be aboard this ship and if there are enough provisions for all of us."

Wynn liked Mrs. Windebank's steady, straightfoward manner, and an understanding seemed to form between them that they would be the spokeswomen for the bedraggled group.

Now the men who had been rescued came down to find their wives, and soon the passengers settled themselves in family units as best they could, though there was little privacy. Then the hatchway opened, and three sailors brought down a cauldron of steaming soup and some cups. When the group had eaten, the hatchway door opened again, and the officer who had carried Wynn across the deck came down the ladder. Even in the gloom of the gun deck, she recognized him because of his height. He had a handsome face, she noted, with a firm but sensual mouth. Again, she noticed the lines etched around his eyes as if he had undergone some bitter experience.

He came into their midst and looked around. Aware suddenly that she had nothing at all on under her blanket, Wynn pulled it tighter around her. As his dark gaze found her, his eyes lingered briefly on her face, and she could tell by the way his gaze flitted over her shivering figure that he too was aware that she was naked beneath the blanket. From the way his lips lifted in a slight smile, the thought seemed to amuse him, and she felt considerably embarrassed.

"I am Officer Robert Lamley," he said. "First mate of this ship. I've come to see that you are made as comfortable as possible. We tried to salvage the ship you were on, but the explosion caused her to fill with water and she has sunk. I'm sorry we couldn't salvage your belongings."

Wails broke out as the women thought about the precious goods they had planned to take with them to the New World. Mrs. Windebank tried to quiet them as Wynn, realizing no one had yet uttered any words of gratitude to Officer Lamley, said, "Thank you." Again he turned his gaze on her. "We are grateful for your help," she began but stopped, suddenly tongue-tied by self-consciousness. Luckily Mrs. Windebank came to her rescue.

"That's right," she said. "We would all be at the bottom of the ocean thanks to those piratical scoundrels if you hadn't come along. Where is this ship bound, if you don't mind my asking?"

"New York," he said.

"There's that then," said Mrs. Windebank. "Our ship was to put in there as well. How long do you figure until we'll get there?"

"Two more weeks, maybe three," he said, his eyes sweeping the group, a look of pain suddenly crossing his features. Surely this present disaster could not be responsible for so intense an expression, Wynn wondered. As a ship's officer, he must be used to storms and rescues, even mutinies.

"Is there anything we can put on when we are dry?" she asked him, feeling herself flush at the mention of her state of undress.

He hesitated only a second before he said, "I'll send the ship's steward with some clothes. We don't have any ladies' clothes, of course; you'll just have to make do with shirts and breeches until we reach port."

Then, apparently deciding he'd said enough, he turned and strode toward the ladder leading up to the deck. Wynn realized that her heart was beating quickly again. There was something about Officer Lamley that both disturbed her and piqued her interest. She could not help but wonder what misfortune had caused the lines of grief that lay about his eyes. But she recognized the strength and fortitude that he seemed to emanate as if he were capable of handling any situation. She thought he must be a very determined man and she suddenly pitied anyone who might cross him, for the combination of temperaments she read in his face led her to believe he must be quick to anger.

The ship's steward brought dry linens and men's clothing. It was an odd assortment to choose from, and some of the women decided to wait until their own things dried to put them on again. Wynn kept a long shirt and a pair of breeches, which she stepped into as Mrs. Windebank and Connie Hinton held her blanket for her.

Thus attired in men's clothing, she hung her sodden dress from a beam above them, letting it dry in the air. She could move about freely in the breeches, and she wandered between the families huddled on the gun deck seeing if there was anything she could do to help them. By the time she bandaged several cuts, saw that everyone was fed, helped make beds from the extra blankets the steward found, and helped sling a few hammocks, she was exhausted. She made her way to a place by the bulkhead next to Mrs. Windebank and lay down. In spite of the hardness of the deck, she was thankful just to be able to stretch out, and among whisperings and thumpings as the rest of the passengers settled themselves, she fell asleep.

The next day passed in a reasonably orderly fashion, and after making herself as useful as she could, Wynn went on deck. They had been fed a nourishing stew, and Wynn felt invigorated by the air as she walked amidships and watched the sailors aloft, the sails billowing to catch the strong breeze that blew them toward their destination.

Since the mutiny she had not had much time to think of her own fate, thankful only that she had not gone to a watery tomb before she had had a chance to do anything that she had set out to do. She had left England two months ago to visit Sarah Kidd, who had been married to her father's cousin, William Cox. Cox had drowned shortly after riding through the night proclaiming the accession of William and Mary to the throne of England. Sarah had been only fifteen when she married William Cox. Her second husband, John Oort, had died in 1691, when she was only twenty-one. Now Sarah was married to a wealthy merchant and captain of a line of sailing ships, William Kidd, her third husband.

Wynn's own family was finding life difficult in England because of their Catholic persuasion. But there was opportunity in the New World if only Wynn's father, Jonathan Cox, could get a foothold there. And so it had become Wynn's mission to visit Sarah and ask if she would like the Coxes to come to New York and work for her. For Sarah and William had several houses and much property to manage, and Captain Kidd was away more than half of the year on voyages. Wynn herself had come on the voyage because she knew she could be an immediate asset to Sarah. Though women did not generally receive much education, Wynn's father had encouraged her to sit in on her brother's tutorial lessons. And so she could write well and do arithmetic. She even had a smattering of Greek and Latin. Wynn could assist Sarah with correspondence and accounts, because Mrs. Kidd could neither read nor write.

She was lost in thought about how to appeal to Sarah Kidd, and felt rueful about the shabby impression she would make since she had lost everything at sea. She did not even own the clothes she stood up in, and was just turning over this fact in her mind when footsteps announced a presence behind her.

She knew it was him even before she turned, and when she faced Robert Lamley, he looked directly at her with something like surprise on his face. For a moment neither of them spoke, but Wynn was again aware of his serious gaze and the firm set of his sensual mouth. She swallowed, suddenly unsure of herself.

"Good evening," she said, realizing she would appear rude if she did not speak.

"Good evening," he returned. His gaze traveled over the loose man's shirt she wore and the sailor's breeches, which came to just below her bare knees.

"I hope you have recovered," he said with a slight frown, and he turned to look toward the horizon.

"Yes," she said, observing the profile he turned to her. He had a high forehead, prominent eyebrows, and a firm jaw. He was hatless now, and his thick dark hair was pulled back and tied with a velvet ribbon at the nape of the neck. Grasping the railing with both hands, he stood with his feet apart to help him balance on the deck.

She frowned to herself. There was something about

him that made her feel shy. She had not seen him smile once, but his concern for the passengers was obvious.

She placed a hand on the rail and followed his gaze out to sea, but she could think of nothing to say. Then it struck her that she ought to use this opportunity to ask some of the questions the other passengers had plied her with.

"You've gone to a great deal of trouble on our account," she said. "I'm sure all the passengers you rescued appreciate it."

"It was no more than any Christian ship would have done to aid another," he said brusquely, but a shadow crossed his face. Realizing that he did not wish to continue speaking of the rescue, Wynn took another tack.

"We will be in New York soon then?"

He shrugged. "Two weeks if the weather holds."

She nodded. "I am most anxious to see it. It is a good-sized town, is it not?" She had read that New York numbered more than five thousand souls and had seven hundred and fifty houses. Although not large compared to the cities of Europe, in a wilderness, it sounded like a respectable population.

"It is a fair port," he said. "My parents live there."

"Do you know Mrs. Sarah Kidd, Captain Kidd's wife?"

He looked at her quickly with interest. "I do, very well. What is your relationship to her?"

"She's my cousin, by marriage that is. I'm going to stay with her."

"I see," he answered. "You must give her my regards. I hope to see Captain Kidd when he arrives in New York."

"You are acquainted then."

"Yes, well acquainted. Captain Kidd is one of the best seamen on this side of the Atlantic. He distinguished himself in the West Indies under Captain Thomas Hewetson against the French."

"So I had heard."

They both fell silent, and Wynn looked down into the waves that had tried to claim her.

"The water was so cold," she said, remembering her fearful experience. "Just think. I might have drowned. I — " and as she turned to communicate more of her thoughts on the harrowing subject, she was caught up short by the look on his face.

He was staring at her with an expression of horror, his tanned face a shade more pale. He gave a curt nod, said, "Good evening," then turned and strode away.

His reaction astonished her, and she would have considered it downright rude, except for something she had read in his brief look — the same bitterness she had noticed when he had carried her across the deck that first day. It was obvious that something in his life had badly scarred him, and as Wynn went below, she continued to think about this strange man who had captured her curiosity.

The passengers adjusted to their circumstances reasonably well, and Wynn took it upon herself to report on their well-being and to request necessities from the ship's steward, a small wiry man with a balding head, called Adam.

Wynn and Adam formed a congenial relationship, and once or twice Adam sent her on to Officer Lamley to get his approval for certain requests. Each time they met, Wynn was careful to speak only on general topics or about the running of the ship. Lamley was instructive and helpful, doing all he could to see to the passengers' comfort, and he listened with interest when she spoke of herself or her family in England. She noticed that when she mentioned Sarah Kidd, he listened even more attentively.

They took to meeting daily on deck, and Wynn found she looked forward to their talks. He told her much that increased her interest in the New World, and finally, one day, a cheer went up from the crow's nest as land was sighted. The passengers came on deck to watch with excitement as the New Jersey coastline came into view, far away at first, then close enough that they could see the rolling, wooded terrain.

The ship followed the coast for eleven miles, then, leaving New Jersey behind, she passed through the narrows, a mile-long tidal strait between Staten Island and the western end of Long Island. Then, as the wind picked up, the ship entered New York's upper bay. Everyone pointed with excitement to the land they passed — with orchards, woods and fields of Indian corn on both shores. The *Leannie* and her passengers had finally reached the New World.

Chapter Two

"There it is! That's New York," said Mrs. Windebank, pointing to the tiny hamlet that covered the tip of Manhattan Island.

"I can't believe we're finally here," said Wynn as the *Leannie* knifed through the water in the upper bay. Even though it appeared to be only a village on the edge of a wilderness, she could not take her eyes from it.

Her heart began to dance with anticipation as she watched the outline of houses, churches and windmills draw nearer. It seemed a civilized contrast to the lush and hostile foliage they had passed on the stretch up from the Atlantic Ocean along the New Jersey coast. Since coming through the narrows, they had passed three smaller islands. First Bedloe's Island, then the privately owned Ellis Island, and now they passed Governor's Island with its lush green grasses.

Wynn leaned closer to the railing, her hair splaying out behind her as she watched the wild duck in the water and the porpoises racing alongside the ship. Henry Hudson had called Manhattan Island "the pearl of New Netherland," and here it was, set where two rivers and a bay poured their mighty waters into the Atlantic Ocean.

Wynn was struck by the bustling activity as the *Leannie* prepared to dock. Robert Lamley mounted the quarterdeck to give the orders. "Stand by," he shouted. So enthralled was Wynn by the teeming harbor life that she forgot to prepare herself to meet Sarah Kidd.

"Oh dear," she said to herself, looking down at her tattered clothes. She had nothing to change into, as her luggage had been lost in the wreck at sea. She hated to appear before her hostess in such a bedraggled state, but there was nothing she could do. She would just have to curb her embarrassment and explain what had happened.

Finally, the ship was firmly moored and the gangplank lowered. Wynn pushed at her hair and attempted to smooth her skirt, which she had put on again after repairing it as best she could. She knew her cheeks were tanned from the wind and sea, for during the voyage, she had spent much time on deck. She had never worried about the sun's effects on her complexion, as many young women did. She'd never had the patience, in any case, always too busy plotting escapades with her brother, James, to worry about her appearance. Instead, she had fed on tales of adventure and romance such as she had read in the twopenny chapbooks that contained popular fiction of the day. Now she felt she was actually beginning to experience some of those same adventures.

When her family had thought of emigrating to the colonies, both Wynn and James had clamored to go. But James's small wage as a carpenter's apprentice was needed at home, so Wynn's mother had reluctantly allowed Wynn to go instead, once she was assured that her cousin by marriage, Sarah Kidd, would be there to meet Wynn at the end of her journey. Her mother had entrusted Wynn to the captain's protection, and Wynn smiled to think of what good that had done.

Apprehension and excitement rippled through her as the passengers prepared to disembark. She followed the other passengers to the dock, and, in spite of a sailor's assistance, her foot slipped a little at the end of the plank. Not that her ruined skirt would be any the worse if she fell into the muddy water that lay in a puddle on the wooden wharf.

"What a mess," she muttered, and then looking up found herself staring into the face of a tall attractive woman with dark curly hair and violet eyes.

The woman was elegantly attired in a currant-colored gown with embroidered stomacher in the vee gap that ended in a point at her tiny waist. The full sleeves of the gown were buttoned up just below the elbow, allowing the tighter chemise sleeves to show. A loose hood covered the dark curls around her face.

"You must be Wynfield Cox," she said to Wynn, who was still struggling with the hem of her skirt. Wynn looked up at the lovely face and immediately blushed at her own dreadful appearance.

"I am. Would you be Sarah Kidd?"

"The very same," said the woman, smiling, appearing not to notice that Wynn looked like a drowned rat. "You must call me Sarah. May I call you Wynfield?"

"Oh, they call me Wynn." Wynn dropped her skirt, taking in the woman's beauty. No wonder she had been the catch of the season when William Kidd married her five years ago.

"Welcome to New York," Sarah said, coming forward to clasp Wynn's hands in hers.

"Thank you. And I apologize for looking such a mess. There was a mutiny, you see, and we were rescued, but not before I, um, fell in. Oh dear."

But Sarah radiated her dazzling smile. "I know. I heard. Thank heavens you're all right. Come, it isn't far to my house. I thought you might enjoy the walk. My lackey will bring your luggage in the carriage. That is . . ."

Wynn pulled a wry face. "I haven't any. It was lost in the wreck."

"Well, never mind. I have some things we can fix you up in."

All around them, workmen and citizens hustled along the wharf. Wynn wrinkled her nose at the fishy smell, the din from the dock workers, children, and merchants on the wharf filling her ears. In that, at least, New York was much like London.

Wynn followed as Sarah led her away from the Great Dock and along a small street, paved with cobblestones along the sides, but with a muddy gutter for drainage and refuse.

"How are your father and mother?" Sarah asked as soon as the crowd had thinned out. Wynn considered how much she should say at this point. Sarah's letter, penned by another hand, had said that Wynn would be welcome in her home when she came over, and that since a sea crossing was so arduous, Wynn was welcome to stay with her as long as she liked. The tone of Sarah Kidd's dictated letter had been polite and friendly enough, but after all, Jonathan Cox, Wynn's father, was related to Sarah's late husband William Cox, and now Sarah was married to the wealthy merchant Captain William Kidd.

"They're doing as well as can be expected, I believe," Wynn answered.

"Oh?" Sarah turned her head toward her young cousin and raised her eyebrows.

Wynn hurried on now that she had Sarah's attention. "My father's luck has turned. He's a good businessman, really, but I'm afraid he was on the wrong side of political and religious factions. His last few ventures were disappointing, and he cannot get backers for any others." Wynn blushed. She had not meant to disclose so much so soon. But it was her habit to tell everything at once. Now she realized that the genteel Sarah Kidd most likely expected to take things more slowly.

They turned into the Strand and walked passed cream-colored brick houses with Dutch-style stepped gables. The quaint homes looked onto the waterfront, as sea gulls careened in the air above them.

"That's our house." Sarah nodded toward one of the largest. Two pairs of windows flanked the front doors, and there were five windows in a row on the second floor and three ornamental dormers in the roof gables. Two fluted chimneys rose on either end of the house.

"The walled garden runs back to an alley that separates us from our neighbors."

"It's wonderful," said Wynn, stopping to admire the house. Truly, it was just as she had hoped. She could see that the space surrounding the waterfront was fast filling up with both Dutch-style homes and English mansions, but there was still a sense of spaciousness, and one could see the sky, uncluttered by a cramped skyline. Beyond the house Wynn could see a half-moon gate in an old wall at the end of the street looking north along the East River.

"What's that?" asked Wynn.

"The Queen's Gate. That wall used to mark the edge of the city, but see how streets have been laid out above it now."

Sarah preceded Wynn up the iron-railed stoop to her front door. Wynn followed her hostess into the cool dark interior and gave herself a moment to adjust her eyes from the bright June sun. Then she followed Sarah through the hallway and parlor that opened onto the family dining room. Here straight-backed mahogany chairs surrounded a polished oval table on which sat two brass candlesticks. Sarah stood on a breathtaking wool Turkey-worked carpet of brick red, black, green, and blue with gold fringe. Against the wall stood a heavy oak press cupboard with intricately carved decoration on the cornice and upper doors.

"Oh my," said Wynn as she began to focus on the sumptuous surroundings. She had not expected this much elegance in the New World, even though she knew that Sarah was married to a successful merchant and sea captain who owned a line of packets and did very well in the import trade.

"You must be tired, and you'll want to change" said Sarah, removing her tippet, the short cape that covered her shoulders. "I'll just tell Elizabeth we're here, and then I'll show you to your room."

'Sarah, I really hope you don't mind my being here," said Wynn when Sarah returned. "When my father suggested I visit you, I knew it was for more than just a family visit, but I was so anxious to see the New World that I took the opportunity. I do not want to impose on you. If there is anything I can do to help you keep house while I am here, I should be glad to do it." Wynn dropped her gaze, nervous that she might insult her cousin. She raised her eyes again. "I can read and write. My father taught me," she said, anxiously raising her eyes to see Sarah's reaction.

Instead of looking insulted, Sarah laughed, her violet eyes sparkling. "Then you can write my letters and help me with the household accounts. I never had the opportunity to learn, you see."

Wynn clasped her hands together, relief sweeping through her. "I would love to assist you. It would make me feel useful and not such a burden to you."

"It's settled then." Sarah held her gaze for a moment, and Wynn smiled. She liked this cousin and hoped they would continue to develop the rapport she felt had already sprung up between them. Sarah sat on a straight-backed walnut and leather settee, but Wynn was afraid to sit on the crimson upholstered chair Sarah indicated for fear she would soil it.

"You'll enjoy life here if you've half the spirit you seem to have," Sarah said. Then she gave Wynn a teasing glance. "Be careful of the sailors, though. The taverns and coffee houses swarm with seafaring men and privateers, even pirates."

"The mutineers on board my ship had turned pirate," Wynn said with a shiver.

"Yes, piracy is condoned here," Sarah said. "The governor fights to rid the seas of piracy, but many colonists came here to escape the heavy hand of taxation in England. Perhaps you are not acquainted with the changes that often occur in our colonial government, but it is so unsettled that laws are often openly violated."

Wynn's spine tingled. It was true, then, that this land held excitement and adventure, even though just at the moment she'd had quite enough of the latter.

"But here, I'm keeping you down too long. A bath and then a glass of Madeira for your throat." Sarah rose and led the way to the stairs. In the entry hall, they passed a brass lantern clock on a wooden wall bracket, its weights swinging slowly on the long chains. Sarah led the way up the narrow stairway, her skirt swishing against the spiral turnings on the stair balusters, which Wynn paused to admire.

On the second floor, Sarah put a finger to her lips. "Little Sarah is asleep. She has a touch of fever, I'm afraid." Wynn nodded and followed Sarah on up to the third floor and into a bedroom at the back of the house.

"Oh, how cozy," said Wynn as Sarah opened the pine door. An ornamented highboy stood against one wall flanked by a painted bannister-back side-chair. A blue-and-white curtained feather bed stood against the back wall, and a china basin sat on the maplewood highboy. A small window looked out onto the garden, shaded by the leafy trees that stood next to the house.

"It's lovely," Wynn said, reaching up to touch the smooth-turned bedposts.

"William has the opportunity to bring home much good furniture from his many voyages. I'll have Elizabeth bring you a bath," said Sarah. Then, by way of explanation, she added, "Elizabeth is William's indentured servant."

An elderly black man, carrying some tools, came up the stairs on his way to the roof. Sarah introduced him. "This is Judson, our other servant," she said. "He's very good to me in the captain's absence."

"Hello Judson," said Wynn.

The black man bowed his graying head. "If I can do anything, you let ole Judson know."

"I certainly will."

"We're lucky to have both Judson and Elizabeth," said Sarah as the elderly man left the room. "William purchased Judson's freedom when he was a slave. And Elizabeth is an intelligent, loyal girl. She'll help you unpack your things."

"I'll be glad of that. Thank you, Sarah. I'm so glad to be here, it gives me such a good feeling."

Sarah patted her hand. "Elizabeth will bring you some clothes. Then, after your bath, come downstairs and we'll talk again. I want to hear more of your father's predicament. Perhaps we can do something about it." Wynn blushed at Sarah's perceptiveness.

While Wynn started to undress, Elizabeth, the young blonde servant girl, brought in a large tub for a bath. Then she filled it with two buckets of water, one hot, one cold, as Wynn disrobed. Wynn thought warm water had never felt so good, as she washed away the grime from the long weeks of the voyage and let the warmth seep into aching and cramped muscles. Her very bones seemed to take in the refreshing warmth.

Elizabeth helped Wynn bathe, all the while amusing her with her chatter. She asked dozens of questions about London, which she had never seen, having come from Cornwall and never having been far from home until William brought her over on his ship *The Antigua*.

"London's a big city, isn't it?" she asked in her country accent, her blonde curls bobbing as she poured more water into the tub.

"Yes," answered Wynn after dunking her hair. "And it's very old. Not at all like here."

"What's it like?"

Wynn laughed. It seemed that no matter where you lived, it was the unfamiliar you wanted to see. "Well, there are a lot of people, and it's very dirty."

"You mean there's a lot of mud? We get that too on the hem of our skirts. That's why we wear them short here, Dutch-style."

Remembering her own predicament with the mud when she had gotten off the ship, Wynn could quickly see the practicality of that. But she returned to the discussion of London. "Not just mud, soot. It clings to the stone walls and gets into your cupboard."

"Oh, I see. Are there very many buildings? Have you seen London Bridge?"

"Of course. The buildings are close together, and some are very old. It's so crowded the streets are dark in some places, even during the day. There are places a young lady like yourself wouldn't want to go."

"Really? Do you ever see the king?"

"Yes, when the king and queen ride in a procession or stand on their balcony to greet the people."

"Are you a Protestant?" Elizabeth asked suddenly.

The question did not startle Wynn. Religion was the reason many people came to the colonies. "My father was born a Catholic. I think that's why he fell on hard times. He supported James the Second, you see, before he was exiled."

"I don't know what religion I am," said Elizabeth as she scrubbed Wynn's back. "That man Calvin said we're all predestined by God to whatever comes to pass."

"How do you know all this?" asked Wynn, amused by the girl's reasoning "Do you read?"

"Nay," she said, shaking her curls. "But I listen to the men talk. There's enough politics and religion bein' talked all the time in the streets. If you're curious, you find out things. But they say New York's not like the other colonies. They say we've got religious freedom here."

"I believe you do," said Wynn. Some people on the ship had told her there was nothing Quaker or Puritan about New York, and although Catholics had been hated at one time, men of any faith were tolerated here. She moved on to another subject, finding Elizabeth a ready source of information about this place.

"Are the Indians dangerous?"

"Not anymore," Elizabeth said. "Though I can't say as I'd blame them if they were. To my way of thinking we make our own trouble with the Indians. There's plenty of land for everyone, and when we leave the Indians alone, they don't bother us."

Wynn had heard wild stories about naked men with red skin and feathers in their hair, and she was anxious to see an Indian, almost as anxious as she was to see a pirate, from a distance, of course. "Will I get to see one?" she asked.

Now it was Elizabeth's turn to laugh. "You probably passed one or two on the street coming here."

"Really?"

"But don't worry," Elizabeth said. "You'll see them. They're harmless, except when they drink alcohol. There's a law forbidding giving it to them. Have you ever seen a man hanged?" she asked abruptly.

"Good heavens no," answered Wynn. At home people thronged to executions, but in spite of her adventurous spirit, Wynn avoided that particular form of recreation. "I have never seen one, and I hope I never will."

"It's a great thing here. They hanged Jacob Leisler five years ago. That was the biggest one. The crowd was so big you really couldn't see anything. They say Mr. Leisler made a great speech before he died. He was a Protestant. I think people are sorry now they hanged him."

Wynn knew about the Leisler Rebellion. When William and Mary had ascended to the throne of England, Jacob Leisler had taken command of the militia and possession of the government because Governor Nicholson was suspected of loyalty to the deposed King James. Leisler proclaimed that he would hold the government in his hands until orders came from King William announcing the successor to the colonial government.

But when the king's man, Governor Slaughter, finally arrived, Leisler hesitated to give up the fort, so he was arrested, tried, and sentenced to death. Four years later, the Parliament of Great Britain reversed the attainder and restored Leisler's property to his son.

"His house was next to this one," said Elizabeth, breaking in on Wynn's thoughts.

"Jacob Leisler's?"

"Yes, but the captain opposed him," she said, speaking of Captain Kidd.

"Did he now?"

"Yes, and he was rewarded for it."

"Hmm," said Wynn, thinking Captain Kidd must be on the right side of politics here. That was the kind of luck her father had never had, she thought with a sigh as she got out of the bath.

After drying herself, she put on a clean fawn-colored gown. It was a relief to finally have a change of clothes. Then she went downstairs, finding Sarah in the kitchen.

Sarah had changed into a more practical cotton dress with a lavender apron. A child who was a smaller version of her mother stood nearby, rolling out dough on the kitchen table. She turned at the approach of the newcomer and looked up questioningly.

"This must be little Sarah," said Wynn. The little girl, whom Wynn judged to be about four years old, had the same violet eyes as her mother and dark brown curls. At four she already looked gently bred and cultivated.

"She's beautiful," said Wynn.

"Thank you. Here, Sarah," said the mother, "cut the dough into cookies, and then we'll sprinkle the cinnamon on top." Wynn looked around her at the shining, well-stocked kitchen. Pots and pans hung within handy reach, and the wooden table was scoured clean. A large cupboard held a splendid array of tankards, chafing dishes, pewter cups and dishes, a coffee pot, tea pot, and all manner of knives, forks and spoons. The aroma of spices added a delicate scent to the air.

"May I help?" asked Wynn.

"Of course," said Sarah, carrying a jar of peaches to the table. "Peaches are in abundance here, so much so that I try to use them in many of my desserts."

"I'm fairly good at making cakes," said Wynn.

"That will be wonderful."

Wynn busied herself for a while over the cookies. "When do you expect your husband to return?"

"In a month or so. He is in London on business. I pray it will not take too long."

"Still, he makes a good living. I understand he owns many ships."

"That he does. Yes, I don't mean to complain. And I have my brother, Samuel Bradley. You'll meet him."

Sarah Kidd had much strength and courage to carve out a life for herself here, especially with a husband gone so much of the time, Wynn thought. Yet she seemed to suffer few of the ill effects that Wynn associated with the married state. Perhaps things were different here in the colonies. Of course, Wynn knew, Sarah was a woman of means. She had been in the fortunate position of being a widow when she married William, for even when a widow remarried, she retained her right to the property left by her former husband.

The two women chatted and baked for the rest of the afternoon. Before they knew it, clouds had stolen over the sky and the cowherd's horn told them that it was sunset.

"The cowherd also wakens the town at sunrise until mid-November," said Sarah, stopping her work for a moment. "In the cold winter, without the horn, it is often difficult to rise."

From the kitchen window, Wynn could see one of the windmills left by the Dutch. Sarah joined her. "The windmills are good luck protection. The Indians are afraid to come near their long arms and the big teeth, which they believe bite the corn in pieces." Wynn smiled at the illusion, then turned back to her work.

"New York is still a Dutch town in many respects," said Sarah, "though the English have ruled it for thirty-five years. Some say little has changed except the flag. Dutch homes, Dutch ways, and in some houses, the Dutch tongue still holds sway. But there is a cosmopolitan smattering of German, French, Spanish, Negroes, mulattoes, and other nationalities, too. And of course the English and Scots."

By the end of the day, Wynn realized she was tired

from the voyage. She looked forward to her first night in a real bed, and with the stillness that came with being on land, she quickly fell asleep.

Just as Sarah said, the sound of the cowherd's horn woke the sleeping town. Burning brush and light pine coaxed the oak logs into hot flames in every hearth, and the smoke rising from each chimney grew to a great cloud over the steep-roofed houses.

The smell of sausage told Wynn that breakfast was ready, and when she came into the kitchen she saw that Elizabeth had spread the table with buttermilk, rye bread, grated cheese, sausage and a pot of tea.

Sarah and her daughter joined Wynn at the breakfast table. "Did you rest well?" asked Sarah.

"Very well. It was a pleasure to sleep in a spacious room after the tiny quarters on the *Leannie*. It took a while to realize I wasn't rocking on the waves."

"You'll be getting your land legs back now. If you like, we can see a bit of the town this morning. There are some new dolls in from London," said Sarah, referring to miniature dolls dressed by cutters and tailors in Paris or London to display the latest fashions. As Sarah smiled, Wynn could see a touch of wistfulness in her eyes. "I'll have a new dress made for the time William comes home," she continued.

How she must miss him, thought Wynn as she ate her bread and cheese. "I'd love to see the town," she said, feeling her anticipation rise.

"And we'll have some clothes made for you as well," said Sarah.

Wynn pressed her lips together. "I haven't any money," she said, embarrassed. "What little I had must have sunk."

But Sarah waved her hand. "Don't worry about the money. You are my guest. I'll take care of everything."

After breakfast the women left the house and walked the few blocks to the center of town. Wynn now wore another of Sarah's good dresses with a silk bodice and slashed sleeves that allowed the white linen to show beneath. Like Sarah, her skirt was open in front to reveal a deeply flounced underskirt. It was a bright June day, and most of the mud on the roads had dried. Droves of pigs ate much of the garbage at the side of the road. Wynn could see the wisdom in Dutch-style short dresses and determined to have all her outdoor gowns made this way to avoid soiling them in the streets.

It was a pleasant walk down the Strand, which turned into Dock Street farther on by the Great Dock. They walked on the stone paving that extended ten feet in front of the houses and shops, which left the center of the street to catch the drainage. As they passed a house with a printing press carved into its wooden signboard, a man in work clothes with grease across his forehead leaned out of the window.

"Good day, Mrs. Kidd," he greeted, with a bow.

"Good day to you, Mr. Bradford."

"Who is that?" asked Wynn.

"That's William Bradford, and that's his printing establishment. The first in town." Wynn could hear the rhythmic thud of the press as they passed.

As they continued down Dock Street, they could see the tall ships in the harbor. They approached the shops, and climbed up on some steps to let soldiers pass on their way to the garrison. Drums and trumpets sounded the march, and the shiny broadblades of horsemen flashed in the sunlight as the soldiers tramped back to their barracks within Fort William.

Wynn's heart thrilled at the sight of the handsome

young men in their buff coats and bandoliers, the leather belts for holding ammunition strung over their shoulders. The men were strong and muscular from the rigors of their training, their faces tanned from life in the outdoors.

After the soldiers passed by, Sarah and Wynn entered a small shop. As they opened the door a bell tinkled, and inside they saw a plump middle-aged woman wearing simple attire and a linen cap sitting behind the counter. She smiled affably as Sarah entered, followed by Wynn.

"Why, my dear Sarah," the woman said. "How nice to see you."

"How are you, Hannah?" said Sarah. "I'd like you to meet my cousin, Wynn Cox, just over from England. And she had quite an adventure on the way — fought mutineers and was nearly drowned."

The matronly storekeeper turned her eyes on Wynn. "Why, I'm pleased to meet you. But Sarah, I thought your family was all in Scotland."

"Actually Wynn is a cousin by my first marriage. Her father is Jonathan Cox, my late husband's brother. Wynn, this is Hannah Luck."

"What pretty coloring you have," said Hannah. "I like a girl with freckles." She looked from Wynn to Sarah, noticing that Wynn's straw-colored hair and blue eyes contrasted with Sarah's dark coloring.

"Thank you, ma'am," said Wynn, taking Hannah's hand and allowing a motherly squeeze. "I'm pleased to meet you." Wynn turned her gaze to the items in the shop. Silver tankards and beakers, silver-clasped Bibles, gold and fine jewelry were displayed on rich velvet. The store also displayed wampum, which Wynn had never seen.

"What's this?" she asked, fingering the strings of shell beads used by the Indians and whites as currency.

"Wampum," answered Hannah. "The Algonquin and Iroquois tribes make beads from clam, conch, periwinkle and other shells. See these purple beads? They have twice the value of the white ones."

"They're beautiful. And they're used for money?"

"The Indians have been using wampum since long before Christopher Columbus discovered the New World. The settlers found the shells valuable, and they are still legal currency here."

"And these belts?" asked Wynn.

"The Indians weave the wampum beads into symbols representing special events. That one is for a marriage proposal," Hannah said as Wynn held up a belt with a design of a woman, a man, two crosses, and four wigwams.

Sarah and Hannah chatted gaily while Wynn examined the other items in the shop. But soon she tired of the confining place and gazed out the window. Across Broad Street stood the King's Arms Tavern with its swinging oaken sign, decoratively painted with a crossed sword and halberd; the sign hung on iron hooks from a wooden pole. As Wynn was staring at the sign, a man emerged and stood against the doorway, shading his eyes with his hand and looking at the sky.

She drew in a breath, for it was Robert Lamley, the officer on the rescue ship. He wore a fitted buff-colored coat, and white ruffled cuffs were revealed by his large turned-up sleeves. As he lowered his hand, he looked in the direction of the shop window.

"Wynn?" Sarah repeated for the second time.

"I'm sorry," she said, whirling around to Sarah, who stepped up to the window to join her.

"Why, that's Master Lamley," said Sarah, gazing after the tall young man stepping into the street. "He's a friend of William's. His family owns property near the farm."

"Oh yes. He was on the ship. He helped with the rescue." Wynn felt her cheeks burning, and in order to direct attention away from herself, said, "I didn't know you had a farm."

"Oh yes, on the Saw-Kill River. I suppose I hadn't mentioned it. We spend summers there. Oh, Wynn, it's so lovely. You can sit on the porch and gaze across the wide river to the palisades on the New Jersey coast. When William comes home we'll go there. It's so good for little Sarah to romp and play." Sarah sighed, and it was obvious as she stared vacantly at the street that her thoughts were on her country home.

"I'd love to see it, when it's convenient of course," said Wynn, her mind still on the man now disappearing down the street.

"The farm was left to my late brother Henry, by my first husband. When Henry died three years ago, the farm came to me," Sarah said.

Wynn watched curiously as Robert Lamley disappeared down the street. She wanted to ask Sarah more about his life, but could not think how to put the questions delicately. It wasn't like her to be staring after a man, she suddenly realized, and, embarrassed, she turned her gaze back to Sarah.

"Come along," said Sarah, who had finished her shopping. She led the way up Broad Street, where stately brick and stone houses with tiled roofs stood on either side of what had once been a canal. Here the streets were paved with cobblestones, and the broad gutters in the center could be crossed by stepping stones when the streets were flooded. At Stone Street, Sarah pointed out the Exchange, where citizens and merchants met to do business. It was so fine a day, she suggested they go up to Wall Street, where the old fortification of the city had been built, then over to Broadway, where Trinity Church was being erected. William had lent his block and tackle to the builders now hoisting stones, and Sarah wanted to see the builders' progress.

As they neared the crumbling old city wall, now standing in disrepair, it was clear to Wynn that it no longer defended the town from anything, and she wondered how effective it had been in its day.

Just as they were approaching the church site, they saw Robert Lamley coming toward them.

As the women watched the tall figure striding toward them, Wynn found herself admiring the handsome tanned face, the long straight nose and the broad shoulders. She self-consciously smoothed her wind-blown curls as Lamley approached.

"Why, Master Lamley, how nice to see you," Sarah said, giving him her gloved hand. He bowed his dark head briefly over it.

"Mrs. Kidd, it is good to see you. May I ask if you've heard from the captain?"

"Indeed I have." Her face darkened slightly as she said, "He's been given a commission by the king for privateering, and I believe he'll be home soon. A letter arrived by packet, saying he was gathering a crew and would sail from Plymouth this month." Then, in a lighter mood, she said, "You wouldn't be looking to go to sea again, would you Master Lamley?"

Something flickered in Lamley's dark eyes before he answered. "I had considered it," he said. Then he turned to Wynn.

"Wynn, I believe you have met Robert Lamley," said Sarah, and to Robert she said, "Wynn is my cousin from England." As Robert's dark eyes met Wynn's, she felt as if he looked right into her soul, so intense was his gaze. She nodded her head as he stared at her, then, offering her hand, realized she was trembling.

"A pleasure to see you again, Miss Cox," he said. "Under more favorable circumstances."

As their hands met, Wynn was stirred by a wave of sensation. In spite of the elegant clothes he wore, he had an untamed look and the strength of his grip testified that he was far more used to pulling lines on a tall ship than holding ladies' delicate hands.

"Robert is an experienced sailor, as you know," said Sarah.

"That's right," he said. "But my father has not been well, I find. I'm afraid I will be land-locked, seeing to his import business for a while."

"But you are chafing to get to sea again," teased Sarah. Then, noticing painful emotions in his eyes, she changed the subject.

"Perhaps you will come to tea with us Friday next," she said. "I have invited a few guests to keep me busy and to meet my cousin."

Robert bowed to Sarah. "I'd be happy to have tea with you," he said, scrutinizing Wynn with a slight frown. Turning again to Sarah, he said, "Send word to the Sign of the Golden Fleece if you should have any more word from your husband. I am most anxious to see him." It was more a command than a request, but Sarah only seemed amused by it. Wynn felt perplexed. There were many questions she still wanted to ask about this man.

"Good-bye then, Robert," Sarah said.

"Good-bye, Mrs. Kidd. A pleasure to see you again, Miss Cox." He bowed, then he was off.

"What a strange man," Wynn murmured to Sarah. "Why is he so gruff? It's as if he is struggling to control himself."

Sarah watched him disappear down the street toward his father's place of business, known as the Sign of the Golden Fleece. "I believe Robert Lamley has had a difficult life. His family is well-off, yet as a young man he wanted to go to sea. He married a girl he met on a voyage, then lost her in a storm on the Indian Ocean.

That was years ago. His father wants him to stay on land and be a gentleman, but Robert is driven to go to sea. It seems an obsession, as if he is trying to conquer something. He will probably sail with William this coming voyage."

"He seems a very complex man," said Wynn. Sarah's remarks helped her understand some of the conflict she had read in Robert's face when she talked with him on deck.

"He is. Would that he could find happinesss one day."

The women continued to the site where Trinity Church was being raised. Sarah explained that William had helped found the church this year and that in another year it would be completed. The Kidds would own a pew. Wynn observed the workmen moving the big stones, but, try as she would, her mind wasn't on the scene before her. She was thinking of Robert Lamley and discovered that she felt apprehensive about seeing him again.

For the rest of the day, Sarah showed Wynn her other properties on Wall Street, Tienhoven Street, and Water Street, which had been built on a landfill. Wynn finally broached the subject on her mind.

"Sarah, with all this property, perhaps you need a manager in your husband's absence?" Her heart pounded as she waited for Sarah's reply. Her family wanted to come to the New World, and Sarah could make that possible.

"I will discuss it with William," Sarah replied. "I am sympathetic to my distant relatives. As a supporter of James the Second, Jonathan must find it difficult in Protestant England. But why doesn't Jonathan want to go to a more Catholic colony?"

"It is the livelihood of his family he is most concerned with, not religion," Wynn said thoughtfully. "He believes New York has the best opportunities for my brother as well." Then Wynn swallowed. She had forgotten to mention James to Sarah. Surely the additional family members would seem an imposition.

But Sarah did not seem to notice the oversight. They now stood at the Queen's Gate next to the East River, where the dark water rippled below them. "Commerce is what makes this town thrive. Unlike others who sought the New World for religious freedom, New York's founders were trading men. It is the spirit of trade that has built farms and town lots and reclaimed land from the waterfront." She turned to Wynn. "It is a metropolitan place, and I do not believe a Catholic would be made unwelcome here."

"That's what my father believes. He would make you quite a good manager, Sarah, if I may be so bold as to say so. It was only prejudice that made his business colleagues turn against him in England. I also believe he wishes to sail to the New World with his family before he is too old. He is only forty-nine and a strong and healthy man yet. He still has a sense of adventure."

Sarah grinned. "You must be right. Yes, I believe we will be able to work it all out. I have more property than I can manage. I really don't know what to do with it all. William takes care of it when he is here, but it would be wonderful to have someone I could trust to look after it year round."

Wynn smiled at her cousin. She knew in her heart that all would go well. As she leaned on the gate staring up at the overcast sky, dark billowing clouds threatened to spill a storm. Yet this was the kind of sky Wynn loved; moving, forming clouds with dark blues and grays, and a wind coming up.

"Come, let's get back to the house before this storm breaks," Sarah said.

Chapter Three

On the day of the tea party, Wynn, Sarah and Elizabeth prepared pickled tongue and beef, sweetmeats, jellies, ornamented cakes, fruit and homemade bread, finally standing back to admire the vast display. No sooner had they changed clothes and come back downstairs than Elizabeth announced the first guest.

"Mr. Portman is here, ma'am. He's in the parlor," she told Sarah with a little curtsy that amused Wynn. Apparently the servants put on airs for company.

"Thank you, Elizabeth. Come along, Wynn. You must meet my dearest neighbor." She led the way to where a thickset middle-aged man stood by the fireplace. He had gray whiskers, pink cheeks and a generous mustache, and Wynn could see the benevolence in his face as he came forward to greet them.

"Well, my dear Sarah, you look lovely as ever," he said, admiring her turquoise damask gown with satin bows at the elbows. The bodice was edged with lace, revealing Sarah's rounded bosom, and the same thick lace bordered her petticoat's small train. It made Wynn feel rather plain in her crisp dimity with ruched underskirt.

"Gerald," said Sarah after he had raised her fingers to his lips, "I want you to meet my cousin from England. This is Wynfield Cox."

Wynn curtsied awkwardly. Nevertheless the gentleman beamed at her, and his warmth reminded her of her father.

"What a pleasure. But you look nothing like Sarah, except that the beauty is equal."

Sarah's tinkling laugh adorned his compliment. "I'm afraid we're related only by marriage," she said. "Through my first husband, that is."

"I see, I see," said Gerald, fingering his lace cravat. "Well, come and have a cup of tea with me, my dear, and tell me about yourself. I understand you are a heroine. Did you come over all alone?"

Wynn followed Gerald into the dining room where the sumptuously laid table tempted those with an appetite. She ignored the reference to her adventure and replied, "I came over alone, but my family will join me as soon as can be arranged," she said. "Sarah has said my father can work for her."

Stroking his whiskers, Gerald chose a sweetmeat. "I am sure he'll be well-employed then," he said. "We need new families in the colonies."

They chatted about London and life in the New World as the other guests began to fill the house, among them Hannah Luck, who nodded in Wynn's direction. It was a large gathering, and Wynn was glad they had prepared so much food, even though the guests took only small portions of each tasty dish. She was so busy meeting the guests that she failed to see Robert Lamley come in. It wasn't until she was seated in a straight-backed chair in a corner of the parlor, laughing at one of Gerald Portman's stories, that she suddenly saw Robert's dark eyes observing her from across the room.

He was dressed in a dark blue, slightly waisted coat. A wide silk cravat complemented the coat and contrasted with his tanned face. A thong held his hair at the neck. His breeches came to below the knee, and dark hose, revealing muscular calves, rose out of his high-heeled buckled shoes. He stood brooding beside a matronly woman who spoke incessantly. As he bit into he scone, Wynn could see that he was only half listening to the one-sided conversation.

Her pulse quickened as she observed him, and she could tell by the way he wore his elegant clothes and viewed his surroundings that he would be more comfortable out of doors, though there was no fault with his deportment. Her throat constricted and she lowered her gaze. She hadn't meant to look at him so long.

"I say," said Gerald. "I don't believe you've been listening to the last words I've said."

Wynn blushed even more furiously at his teasing. "I'm sorry. What were you saying?"

But Gerald, who had followed her distracted gaze, was not surprised by her air. "Nothing of importance. But then I've been dominating your conversation. Perhaps you would like to visit with some of the other guests?"

"Oh, no, no." But it was too late. Robert Lamley had crossed the room and stood before them.

"Miss Cox, I believe," he said and bowed.

She found her voice, hoping her cheeks were not as red as they felt. "Yes, Mr. Lamley. How do you do? Do you know Mr. Portman?" As Gerald rose from the velvet-cushioned chair, Wynn noticed that he was several inches shorter than Robert.

"Yes, we are acquainted," said Gerald. "How are

you, Robert?" The men shook hands, but neither smiled.

"I am well, Mr. Portman, except for the annoyances of my father's business."

"Ah, Robert, when will you give up your adventuresome spirit and stay on the land?"

"Never, I hope, sir. I cut my eyeteeth hanging onto a tops'l yard while trying to fist billowing canvas in a gale. I'm afraid life on land is too tame for me."

"Aye," said the older man. "You've dodged many a French cannonball as well, I'll wager. Still, there are also rewards to be won staying at home."

Robert nodded curtly in acknowledgment.

"Perhaps you'd like to speak to Miss Cox?" offered Gerald reluctantly.

Robert turned to Wynn. "I find I need some fresh air. Would you care to take a walk?"

Wynn was startled. "Wouldn't it be rude to leave the other guests?" she asked, although she knew she, too, would like to quit the stuffy room.

"It is stifling in this room," he said. "Perhaps you will accompany me to the garden?"

She glanced at Sarah, who was caught up in conversation, then she nodded. "I'll just excuse us for a few minutes."

She led the way past Sarah and bent to whisper in her ear. "I'm showing Mr. Lamley the garden, if you don't mind."

Sarah looked up, assessing Robert, then said, "Don't stay away too long," and returned to her conversation. Words about fattening geese and using their feathers for comforters reached Wynn's ears as they passed by.

Outside, Robert took a deep breath, inhaling the air as if it were giving him new life. He stretched his shoulders as if he found his suit confining and led Wynn to a small bench under the locust tree, whose blooms scented the air.

"It is more pleasant here, is it not?" said Robert.

"Yes, of course," she answered. "But to be within the confining walls of the garden is not as much to your liking as walking the planks of a ship, I surmise."

"I'm afraid you are right," Robert said with an odd smile.

"And yet your father is a merchant. How did you happen to go to sea?"

Robert shrugged as he gazed over the garden wall at the pink sky beginning to cast a glow over the water. "My father was the younger son of an old and impoverished noble family. He came to America to build his own fortune."

"And did he succeed?"

"Modestly. But to answer your question, I first sailed to look after the goods my father traded. The ocean became for me a great system of canals linking the continents. Then I fought the French. Once the sea beckons . . ." He stopped.

"I'll sail with Captain Kidd when he docks here on his way to the Indian seas," he continued.

"Why must you go?" she said impulsively.

"It's the only life for a man," he said. "To feel the swaying of a ship under your feet, to hear the creak of timbers."

"What about the danger?" she said, remembering the pain he must have suffered when he had lost his wife.

Robert's eyes darkened. "I've met danger head on. I've seen man powerless before the mighty sea" — the muscles in his face tensed — "when it becomes a monster, waves breaking against timbers. The ship tossed in the hands of God." He turned to Wynn, whose heart was pounding, so afraid was she that she had said the wrong thing to him. "I've met her danger, but she cannot force me to surrender to it. I've conquered the sea before, and I will conquer it again, a thousand times before my death."

His words made her tremble. She could see he was fighting an inner battle, perhaps trying to conquer some deep emotion within himself, rather than the sea. Yet she did not know him well enough to voice this belief, so she remained silent, only gazing at him with her blue eyes.

The eyes that looked at Robert held compassion, and he saw it as he stood above her. His glance took in the brightness of her complexion, the determined set of her chin, then he turned away, berating himself for paying any attention to this bewitching girl. He had loved once and lost his wife to the monster sea. He would not love again. Nor could he merely dally with a guest of his friends. She would be far too protected for that. Nevertheless his eye had not missed her straining bosom, the trim waistline and turn of ankle that she took no care to hide under her skirts. He must put these thoughts aside. When his body drove him to it, he had found satisfaction among women that he could use and forget, but he went for months at a time before doing that, feeling somehow that it defiled the memory of the wife he had loved so passionately.

This woman could not be used that way, and he would not love again. It was his fate only to do battle with the sea until he had purged himself of both his love and hatred of it. He stared silently out at the river.

Perhaps if he could unburden himself to her, Wynn reflected, he would find that life need not always seem so cruel. Her next words startled him out of his reverie.

"Perhaps you will show me the ships you've sailed on," she said. "A woman is not safe walking about the docks alone."

He looked at her curiously before answering, as if debating with himself. "If you would like to see the craft that line the harbor, I will show you. You would be safe with me."

She averted her eyes, unable to meet, for long, his

intense gaze. "Very well. I would be pleased if you would escort me. But I believe we should be returning to the guests."

He removed his foot from the bench where he had been leaning with his elbow on his knee. "I will take you to the docks on Sunday then," he said, watching her closely.

"Sarah and I will be at home after church. We will be happy to see you then," she said, afraid her voice would betray the fear she now felt about her request to him. She gave her hand to him so that he could lead her back to the house, and when he took it, a burning sensation assailed her. She was glad for the company inside to distract her. There was something she could not quite name about the way he made her feel, but it held the promise of adventure that she had come to the New World to find.

Yet she realized she would never fall in love with such a man, for he would never be capable of tender feelings. And she pitied the woman he might one day marry, for she would be left at home while he sailed on the great oceans linking the continents.

On Sunday Wynn dressed with care. Her close-fitting green bodice was tightly laced, sloping to a point in front, and the low-cut neckline bared her neck and bosom. For modesty's sake she wore a lacy waist-length tippet, tied at the throat, which covered her shoulders and bodice like a short cape. As she brushed her straw-colored curls, she pondered the events that had brought her to this outing.

She could not suppress the excitement that raced through her at the thought of seeing Robert Lamley today. She told herself it was out of pity for the man. Surely he was lonely, and perhaps even a little mad, but maybe a little company would draw him out. She pressed her lips together. This feminine instinct was new to her, and she wondered at the change. What would James say if she told him about Robert as she had told him about everything that touched her life in the past?

She studied her innocent, open face in the mirror above the highboy, her stomach churning as she tried to view herself as Robert must view her.

Perhaps she ought not to have suggested walking out with him. What would she say to bring him out of his shell? He had such a moody temper, and his fixation on conquering the sea was such nonsense.

Wynn did not have long to ponder about Robert, however, for Elizabeth poked her blonde head in to announce that Master Lamley had called and was waiting in the parlor. Wynn fingered the ringlets that hung gracefully over her shoulder and followed the servant girl down the stairs.

Robert, who had been facing the window looking out at the waterfront, turned as Wynn entered the parlor and took in her approaching figure. As she felt his blatant stare sweep her bare of any covering, she swallowed in embarrassment, horrified at the catch in her throat.

Just then Sarah entered, her linen petticoats swishing softly. She greeted Robert with outstretched hands.

"My dear Robert, how nice to see you," she said as she walked toward him. He took her hands in his and bent to kiss them. Then he raised his dark eyes to Sarah's violet ones.

"Mrs. Kidd, I hope you are well today. I have not thanked you for the tea on Friday." He spoke politely, but with a certain moody arrogance that, in spite of sounding stilted, made him seem even more attractive. Sarah simply returned the flattery.

"A few hours of social fellowship keeps me from utter boredom when William is away," she said.

"I pray that he will return to you soon, madam."

"Ah, Robert," Sarah teased. "You do not fool me. You want him to return for only one reason, so that you can set sail with him when he leaves again."

Allowing himself to be cajoled, Robert smiled, but he pleaded his case. "I cannot fool you, Sarah. I wonder that you know me so well. But you make out that we poor sailors are guilty of destroying the joyful experience of matrimony." Sarah laughed lightly, as if she had had this conversation many times before.

"You know there is no malice intended. What a man does is his own business. How well I know that the lure of the sea is as strong as the lure of a woman's arms. William has enough property and business to retire to the land for the rest of his life, and yet I know he will never do it and I imagine the same is true for you."

Wynn found herself blushing at Sarah's vivacious frankness.

"Ah, but do not let me keep you," Sarah entreated. "The day is not half over, and there are sights to see. Do take care of my cousin, Robert. I expect I shall see you some hours from now." She turned to Wynn. "Enjoy yourself, my dear," she said, kissing her cousin on the cheek.

"I will, Sarah," said Wynn, and with that Sarah took her leave, her skirts bustling as she walked out of the room, leaving Robert and Wynn together.

After leaving the house, Robert and Wynn walked in silence down the Strand to the Great Dock where the tall ships were moored, two- and three-masted sloops with raised quarterdecks; single-deck pinnaces with high, sweeping bulwarks; seven-hundred-ton East Indiamen, the ships that brought home the treasures of the Orient — silks, spices and jewels. Robert pointed out the differences between the complex riggings.

Swept up in his words, Wynn walked beside him, listening as he described the various aspects of his voyages. Here on the docks, his brooding face and dark eyes came alive. "With one of these vessels under our feet, a good crew can ride even the roughest sea," he said with pride. "To be a good sailor is to master it."

She paused on the wharf, facing him, her hair blowing behind her in the strong breeze. When he looked at her as she stood silhouetted by the great ships, excitement flickered in his eyes. The air blew through his black hair, loosened from its thong, and his tanned face seemed all the more virile in this setting. Wynn felt drawn toward this strange man whom she strangely understood. Perhaps it was because she, too, had been willing, even anxious, to leave her familiar home in London and voyage to the New World where people shared a sense of challenge.

For Robert, the challenge was the sea — a sea that had taken a wife from him and with which he still did battle. She could picture him riding above the waves, the sea submissive to him. But to her way of thinking, he fought a useless battle.

A feeling of resentment ran through her. A man like him would always be on a quest. But she, like other women, was destined to wait on the land. She tried to imagine herself waiting for a man like Robert, but then the other side of her nature rebelled. She knew she was expected to lead a settled life, to someday run a household and raise children to climb on their papa's lap at night. But she had always yearned for something else, although she did not quite know what. But alas, she was only a woman, and she would never be able to voyage to all the continents like a man.

As she reflected on these things she did not realize that she was still staring at Robert, but his gaze did not leave her face, and he took a step closer to her. For long moments they looked into each other's eyes, as the clouds sailed overhead in the blue sky. They could hear the sounds of children playing in the distance, while on the docks, sailors heaved crates onto ships. But time seemed to stop. In that moment, Wynn had an odd premonition that Robert's fate would somehow be linked to hers, even though she struggled against it. She backed away a step as she foresaw the obstacles that would come between them, and the strange feeling passed.

Robert turned away and moved toward the giant ship that was docked near where they were standing. Emotions he had not known in some years struggled within him. This was not advantageous at all. He was not planning for a woman in his life, and yet he had let her tempt him to see her again. He was just now fighting off the other responsibilities incurred by his family's business. He could not let himself be tied to land by a home and a wife as well. And he could not take a woman on a voyage. That had cost him dearly already.

With his hands in his belt, he lifted his shoulders and shook his hair backward, the gesture expressing his frustration. He looked back at Wynn's fresh face, her cool blue eyes and straw-colored hair, the ringlets blowing above her modest short cape, and the vision of her standing there pulled at something in him that he had thought long since buried.

He took her elbow and propelled her away from the dock in the direction of the Governor's Garden. They walked for a while, hardly aware of passers-by, finally stopping on a rise of ground covered with forest that afforded a view of the Hudson, its surface unbroken except for a lonely canoe and a small skiff drifting downstream. Wynn sensed Robert's annoyance, but she knew she had neither said nor done anything to offend him. Nevertheless she was beginning to be able to measure this man's chameleon disposition.

They stood for a while next to each other, viewing the scenery, and again Wynn felt awed by this new land, a vast wilderness to be explored. There seemed to be little to say, so they walked slowly back to the east side of town, nodding now and then to acquaintances and eventually came to the Queen's Gate, where the Strand met the old wall that had once fortified the town.

"We may be going to the farm soon," said Wynn just to fill the silence. "Sarah has had word that the captain is due in a matter of weeks, and the heat is starting to bother her. I believe your family has property next to the Saw-Kill farm?"

"Yes, that is true. My parents are there now."

"Do you like it there?"

"The country and fresh air are bracing."

"I am anxious to see the country. Do you go there often?" she asked, and then bit her tongue, afraid it sounded as if she wanted to see him there.

"I am mostly tied to business here, when I am not at sea," he said.

She turned and gazed out toward the harbor. Directly east lay Long Island, and she remembered the rich green foliage she had seen on Staten Island as they passed through the narrows on the way in.

"What is the farm like?" she asked.

"It is on the Hudson River, where the banks are too steep for commerce but pleasant for leisure," he said.

"You will see it," he said, stopping rather abruptly.

As they stood by the gate, Wynn noticed several of Sarah's neighbors pass by. She wondered what they would think seeing Robert and her together. In England when a gentleman called on a lady, it meant he was serious about her. Here, she somehow felt, there might be some speculation as the neighbors sat on their stoops gossiping in the warm evenings, but the relationship would not be taken seriously. If what Sarah said was true, everyone's business was everyone else's, but there was not much time for idle conversation, as people had to spend so much of their time fighting for their daily survival.

"Perhaps we should go in," she suggested to Robert. "Sarah will be putting on tea."

Robert nodded, and she slipped her hand into the

crook of his elbow. His arm felt strong as he led her down the street and up the steps to the house.

Inside the house, Robert accepted tea and conversed with Sarah. Seated in the armchair, he relaxed and seemed to make an effort to entertain Sarah and her daughter, the hard lines of his face relaxing into a teasing expression when little Sarah climbed on his knee.

Wynn scarcely noticed the passage of time, and when she looked out the window, she saw the sky had darkened. Robert finally stood to take his leave, bowing first over Sarah's, then Wynn's hand.

"If I may be of service to either of you ladies in the captain's absence, please call on me. I will be at your command."

"Thank you," said Wynn.

"I might ask you to hold the wool while I knit," quipped Sarah.

Undaunted by her teasing, Robert smiled. "I shall be here to hold your wool whenever you summon me, provided, of course, that business allows." Wynn wondered at the lightness of spirit Robert seemed to experience under Sarah's warm roof.

Then a painful thought crept into Wynn's mind. Perhaps it was not the home but Sarah herself who warmed Robert's spirits, as she did all her guests'. An unfamiliar pang of jealousy tore through Wynn's heart. She suddenly doubted that she could ever bring such warmth to Robert's eyes, and the thought so distressed her that she found it hard to carry on the banter as Robert prepared to leave. Even more distressing was the fact that this man could have such an effect on her.

After Robert left, Sarah did, indeed, go after her knitting needles and Wynn sat with her on the settee in the parlor keeping her company. Her eyes lowered, she made conversation about the wool as little Sarah played with some pieces of yarn on the floor.

"Thank heavens we don't keep sheep," Sarah was saying. "Many of our neighbors do, and I've watched them prepare wool from the fleece. It's a tedious job — cleaning, washing, dyeing, carding, greasing, and rolling. Then you have to spin, wind and rinse it. Finally there is the knotting."

"All that makes knitting seem the easiest part," said Wynn, still concentrating on the yarn in her lap.

"Indeed," said Sarah, "except for the sheep, who have the easiest job of all." Her knitting needles clicked as a stocking began taking shape. At eight o'clock the curfew rang from the church belfry, and she rose to take little Sarah to bed.

Wynn sat by the windows, which were open to let in the breeze from the river. She stared at the water lapping lazily on the shore, thinking of her home in England. How she hoped her family would come soon so they could all be together again. She wished her brother, James, were here now. In the past, they'd shared everything, but she wondered if she'd be able to explain to him how she felt now. When she heard the rattle of the night watchman, she started up to bed.

Outside, the watchman sighed and lifted his lantern so he could see the large brassbound hourglass. He hoped no small boys would taunt him tonight. It made his hair stand on end when one of them shouted "Indians," only to laugh and run away. One day there again might be a real threat from the Indians, and then where would they be if he didn't take the cry seriously? A dog barked, and the watchman rang his bell, proclaiming the weather and the hour of the night.

Wynn pulled back the covers of her feather bed and laid her head on the pillow. The branches outside brushed the window panes as wind swept over the silent house. Already she felt that the New World was more suited to her spirit than England had been, and in spite of her nervousness about her feelings for Robert Lamley, she felt exhilarated and alive.

Chapter Four

The month passed, and one July day the cries of young boys as they clattered up the steps of the house brought Sarah and Wynn out of the kitchen, where they had been adding up accounts at the kitchen table. Elizabeth was in the hall scolding the small urchins who were falling all over each other trying to deliver their message.

"Missus Sarah," panted one small cherub with very tousled hair. "We gotta see Mrs. Sarah, the captain's wife."

"Yes, yes, what is it?" Sarah said, walking quickly into the hallway.

"There she is," said the other boy, escaping Elizabeth's grasp and pointing to the lady of the house. "It's the *Adventure Galley*, missus. Joe down at the dock said to run and tell you."

"Oh," Sarah gasped, one hand flying to her heart. She ran to the window to stare out at the tall masts sailing into the harbor and hastily untied her apron. Wynn, sharing in her excitement, ran upstairs to get little

Sarah. How wonderful, the captain would be home at last. She brought the little girl downstairs to find that Sarah had already run out of the house.

Just as Wynn emerged from the house with little Sarah, she heard a man's voice calling to Sarah. "Hey ho," he shouted. It was Sarah's brother, Samuel Bradley, dressed like a sailor in work pants and a shirt open to the chest. He was dark and lean like Sarah, but with well-developed muscles in his arms and chest from the hard work he did. He motioned Sarah toward the docks. Wynn had met Samuel when he had come to help Judson with some of the heavier jobs around the house. He was a taciturn fellow, but strong, and full of affection for his sister.

Sarah ran along the waterfront down to the Great Dock — her daughter and Wynn following at some distance. As Wynn neared the dock, she saw that another of the captain's friends had also come to meet him. Robert Lamley, dressed as elegantly as ever, stood at the edge of the dock, one foot resting on an ironbound crate, which was ready for loading.

Sarah had gone all the way to the end of the dock and now watched as the *Adventure Galley* bore down on them. The ship was fast and graceful, and everyone on the dock stood watching as the impressive vessel skimmed the water of the upper bay.

Robert stood rigidly, only his eyes moving, as he kept pace with the boat. As she moved closer, other ships in the waters gave her the right of way. She was a hybrid vessel, combining modern hull and sail rig with the ancient concept of oar power. Built for combat, she looked heavy for a ship of her size but still maneuverable with lots of fire power. As she approached, those on dock began to cheer. Sarah turned and called for her daughter, and Wynn let the girl run to her mother. Sarah lifted the little girl up so she could see the great ship that brought her father. Samuel moved closer, squinting to get a better view of the new vessel.

Wynn took a few steps forward, and Robert caught her eye. He lowered his foot from the crate and looked at her with joy in his eyes. Wynn's heart leapt at his expression, and words seemed unnecessary as she simply moved to him, caught up in the excitement. He took her arm and pulled her gently toward him as if he sought a physical expression of his feelings.

From the ship, men yelled orders and lines were thrown ashore. Then the pilings crashed with the weight of the ship as the lines were pulled tight. Robert and Wynn balanced themselves on the floating dock as it rode with the waves while they watched the crew secure the lines.

A tall man dressed in captain's garb stood on the quarterdeck, issuing orders. When all was secure, he ordered the gangplank lowered. The crowd made way so that the captain's wife could go aboard. Wynn and Robert watched as Sarah and little Sarah tripped lightly up the gangplank, with Samuel Bradley following. The captain had come down to the upper deck and stretched out his arms to embrace his family.

"Ho there, Samuel," he called to his brother-in-law as he reached to grip Sarah's brother by the arm.

Wynn's heart fluttered, and without realizing it, she moved even closer to Robert. She stared at the beautiful lines of the ship and her eyes became moist, whether from the sea breeze or from the emotions she felt, she did not know. Then, becoming self-conscious, she looked up at Robert. He must have been feeling something of the same thing, for his eyes were damp as he looked into hers. His hold on her tightened as he stared at her. Then he lifted his hand to brush her hair away from her forehead, and a rush of sensation overwhelmed her. Still, his grasp tightened, and he seemed about to speak, but then he stopped as if he thought better of it.

That he was attracted to her was obvious, and his tight hold on Wynn made her feverish. But that he struggled with himself was evident too. Finally, he put his lips to her forehead and placed a kiss there. She shut her eyes, her head against his shoulder, her heart throbbing violently. He sighed then, and loosened his hold on her. She stood gazing at him until she was distracted by the commotion that told her William and Sarah were approaching.

Raising an arm in greeting, Robert turned and walked toward the captain, who was tall and broadly built with a sandy head of hair flecked with grey. Sarah looked absolutely radiant, as the captain, with his daughter in his arms, beamed upon the crowd who cheered him. He put little Sarah down and extended his arms as soon as he saw Robert.

"Robert, my old friend, it's good to see you," he said as the two men embraced.

"Welcome to New York," said Robert in a reserved tone that nevertheless managed to express his gladness. Wynn watched the two men shake hands after embracing and clapping each other on the back. As they eyed one another, she could see that they were of equal height and equal in presence, although Robert was the younger by about ten years. They both exuded the same sense of bravado, a daring and self-confidence that seemed to outshine other men.

"You must join us at the house, Robert. I have a lot to tell you," Kidd said, clapping him on the shoulder again.

"I've been anxious to discuss some matters with you myself," said Robert. "But I wouldn't want to take you away from your family, William."

"Nonsense, man. I'm sure Sarah will agree, we must

all celebrate together this evening." He gave his wife a wink and squeezed her shoulders. "I have all night to enjoy my wife." Sarah laughed, a gay, throaty laugh, unembarrassed by the suggestive remark her husband made.

"We'd be most pleased if you'd join us, Robert," she said. "You know you're always welcome at our house. Samuel will be there too. And William, you have not yet met our cousin. Did you receive my letter telling of her arrival? She's been the best companion I could ever have, and I want you to meet her. Cousin?" She turned to Wynn, motioning her to join their group.

As Wynn stepped toward them, admiration flickered in William's eyes. He seemed to assess her qualities at one glance. Wynn smiled politely and held out her hand. She liked the alertness in his eyes and the patrician face, deeply lined from years of responsibility. William bowed gallantly to her.

"Welcome, Cousin Wynn. I did indeed receive my wife's letter, and I am indebted to you for keeping her company. I'm afraid being a sailor's wife is a lonely occupation. Any companionship and distraction you have provided is more than appreciated."

"It has been my pleasure, sir, and I thank you for opening your home to me. When I first came, I did not know how welcome I would be, as I am a stranger to you all and only distantly related."

Sarah broke in on them. "Enough of this exchange of compliments. Let's all go to the house and Wynn and I will oversee a delicious meal while you gentlemen exchange confidences in the study. We have the whole evening." She clasped her brother's arm and leaned down to smooth little Sarah's hair while Captain Kidd fell in beside Robert and led the way, already deep in discussion with his seafaring friend. This left Wynn to carry little Sarah and trail along behind the girl's mother. The Kidds nodded hello to passers-by who turned to look at the celebrated group, for Captain Kidd was well established in society and business in New York. Wynn was aware that he had been honored by the governor for fighting the French in the West Indies, for Elizabeth had told her about this. Robert, too, had distinguished himself under Kidd's command, but Elizabeth was unable to tell her much about this, except that it was shortly after that time that Robert had married and lost his wife.

When Captain Kidd's entourage reached the steps that led up to the house, Robert turned to offer a hand to Wynn. Their eyes met as their hands touched, and a shiver went down her spine. Already, unspoken feelings passed between them. When she met Robert, she had believed it was only pity and curiosity she felt for him. Perhaps she had been fooling herself, she told herself now. She had been attracted to him from the first, but she had not allowed herself to admit it. Now apprehension struck her heart. She had not meant to fall in love with this man; it could only mean heartbreak and loneliness. As they entered the foyer of the cool house, Wynn realized there was only one way out: If Robert went to sea very soon, her emotions would have time to settle, and she would get over her infatuation.

In the shadowy hallway, Robert put his hand on her waist and squeezed it briefly. He could not help the desire that filled him, and as he gazed at her half-parted lips and the soft curve of her breasts, the blood throbbed in his loins and made them ache for her.

Wynn's resolve melted. She wanted to fall against him and feel the strength of his shoulder, but she steeled herself to remain rigid instead. She would have to fight these emotions if she were to do what was best for her future, she thought to herself. If she had misled Robert into thinking she held affection for him, she would have to clarify her position. He might be angry, but it was better to make her feelings known now than to entangle herself in a relationship she would later regret.

Robert left her then and followed William and Samuel to the study across the hall from the parlor. Elizabeth had dusted and made it ready just this week, in anticipation of the captain's return. She stood by the door and curtsied. "Welcome home, sir."

Wynn noticed how slight the girl looked standing among the three tall men.

"Thank you, Elizabeth," William said. "I'm glad to see you've kept things in good order here."

"I've tried, sir. Can I bring you anything?"

"A glass of Madeira for Mr. Lamley, Mr. Bradley and myself, thank you." The girl curtsied again and hurried off to get goblets and a decanter.

"Thank you, William," said Samuel, "but I'd best bathe and change. Sarah'll be wantin' me clean for supper. I'll have that glass when I come back." He shook hands with the captain and with Robert and, tipping his hat to Wynn, left by the front door. Then William ushered Robert into the study.

"I have a commission from the king," he said as he closed the oak door behind them. As Wynn watched the door close, a shiver of foreboding passed through her. Having learned a few of the details from Sarah, she knew Robert was going to join this venture of Captain Kidd's and that it was already fraught with problems. However, it was not her business to pry into these things, especially since she'd made up her mind that there was no future for Robert and her. It would be best if he went to sea and got out of her life.

She went out to the kitchen, her linen skirt and petticoats rustling as she walked. She replaced the apron she had thrown down when they all rushed to the dock, and silently bent over her work, helping Sarah and Elizabeth prepare a feast. How could Sarah sing, wondered Wynn? Granted, her husband was home at last, but only to take care of whatever business he had here and then leave again. There was no peace for the family of a seaman, yet Sarah seemed to accept this life. She was at home with the rules of this society, within which she'd developed her remarkable character and wit as well. But on occasion Wynn had noticed an underlying sadness, which revealed the true state of her emotions.

Wynn took the vegetables Elizabeth brought in from the pantry and cut them with annoyance. If the New World offered adventure and opportunity, there was also turbulence to be had as well. And yet, wasn't her own impetuousness to blame for the feelings of dismay she now felt?

Captain Kidd walked around the large walnut veneer desk and heaved himself into his big double-nailed leather armchair. "Ah," he sighed, "the comforts of home. It's odd how you get used to being without them at sea, then when you near shore you don't know how you could have stayed away so long."

Robert crossed to the window and put one booted foot on a small turned stool, glancing first out the window, then at Kidd. He smiled wryly at the captain.

"And how long will you be enjoying the comforts of home this time, my friend?" asked Robert.

"That is what I have to talk to you about. I had bad luck in London."

"Surely you don't consider your Great Seal Commission bad luck?"

"No, no, of course not, but it was what followed. Ah, Robert, I fear the Furies are after me this voyage. I sincerely hope it will be my last. I am ready to retire and enjoy my family and my property on land."

Robert looked questioningly at Kidd. "If the terrible

winged goddesses are chasing you, sir, what was your misdeed? Those goddesses pursue and punish doers of unavenged crime."

"Well, perhaps I spoke too grandly. It was not a crime, merely an oversight. I failed to salute the king's yacht while sailing down the Thames. To make matters worse, my men insulted the royal naval crew by slapping their backsides. It cost me dearly."

Robert stared at Kidd then broke out in booming peals of laughter. Just then Elizabeth brought the Madeira, nervously watching Robert's merriment as she placed the tray on the captain's desk.

"That will be all, Elizabeth, thank you," said Kidd. After she had left and closed the door behind her, Kidd reprimanded Robert in a teasing tone.

"Really, my dear fellow, we can't have you carrying on so in the house. What will the servants think?"

"More to the point, what will everyone think when they hear you blundered with the king's vessel? Why didn't you salute?"

"I thought my commission released me from such deference. But it seems I was wrong. For at the Nore, Captain Stewart of the H.M.S. *Duchess* pressed all my ablest men into naval service."

"You should have been aware," said Robert, "that the Nore has always been a favorite place for the king's ships to lie in wait for merchantmen and press them into service, often against their will."

Kidd took a sip of Madeira, which he had poured from decanter to goblet. "I was not concerned. I had my commission to protect me."

Robert threw back his head and laughed, more in derision than in humor. "But again you were wrong. The naval vessel took your men, then?"

"Of course I set out to find Admiral Russell, who arranged to get my men back. But I was cheated. Captain Stewart exchanged his bad eggs for my good ones.

So I am left with a ragtag collection of men, who, when faced with pirates, may disappoint me."

"Then how can you set sail?" Robert became more serious.

"I will add eighty men to the crew here. And that, my dear Robert, is where you come in."

"Ah, I though so." Robert came to stand before the captain's desk. "Tell me more."

"I can trust you, Robert, and you inspire confidence in men. Join the crew as first mate, and my conscience will rest easy. We can dispel any trouble that might arise. Of course my brother-in-law, Samuel Bradley, will go with us too."

"A good man," said Robert.

"And an able seaman." Kidd reached into his coat pocket and extracted some papers; unfolding them, he pushed the documents across the desk for Robert to see. "I have two commissions," he continued. "This one is the Admiralty Commission. I am," he quoted, "to apprehend, seize, and take ships, vessels, and goods belonging to the French king and his subjects or inhabitants within the domain of the French king."

Robert nodded. "And the other one?"

"The Great Seal Commission. The king charges me to sail as a private man-of-war and to apprehend pirates."

"It is doubtful that any privateer has ever been granted letters of marque with so much royal authority and official sanction," said Robert. "You are to be congratulated." Finishing off his wine, he returned the goblet to the tray on the captain's desk.

"With these commissions I rank equal to the authority assumed by the captains of the East India Company," said Kidd.

"Who assume the right to wear uniforms and swords and are saluted by cannon from the forts when they step ashore at one of the Company's factories in India," said Robert with a trace of irony in his tone. "Still, you hold no navy rank."

"That is true. But I have authority very near that of a king's officer."

Robert thought the captain a bit too sure of himself, but he kept these reservations to himself as he poured himself another glass before taking a seat in a straight-backed side chair in front of the desk. "Tell me then: Who are your backers and what part does the king play in this? What are the arrangements?"

Kidd shifted forward in his chair. "No purchase, no pay," he said. "The crew will get no pay until we've captured booty from an enemy vessel or pirate ship. And the lion's share goes to the noble lords."

"Who are?"

"Henry Stanley, the earl of Romney, master of the king's ordinance," Kidd began.

"He was secretary of state in 1690, I believe, and lord lieutenant of Ireland two years later," Robert said.

"Correct. But let me continue. Admiral Edward Russell, the man who interceded to get my crew back from Captain Stewart. He made several voyages in the cause of King William the Third, but it is rumored that he also intrigued with James the Second."

Robert frowned, trying to assess the men named by Kidd.

"Still, Lord Russell got me the same number of men taken from me at the Nore," said Kidd.

Robert made no comment, but stared into his goblet as Kidd went on.

"Charles Talbot, secretary of state, and a shrewd man, if I do say so."

"Yes," said Robert. "And Bellomont?"

"Oh yes, Richard Coote, Lord Bellomont, recently appointed governor of New York and New England. He's a favorite of the queen."

"An ambitious Irishman," said Robert.

"He does seem rather the opportunist. He was a Jacobite under the Stuarts, then a Roundhead under Cromwell, then a Jacobite again after the Restoration.

Finally, he plotted to bring over William of Orange from Holland."

"Well, that's not saying much; almost everyone did who wasn't Catholic."

"My dear Robert, you exaggerate. In any case, it is a wonder he maintains his position. His wife's escapades are the talk of London. Personally, I think he is counting on this venture to pay his debts."

"Hardly a good reason to set sail chasing pirates — to settle another man's debts," said Robert cynically.

"That isn't the reason I'm doing it."

"I'm sorry, William. I don't mean to discourage you. I want this voyage as much as you do. I need to get away to sea right now. The land constrains me." He set his goblet down hard, sloshing the ruby liquid as he did so. "I just want to know the facts."

Kidd took another sip from his goblet and continued his recital. "I nearly forgot John Somers, Lord Keeper of the Great Seal. He is the clever debater they all speak of."

"And how did you meet these noble gentlemen?"

"I barely did," said Kidd. "They're all a bit too aristocratic for my taste. It was Livingston who persuaded me."

"Robert Livingston? He was in London then?"

"Yes. He told me the governor was very interested in suppressing piracy in northern waters. And the East India Company has been plagued for many years by pirates in the Red Sea."

"They sizzle under the royal anger of the Great Mogul of India, who must be thoroughly mystified by the goings-on of the English. A black market of East India pirate goods flourishes here."

"So it does," replied Kidd. "And the East India Company has desperately petitioned King William for aid."

"The commission, then, is his answer," concluded Robert. "And Livingston?"

"If you ask me, he simply wants to make a fortune." Kidd smirked. "He always did cultivate friends in high places."

Robert turned round and leveled his gaze at Kidd. "A very Whiggish crowd, hmm?"

"Livingston wasted no time in telling Bellomont he had run into me. I was taken into his confidence and that of the promoters and my advice was sought as to the choice and purchase of a ship. Bellomont offered to find four-fifths of the sum needed if Livingston and I found the rest."

"Ah, this brings us again to the division of the spoils. Just what is the agreement?" asked Robert.

"The first ten percent goes to the Crown," Kidd said.

"That is customary," Robert commented.

"The remaining ninety percent is split three ways — sixty percent to Bellomont's backers, fifteen percent for Livingston and myself, and twenty-five percent for the crew."

"My God, man, you'll never get a decent crew for that. A regular privateering agreement gives sixty percent to the crew."

Kidd nodded resignedly. "And there's to be no sharing out of the spoils during the cruise, only after it has been properly counted by an admiralty court." He laid a palm on the smooth desk and raised an eyebrow.

Robert's face took on the angry quality so familiar to those who knew him. "And if there is no booty?"

"Livingston and I pay back every farthing our backers put into the venture." He raised a palm. "But that is unlikely. And if the prizes taken amount to one hundred thousand pounds, the *Adventure Galley* is mine."

For a moment Robert was silent. Both men knew the odds were against such a venture, but they also knew how profitable it could be if it were successful.

"Why did you say you'd do it?" Robert finally asked.

"Have you ever said no to a king?"

Outside, the light had faded. The two men sipped their wine, each deep in his own thoughts. The venture was quite mad: one ship against a sea of pirates. But by asking a seasoned captain like William Kidd, the noble lords must have been almost certain he would have the courage to take it on. And Kidd, by asking a man like Robert Lamley to be his first mate, was almost assured of a positive response. For to Robert, who never turned down a challenge, this was just one more battle to be fought. It hardly mattered whether it was privateering or a clash of arms. To him it was the same — to pit himself against unfavorable odds, and to win in the arena that had made him pay so dearly — the sea, where he had proved again and again that he was master. He would not say no to William. This man had broken him in before the mast and he felt a loyalty to him such as he felt to no other man.

Only briefly did Wynn's face flash before his eyes, but he forced his thoughts elsewhere. He had tired of the import business. His family was well-to-do now, and there were other men who could manage it in a trustworthy fashion. Yes, the time was ripe. If he wanted to keep his hand in, he must sail now. He must help Kidd with an unruly crew, break them, if necessary, into obedient sailors who depended on each other for their lives as well as the success of the venture.

Elizabeth knocked on the door to announce dinner. Kidd rose. "It's agreed then?" he asked before leaving the room.

Robert reached out his hand for Kidd's grasp. "Agreed," he said firmly. Then they left the gloomy study together.

The ladies changed for dinner. Sarah chose a deep burgundy taffeta gown with fitted bodice and lace below the elbow. Her breasts gleamed white above the low straight neckline. Wynn donned a green silk gown with a square-cut neck, deep folds in the underskirt, and chemise sleeves showing beneath the turned-up cuffs. With Elizabeth's help, she had made the dress over from one of Sarah's and was pleased with its effects.

A half smile played over her lips as she descended the stairs, and she told herself she had chosen to wear the dress to help celebrate the captain's return — no other reason.

Samuel Bradley arrived, having changed into a brocade coat and knee breeches. He joined the men in the foyer, where they were discussing the venture in low tones as Wynn passed into the dining room where Sarah was just lighting the candles.

When the men came in Wynn kept her eyes lowered, trying to avoid looking at Robert's face. She did not know what plans he and William had made, and though she was determined not to concern herself with them, she couldn't help but feel curious. Evidently, they had discussed their voyage, and now they were filling Samuel in.

Elizabeth served oysters in Sarah's own special sauce, and then they turned to the roast duck, complemented by carrots and parsnips. For dessert there would be pumpkin pie, raisins, nuts, apples and oranges.

"Wonderful, my dear," said William, licking his fingers over a piece of duck. "I don't know how I last those months at sea without your cooking." He leaned across and pinched Sarah's cheek. Wynn stole a glance at Robert as he averted his gaze from William and Sarah and concentrated on his plate of food.

"May I ask how long you will be feasting on my cooking before you go to sea again, my dear?" asked Sarah. William chuckled and leaned back in his chair. Wynn thought he looked as if he wanted to avoid the question but knew he could not.

"I should think it will take a month, at least, to find the rest of the crew," he said.

"Aye," said Samuel. "Not many hereabouts wantin' to fight pirates."

Sarah breathed more easily. "Then we will have time to go to the farm," she said. "I want Wynn to see it."

William pressed his wife's hand as Samuel spoke again. "Robert and I can enlist the men while you and Sarah go on to the farm."

"Thank you, Samuel," said William. "Providing things go as planned, we can all spend some time at the farm."

Wynn caught Robert's gaze across the candlelit table, then hastily dropped her eyes. How she wished these maddening feelings she had in his presence would desist. The dinner seemed endless to her.

After dinner, they took coffee in the parlor, where Sarah played the virginal. Wynn sat straight against the back of the settee with Samuel on her left. Again, she felt a pang of jealousy when Robert gazed appreciatively at Sarah's radiant face as she played and sang in a lilting voice. The moonlight coming in over Sarah's shoulder flattered her complexion, giving it a soft glow that contrasted with the brilliance of her eyes and her dark hair, which fell in ringlets over her bare shoulders. Was there anything Sarah couldn't do, Wynn asked herself, momentarily forgetting that Sarah could neither read nor write.

Wynn herself could only sing and play passably. She had learned a minimum of music, always being more interested in her brother's Latin and history lessons. Not fitting subjects for a woman, she knew, but her father had indulged her and allowed her to sit in on James's lessons, where she and her brother had often competed in their progress.

It never occurred to Wynn that Robert gazed at Sarah to keep his eyes off Wynn. Now that he had business matters to attend to, he could no longer allow her to invade his thoughts the way she had prior to the captain's return. He could understand his lust for her, for he had been without a woman for months. Thus he was afraid to look at her for fear he would give in to his masculine needs and seek an opportunity to seduce her. But he could not do that. Sarah would never forgive him. He frowned, his fingers idly tapping to the music on the arm of the great chair in which he sat.

Wynn felt herself becoming increasingly irritated. Why was Robert behaving this way? He had certainly been more attentive this afternoon. Indeed, she had thought for a few moments, at least, that he was becoming attached to her. But she had forbidden herself such thoughts. Her face began to flush, and she decided she needed some air if she were to bring her mind under control. She stood suddenly. Sarah continuted to play, but Wynn glanced quickly at the others.

"I need some air, if you'll excuse me." And she walked through the house and out to the garden.

"Ah," she sighed aloud, once alone in the garden with its sweet fragrances. Here it was dark and quiet, and she could calm her unruly emotions. She must rid herself of this man with whom she had made the infernal mistake of becoming acquainted. Thank heavens he was going away. A month wasn't soon enough.

But she was being uncharitable, she realized, as she sat down on a cold stone bench. To want William to leave Sarah any sooner was unthinkable. And Wynn needed to stop these waves of jealousy she was feeling for her hostess. It was insane. Sarah loved William, but with her graciousness and femininity she could not help but win the admiration of many men such as Robert. Any man would admire her good looks, beguiling temperament, and ready wit. Even if Wynn was more literate, she did not feel equal to Sarah's cleverness.

She was so wrapped up in her thoughts that she failed

to hear the footsteps that announced a presence near her. She gasped as Robert bent over her, and stood up in alarm.

"Why didn't you say something? I thought you were in the house with the others!" she said.

"It seemed an opportune time to leave the loving couple alone when Samuel took his leave," said Robert.

"Of course," said Wynn. "I didn't think of that." He was so near she could smell the wine on his breath, and she remembered he had drunk several glasses at the meal.

"Perhaps you were thinking of something else then?" he asked, a slight growl in his voice.

"I don't know what you mean."

He shrugged and turned away, speaking to her over his shoulder. "It doesn't matter. The fact is, I've come to apologize."

"For what?"

"The manner in which I displayed myself toward you earlier. It was not my usual behavior." His words were slightly slurred as he delivered the speech he had planned, and he swayed slightly.

Wynn thought she could see what he was apologizing for. He did not care for her; he had only been moved by sentimentality at the dock earlier. Nevertheless, his apology insulted her pride. She had wanted to reject him, not be rejected by him.

"I would hope you do not act that way with every female whose company you are in," she said, attempting to mask the disappointment she felt.

"I do not, I can assure you." Even in the alcoholic stupor threatening to overtake his brain, he was all too aware of her nearness; of the heat he felt every time he looked at her tempting figure, the ripe fruits of her breasts. Even now he envisioned his lips on hers.

"You have nothing to apologize for," Wynn said stiffly. "It was I who was unladylike. I had forgotten my upbringing. I can assure you it will not happen again." She burned with hurt and embarrassment. What an insidious man he was, and how horrid he must think her. She must get away, but where? She could not interrupt William and Sarah's privacy, nor could she remain here. The only escape was her own bedroom. Very well then, she would retire early tonight.

"Rest assured, I do not think ill of you," he said.

She looked at his face, now profiled, outlined by a soft moonlit sky, and her heart pulled at her in spite of her unhappiness. She uttered a small cry before her hands flew to her lips to still the sound.

"What?" asked Robert, turning full round in fear that she had hurt herself.

"Nothing," she said. "I'll go now, if you'll excuse me." But Robert blocked her path.

"I apologize if I've offended you," he said.

"I repeat, you have not," Wynn said, clenching her jaw. Obviously he did not want an involvement, but she was dismayed that his insults had such power to hurt her. She had to push by him. Surely he did not expect her to stand here and cajole him.

"Please," she said, "we have agreed to drop the matter."

"Yes, we have. But not before this." And he reached for her, pulling her harshly to him and clamping his mouth on hers.

Wynn stifled the cry that rose in her throat as his angry mouth burned its imprint on hers. As his hands sought her waist, her bodice, she gasped. He had ignited a fire that began deep in her body, its intensity shocking her. She was powerless to move, but opened her lips as his tongue caressed her mouth.

He sighed deeply as his hands came up to her shoulders, and she found herself clinging to him. Then his fingers sought entrance to the bodice of her gown, and she cried out softly, gulping for air.

"Robert, no," she said, lowering her head to his chest. This was mad. She had never experienced such feelings. No man had ever done this to her. They swayed together, and then a great tremor seemed to go through his body as he removed his fingers from her gown and held her away.

"I apologize again," he slurred. "It was the wine. I fear I have had too much."

She gasped for breath and steadied herself against the bench. "I'd best go in." She couldn't look at him.

"Yes," he said and stepped aside. Although she had wished to escape him, she felt a surge of sadness that he was so easily allowing her to leave.

"Good night," he called after her. The deep tones of his voice pierced her heart. To think that he had held her so intimately, and yet he did not care for her. It was the wine — that and her own ill-concealed emotions, she thought in shame. For already a part of her wanted to turn and run back to his arms — arms that did not love her but would only use her. She rushed into the house.

Robert stood there, watching her go, fighting himself, cursing her. "Good riddance," he said to the night air, though his heart and his body told him otherwise.

Wynn sneaked upstairs before William and Sarah could wonder what had happened to her. She shut the bedroom door, quickly undressed, and slipped into bed. The linen under her feather comforter was cool. Blowing out the candle that Elizabeth had lit for her, she lay trembling and stared out the window. The moon was a giant globe lighting the night sky. She shut her eyes on the scene, trying also to shut out the visage of the insolent Robert Lamley, her body burning with desire and shame at the thought of the touch of his long fingers on her skin.

Eventually she fell into a fitful sleep. She dreamed of her father talking to her of the coming voyage. She saw her brother handling sail on the yardarms of the *Adventure Galley*. But her brother was in England, she argued in the dream. The visions clouded over, faded. Finally, she slept peacefully.

William sat back in his great chair and filled his long-stemmed pipe with tobacco. His daughter was in bed and he sat watching his wife who was plying her knitting needles.

"Would you like some mulled cider?" Sarah asked.

"Later, perhaps, my dear. Right now I am content."

"Content, is it?" she teased him.

"Just to look at you. I am a lucky man." She dropped her work to her lap and looked up at him.

"And I am a lucky woman," she said.

"What? With a husband gone half the year?"

"That is true," she said. Then she put her work down and came to sit at his feet, placing her head on his knee. "But I married you for love. That is something no one can take from me, no matter where you are."

William caressed her dark tresses with his weathered hand. The house was silent. "You do get my letters."

"Yes. Sometimes months after you've written them. By the time I get the letters, everyone else from here to Boston knows Captain William Kidd has written to Sarah."

He laughed heartily. "Do they also tell you what the letters say?"

"No, the seals are unbroken. Besides, what could you write to your poor wife that anyone would need to know about?"

"I hope it remains so. I truly do." William sucked on his pipe and cast a troubled gaze at the windows, which looked out to the dark waters of the harbor.

"This privateering voyage sounds rather chancy,

don't you think, William?" Sarah asked, raising her head. "If you want to catch pirates, why don't you just go down to the local coffee houses?"

"It's true that piracy is endemic in the colonies. But I think Governor Bellomont is determined to change that. It is my hope that with a more favorable contract than the one I have to offer, I will draw men of the quality I wanted in England — settled family men. I shall write Livingston that I am constrained to make new contracts with the crew."

"I do not understand these Articles of Agreement between Lord Bellomont, William Livingston, and you," said Sarah, "but I rely on your judgment, my dear."

He sighed. "Let us hope your faith is justified."

"Robert has agreed to go with you? I'm almost sorry," she said.

"Whatever for?"

"I thought he and my cousin were getting on rather well together, but with a voyage to attend to, he will probably lose all thought of her."

"Do you think the *Adventure Galley* has more allure than your cousin?"

"I know it does," said Sarah. She tweaked William's ear.

"Aha," said the captain. "Outsmarted by my wife again." He took her in his arms and kissed her warmly, his hand seeking the fullness of her breast.

Love and desire flooded through her, and her body trembled in his arms. Even after years of marriage and bearing him a child, the touch of this man brought a tingle to her skin. "To bed with you," he groaned between kisses. They rose together, and she led him to the stairs.

Chapter Five

William spent several days on the waterfront gathering a crew while Robert went over the *Adventure Galley* inch by inch, impressed with her seaworthiness. They also sold the cargo of a small French vessel Kidd had taken as a lawful prize en route to New York. The proceeds were expended in laying in a further stock of provisions for the coming voyage, and Robert spent many an hour at the ship's chandler inspecting sailcloth and cordage.

He and the captain spent late nights in the study drafting new Articles of Agreement with more liberal terms for the crew. Now forty shares would go to Kidd and the partners, leaving sixty shares for the crew. Livingston, who happened to be in town, approved of the new arrangement on behalf of Bellomont after Robert persuaded Livingston that this was the only way to get a crew, and they could not sail without one.

Sarah and Wynn were meanwhile preparing the household for a stay in the country. They were packing linens to take to the farm when Sarah stood up abruptly and stared straight ahead.

"What is it?" asked Wynn, looking up from the chest she was just shutting.

"I felt something," answered Sarah, a glassy look in her eyes. "A premonition. Oh Wynn, I don't like the idea of this voyage. I don't think William will be safe, yet I cannot tell him that. Oh dear." She sat on the bed and covered her face with her hands.

Watching Sarah reminded Wynn that this was why she had shunned any involvement with a sailing man. Always these fears that a voyage might be his last — that he would never reach home again. She sat next to Sarah, putting her arm around her waist.

"Is there anything I can do?" she asked.

Sarah shook her head dejectedly. "I don't think so. I wish I knew. I don't know how to say these things to William. He knows more about them than I do. I thought I was used to being married to a sea captain." She tried to smile through her tears. "I see that I am not."

Wynn gave her shoulder a squeeze. "I don't think it matters what a man does," she said, trying to believe her own words. "There is always some danger associated with it, isn't there? Still, you've got your daughter to think of. Don't worry, Sarah."

"I know, I know. There's nothing I can do. I wish I'd been in England. I could have said no to that King William."

"I believe you could," Wynn grinned.

"I've already lost two husbands, one on his account. Surely I don't owe the king another one. And my brother will be going on this voyage too."

Wynn's good humor deserted her as Robert's face appeared in her mind. If there was the possibility of danger on this voyage against pirates and England's enemies, then Robert would have to face it too. Would he come back?

Remembering the warmth of his arms around her, Wynn closed her eyes and took a deep breath. She had to forget him. She reminded herself that a woman in love and a woman who married became man's mere vassal to be used and ordered about as he pleased. She opened her eyes and began to fold a sheet, thankful for something to do. She had the farm to look forward to. And when they returned there might be word from her family. She had written two letters for Sarah, in which she urged them to come to New York.

But try as she might to remain aloof to the undercurrents in the house during the next few days, she could not help but read the signs that passed between Sarah and William. She could see the affection they had for one another as William tweaked Sarah's chin or patted her derriere when he thought no one was looking, and she saw the way Sarah's eyes followed her husband whenever he left the room. And she could also see how worried they both were about the coming voyage.

Robert often accompanied William home to share a glass of Madeira in the study. Once, Wynn passed by the door, which was left ajar, and she caught William and Robert deep in conversation.

"But one ship against so many . . . parlous situation . . ." The rest of Robert's words were muffled.

". . . few French in the Eastern Seas . . ." came William's comment ". . . elusive pirates . . ."

"Crown's gainsaying of pirates futile in the colonies . . ."

"But it would have been disloyal to the king not to accept," said William.

". . . might vitiate the enterprise . . ."

". . . promised to stand by me."

Wynn shivered at their words and hurried past.

Often Sarah invited Robert to stay for dinner. Usually he declined, but when he did stay, Wynn found it difficult to face him. Although they spoke rarely, she occasionally caught him staring at her strangely. She endeavored to treat him as she would any other guest, but his responses to her overtures were either abrupt or puzzling, so she gave up trying to converse with him at all. Instead, heavy silences accompanied them when they were left alone for a few moments while awaiting one of the Kidd family members. Only in Sarah's presence or with little Sarah did Robert's hard facade break down. But mostly he favored William's presence, so they could map out their route.

Late in July, with Judson driving the carriage, Wynn, Sarah, Elizabeth and little Sarah left for the farm. William was to follow as soon as business allowed.

As their carriage bounced along the rutted road north, Wynn admired the scenery. Grassy meadows undulated along the river, and leafy elms and hickorys arched over the road, brushing the top of the carriage as they passed from sun to shade. Here and there neatly kept farms dotted the wilderness, and animals grazed in the mid-day sun. Pleasure craft and small sailing vessels sailed up and down the East River, now visible, no longer hidden from their view by the rolling landscape with its thick foliage where fields had not been cleared. Sarah was pensive, and the little girl played with her doll, so Wynn did not try to make conversation.

In the early afternoon, the carriage slowed and turned off the main highway. Sarah roused herself from her reverie to point out the signs along the bumpy road to Wynn. Sheep grazed on a large meadow to the south of the road, and Sarah waved to some field laborers who recognized the carriage.

"There's the stream," said Sarah, pointing to a brook that rushed noisily along a rocky riverbed. "See the wild cherry trees that grow on the side."

Wynn looked eagerly at the unspoiled surroundings.

The breeze was cooler here than in town. The carriage bounced along the curving lane and at last they glimpsed the three-story clapboard house set in a lush green clearing. Here the cockleburs, goldenrod and chickweed gave way to a neat lawn surrounded by a picket fence. Japanese magnolia and forsythia surrounded the house, which was nearly as large as the one in town. A central chimney rose from the pitched roof and three dormer windows topped five bays. The dark-stained raised-panel double door was framed by two wooden columns topped by a molding that curved up in the shape of a scroll. Other than that, the house lacked ornament.

The carriage pulled up to the small gate, and Judson climbed down to open the door for the ladies. Little Sarah tumbled out and ran straight through the opening in the coppice at the edge of the yard and headed for the grove of trees behind the house.

"She does love it here," said Sarah, watching her go.

"I can understand why," said Wynn, breathing in the scent of cherry blossoms. "I hope the captain can join us soon."

"So do I," said Sarah. "Well, let's go in."

Inside, Wynn found cool rooms furnished with sturdy furniture that was both tasteful and practical. Baluster-backed side chairs with rush seating surrounded a large gateleg table with turned legs in the main hall. In the sitting room a leather armchair and great chair with cushions were drawn up around a blue and white delft-tiled fireplace. An upholstered daybed sat near a window looking out over the front lawn. The hardwood floor was bare except for a small Turkish rug between two chairs in front of the fireplace.

The largest and most often used room in the house, however, was the kitchen. Large iron pots hung above a fire shovel, tongs and a spit for roasting in the giant hearth with an oven in the back. A long trestle table with joined benches on either side filled the center of the room. A tall spice box with paneled doors stood next to a slate-topped table that held a large porcelain pitcher and bowl. A spinning wheel rested in the corner. From the kitchen window, Wynn gazed out over the secluded clearing. Through the openings in the trees beyond, she could see the rolling fields dotted with sheep, and she wondered in which direction the Lamley property lay.

Elizabeth showed Wynn to a cozy room upstairs, where white dimity hangings enclosed a four-poster feather bed. "You'll need the blanket," said Elizabeth, "for the nights are chilly."

They opened the window to let in fresh air, and then Elizabeth helped Sarah and Wynn unpack.

It wasn't until dusk that Wynn found time to steal away by herself to do a bit of exploring. As she wandered past the coppice at the edge of the yard and down to the stream, she realized how much she had needed some time alone. It had been a strain to be in Sarah's house these last weeks. Although she felt only gratitude for the Kidds' hospitality, she had difficulty being with them, knowing that their lives were filled with worry on William's account.

All the while she struggled with her own feelings. Her young body and lively spirit were blossoming and she felt longings that she didn't know how to control. And always associated with these longings were thoughts of Robert Lamley. Even here, in the fading light, leaning against a sturdy oak tree, she could not forget him. She wandered along a path and sat on damp grass for as long as she dared. Then she found her way slowly back to the house and returned to the bright kitchen where a pot of tea was steeping by the hearth.

Sarah looked up from her needlework, glanced at Wynn, then out the window. "I'm glad you've returned," she said. "It'll be dark soon."

"I'm sorry if I worried you. It was so peaceful."

Sarah smiled sympathetically. "Yes, it is, isn't it?" She picked up her embroidery while Wynn went into Sarah's sitting room, lit a lamp, and began to write a letter to her brother. She tried to explain something of her confused state of mind, but the words looked stiff, and anyway, she had never talked about these kinds of feelings with James before. When the ink began to blur before her eyes, she returned to the kitchen. Little Sarah had fallen asleep on her mother's lap, and now Elizabeth carried her up to bed. Wynn took a candle up to her bedroom and lay down on the bed. She thought of England, and of friends she had known there. In her mind's eye, she saw the face of her dear mother and fervently wished she were here now to comfort her in this confusing time. She badly needed someone to guide her.

Life had been easy at home, where she knew exactly what was expected of her by her family. But she had wanted to leave all that, she reminded herself before she drifted off to sleep. She had wanted to cross the ocean and see this place one heard so much about — England's colonies, a new land that stretched so far, no one knew exactly how big it was. When she thought of the explorers who had found their way across it, she remembered how she had envied the fact that men could seek adventure, while women could not. Now she wanted nothing more than someone to comfort her. Comfort, she said to herself, comfort was what she desired most of all.

Wynn was on the lawn playing with little Sarah when a carriage turned into the lane and rumbled toward the house. As Wynn watched its approach, the little girl ran to the edge of the yard, jumping up and down and yelling, "Daddy, Daddy," as the carriage stopped, and William got out.

He knelt to pick up the squealing child. Then he put

her down and came to greet Wynn, who was pulling a twig from her hair that she had gotten in her tussle with the little girl.

"Hello, Cousin," he said as he took her hand.

"Hello, Captain. I'm glad to see you. How was your journey?"

"Fine, fine. Robert Lamley accompanied me as far as his parents' estate."

"Oh," said Wynn, her face clouding over. She had just begun to feel refreshed and revived by the country, and now she supposed she would not be able to avoid seeing Robert again.

"Why, my dear," said the captain, taking her arm as they walked through the gate, "one would think you were disappointed. I rather thought you and Robert had taken a liking to each other, hmm?"

She looked at him quickly, "What makes you say that?"

"He speaks of you often, you know."

She looked straight ahead, a firm set to her chin. "No, I didn't know that. I don't know why he should."

William dropped her arm and stopped, facing her. "I can see why he does. I see in him the same signs I felt when I first met Sarah."

"But, Captain," Wynn said, her face reddening. "He has made it quite clear to me that there is nothing between us at all."

Wiliam gave a chuckle. "You musn't believe that, my dear."

"Why not?"

"Because these things don't come easy to men Robert's age, and especially to a man like Robert. You must know of his unfortunate loss earlier in his life."

"Yes, I know that — to my own misfortune." She hurried to explain. "I became friendly with him, thinking he needed someone to talk to. I only wanted to help him." She shrugged, looking away. Her explanation sounded weak, even to her.

"I'm sure he did need your friendship."

"Well, I don't mind being friends with him, but he is dangerous to be near." She blushed. She did not mean to share such intimate knowledge with Captain Kidd. Yet she found him easy to talk to, much like her father or the affable Gerald Portman. But she shouldn't say too much. After all, William and Robert were friends. William might not mean to betray the trust of a young woman who was kin to his wife, but he might hint at Wynn's feelings to Robert if she betrayed herself. Still, she needed to make her position clear.

"I shouldn't have said anything," she said. "But I want you to understand something, Captain, and Robert too." She raised her head defiantly. "I'll never love a sailor. I . . . I don't have Sarah's strength and patience. I'm sorry if I sound bold. I don't mean to be insulting. It's not that I don't admire what you do and what you have done for your family. It's just that I want something different for myself."

Just then Sarah appeared on the steps and William's attention turned to her.

"Hello, darling," said Sarah, tripping down the steps and into her husband's arms. They embraced and William planted a kiss on her mouth that lasted several moments. Wynn turned away, fighting back inexplicable tears.

"Oh damn me, where do these wretched emotions come from," she whispered and ran into the house and up the stairs, flinging herself onto the bed. Although her words were proud, her heart told her something else. At that moment, she wanted only one thing — to be in Robert's arms the way Sarah was in William's. Her temples throbbed, and she buried her face in a pillow, trying to blot out the painful thoughts.

After a nap, she felt better. She bathed her face in cool water brought from the stream, and then she helped Sarah and Elizabeth with supper. Suddenly, the quiet of the country and long evenings ahead seemed oppressive to Wynn. Loneliness assailed her. In town she had longed for solitude, but now in this idyllic setting, she longed for people around her once again. Sarah and William were content with each other, and though Elizabeth gossiped with Wynn when she got the chance, the girl wasn't the kind of company Wynn needed. She wanted the companionship of a loved one, and this need compounded her homesickness. She hoped her family would set sail soon, so that at least she and James could conspire together. It would take her mind off her troubles.

The next day Judson volunteered to take Wynn to look at the sheep, and Wynn decided that it would be far better than an endless day reading a chapbook on the daybed in the parlor.

Elizabeth packed a lunch, and Wynn put on sturdy walking shoes that laced up her ankles and carried a sun bonnet, for Judson said they would have to walk a mile or so. The day was bright, and already the sun heated the countryside with warmth that promised an even hotter afternoon. Perspiration dripped from Wynn's forehead, and by the time they reached the plateau of the small hill the back of her cotton dress was soaked with dampness.

"Judson, let's sit down here. I can't go any farther," she pleaded.

The black man chuckled. "I thought you wanted to see de sheep," he said. But he spread the blanket and lowered the basket to the ground.

"I can see them from here. Look," she said, pointing to the flock grazing on a distant hill. Their shepherd lounged against a tree, carving a piece of wood with his knife.

"Yes, ma'am, whatever you say," said Judson. He

started to withdraw once he had spread the blanket, but Wynn patted a spot beside her.

"Come sit here, Judson, and help me unpack the basket." She wondered about Judson. She only knew that he had been indentured to Captain Kidd, who had freed him of his servitude. Now he was paid a regular wage in addition to his living quarters at the back of the house. He was devoted to the Kidds, as he had no family of his own.

Slave trade was a major business in New York, and Wynn knew it must be fearsome for the Negroes like Judson. She had heard from her brother awful stories of how the slaves were thrown in the bottom of ships with no freedom to care for themselves in any way. The expression in the eyes of some of the slaves she had seen bore out of these stories. She looked now at the wizened but gentle face of Judson, who carefully laid the food on the tablecloth she had spread, and she wanted to ask him so many things. But she didn't know how to begin.

Judson kept his eyes lowered. He seemed to like her, she thought, and he had told her he hoped she would stay on with Missus Sarah.

"Do you come to the farm often, Judson?" asked Wynn, chewing on a piece of bread she had buttered generously.

"Summers mos'ly," he answered. "Miz Sarah, she usually needs me for the yard work and such like."

"I'm sure she couldn't get along without you, Judson," said Wynn. For a few moments she chewed in silence, then she insisted Judson help himself to a piece of chicken.

In the next moment, a horse and rider crested the hill where the sheep grazed. The rider paused briefly on the top of the hill, then his horse picked its way along the horizon and followed a trail near the trees. Wynn watched the rider idly, then bit her lip as she asked, "Who's that coming toward us?" She was sure she already knew the answer.

Judson stood and shaded his eyes, as the rider, on a thoroughbred black horse, rode on at a relaxed pace.

When he was near enough to be identified, Judson said, "Why, it's Master Lamley. His folks' place lies just yonder. I reckon he's come to see the cap'n."

Wynn lowered her gaze. "Yes, I suppose so." The food in her mouth became suddenly dry, and she brushed the crumbs from her lap. When she heard the horse's hooves nearing, she looked up with a frown. Dressed in a tan riding habit, his feet encased in tall black leather boots, his hair caught with a thong at the back of his neck, Robert reined to a stop some thirty yards from them and, dismounting, let the horse's reins dangle onto the ground.

"Good day," he said as he advanced. Judson moved off toward the trees.

"It's all right, Judson," said Robert. "I don't mean to interrupt your picnic."

"Why did you stop then?" said Wynn.

Robert cocked his head and looked down at her. "Well, I wouldn't have, if I'd thought it would offend you. Perhaps I should go on. I was exercising Valiant. He's a beauty, don't you think?" he asked, turning to admire his horse.

Wynn looked at Valiant's fine lines as he grazed on the rich grass.

"He is beautiful," she said. "I didn't mean to be rude. Please accept my apology." Then she remembered her manners. "Would you care for something to eat?" she asked. "A leg of chicken or a piece of pound cake?"

"No, thank you," he said. "But it looks delicious. Did you make it?" He sat down.

Judson cleared his throat. "If you don't mind, miss, I'll just walk over to have a look at those sheep."

"Of course, Judson. We'll be all right here." The servant bowed to Robert and took his leave.

Robert stretched his long frame on the blanket, near enough for Wynn to touch. His nearness made her tremble, and she unconsciously moved away from him.

"I am surprised to see you," she said, looking away from him.

"But you knew I came up with the captain."

"He said as much, but I thought you'd be spending your time with your parents."

"So I have been, but our properties join on the other side of that hill, so I came for a ride. I thought I might stop and inquire of your household."

So that was it, thought Wynn. He wanted to see the lovely Sarah. Wynn knew there would never be anything between Robert and William's wife, but she could not help but notice the way Robert relished Sarah's company. Of course any man would find her amusing, Wynn thought. Even though Wynn knew Sarah's own spirits were, at times, heavier than she would let on, to society, she was always the gay and capable Sarah Kidd.

Sarah's vivaciousness made Wynn feel rather plain by comparison. Who wouldn't prefer Sarah's dark beauty to Wynn's own straw-colored hair and turned-up freckled nose? Sarah wore clothes that complemented her violet eyes and fair skin, whereas Wynn's modest new wardrobe made her appear no more than a shy girl. It was at times like this that Wynn felt the urge to shine in her own light, but she didn't know exactly why she wanted to parade her own attributes.

Robert lay on his back and closed his eyes to the warm sun. If Wynn had moved her hand only slightly, she could have drawn her fingers through his hair, but she began packing away the chicken instead.

"The farm is really quite nice, I think," said Wynn to break the insufferable silence that lay thickly between them.

Robert sighed. "It is pleasurable. I forget how

relaxed I can be up here. When I'm in town, all I can think about is work, and now, the voyage," he said with obvious irritation.

"How are plans coming for the voyage?" she asked, trying to sound polite.

Robert threw one arm behind his head. "As well as can be expected under the circumstances."

"I see." She bit back the questions that she wanted to ask.

"If I could only get William to settle his affairs. At this rate we'll not sail until September."

"I'm sure he enjoys being with his family. Perhaps he is not anxious to leave."

"I am afraid that may be true. But the sooner we leave, the sooner he'll return."

"Only to leave again."

Robert rolled on his side so he could see her face. "Do I detect bitterness in your reply?"

"Only that I do not see how Sarah stands it, having her husband absent all the time."

"Even though she loves her husband?" The seriousness of his tone startled Wynn. Whatever could he mean?

"That has nothing to do with it." To conceal her nervousness she continued to pack the basket.

"Wynn," he said abruptly, reaching for her hands to still their motion, "I was rude to you in the garden the night William came home. I was drunk. I ought to ask your forgiveness."

"Ha, you put it strangely — you 'ought to ask.' "

"Will you forgive me?" he persisted.

"For what? You were right. We had become rather, well, I suppose we lost our heads." Feelings choked her as she attempted to go on. "It was unbecoming, don't you think, for two people who know each other so slightly to behave that way?" Her face felt hot as she spoke so frankly to him.

"I did not think so."

Wynn trembled as his hold on her hands tightened. "Robert, please, let go of me."

But he sat up and pulled her toward him, his lips quivering, his eyes dark pools of emotion.

"Must I? I thought so as well. I told myself I have no room for this. I loved once and lost, so when I met you I tried to resist those sea-colored blue eyes. But I have tired of this battle. I am a man after all, and a man has needs. I can no longer deny them."

He breathed heavily, his breath sweet and warm on her lips. Her body trembled and her senses spun as his arms tightened their grip around her, pulling her to his chest. One hand reached around her hips, pulling the lower part of her body closer to his legs. Gently, he lowered her to the blanket, while her heart hammered in her throat. She opened her lips in confusion just as he lowered his mouth to kiss her.

The kiss seemed an answer to everything Wynn had longed for these past few weeks. She gave up fighting and reached her arms around his neck as he ravaged her mouth, then moved to lie on top of her. She felt his strong thighs against her skirt, his torso like rigid steel, but he held his body gently over her so as not to crush her under his weight. When his mouth left hers, she gasped for breath. Part of her mind still struggled with the fact that she was contradicting her vow to forget him. But she was unable to resist. Then a sudden fear shattered her euphoria. Supposing she did let him introduce her to those secret things that passion had hid from her till now. He would never marry her, he had said as much, or nearly so. He would only use her for the pleasure they were so obviously capable of giving each other. Then he would leave for the Indian Seas.

These and other thoughts swam in her mind as his warm lips sought her neck, her breasts, while his hands massaged her side, her hips. It took all her willpower to make him halt. "Robert, Robert, please, you mustn't do this."

"What, my love? Don't you want this too? I've seen the way you try to avoid me. If I didn't affect you the way you affect me, you wouldn't have to fight so hard to ignore me. Let me show you what pleasure we can take in each other. Let me forget my agony for once."

If she truly thought he could forget his agony with her, she might have allowed him to continue. But it was only so many words. Her passion began to wane at the disappointment she felt in his lack of love, and she squirmed under him.

"You want to take pleasure in me and then what? What do I get in return?" He rolled onto his back and she brushed her hair with her hands. Embarrassed to see the boldness of his manhood under the cloth of his pants, evidence of his desire, she looked away.

"Pleasure, my dear. You would get the same pleasure as I. I'm sorry if you are shocked. I am aware that a girl of your upbringing must be unfamiliar with what passion can bring. But," he said, turning to look boldly at her. "The pleasure is not all one-sided."

"I am not shocked. I am not so unfamiliar with the desires you speak of," she said a haughty attempt to defend her unworldliness.

"Oh?"

"But it is callous to want to use a woman and give nothing in return."

"You are right, I suppose," he said with a sigh of apathy. "It would not be right." He lay on the blanket.

Wynn felt too dizzy to try to move.

"I loved once," he said, as if he had a need to speak of it.

"I am aware of that."

He rolled toward her again, tracing the threads on the blanket with his fingers. "She was like you, in many ways."

It hurt her to hear him say this. She could not bear to hear of his feelings of love for another woman, when all he felt for Wynn was lust. It made her angry to be thus compared.

"But you are very different in other ways," he continued, more to himself than to her. "And I am very different now." He lay back again and caressed a corner of her skirt with one hand.

Pity and passion mingled in her and she longed to bend over him and smooth the lines of pain from his face. The urge to give him comfort was very strong, but she knew it would be wrong to encourage him further.

"Perhaps we should go to the house," she suggested.

"I am not ready," he said. Then he grabbed her hand, which had strayed within easy reach of his. "Stay here with me a bit, Wynn. Don't worry," he said in a mocking tone. "I will not try to seduce you again. I see now that you do not want it, and I would never force you."

She refrained from answering. Still, she found an odd contentment in just sitting with him. There was no need to speak now, perhaps because he had revealed so much of himself to her.

When the sun had crossed the sky and had begun to drop toward the western horizon, Judson returned. Wynn pulled away from Robert and smoothed her tangled curls.

"Come, Judson," she called, getting up. "Help us with the blanket." Robert rolled from his place as she began to put the rest of the things away. He whistled to the black stallion, and Valiant trotted to his master, then stopped a few feet away, pawing the ground.

"Is he always so obedient?" asked Wynn.

'He knows who is master," answered Robert in a teasing tone. Then he went to the horse. "Judson, please take the basket and the blanket back to the house. Your mistress will ride with me."

She was about to protest, but Robert's look silenced her. Judson did as he was told, and as soon as he was well on his way through the woods, Robert led Wynn to the horse. Then he lifted her onto the horse and climbed on behind her. Encircling her waist, he took the reins. They raced off at a canter down the hill, and when they came to a stop in front of the house, Wynn's heart was beating wildly from the thrilling ride.

Robert dismounted, then reached up for her. As she slid down, he held her close to him for a brief moment, and his eyes seemed to command her not to resist.

But when her feet touched ground, she lowered her gaze. She would not let herself be drawn into the trap this man was setting for her. So what if her body was alluring to him and her feminine instincts were just beginning to bloom? She would not waste her womanhood on a lonely, half-crazed man who would enjoy her body and then leave her bereft when he went to sea.

She tossed her head haughtily and began to push past him, but his arms imprisoned her against the horse. He leaned toward her and as she raised her eyes to his, she saw the torment there. His body smelled of healthy male sweat, and her blood, still rushing from the ride, coursed through her veins in response to his nearness.

As he lowered his mouth to hers, she tried to protest. "Don't resist me, Wynn," he pleaded. "I promise this won't hurt you. I need you." He placed his lips on hers gently, then his left hand slipped up her side to cup her breast. A tingling sensation began deep within her, and she had an uncontrollable urge to thrust against him and open her mouth to his insistent tongue.

"No, no," she whispered hoarsely, and flinging herself away from him, she ran into the house, confusion filling her. She didn't care what kind of spectacle she was making. She simply had to get away from him.

Upstairs she flung herself across the bed, tears running down her cheeks, tasting salty as they landed on her lips. What did he need her for? He would probably find his fill of exotic women in faraway ports who would be willing enough to serve him. A jealous rage filled her as she thought about him in the arms of native women. "It isn't fair," she cried, clenching a fist full of bedspread. A man had the freedom to do as he pleased, love as he pleased. But a woman had to live within such strict confines.

Standing with his feet astride, Robert watched Wynn run into the house. Then he grabbed Valiant's reins, flung himself into the saddle and, kicking the horse in the ribs, set off at a gallop.

Looking up from the daybed in the parlor where she'd been knitting, Sarah saw Wynn rush by, and now she watched as Robert raced away. She sighed deeply and wondered if she ought to interfere. She knew something of what the young lovers felt for she remembered her own awakening to passion. She had been very young when she'd first married, a mere girl who knew nothing of such matters. But the rewards, Sarah thought, as she contemplated the wild emotions she had glimpsed in Wynn and Robert, the rewards for learning how to please a man were worth everything one suffered for love.

Chapter Six

The Kidd household returned to New York in August so that William could make the final arrangements for the voyage. When Sarah expressed concern for Wynn's state of mind, Wynn refused to talk about her feelings for Robert.

"There's nothing to discuss," she said as they worked in the kitchen one evening, putting up preserves from the fruits they had brought back from the farm.

"Men are hard to understand, sometimes, Cousin," Sarah said in her forthright manner. "I cannot have been married three times without having gained experience in these matters."

Ugly thoughts twisted Wynn's face into a glower, which she directed to the jars on the square oak table.

"I don't mean to be ungrateful, Sarah," she finally said. "But I simply have not found a man worth asking advice about."

"My dear Wynn," Sarah said as she moved between the open hearth, where the water boiled in an iron pot, and the table where she had set the jars. "You have been torturing yourself these last weeks. It is as plain as day. When you are with Robert Lamley you will not converse with him for fear of giving yourself away. Yet when he does not come to see us you pine like a lost puppy. Something must be done about it."

"What is to be done?" Wynn said, sealing a jar with wax and moving on to the next one. "He does not love me, and I do not want him to. That is final." She fetched more sugar from a shelf in the pantry.

"I happen to think he cares for you," said Sarah, determined to air the subject for Wynn's own good. "Has he not said as much to you?"

"Of course not," Wynn said, looking up, surprised.

"Would that change things?" Sarah gave Wynn a knowing look.

The stormy expression returned to Wynn's face, on which angry blotches betrayed her feelings. "No, it would not. I do not intend to attach myself to a sailor."

"Is that why you spend so much time in Gerald Portman's company? It makes Robert jealous to see you walking out with anyone else, you know."

"I hadn't noticed."

Sarah wiped her hands on her apron. "Oh, Wynn, why must you be so stubborn? All the Coxes are. You must try to understand Robert."

"Why?"

"Because he needs you. I can see it written all over him. He is not so unlike William, you know."

"I don't think so." In spite of Wynn's determination not to listen, Sarah had a way of putting things that made it hard to refuse to hear her out.

"That is because you have not yet seen how Robert could be with a woman he truly loves. He wants the same thing any man wants."

Wynn flushed. "Oh, he has made that abundantly

clear. Don't think I am naive about such things." She mashed the preserves with all her strength, venting her emotions on them.

"Oh, silly girl. I don't mean that. Of course all men want that." A devilish smile appeared on Sarah's red lips. "I mean a home and family. Robert needs love. He just doesn't know it."

"And I suppose you are going to tell him."

"I may have to, if someone else doesn't," said Sarah, returning to her preserves, exasperated by Wynn's obstinacy.

"I'd appreciate it if you didn't," said Wynn, crossing to the water bucket to wash her hands. "I don't need any help in this affair. He will go to sea and that will be the end of it."

"For eighteen months, anyway."

Wynn paused, her hands over the water. "That long?"

"You see, it does concern you. Yes, that long. Oh, Wynn, I know it's hard. No one knows more than I do what it is to be married to a sailing man. But there's nothing as wonderful as the love he gives me in return for it."

"Robert doesn't want to marry. You don't expect me to love a man any other way, do you?"

"Of course not. But he does want to marry, he's just afraid to. It's time he got over the loss of his wife. It's been well over six years."

The idea of Robert Lamley being afraid of anything would have amused Wynn if she had not felt so miserable at that moment. "I'm sure he's consoled himself elsewhere."

"Well, bachelors are not monks. But what satisfaction is there for a man who uses a woman for bodily urges alone? He is still a lonely man. Can you not see that?"

"Robert's loneliness is no concern of mine." By her look, Wynn forced Sarah to understand that the conversation was a futile one. Wynn half admitted to herself that her own emotions may have been blinding her to Robert's thoughts and feelings, but it had been her concern for him that had led her astray in the first place. Now she had to protect herself against his charms. She thought with embarrassment of her temptation the day Robert had found her with Judson in the meadow. How readily she might have surrendered to him then if she had not gathered her wits about her at the last moment.

On an evening when William was smoking his long-stemmed pipe next to the fireplace in the parlor and little Sarah was handing her mother tulips to arrange in an oriental vase, Robert appeared, unannounced. Elizabeth led him into the parlor.

"Uncle Robert," said the girl, dropping the flowers to the floor and going to him. "Can I have a kiss?"

Wynn looked up from the book she was reading as he laughed and bent down to plant a kiss on the little girl's cheek. Wynn felt her own cheeks turn a dark shade of red.

"Don't get up," he said to William, who started to rise.

"What brings you here this evening, Robert?" said the captain, sinking back into his great chair.

"We haven't seen you in a week," said Sarah. "Where have you been keeping yourself since you returned to town?"

"I had work to do," he said. Then he turned to Wynn, who had tried to bury her nose in the book again. "But I've come to see your cousin."

Her blush deepened as she put down her book. She could hardly protest in front of everyone. She rose. "I was just thinking of a walk. Perhaps you would escort me outside. I have a need for some fresh sea air."

"I thought you did not like the sea air," he said, mocking her.

Not to be outdone, she said, "Only that in the upper bay." She fetched her cape, for it was windy out, while Robert waited for her in the hallway.

They walked down the steps and turned into the Strand. He offered his arm, and though Wynn was reluctant to take it, she decided that was a better alternative than tripping across some refuse in the street. Although the ships in the harbor made a pretty sight tonight Wynn did not find the view particularly appealing.

They passed through the Queen's Gate and on out toward Maiden Lane, an old road that now intersected new ones being laid as the town stretched northward.

"How far do you think New York will grow?" Wynn asked to take her mind off her disturbance at the way Robert tucked her elbow to his side, forcing her arm to feel the warmth of his body.

"Some distance, I expect," he said in answer to her question. "It is a fast-growing place. Commerce here never seems to lag." Then he asked, "Will your parents be coming over soon?"

"Yes, but not before you set sail."

"I'm sorry."

"Why?"

Steering her nearer the riverbank, out of the traffic of passers-by, he planted his feet in the moist soil and took her by the shoulders. As she tried to move away, he said, "Don't try to wriggle away. I only want to face you. I wish your parents were here because I want to ask for your hand in marriage."

"You what?"

"I want to make you my wife, Wynn. Will you marry me?"

"Whatever for?" She was startled by his way of putting it, and his manner was so unfeeling that it reminded her of his earlier curt behavior with her. He certainly knew little of wooing a woman, and she wondered briefly if this was how he had acquired his first wife.

"Because I cannot get you out of my mind," he went on in a gruff tone. "I tried to, but I see I cannot. It is ridiculous for two people who want each other the way we do to keep ourselves apart, no matter what the reason. I am prepared to marry you."

"But I am *not* prepared to marry you. Please, let go of me."

He loosened his grip, but he still held her. The brooding quality in his eyes had not lessened, and as his dark hair blew around his face, Wynn was aware of his compelling masculinity. Still, he had said nothing of love. It was as if he were willing to pay the price of marriage only to satisfy his lust. This was not the gentle courtship she had imagined, but seemed more like a business arrangement, and she was not for sale.

"Will you explain yourself?" he demanded.

"I don't have to explain myself. I told you I will not marry you."

"But you want me, I can see by the way you respond to me. You are a passionate woman, Wynn, I can feel the tremors in your body when you are next to me."

"You flatter yourself."

"Oh stop it, Wynn Cox. I know the magnetism between a man and a woman who is meant for him, as you are meant for me."

She glared at him and through gritted teeth said, "You are the most arrogant fool I have ever met. Now take your hands off me and never come near me again. I don't know what kind of man you think you are, but I find you contemptible. I am surprised you ever married at all. I am quite sure you have a heart of rock and you are totally insensitive to any but the most base kind of woman. If your wife ever loved you it was probably because you used her and then left her with no choice."

Wynn had no idea where the words sprang from, as she continued to hurl insults at him, but she was so angry she would have said anything to get out of his grasp. How selfish of him to think that he could marry her, have his way with her and then leave on a voyage, all without a trace of love, or even compassion. He was the hardest man she had ever known, but she was determined to be a match for him.

The black look on Robert's face finally frightened Wynn into silence. Then, slowly, he drew back his hand and slapped her face so hard he knocked her off balance, leaving her cheek smarting with a red tinge.

"Oh," she cried out as he pushed her aside and stormed away. He had gone several paces when he stopped and turned back to Wynn, who was leaning against a stone marker, gathering her strength.

"I ought to kill you for speaking of my wife that way," he said, his breathing labored as he grasped her violently. "If you ever insult her memory again you will regret it. To think that I humiliated myself by making you a proposal of marriage. You're not worth it."

She thought she'd never seen such hate in anyone's eyes and instantly regretted her words. He was right. She could say what she liked about him, but it wasn't fair to insult a dead woman of whom she knew nothing. She lowered her head, tears gathering as she said, "I'm sorry. Not about what I said in regard to your insolence, but about your wife. Please forgive me for that. I should not have said it."

Robert released her, throwing her off balance again. Then he paced nearer the river, his hands on his hips. Finally he turned to face her. "I'll accept your apology," he said, and she could see the pain in his eyes.

"But I withdraw my offer of marriage. I could never be happy with a woman who fails to understand me."

She stood by the marker holding her cheek where he had slapped her and watched him stalk away. When he had passed through the gate, she moved onto the road and started slowly home.

"Wynn Cox?" Gerald Portman, on his dapple-gray mare, dismounted and bustled toward her. "What are you doing out here alone? Allow me to escort you." He tucked his riding crop under one arm and looked at her face with alarm.

"Thank you, Gerald. I must look a sight." Her emotions were still creating havoc inside her, and now anger and cynicism overlaid her grief and shame.

"May I ask how you came here?" he asked hesitantly, taking her elbow.

"I was with Robert Lamley. But it doesn't matter. I'll never be seen with him again. I despise the man."

"My dear, what did he do to you?" Gerald pulled himself up as if ready to challenge the younger man to a duel.

"He proposed to me."

This seemed to take some of the bluster out of Gerald. "Then he did nothing dishonorable?" He sounded almost disappointed.

"Not unless you call proposing to marry without love dishonorable. Oh, I'm sorry, Gerald," said Wynn inconsolably. "I shouldn't be confiding these things to you."

He patted her hand. "Yes you should. I am your friend. I care a great deal about you, Wynn, dear. More than you know. If anyone has offended you they'll have to answer to me." Again he drew himself up as if ready to take on an opponent, jutting his bearded chin out so that the hair on his face caught the breeze.

"How good you are," she said. "Yet I don't deserve

it." She looked up at him with a tear-stained face. She did feel affection for him. It was nothing like the unruly passion she always felt in Robert's presence, but the feelings she had for Gerald were more in keeping with what she might expect in a marriage. And it embarrassed her that Gerald should see her this way.

It would serve Robert right if Gerald proposed to her and she accepted. Of course, he was older, but he could offer her a good home and he would be devoted. Yes, when she was ready for a home and marriage, Gerald Portman was a very likely candidate. She knew her parents would be relieved to see her settled with a man like Gerald, although when she had sailed to the New World she was most certainly not looking for a husband. It was only to protect herself from the likes of Robert Lamley that she now considered marriage.

Pain still raged in her heart, and Gerald was so soothing to be with. And she could not put off marriage forever. She sniffled, and Gerald offered her his lace handkerchief.

"Thank you, Gerald," she said. "You are so kind."

"Of course, my dear." He squeezed her elbow and when she saw the compassion in his eyes, she felt so embarrassed that she had to turn away.

They walked in silence, Gerald leading his horse by the reins. When they reached the stoop of Sarah's house, Wynn went up alone.

"Thank you, Gerald," she said from the top step. "Please come to tea soon. Sarah enjoys your visits."

"When does the captain sail?"

"Two weeks from now."

Gerald raised a hand. "I'll call before then."

Wynn walked sadly into the house and up to her room to freshen up. She bathed in cool water from the china wash basin and relaxed by brushing out her hair. Just before bedtime, she tiptoed downstairs to have a cup of tea. No one was about, so she was not called upon to make conversation.

Finally she left the warm kitchen and went to bed.

The next two weeks were agonizing for Wynn. The *Adventure Galley* was nearly ready to sail. Whenever Robert Lamley appeared at the Kidd house, Wynn went up to her room, making no more pretense at socializing. At night she lay on her bed staring out her window at the moon or trying to read. But she found it impossible not to think about Robert and his desire for her. It moved her body in strange ways. Still, she lamented, it was not love that attracted him to her. If he loved her, if he could forget about his wife, perhaps she could forgive his arrogance and harshness and marry him. If only there were a tiny crack in the iron surrounding his heart. But there was not, and she reminded herself that it was better so. For surely she would be miserable without him for eighteen months.

Sarah moved about the house as cheerfully as possible. But when Wynn saw her in unguarded moments, she knew the suffering she must feel. The two women spoke less when they were together, relying on little Sarah to amuse them. How Sarah must rue the day the ship weighed anchor, Wynn thought, finding her own feelings about the departure more and more ambivalent.

At dawn on the sixth of September, Sarah knocked on Wynn's door. Wynn lay in the twisted covers with her eyes open. "Come in," she answered. "I'm not asleep."

"I thought you might like to watch the ship weigh anchor," said Sarah. There was nothing Wynn wanted less, but she could not let Sarah go alone.

"Yes. I'll dress and come down." Wynn's heart felt like lead as she dragged herself from bed and hugged herself against the chill morning. Downstairs she found the kitchen already alive with activity. William had been away all night getting the ship ready, and now everyone was up, excited to see the big ship sail.

"Why can't we go with him, Mommy?" asked little Sarah, rubbing her eyes with her small fist. The mother picked up the little girl and hugged her tightly.

"I, too, wish we could go with him, darling. But a sailing voyage is no place for a woman. Daddy will be chasing pirates."

"Will Uncle Robert chase pirates too?"

Sarah smiled and glanced at Wynn, who was warming her hands around a pot of tea. "Robert will be with Daddy, yes," Sarah answered the child's question. "And so will Uncle Samuel."

"Will it be dangerous?"

"Oh!" muttered Wynn as she scalded her hand on the tea pot. Her heart thudded in her chest. Danger. So wrapped up in her own selfish problems, she had given little thought to the actual danger the men would face. Yes, Robert would be in danger, she realized, a wave of emotion sweeping over her.

"There will be danger, dear," the mother said softly to the child. "That is what a man thrives on. He has to fight the sea and the storms and the pirates and England's enemies. But Daddy and the other men are very strong, and they work together to win against their enemies."

"Does Daddy like it?"

"Yes, he does. All the men of the sea feel the same way." She looked at Wynn, tears glistening in her violet eyes.

Wynn swallowed a lump in her throat and fetched her cloak. She was glad she had risen to bid the ship bon voyage. She wanted to see Robert after all, to wish him well. She wanted to tell him she would say a prayer for his safety. If anything were to happen to him during the voyage, she had only their last hateful encounter to remember, and it would make her feel bad. It was not the right way to part.

"Are you ready?" asked Sarah when everyone was cloaked and standing in the hallway.

"Yes," answered Wynn. Suddenly Sarah hugged Wynn to her. Wynn stifled a sob. Surely Sarah knew what Wynn was feeling at this moment. Though she had refrained from mentioning her innermost thoughts these past weeks, she knew there was little she could hide from Sarah.

Light tinted the eastern sky and the air smelled fresh with the salty sea breeze as they walked into the empty Strand. Closer to the dock, the work day was already in progress, orders being shouted as the sailors made ready to cast off. The great ship rode the gentle waves that washed against the bank, as Wynn and Sarah walked out on the wooden wharf toward it. Seeing them approach, the captain broke away from a group of men, Samuel Bradley among them. He joined them silently and took his family in his arms. Then he gave Wynn a hug as Samuel bid his sister good-bye.

"Take care of Sarah," William whispered to Wynn.

"I will," she promised. Then, over the captain's shoulder, she glimpsed Robert Lamley. How different he looked in his officer's garb, complete with tricornered hat and gold frogging on the dark blue coat.

From the upper deck, he caught her gaze and hesitated. She moved forward a step, the wind catching her hair and lifting it off her shoulders. Robert advanced toward her down the gangplank. His fierce look masked any gentler emotions he might have had as he stood in front of her.

"Why have you come here?" he snapped.

"I came with Sarah," she said slowly, then added, "to wish you bon voyage." He moved closer to her and seemed about to grip her arm.

"Why should you do that? You told me in no uncertain terms that you wished never to lay eyes on me again."

"I'm sorry, Robert," she said as she moved a step closer, realizing that if she had anything to say to him, it must be said now or never. "I didn't mean the things I told you. I was hurt, and I was trying to get back at you. You didn't deserve to be spoken to that way. I —" she paused, her lip trembling, "I care for you, Robert."

Robert gripped her arms. "Why did you wait until now to tell me this?"

She raised her head, her face a dark shade of red. "I didn't know how I felt before."

He grabbed her by the waist and pulled her toward him. "I ought to throttle you. I will never understand why women toy with men's feelings and claim innocently never to know their own. All I know is that you have possessed me. I cannot live without you, Wynn Cox. I finally offered you what you wanted, marriage, but even then you refused me. Yet you stand there and look at me with mournful eyes, full of the same desire I feel for you. I do not understand any of it."

Then he clutched her to his chest and bent over to kiss her savagely. As he moved his mouth hungrily against hers, Wynn stifled a little moan. She folded herself to him, tears running down her cheeks. Oh why, why did she love him so, she wondered. And why did he not love her, or if he did love her, why did he not say so?

It did not matter, she thought. She would give herself to him even though he did not love her. If only she had understood her feelings sooner, they could have spent these last weeks together. Now it was too late. He was sailing, and the chance of his returning to her, safe and still desirous of her, was slim. She turned her face so that her cheek rested against his shoulder and sobbed bitterly, while Robert kissed her hair and caressed her, letting her spend her emotion.

"What is it, my love?" he asked her tenderly.

"I did not know, I did not know," she sobbed. "I should have married you when you asked me."

Robert uttered a deep frustrated sigh. "Do you still want to marry me?" he asked, not loosening his grip on her.

"Yes, yes," she sobbed.

"Then we shall marry, my sweet. You must wait for me."

"But you will forget me, Robert. You wanted me because my nearness to you provoked your longings. But when you sail to the southern seas, you will be in different lands. You will see exotic, dark-skinned women, You will want someone else."

He lifted her chin to look at her tear-stained face. "I'll want no one else," he said. "Listen to me, my wild one. I have seen and tasted many women the world over, and I have learned what I want. I loved once very deeply and I thought when I lost her that I would never love again. I shut off all feelings and only went with a woman when my body demanded it. But when I met you all that changed. I was compelled by your character, your spirit. It was not only your tempting young body that I desired. I found that I wanted you more than I had ever wanted another woman before. Do you understand what I am saying? I wanted you more than anyone." He pulled her to his breast again.

"I fought it, of course. I thought at first that if I had you, if I satisfied myself with you just once, I could get you out of my system. But that was not to be. I could not deflower the girl who was staying under the roof of my captain and his wife. So I told myself I must marry you. But I knew all along that I had been afraid of loving again. Afraid of losing again."

"But you did not seem to love me," said Wynn, ashamed and miserable.

"But I did love you, my little one. Don't you see it

now?" he said, his voice quavering with emotion. "I had closed my heart for so long it was not easy to open it again." He lifted her chin. "I could not say it then."

"You seemed to have eyes only for Sarah. I thought I could not rival her beauty and accomplishments," she sobbed, clinging to his shoulders.

"I looked at Sarah only because I could not bear to look at you. I see now that I was foolish."

Wynn lifted her head and tried to smile through the tears. "We have both been foolish. What shall we do?"

"You will wait for me. In eighteen months I will return and we will wed. You must promise me."

Wynn gulped. How hard it would be to wait. This was why she had fought so hard against falling in love with a man like Robert. Yet wait she must. She had no choice now. She loved him more than anyone, and she had told him so.

"Yes, Robert, I'll wait."

He bent to kiss her then, long and passionately, holding her close to his body, so his physical desires could be felt against her soft thighs. He held her as if he would never let her go.

"Oh, Robert, tell me it will be like this when you return," she pleaded. "Tell me you will not forget me."

"I will not forget you," he said, kissing her again.

Only the captain's call broke them apart. Robert gently released her and stood gazing at her for a long time. "I love you, my dearest," he said.

"I love you, Robert," she said, choking back her tears. When he turned and walked away, she thought her heart would break with both happiness and misery.

Sarah joined her as the ship cast off. They held each other, drawing strength from each other as the little girl huddled against their skirts. The oars were manned until the ship got under sail, and Wynn and Sarah watched, breathless as the well-coordinated crew became one instrument, navigating the sturdy ship out into the harbor.

"Away aloft!" came the cry as William's orders were passed on to the crew. The sails unfurled, and the ship picked up speed, heading for the narrows, where she would travel at a fast clip down the New Jersey coast past Sandy Hook, making for the Atlantic Ocean, and then for the coast of Africa.

Africa, thought Wynn, and then India. The other side of the world. She gripped Sarah even tighter and laid her head on the other woman's shoulder.

"Is it ever any easier than this?" she whispered to Sarah.

"I suppose it isn't," Sarah responded in a faraway tone. "One simply learns to live with it."

When the ship was out of sight and the sun climbing the eastern horizon, its light now blinding them, the two women walked back to the house, holding onto each other. By now the town was awake, bustling with commerce. The citizens of the town carried on the usual routines of life, but for Wynn and Sarah, life had changed forever.

Chapter Seven

From the moment Robert had said he loved her on the dock before he sailed away, Wynn had been left to struggle with the emotions of hope mingled with despair. For on only one declaration of love, she would have to nurture hope for the next eighteen months. She did not know how she was going to be able to get through the months of interminable waiting. There would be letters, of course, but they would be few, she imagined, and there would be long weeks without any word of Robert.

In October there was news from other ships coming into port that the *Adventure Galley* had safely crossed the Atlantic. At Madeira she had met a storm-damaged Barbados brigantine, and Kidd gave her a new mast, rigging and canvas to help her on her way. A few days later, Wynn received a letter from Robert.

"I believed it was the sea I was fighting," he wrote. "I find it was myself. Send greetings to your family for me, and tell them of your husband-to-be." However,

Wynn's mother had written to say she was not well and that their voyage would be postponed until spring, so Wynn's loneliness increased.

Gerald Portman saw to it that the women were not left alone when they needed company, but when Wynn told him she was engaged to Robert Lamley, he congratulated her regretfully.

On Christmas Day, she walked home from church with Gerald, who still looked after her in a protective manner. It had snowed two days before, but now the snow was splotched with mud from the streets. Wynn held Gerald's arm with one hand, to avoid tripping, and with the other held her skirts, now shortened, out of the mud.

"I think I can smell the roasting goose from here," he said.

"I imagine Sarah's table will be one of the fullest in town," said Wynn, thinking of the guests that were gathering at the Kidd house for dinner today. Sarah had outdone herself preparing a luscious feast of one of the fattened geese.

"It's a pity the captain can't be here," said Gerald.

"Nor my fiancé," she reminded him.

"Do you really plan to marry that man when he returns, my dear? I thought perhaps after several months of absence you might have changed your mind," he said, looking straight ahead.

"I won't change my mind, if Robert doesn't," she said.

"I suppose they're rounding the Cape by now. Have you had any word?"

"Not as much as we'd like. But I'm not worried. I'm sure they'll do very well," Wynn said as she gathered up her skirts to go up the steps to Sarah's house. Inside, the air was redolent of the delicious scents from cooking and baking, and several neighborhood children stood admiring the table, which was laid with fabulous goodies. Wynn turned to give Gerald's cheek a peck.

"Merry Christmas, Gerald. I do hope you'll be pleased with my cinnamon cakes."

"I'll try to save them a special place in my tummy." He laughed jovially and patted his round middle under the embroidered silver vest he wore beneath a gray surcoat with commodious sleeves. Wynn felt sorry for him since she had fallen in love with the dashing Robert Lamley. She could never feel for Gerald what she felt for Robert, and she was powerless to change that. Still, she wanted Gerald as a friend. He was someone to talk to during the lonely times. She sighed as she turned to help Sarah greet the other guests. She couldn't please everyone. If Gerald was still a bachelor, it wasn't her fault.

Soon laughter and conversation filled the house. Wynn did not know how Sarah planned to seat them all around the large oval table in the dining room, but somehow she managed. They stuffed themselves with turkey, goose, mutton, lamb, veal, sausages, and an array of vegetables. All this was washed down with Madeira, punch, cider or beer. For dessert there were puddings, as well as Wynn's cinnamon cakes and apple pie.

After dinner everyone gathered in the parlor to sing Christmas carols, accompanied by Sarah on the virginal. She looked ravishing in a red taffeta dress that revealed bosom and shoulders, while Wynn was dressed in lime green brocade that complemented her complexion and light hair. She found a seat by the window and sang softly to herself, looking out at the harbor. Even with William gone, Sarah managed to create a festive atmosphere. This was exactly the kind of Christmas Wynn loved, and it would have been perfect if only Robert had been present.

The holidays brought good cheer to New York. All the colonists greeted the New Year with a flurry of parties, somewhat less elegant than entertainments in Merry Old England, but their enthusiasm made up for the lack of refinements. Wynn tried to enter into the spirit of the season, but often she walked alone, staring for long periods at the turbulent waters lashed by the winter wind. Sometimes she could almost feel Robert's presence, but at other times she felt bereft. She would stand at the edge of the water and strain her eyes looking out to sea as if by looking hard enough she could see the *Adventure Galley* sailing the southern seas.

When she grew tired of trying to make herself useful at Sarah's house, she would go out with Sarah to the coffee houses or visiting neighbors. All New York was abuzz with the news that Governor Bellomont and his wife, Kate, a countess and much talked-about because of her notorious love affairs, would soon arrive in the colonies.

While New York awaited a new governor, on the other side of the world, the *Adventure Galley* reached Madagascar. Wynn read William's letter aloud to Sarah as they sat over their needlework in the parlor one damp night while a fire flickered in the stone fireplace beside them. The news was not good.

"I was forced to sail with Captain Warren's fleet for a week," William wrote. "Captain Warren refused to give me new sails to replace the ones we had lost in the Atlantic storm. I argued that my commission entitled me to aid. Otherwise, I would have to seize the sails from the first merchant ship I encountered."

Sarah closed her eyes and shook her head. She knew what could happen when her husband lost his Scottish temper. "Go on," she said.

"Commodore Warren threatened to press thirty of my men. At last, we were obliged to sail away at night, under oars." Wynn looked up, picturing the mighty ship gliding sowly under the cover of night, with only the splash of oars heralding its departure.

"This does not bode well," commented Sarah. "I wonder if he will be as untactful with the East India Company. He has always felt the East Indiamen do not have the right to fly a navy pennant, and he said if he saw one doing so he would order them to strike it. Oh, Wynn, I fear for him. His royal commission has gone to his head."

"But surely he has authority."

"Authority in England or the colonies is one thing; I fear they will not listen to him in the East. Men there seem to have a law of their own. I'm sorry, Wynn," she said. "I shouldn't burden you with my troubles. You have enough to think of. I have lived through this before. You have not."

"You are right to tell me what is in your heart, Cousin. If there are things about this voyage I should know, do not be afraid to speak of them. After all," she said, laying the letter in her lap. "I must learn to live through this too."

"This may be William's last voyage," said Sarah, but the manner in which she said it made Wynn shiver.

The men had not yet taken any booty, which made Wynn fear they would be longer than eighteen months at sea. Sarah was following a similar train of thought.

"It's been four months since the ship set sail from New York, and neither my husband nor any of the crew has earned a penny. Provisions must be running low. Oh, Wynn, I have the most dreadful premonitions. What does my brother say?"

Wynn read the letter Samuel had written, but he had little to say, merely repeating the events William had described. His usual bold script looked weak, however, and Wynn feared he might be ill. There was a letter from Robert as well, which Wynn had already scanned hastily and would savor later in her room.

Sarah hesitantly voiced another thought that had been plaguing her. "The *Adventure Galley* is on the western coast of Madagascar, yet even I know that the most notorious pirate stronghold is in the eastern waters of that island. Why are they waiting on the western side?"

"It's almost as if they are avoiding the pirates," Sarah said, more to herself than to Wynn.

As spring came to New York, flowers pushed up from the ground, and buds sprang out on the trees. The night chill, however, still threatened to freeze the new blossoms. Nevertheless, the budding trees and beckoning out of doors did much to relieve Wynn's boredom and lift her spirits. As the ice melted on Collect Pond, she stored away her winter attire.

When she went to collect the mail at the White Rose Tavern, where it was distributed, she was full of hope. Surely by now the *Adventure Galley* had a prize. For she too was worried about how much the voyage was earning.

Standing outside the tavern, she read Robert's letter with growing horror. In March, he wrote, they made for the island of Mehila in the Comoros, where they had the ship careened to scrape away barnacles and repair leaks, but in the space of a single week, a third of the crew sickened and died. However, both Robert and William were all right, and Samuel sent his love.

Heartsick, she dropped the letters into her skirt pocket and looked toward the house. How could she break this latest catastrophe to Sarah? She wished suddenly she had never become involved with the kind of man who sailed on such a dangerous venture. Her worst fears were coming true, and tears stung her eyes as she thought of Robert. If he survived this voyage, she would make him give up the sea — she would not marry him if he refused.

When she found Sarah in the kitchen, her own expression communicated the news, because Sarah immediately dropped her work.

"Is it bad news? Is William all right?"

Wynn nodded, pushing down the lump in her throat. "They're all right, Sarah, but I'm afraid they've lost a third of their crew. Fifty men died from the fever at Mehila Island last month."

"Oh no." Sarah sat down. "What else does he say? How are Samuel and Robert?"

"They both send word. But Sarah, I'm so worried. I can't quite describe it, but I know in my heart that something is wrong."

She read the letters out loud to Sarah. It seemed the *Adventure Galley* had met up with an English ship and so had gotten their Christmas letters. When she was finished, she looked at Sarah, who stared into space as the afternoon shadows filled the room.

"What next, Cousin. Mutiny?" Sarah's voice was icy, and Wynn shivered at the fateful foreboding.

"Oh don't say that, Sarah. So much bad luck cannot last."

"This voyage was ill fated from the first," said Sarah. "I hear the rumors. Lord Bellomont is displeased at the lack of success the voyage has had thus far. He is a two-faced man, and I fear what he will do. I told William he should not trust him."

"I suppose he had no choice."

Sailing northward the *Adventure Galley* dropped anchor off the island of Perim in the narrows at the mouth of the Red Sea. Stripped of their shirts, cloth bands tied around their heads to soak up the dripping perspiration, Robert and William stood on deck, looking out over the still water as the sun parched them and the humidity rose to a saturation point.

"It looks like a good enough spot to ambush pirates," Robert said, lowering his spy glass.

"Pirates will be waiting here for the big convoys of Arab merchant ships from Mocha," said Kidd, speaking of the chief port of the Yemen coffee trade. "Here we are sure to catch either pirates or French prizes."

"How long will we wait?" asked Robert, shading his face against the burning sun.

"I've sent a small boat to Mocha. She'll return with word when ships appear ready to sail. Then we'll ambush any pirates or Frenchmen."

Robert was silent. He fully realized their equivocal position. The captain's letters of marque empowered him to take French vessels. But in these waters, a ship often flew the colors and showed the passes of whichever nation it found convenient. It was not easy to discover a ship's true identity, and if Kidd set off in pursuit of a strange sail and that ship resisted them, what then? Lives could be lost. And what if the ship turned out to be neither pirate nor French, but Dutch or, God forbid, English?

He caught a line of standing rigging in his hands, pulling against its tautness. He wondered why he had been so anxious to come on this voyage. Even though he had known the risks from the start, it had been far less glorious than he had anticipated, and they dared not go home empty-handed. The financial arrangements of their contract were much too onerous for that.

Robert had also begun to question William's wisdom, knowing that he would have managed things differently if he were captain. He hesitated to criticize his captain and friend, and he would never do so in front of any of the crew. He owed William his respect, even if he didn't always agree with his moves, but, so far, those moves had not led to any prizes.

As the *Adventure Galley* lay in wait on the hot sea, Robert became convinced that Kidd was nearing the decision to sacrifice reputation and position for the dubious fortune to be won by robbing Moorish ships. Legally that was piracy, but Robert knew the authorities in England had winked at the practice in the past, and they might do so once more, since the noble backers were so anxious for their money. Moorish ships were regarded as fair prey by captains on Christian privateers. It was a thin line, thought Robert as he paced the quarterdeck in the hot sun. Out here one's reason began to reverse itself, and it became harder and harder to relate to the rules back home. He wondered if William would actually turn pirate rather than sail home empty-handed. And if so, would he be forced to turn pirate too?

He lay in his berth at night, Wynn's face hovering sweetly above him. Only thoughts of her kept him sane. The rising pressures coming from a crew that demanded they take a prize and his concern for William made it difficult for Robert to come to any decisions. There had been a time when he might have been tempted to throw in his lot, turn pirate if fate ruled it. But what then of his love? No longer obsessed by the sea, he now looked forward to the comforts of home and the love of a woman. Soft flesh, eyes that melted his heart, these were the things that now drove him on. Clenching his teeth as the heat of desire flowed through his veins, he was determined to reach home and his beloved if possible.

Robert stood with Kidd as they waited off Babs Key for the Mocha fleet. Finally they sailed out flying

English colors, Dutch colors, but no French flags. Robert's muscles tensed as the *Adventure Galley* rolled on the waves.

The entire crew stood at the ready, hoping for a prize at last. They sailed even with the fleet now, showing no colors of their own, only a broad red pennant. They were coming near a large Moorish merchant ship.

"No pirates to be seen, damn all," swore Kidd, beads of sweat standing out on his forehead as he watched the Moorish vessel. "She'd make a good target."

A hundred yards away, the *Sceptre*, one of the well-armed English East Indiamen escorting the convoy, came abreast, hoisted her English colors and opened fire on the *Adventure Galley*.

Swearing, Kidd ordered fire to be returned, and they leveled a broadside, hitting the Moorish ship in the hull, sails and rigging. There was the crunch of timber, a flash of smoke, then the cries of the men on the Moorish ship filled the air.

Catching William by the sleeve, Robert yelled above the din, "They outnumber us, sir! Break off."

Kidd turned to him, glowering. "You are right," he said, and ordered his men to disengage the fighting.

Robert leaned against the bulwark and drew a deep breath. He hoped Kidd realized that he was not afraid of fighting, only frightened that Kidd would do something foolish. It would be far better to save their bravery for a just cause, and he prayed that the captain would resolve to wait until this was possible.

"We'll sail for the Malabar Coast of India," said William, going below to his cabin as they retreated under sails and oar.

That night Robert stood watch listening to the grumblings below decks. That they had taken no prize was lowering Kidd's prestige among the men. How long would the men remain loyal? His temples pounded as he contemplated the alternative.

"Ship ahead, sir!" cried the watch in the early light of day. Robert mounted the ladder to the fo'c'sle deck to get a better view, and though his glass sighted a Moorish ketch flying English colors. He felt a sense of foreboding as the ketch approached. Before William could give any orders to stop the ship, Robert hurried to the great cabin. He found Kidd poring over the ship's log.

"Moorish ketch ahead," Robert reported. Kidd raised his eyes, and Robert did not like what he saw in them. "But she's flying English colors, sir," Robert cautioned.

"Might be a ruse in these waters." Kidd stood and gazed out the porthole of the cabin. It did not take him long to reach a decision.

"Board her," he ordered Robert. "She might have something of use to us."

"But we have no right," Robert began.

"That's an order," said Kidd as he strode out and up on deck. All eyes turned toward the captain as he mounted the quarterdeck, where he took the glass from Robert, who had followed him. The crew was silent as the *Adventure Galley* rocked in the sea and the captain eyed the Moorish ketch. Then a sailor called from aloft.

"Are we goin' after her, Captain?"

Angry shouts went up from the crew as they clamored to board the ketch. Months of hardship with nothing to show for it had so exasperated the men that both officers knew, with growing dread, that if they let this prize go by, there would be a mutiny. It was in the very air they breathed. As he gave the order to signal the smaller vessel, William could not look Robert in the eye.

"Prepare to board," he shouted, and a great cheer went up from the crew.

As they neared the vessel, they could see that although it was manned by Moors, two Europeans stood on deck.

Kidd saluted the captain of the ketch as they came alongside. "Request permission to board," he said gruffly.

"Permission granted," said the other captain grudgingly, in an English accent. "I am Captain Parker." Beside him a taller man with olive skin stood silently by. He did not salute as Robert and a party of five men followed Kidd over the gangplank to the other vessel.

"What cargo do you carry?" asked Kidd.

"Sir, we sail under English colors," said Parker. "We carry a cargo of pepper, coffee and myrrh."

"Any money?" asked Kidd, as a murmur went through the crew, their knives glinting in the sunlight. Robert's hand went to his own weapon, an ivory-stocked wheel lock pistol, as the sailors from both ships hurled murderous glances at each other, but neither captain gave the order to fight. The *Adventure Galley*'s guns remained leveled at the Moorish ship as Kidd showed his letter of marque to Captain Parker, who frowned over it. "What right does this give you to search our ship?"

'The king's right," said Kidd, then turned to his men. "Search this ship," he order. "There must be money on board. Take the money for the king's duty."

"Order your men to remove one dozen bales of pepper and a like number of coffee to my ship," Kidd ordered the captain of the ketch. "And you, I think I'll take you along with me as pilot. This Moorish ship is no place for an Englishman. You belong in the king's service."

"I am in the king's service," protested the angry captain, the tendons in his neck tightening.

"Who is this man?" asked Kidd turning to the other tall European who stood beside the captain.

"A linguister," Captain Parker replied. "He is Portuguese."

"An interpreter, hmm," mused Kidd. "Useful in these strange waters. Have him go aboard with you." He gestured to his own ship.

"But sir," the English captain protested indignantly.

"You'll do as I say unless you want my cutlass through you."

Robert's temples throbbed. It was too late to stop William from this disastrous action, but he was ready to spring to his defense if anyone had laid a hand on the captain.

Hugh Parrot, one of Kidd's crew, came to report. "No money, sir, but we have several bales of pepper and coffee as ordered, as well as some myrrh."

"Very good. Take them," said Kidd. Behind him the crew on the *Adventure Galley* let out a wild, "Hurrah!" as they licked their lips in anticipation. Booty, at long last! But Robert suddenly wondered if the king would ever see it. He stood rooted to the deck, sick at what he knew was a blatant act of piracy.

He fought to keep from lashing out at Kidd for he had vowed never to reprimand his commander in front of the men. He knew that if one false move was made, both bloodthirsty crews would be at each other's throats. He must try, at all cost, to avoid useless bloodshed.

Kidd made for his own ship, and for all their protesting, Robert noticed that the English captain and Portuguese interpreter did little to avoid their present predicament. He wondered if perhaps they preferred service on a privateer to the Moorish ship they manned.

When all was secure on the *Adventure Galley*, Kidd let the Moorish ship sail away, and sent his new prisoners below.

"What will you do with them?" Robert asked.

"They'll be useful to me," was all the glowering captain told him before he went to his cabin. William's manner had become very distant, and Robert knew he must rue the day he set out on this voyage.

The small ship wandered in an empty ocean as Robert sat in the first mate's cabin, trying to discipline his mind to think clearly. He sat at his small writing table trying to compose a letter to Wynn. Now he had only her image to remind him that there was a world back home. Here, on the other side of the ocean, one could easily forget the streets of New York and the courts of London. No wonder William was seizing ships unlawfully. It had become a matter of survival, yet it was hard to fathom just what was in Kidd's mind. How did he expect to justify his acts? Robert's head ached as he tried to reason it out.

He dipped his quill in the bottle of ink. He had decided there was no use keeping the truth from their loved ones back home. They ought to be forewarned. It had crossed his mind that so much bad news might discourage Wynn from waiting for him. But it was better to give her the truth, so she could make a decision. Perhaps she had been right not to want to marry him. The thought was painful to him and he wondered if he could convince her that this would be his last voyage, that her love for him had helped him conquer his useless obsession with the sea.

He continued the letter he had begun. "We've had two deserters," he wrote. "Then a third, Benjamin Franks, who persuaded William to let him go ashore by leaving behind his beaver hat. I do not know what was in William's mind, for this Franks will not come back. The captain is ill disposed to let anyone go ashore for fear of their escape." He went on to describe the strain felt by all the crew. The letter, which was posted at Carwar, left on an East Indiaman bound for New York.

Chapter Eight

Thirteen thousand miles from the *Adventure Galley*, on the Strand in New York, Wynn Cox and Sarah Kidd began their day as they had every day since their men left on the voyage. Although Wynn had not grown used to Robert's protracted absence, the pain had dulled, and Sarah seemed content, with only a trace of sadness in her eyes.

How could she be so resigned? Wynn wondered. *I can never be that way*, she thought as she turned into the street. *I must have been mad to love a sailing man.*

Surely if his letters meant what he said, that he loved her and wanted nothing so much as to return to her, he would never set sail again, especially on such a dangerous voyage. But a little voice argued inside her. Wasn't it wrong to expect a man to change? For most men never did. If she truly loved Robert, she would have to take him the way he was, she told herself.

Now her days were not only filled with her duties to Sarah, but also with helping her family, newly arrived from England. The Coxes had disembarked one cloudy day late in the spring. They had rented a little house on Church Street while Wynn's father and brother, together with some hired men, built their own house out past Maiden Lane. She was on her way there now, having finished writing letters for Sarah this morning. She was anxious to talk to James today. She smiled to herself, remembering her impression when she'd first seen him after a year's separation. He seemed to have grown an inch, and he had filled out. With his laughing blue eyes and boyish good looks, he was the only bright spot in her life just now.

Just then a voice calling her from down the street, interrupted Wynn's reverie. She turned to see Hannah Luck, her wide wimple flapping in the breeze, hastening along the water's edge toward Sarah's house. Wynn wondered what could be hurrying the little lady along so.

"There you are," said the older woman, panting for breath. "You must come with me to Madam Sarah's, for there's news she must hear."

"What is it?" asked Wynn.

"There's been a deposition made, at Bombay, before the secretary of the East India Company by a Benjamin Franks, who declares he was only on Captain Kidd's ship because he wanted to go to the East Indies to establish himself as a jeweler. He left the crew at Carwar and his deposition was sent to London." She stopped for breath.

"How do you know all this?" Wynn could not believe that the woman could keep so many facts in her head for any length of time.

"There's a circular," she said, producing the paper, printed on one side. Wynn snatched it from her, horror mounting as she stood reading it.

"Deposition of Benjamin Franks," it said, "confirms piratical acts of William Kidd, Robert Lamley and crew," Wynn's heart pounded as she read the horrible document which described the entire voyage, detailing much of what she already knew. Franks had joined the crew, it said, because he had losses of above 12,000 pounds sterling by "the Earthquake and Enemyes and through misfortune." Kidd was on his way to the East Indies and told Franks he would put into some of the ports where Franks could follow his profession as a jeweler, so he joined up.

Franks detailed the meetings with the other ships, and how after taking on water at St. Johanna, he lay sick with fever, ague and flu. He was still ill when the *Adventure Galley* lay in wait for pirates off Babs Key, and later he heard all that happened when Kidd took the English captain and the Portuguese linguister aboard. Later Franks crept up to the Portuguese to ask what news, and the man told him about the booty Kidd had taken from the other ship.

Finally, when Franks was recovered from his illness, he asked the captain if he could go ashore at Carwar, where the *Adventure Galley* put in for wood and water. He said that Captain Kidd was afraid to let anyone go ashore except those he could trust.

"Dear God," Wynn said. "That is exactly what Robert wrote," Hannah looked confused, not knowing to what Wynn referred.

"This I do swear by the Old Testament to the best of my knowledge and what I have heard of the seamen, that all the above written is true. Benjamin Franks."

The deposition seemed to hammer shut Robert and William's fate like nails into the lid of a coffin.

"Let us hurry," she urged Hannah, who was vexed at having to wait so long for her. Wynn walked quickly back to the house. She dreaded giving bad news to Sarah, but she knew it must be done. If Robert and William had become pirates, perhaps there was something she and Sarah could do to save them. She did not know what exactly, but the urgency in her heart told her she could no longer sit peacefully by, doing nothing.

Her heart raced as they ran up the steps and through the cool foyer of the house. Sarah was in the kitchen, and when she saw the look on Wynn's face, she dismissed Elizabeth.

"There's been a deposition," said Wynn, sinking onto one of the wooden kitchen stools to read it aloud to Sarah.

All too aware of Hannah's presence, Wynn wished the woman would leave. This was too personal, and Hannnah, well-meaning as she might be, would gossip. Talk in the colony spread from one set of lips to another faster than the subjects of the gossip could act. Just now Wynn wanted to be alone with Sarah to think.

Wynn read the circular, wiping her fingers on the apron. Some of the ink was still wet, since the printing house was only a few doors away, and Hannah had rushed it to her so quickly.

"So," said Sarah, when Wynn had finished. "They really are accused of piracy. Oh my Lord, what will we do now?" And she too sank slowly onto a kitchen stool.

"Well now, my dears," said Hannah, "I'll leave you to think out what's to be done. But if there's anything I can do to help, you must let me know. I'll be here on a moment's call, though I don't rightly know what can be done with the captain and Mr. Lamley on the other side of the ocean." She rose, kissed Sarah's cold cheek and, with a rustle of petticoats, was gone.

Sarah remained seated, staring at the deposition as if it were a poisonous snake.

"I had heard that they were accused of piracy, but I had hoped it was only jealous tongues wagging."

"Surely it isn't true, Sarah? Robert and William would never turn against the king," said Wynn, tears escaping her eyes and running down her cheeks.

"They may not consider themselves pirates, dear

heart," said Sarah, taking Wynn's clenched fists in her cool white hands. "For what they have done and what the law says they have done can sometimes be very far apart, especially if you're as far away from England's justice as they are."

Wynn's face trembled as she looked into the solemn violet eyes across from her. "They will come home, won't they? Surely this is all a mistake. If they are here to explain themselves, surely they can prove themselves victims of an unruly crew, and driven to these acts of, of —" She found it hard to utter the word "piracy," so filled was it with the threat of punishment.

"If only they didn't have to answer to the king and those Whig lords," said Sarah, standing up and pacing the kitchen. "But they must either fulfill their contract to our dread sovereign or face disaster," she sighed. "Their only hope is to, indeed, catch some pirates or plunder enemy vessels. Dear heaven, I do not understand why they have not done that already. What can be in their minds?"

Once again, she stared into space, as if trying to establish some mystical contact with her husband, so far away. Wynn did not interrupt the other woman's thoughts, but considered her own dilemma. She had tried without success to forget Robert, both before and after he had declared his love for her. Visions of him rose before her now. Robert, standing in front of the White Rose Tavern the day she first saw him; Robert glaring at her across the parlor; then holding her close on the wharf. If only she could reach out now and touch him. If only by some miracle he were standing beside her, here in this kitchen. She would do anything to see him once more. She could not just abandon him to his fate.

She took a deep breath and faced Sarah again. "What can we do?"

The question brought Sarah back from wherever her mind had wandered. "Do? Why we can do nothing."

"No," Wynn said. "I cannot accept that." And she stood, angry now at the turn of events. She would not sit still, and she did not see how Sarah could. For the first time, Wynn felt stronger than her cousin. She had always looked up to Sarah as an example of how one dealt with being a sea captain's wife. But Sarah had turned inward, finding her solitude there. Perhaps she had been through so much hardship already that she had gotten used to it. Perhaps she derived her inner strength from steeling herself against bitterness, not fighting the outcome.

Not so for Wynn. She was too young. She would not give up easily. There must be a way to help Robert. She didn't know how yet, but she would find out, she told herself as she passed through the parlor and outside.

Just then little Sarah came running down the street, laughing as she chased a little boy with mud on his breeches. Passers-by smiled at the children, and Wynn's heart contracted. How she pitied Sarah's child. What would the little girl do without a father?

"Oh no," she gasped and began running down the Strand until she reached Maiden Lane and turned toward the house her family was building. She slowed only when she saw James hammering planks into place for the second story of their new house.

"Hey, Sis," James greeted her, dropping the plank he was setting in place and wiping his hands on the apron that covered his kersey breeches. His flushed cheeks and windblown hair, the same straw color as Wynn's, emphasized his youthful appearance. His white shirt was damp with perspiration from the labor, and the front was half unbuttoned, revealing his well-developed pectoral muscles. He lifted a muscular arm and wiped his forehead with his sleeve.

As he came close enough to see that his sister was troubled, his cheerful expression became sober. He signaled for her to follow him to the base of a spreading elm, then heaved himself against it and slid to its base. She knelt down next to him on the uncut grass, spreading her muslin skirts around her. The warmth of her brother's presence comforted her. It always had.

"James, whatever am I to do? I have heard that Robert's sure to be arrested for piracy."

"Hold on, Sis, what's happened? I can't help you unless you tell me everything from the beginning."

As Wynn told him about the deposition and how the news was spreading that Captain Kidd and his men had turned pirate, he frowned in concentration.

"Here on shore there's little to be done, it seems," she said. "But there must be something, James. I am determined to help Robert out of this situation."

"You mustn't endanger yourself," said James, taking her hand in his. He had not met this man Lamley, but although he had some idea of him from what Wynn had told him, James had decided to reserve judgment until he met the man in person. As for William Kidd, he could not understand him, nor did he know why Robert was so loyal to him. But of course he was prejudiced. He cared first of all for his sister's happiness.

Having revealed all of her emotions in the narrative about the morning's occurrences, Wynn now stared resolutely at her fair-haired brother.

"I must go to him," she said.

"Don't be foolish, Sister," James said. "You couldn't help him by going to him, and it would be dangerous for you. Why the *Adventure Galley* could be anywhere, for all you know." He caressed her hand idly with his thumb and spoke more gently. Wasn't this the same strength of character that had driven her to cross the ocean as her father's emissary to the wealthy Sarah Kidd? Still, he did not want to see her in danger.

"Robert wouldn't want you to endanger yourself," he cautioned. "These issues may be resolved here on land."

"He thinks I might not wait for him."

"That is for you to decide, of course," said her brother, but one look at her eyes and he knew that not only would she wait for the handsome sailor, but more than that — and this frightened James — she would journey to the ends of the earth to find him if she thought that was the only way. As he stared into her blue eyes, he realized that the woman in her had come to full bloom.

"What does Sarah make of all this?" he asked as he arose, pulling Wynn to her feet as well.

Wynn shrugged. "She seems resigned to whatever happens. I don't quite understand it. I know she loves her husband, and yet she doesn't fight back. She just lets fate take its course."

"Perhaps that is the way you should look at it."

"No," said Wynn. "I will not. We make our own fate. I do not believe the ideas about predestination. I cannot. If everything were figured out by God beforehand, why we might just as well lie down and die right now. I cannot believe that God is that cruel."

James did not argue. Wynn had always taken on life this way, refusing to bow to anything she could not understand, while he was content to live from one day to the next. A good day's work, good drink, a lass to dally with, and James was happy. He had no desire to twist destiny in any way.

But then, he mused, as he regarded his strong-headed sister, perhaps it was because he had never had a cause. A cause filled people with fire — the determination to do something in spite of the odds. And after all, that was what this new land was all about. That was why they were here at the edge of the frontier instead of home in England. The New World offered a chance to shape destiny and carve out a place for oneself.

"Come on," he said, brushing the dead leaves off his breeches. "Let's go see what Mother's made for us to eat."

Life aboard the *Adventure Galley* worsened daily. When William Moore, their gunner, had proposed that they plunder an English ship, the *Loyal Captain*, Kidd had stopped her, examined her papers, but then let her go. Now Moore sat grinding a chisel on the deck as overhead, the sun glared down. Robert watched from the quarterdeck as William strode in front of Moore on the deck below.

"Captain," Moore shouted. "I could have put you in the way to have taken that ship and never been the worse for it."

Glaring at the gunner, and muttering under his breath, Kidd went below, as Moore continuted to hurl insults after him.

Robert climbed down to the deck where Moore sat and, placing himself in front of the truculent man, said "Shut your mouth or I'll have you in irons."

Moore turned up his snarling face. "I wasn't complainin' none about you, Master Lamley. Yer a strong man, I can see that. But the cap'n 'ere, he's weak, that's what he is." Then he raised his voice as Kidd reappeared at the hatchway.

"You have brought us to ruin, and we are desolate," cried Moore from his crouching position by the railing as Robert kicked his shin with his boot in an attempt to shut him up.

"Have I brought you to ruin?" said Kidd, striding to

where the first mate stood over the man. "I have not done an ill thing to ruin you, and you are a lousy dog to say those words."

Robert tensed, ready to spring between the two men if a fight broke out, while out of the corner of his eye he gauged the reactions of the rest of the crew. He noticed that a sailor, one Darby Mullins, who was making a bight splice nearby, had stopped his work to watch the argument.

"If I am a lousy dog, then you have made me so," Moore grumbled.

Kidd seized an iron-bound bucket that stood nearby and, before Robert could stop him, crashed it against Moore's head, "Have I ruined you, you dog?" roared Kidd at the man who lay prostrate on the deck.

"Damn him for a villain," moaned Moore as he was carried off by several of the crew.

As Robert watched the men go below, Kidd turned to him, the anger still flashing in his eyes. Although brutality on board most ships was common, it was dangerous with such a dissatisfied crew as theirs, but decorum prevented him from saying anything unless he himself wanted to be accused of mutiny. But as he looked into his friend's eyes, Robert felt pity. God knows, he himself had been close to ringing the gunner's neck. But if William was losing control of the crew, it was up to Robert to be on the alert. He decided that he would stay armed at all times from now on.

The next day, Robert was alone in his cabin when his servant, Will Jenkins, knocked on the door.

"What is it, Jenkins?"

"It's Mr. Moore, sir," said the servant, his knobby fingers loosening the scarf at his neck as if to breathe easier.

"Well, what is it?"

"He's dead, sir. Doctor says he fractured his skull."

His stomach tightening into a knot, Robert turned

away. "Thank you, Jenkins," he said over his shoulder. "I'll tell the captain."

Robert paced the small cabin, taking stock of the crew. If there was a mutiny, who would stand by the officers? Richard Barlicorn, William's servant, was loyal. So were Hugh Parrot and Tom Perkins, able seamen, and Will Jenkins. He numbered others who would probably stand loyal rather than turn pirate, but he couldn't be sure. Hungry men in a hot sea could react more like animals than loyal followers.

Robert guessed that below decks some of the men were murmuring "murder," but he knew that Kidd had not meant to kill the man, only to discipline him. He prepared himself to face William with this latest news.

"Come in," said Kidd when Robert knocked. He found the captain staring morosely over the ship's log as he sat at the mahogany table that was bolted to the floor of the cabin.

"It's Moore, sir," said Robert. "He's dead."

William said nothing, only continued to stare ahead, his eyes gazed, until he finally motioned Robert to leave him alone.

It now took all of Robert's strength of will to continue to hold the crew together. When he retired to his cabin each night, he was tortured by thoughts of Wynn and fears that he would never see her again. There were times when he cursed his love for her, cursed the fact that, once again, he had fallen under the spell of a woman. Then, as exhaustion overtook him, he would whisper, "Forgive me, my love, it is not your fault. Surely I am a doomed man."

Gerald Portman sat with Wynn and Sarah in the Kidds' parlor, uncomfortably aware that he held no place in any woman's heart. Still, the Kidd household provided him with emotional warmth, and he was a comfort to the desolate women, he knew. Wynn seemed to want him as a confidant, even though she talked mostly of Robert, and he listened stoically, steadfastly hoping that she would come to her senses and change her mind one day.

Idly turning the pages of a book of poetry, Wynn surreptitiously watched as Gerald sat on the settee with Sarah and the little girl. She wondered if he would make her another proposal now that the news was out about Robert's supposed piracy. She felt sorry for Gerald, and she honestly liked him, but she knew she could never marry him. Ever since she had acknowledged her love for Robert, she had known that her fate was linked with his.

But what if Robert never came home? What if the accusations of piracy against him held? Lord Bellomont had finally arrived in New York to serve as governor of New England and New York, and it was he — that hated man — who was responsible for Robert and William's present folly. She *had* to find an opportunity to speak to him — and soon, before he moved on to Boston. She dropped the book and stared toward the window, noticing dusk had fallen.

"Time to go to bed." Sarah's voice broke into Wynn's consciousness.

"Do I have to, Mother?" asked little Sarah. She was a pretty little thing with brown curling eyelashes that would have touched her father's heart if he had been there to see her. The little girl came dutifully toward Wynn, and she leaned down to receive her little kisses. As she caught Gerald Portman's eye, she saw a flicker of emotion, and guessed he was envisioning his own home with a wife like Wynn and girls like Sarah's small daughter.

As Sarah stood to walk upstairs with the child, the servant, Elizabeth, appeared. "If that's all, ma'am," she said, "I'll be going to me room."

"Good night, Elizabeth," Wynn said.

When the others had left, she cleared her throat nervously. Gerald eyed her cautiously, then looked away. He was not bad-looking for a man his age, Wynn thought. Certainly he was kind and full of compassion. But when she compared him to Robert — no, there was simply no comparison.

"Gerald," she began, folding her hands in her lap.

"Yes, my dear," he answered.

"I must speak to you of my feelings." His look of pain told her he knew what was coming. Nevertheless, she continued.

"I want you to know how much I appreciate your friendship." The pained look receded, and in its place hope appeared. "But please don't mistake my intentions," Wynn hurried on. "I still intend to marry Robert Lamley, and I — that is — I know you hold affections for me." She glanced down at her hands. "I wouldn't want you to be disappointed."

Gerald was silent for a while, as if gathering his thoughts. "I know you have promised yourself to Robert Lamley," he finally said solemnly. "You have told me as much. But surely you will not sully your reputation by remaining loyal to a man accused of piracy?" His voice sounded strained, and he could not look her in the eye for more than a few words at a time before glancing down with a frown. "I cannot let you ruin yourself even if you believe yourself to be in love with the man."

He continued, seeming to gather courage as he spoke. "If he is accused of piracy, tried and acquitted, and if he then makes you his own in an honest way, then I am prepared to stand aside. I am not by nature a jealous person. But I cannot help but nourish hope, you must understand that," he said.

Wynn stood slowly, placing her book on the side table near her chair. "You must not, Gerald," she said.

"Robert will return."

"My dear, I know you hope as much," he continued. "But I have seen far too many young women's hopes dashed over just such a situation. If he returns he will have to answer for these piratical acts now that Governor Bellomont is in New York, and until he comes to claim you, you need a protector. I wish to be that protector. If indeed he does come to claim you honestly, I will interfere no more."

"My dear Gerald," she said. "You must not wait for me. Surely there are other young women who would make you happy and whom you could please as well." She felt the crimson color rise in her cheeks. She could not avoid thoughts of the intimate details of a marriage, for her body had felt urgings that she could not deny when she thought of Robert's arms around her. But thinking of Gerald in these same terms embarrassed her. She couldn't even imagine it. And surely he would demand the physical side of love, since he seemed to want to produce children. This much she gathered from the pleasure in his eyes when he looked at Sarah's daughter.

"Please sit beside me, dear Wynn," he said, patting the leather seat on the settee. "You know I will not press you." This she knew, for his chaste embraces never threatened her in any way. She felt the same warm response to his nearness that she did to her brother's or father's. Beside Gerald she felt like a child, whereas Robert made her feel like a woman, ready to fulfill a man's desires.

"Gerald," she asked softly, "would you do something for me if I asked it?"

"Of course, my dear. What is it?" She knew his answer was not quite true. He would help her only if he knew that what she asked would be for her own good.

"I — I'm not sure yet. But I might need a favor soon, and I want to be able to count on you as a friend."

"Of course I am your friend. You may rest assured of that."

"Good. You put my heart at rest."

He picked up her hand and held it between his own. "My poor little one. Such heavy sorrows." He contemplated Wynn and Sarah. Both were made of sturdy stuff in their own ways. Neither was like the cosseted beauties in Europe who would never face such dangers, much less wait for them to pass. For that he had to admire Wynn. He sighed. He did not know why he loved the girl at his side with her determined chin and her proud expression. She brought out in him some latent emotions he barely remembered once having, his own youth being so far away.

The soft footsteps coming down the stairs warned them of Sarah's approach. She came in, her full-length dressing gown trailing softly over the polished wood floors.

"I'm sorry if I'm interrupting your conversation. I just thought I would sit up for a while."

"I'll be going," said Gerald, standing and smoothing his waistcoat. "If there's anything I can do —" he left the sentence unfinished.

Wynn nodded and saw him to the door. Outside, the clouds were coming up, covering the moon. She shut the door as he walked away into the night. She returned to the parlor and saw that Sarah had taken a seat and picked up her needlework. At first Wynn thought she would go to the woman, but then she thought better of it. They had consoled each other many times before and had run out of things to say. Nothing she could say to Sarah would make any difference in what happened now, so she bade her good night, threw her cloak around her shoulder, and stepped outside to walk to her parents' house alone.

Chapter Nine

As Wynn walked past William Bradford's printing house on her way up the Strand, she noticed a stubby-looking Dutch ship unloading an immense cargo from Madras and Surat.

She was standing observing the ship when a small boy approached her. Although skinny and dirty, he held his head in a jaunty position, and from the belligerent way he addressed her, she could tell that he was already used to making his way in a hard world.

"If ye be the lady Wynn Cox, I've news fer 'e from my master, Old Man Drago," he said.

"Who sent you? Who is this Drago?" she asked, grabbing his shoulder.

Grimacing, he shook off her hand and said, "Drago Calicut, lately of the *Mocha Frigate*. His cap'n sent him ashore when he came ill."

"And why does he want to see me?" she asked.

"He brings word of Robert Lamley, Cap'n Kidd's first mate, if you want to hear it."

She clutched the boy again. "Where is he?" she demanded.

"There's a price," said the boy, his eyes shifting from side to side.

"I'll pay," said Wynn impatiently. "Take me to him."

"He's at the Boar's Head Tavern, down by the docks. I c'n take you there now, if you got the money."

Wynn knew the Boar's Head Tavern — a seedy place haunted by pirates and other disreputable persons. But she decided she would surely be safe enough in the middle of the day, and if there was news of Robert to be had, she would take any chance.

"Take me to this Drago, and then I'll give you more coins to go and tell my mistress, Sarah Kidd, where I've gone."

The boy nodded sullenly and started off down the street, a few paces in front of her. She followed him past the docks to where the Strand turned into Pearl Street. There, set back from the main thoroughfare in a grassy plot, was a small wooden structure, formerly used as a warehouse. Sailors and drunkards leaned or sat about, and Wynn kept her eyes averted from them as she followed the boy through the weedy tavern yard. The men lying in the grass made lewd comments as she passed, some of them clutching at the hem of her skirt, but she ignored them — the need to hear news of Robert drove her on.

The door creaked open as the boy slid through, and she stepped into the dark interior. For a moment there was a hush, as sailors, pirates and black market traders paused from their discussions to peer at her through the smoky air. The boy gestured for her to follow him to a corner of the room where his master sat drinking alone behind a small wooden table.

Drago Calicut, a wizened little man with a scarred face, was hunched over a tankard of beer. When the small boy rolled up a beer keg and turned it on its end so Wynn could sit down, she instructed him on where to deliver her message to Sarah, paid him and then sat down, trying not to shudder at Calicut's repellant face.

"What have you to tell me?" she asked, noticing that the other patrons in the tavern had gone back to minding their own business.

"What's it worth to you?"

Wynn sat silently, summing the man up. If he really did have a message from Robert, she knew her fiancé had probably already paid him to deliver it.

"How much did Mr. Lamley pay you?" she asked. She saw the flicker in his eye and knew that she was right.

"He promised me ten shillings, paid me five, said you'd give me the other five." Wynn doubted this was true, but the man was shrewd and she had little recourse but to agree.

Placing three shillings down on the table, she said, "You'll have to send your boy for the rest. I don't have any more money with me." Indeed, she had only very small change on her, as she had just paid some of Sarah's bills in town.

Calicut grunted his approval and, ordering a second tankard of beer to keep his tongue loose, began his story in a voice that, although it was scratchy, was also compelling.

"Your man Lamley sailed with Captain Kidd. Ah, that man's headed for a nasty fate, he is. Made many a wrong move, he did, on the other side of the world." Wynn already knew this, and she hoped she would get more than these wild rumors for her money. But what he said next gave her hope.

"I was with the crew at Madagascar. But I can tell you the events since the death of William Moore, for that I seen with me own eyes. Evil ran rampant on the ship then," he said, describing Kidd's thrashing of

Moore with the iron-bound bucket. "The crew held the captain guilty of murder. Some say it was an accident. Nobody would speak, but there was much grumblin'."

Wynn swallowed hard, wondering about Robert, but she let Drago continue to tell the story his own way.

"Aye, the captain and his men had already taken two prizes when they came upon their last prize."

"What ships?" asked Wynn, for she was unaware of these latest prizes.

"The *Maiden*, some call her the *November*. We did take her off the port of Calicut, my namesake, in November last. She was flyin' French colors and we chased her under French colors of our own. The captain wished to let her go, her cargo being of very little value, but the crew demanded to make her a prize. It would have been mutiny if he hadn't taken her."

Mutiny. Although the word made Wynn cringe, she was glad that William and Robert had given in to a mutinous crew rather than be killed. At a trial they could be proven innocent if they had only done that much, surely.

Drago continued. "Two horses, twelve bales of cotton, some quilts, and sugar," he said, rattling off the booty. "The master, a Dutchman, with two other Dutchmen and eight or nine Moors came aboard, declaring it was a Moorish ship. They handed the captain a French pass. Kidd put the Moors in the longboat. He sold the cotton and the horses on the coast to the natives for gold and coin and took the ship along with him as a prize."

Wynn frowned. Why didn't he bring the prize back for England as was stipulated in the Articles of Agreement? But perhaps they were so desperate they needed the money to feed the crew.

"Three days after Christmas, to my recollection, they seized a Moorish ketch off the Malabar coast and took candy and coffee. Twelve days after, they plundered a

Portuguese ship of East India Company goods — gunpowder, opinum, rice."

"But what of Master Lamley? You said you had news of him?"

"A tortured man he was in those days. Loyal to the captain to the last, but troubled by the rest of the crew, and I don't blame him. He took to walking the deck armed at all times, and I don't wonder he seldom slept." Drago looked straight ahead of him, as if reliving the scenes.

"Then they took the biggest prize of all." He paused. "The *Quedah Merchant*. Five hundred tons of merchantman outward-bound from Bengal to Surat. A rich cargo she had of silks, muslins, sugar, iron, guns and gold coin, and she was making heavy weather off the Indian coast, ten leagues it was, north of Cochin.

"We pursued 'er four hours. Then we came upon 'er and fired across 'er bow. An old French gunner posed as her master and came aboard. Captain Kidd ran up the English flag and claimed her as a prize. She had Armenian owners, so it seemed."

Wynn followed the narrative as best she could. It seemed the rules at sea were complicated by the fact that ships identified themselves under whatever colors appeared most convenient at the time. Just because the ship had a French pass did not make her a French ship. Evidently this *Quedah Merchant* was Armenian, and Wynn wondered if that made her a lawful prize.

"The owners offered to ransom the ship for three thousand pounds," Drago went on. "Master Lamley stepped in and agreed. He tried to persuade the captain. But Captain Kidd refused. I guess bein' so long at sea with so little prizes made him greedy; that or fear o' his unruly crew. Kidd scorned the three thousand pounds offered and sold some 'o the cargo on shore for eight thousand. Ah, Master Lamley remained silent, but you could see it in his eyes, you could, that he knew this was a dangerous move. All that time it was the first mate who kept the crew down. He served as the captain's bodyguard of a sort, for the men were afraid of Master Lamley's temper and his evil stare when he got mad."

With a leaden heart Wynn realized that Robert and William were in a situation that had become increasingly desperate, and she chafed to do something. She let Drago continue, however, for she had not previously pieced together as much news about the fateful voyage as she was now getting. With Drago's information, together with the sparse letters she had received, and the rumors she had heard, she could finally form a true picture of Robert's condition and that of the *Adventure Galley* crew. As Drago continued she forced herself to focus on his story.

". . . divided the take among the crew. Kept them quiet, he did. I heard him havin' a row about it with Master Lamley. The first mate said somethin' about takin' it all back to England, for it was England's prize. But the captain muttered to him about satisfyin' the crew. Seems all the backbone had gone out o' the captain, and there was nothing his mate could do about it."

Wynn could imagine Robert's anger and, remembering his brooding eyes, she was glad at that moment that she wasn't Captain Kidd — except, her heart cried out, Captain Kidd at least was with Robert, and she was not.

"It was five or six days before the captain of the *Quedah Merchant* appeared, and Captain Kidd found out he was English. His name was Captain Wright. Kidd stayed in his cabin lamenting he had captured an Englishman, for this he had sworn he would not do. I heard him make a speech to the crew then. He said the takin' of this ship would make a great noise in England. He proposed they hand her back to her rightful owners, but the crew refused to allow this, and so the three ships continued on their course.

"I was a sick man then too," Drago said. "I knew it

were better for me to get home where I had business to attend to. I ha'nt got long to live, my heart was tellin' me, and I needed to tend to my affairs."

Wynn wondered what possible business affairs this dilapidated man could have and surmised it was more of an excuse to get away from the compromised captain than anything else, but she did not voice her judgment.

"Where are they now?" she asked, her heart pounding harder.

"Headin' for St. Mary's in Madagascar, last I heard of 'em. They got to wait five months for the northeast monsoons to blow 'em around the Cape."

"Five months! I cannot wait five months." She stopped herself, knowing it did not matter to Drago Calicut how long she waited, as long as he got paid.

"What will they do there?" she asked as a final question.

"Got to fit out the *Quedah Merchant* to voyage far. The *Adventure Galley*'s too seaworn. It won't be easy recruitin' a crew from those that drift that island."

"But surely they want to get home." She thought of Sarah and her little daughter and of Robert saying he wanted to come home to her. And yet it was now dangerous for them to return home. She was certain that with so many apparent acts of piracy, it was only a matter of time before orders would be issued for their arrest. She had no confidence that the high-placed Whig lords who backed the voyage would do anything to help. The venture had been a failure, and they would turn a deaf ear to Kidd, she was sure. She sat silently, wondering if Kidd and Robert knew the extent of their plight. If they tried to come home, they might be hanged.

She wondered if they would be daring enough to come home anyway. Surely Captain Kidd would stay at sea until he achieved a modicum of success for the king, or until he met his fate. And he would keep Robert with him.

She cursed under her breath. Knowing that Robert would never desert his captain, there seemed only one thing to do if she ever wanted to see him again. She would have to run away, for none of her family or friends would approve of what she had decided to do. But life was not worth living with Robert on the other side of the world and likely never to return. She had no choice. But even as she thought it, she realized she did not know how she would carry out such a plan.

"Thank you," she said to Drago. "I'll pay you well for this information if you'll send the boy with me."

The man nodded, sipping his beer. He motioned to the youngster, who had reappeared to follow her home.

Emerging into the sunlight, Wynn took a deep breath of fresh air. She had not realized how stuffy it was inside the dark tavern, and yet she realized, as the smell of fish assailed her nostrils, if she were to join Robert, she might have to suffer far worse surroundings.

From the raised platform at the end of the Long Room upstairs in the White Rose Tavern, a flute, clarinet, French horn and drums set in motion the assembly of dancers gathered for entertainment. Elegantly clad ladies in their low-cut satin and lawn gowns that came to the floor and gentlemen in brocade waisted coats and ruffled shirt-sleeves bowed, turned, smiled, stepped and glided gracefully around the room. Spectators fanned themselves on pine-slab benches lining the walls.

In the hallway guests refreshed themselves from delft punch bowls or with glasses of Madeira or rum. A cold supper of meats, biscuits, chocolate and cake was laid out on a trestle table, and across the hallway from the dancing some of the men sat smoking and sipping brandy.

Governor Bellomont was among them, his gouty leg

raised on a stool under the table where he sat. Smoke floated around his head as he talked with the leaders of New York, who puffed on their white clay pipes. He was dressed in a brocaded tunic and his linen cravat, which reached to his chest, was trimmed with a border of lace. A curled wig sat on his head and his puffy red cheeks were clean shaven. But in spite of his foppish dress and effeminate manners, his presence was commanding.

Over the din of conversation penetrating every corner of the room, he talked with his companions, but from time to time his pale eyes wandered toward the door. Across the hall his young wife, Kate, the countess, ostentatiously gowned in tight-fitting cherry-colored satin with black silk petticoat, her voluptuous breasts pushing against a black lace bodice, threw back her head and laughed. Lifting her petticoats higher than the more modest ladies in the room, she exposed her ankles while dancing in showy, complicated steps.

The revelry had been going on for some time, and most of those present had had plenty of time to imbibe. Although the company had gathered to fête their new governor, his own indulgent manners and his wife's uninhibited spirits encouraged the tongues and the roistering.

Wynn caught her breath as the music finished. She curtsied to her partner, a gaunt young man named Clarence with brown hair that fell over his ears. Over Clarence's shoulder, she caught a glimpse of James's blond head as he laughed gaily with a young woman dressed in a simple gown of embroidered cotton. The waist of her dress was pulled tight with drawstrings that crisscrossed up the bodies, and her white chemise opened to reveal plump breasts. Wynn saw James lean down and whisper something in the girl's ear, causing her to clap her hand over her mouth and giggle. Then

James reached his arm around her waist to lead her away, his face still flushed and his breath ragged from the dance.

"I think I'll get some wine," Wynn said to her attendant, who was already looking about for another partner. She moved toward the door, and as she turned into the hallway, she saw James and the girl running up the stairs. The girl paused at the top of the landing, thinking herself hidden from view, and turned back to James, who pulled her close, one hand sliding up under her flounces, exposing her thighs. Then they broke apart, laughed, and ran up the stairs.

Wynn's cheeks flushed with embarrassment. Watching the two young people caused a heated feeling deep in the center of her body. It spread from between her legs to the tips of her breasts, which felt suddenly tender and desirous. As she watched James and the girl in their shameless embrace, she had pictured herself with Robert. She hoped that if anyone were watching her, they would assume it was the dancing that had brought the color to her cheeks and caused her uneven breathing.

"May I bring you some refreshments?" came a familiar voice over her shoulder. Gerald Portman hovered close behind her, and she could feel his light breath against her ear.

"Thank you," she said, glad that her back had been to him so she had time to compose her expression. Other guests stood about the table laid with the cold collation, as Gerald moved to pour Wynn some punch made of rum, brown sugar, fruit and lemon rinds.

Just then a loud female voice distracted them, and they both followed the sound to its source with their eyes. A few feet from them, a handsome gentleman in fitted waistcoast and silk stockings was bowing to kiss the countess's bejeweled hand.

"Oh you flatter me, young man," the governor's wife said in a suggestive tone, touching his dark hair as he lingered over her hand. Wynn noticed that when he raised his head, his eyes were focussed on the countess's ample bosom, which was only inches away from his lips.

The governor's wife had been the subject of many rumors in New York months before the governor had set foot on this shore. It was said that she spent outrageous sums of money on extravagant jewels, clothes and imported furniture, and that she had gambling debts as well. If the way she was flirting with the gallant in the dancing room was any indication of her amorous encounters, Wynn could believe the gossip about her infidelities was most likely true.

She turned from the sight. What the countess did before or away from her husband's watchful eyes was no concern of Wynn's. She had her own affairs to think of, and she was more interested in the governor himself, who sat across the hall talking earnestly with several important-looking gentlemen. Among them Wynn recognized Robert Livingston, the man who had introduced Captain Kidd to Governor Bellomont. She had seen him when he'd come to Sarah's once or twice. She crept closer to the door, trying to assess the situation.

When Sarah had told Wynn they were invited to a party for the governor at the White Rose Tavern's Long Room, Wynn had realized that the occasion would be a propitious one to meet Governor Bellomont, and she had laid her plans immediately. Determined to find an opportunity to speak to the governor, she had come to the entertainment escorted by her brother.

It was a bold plan, for she had no doubt that the governor did not seek the counsel of a mere girl. But she had made up her mind to find a way to induce Bellomont to promise that Robert and William would be given a chance to plead their case if they brought the

Adventure Galley home along with the *Quedah Merchant* and their other prizes. She had no idea whether Bellomont would treat them fairly, or if he had already made up his mind that they were pirates.

But how was she to approach the governor? He had not moved from the room in which he sat all night. She glanced sidelong at Gerald, wondering if he might help her somehow. But just then Robert Livingston rose from the stool where he had been sitting next to the governor. He took a last sip of brandy, tilting his head back to empty the glass. Then he wiped his mouth with his cuff and bid the governor adieu.

As he walked toward the door, he spied Gerald Portman, and though Wynn had no idea the two men were acquainted, he called out in his Scottish accent, "Gerald Portman, you dog, where have you been all evening? Surely you haven't been boring this lovely lady with your opinions on commerce."

He bowed to Wynn. "May I have the honor of knowing this lovely young lady's name?" He teased her with eyes that darted over her from beneath bushy gray eyebrows.

Gerald shook Livingston's hand. "May I present Miss Wynn Cox? Her family has newly arrived from England, and they are in the employ of their cousin, Mrs. Sarah Kidd."

"Ah," said Livingston as the light of recognition came into his eyes. "Then I believe we have met, or perhaps Mrs. Kidd's description was so enthusiastic that I felt I knew Miss Cox already." He took Wynn's hand and smiled again.

Livingston could be the solution to her dilemma, Wynn realized quickly.

"Thank you, sir," she said. "I have heard of you from Mrs. Kidd, and from her husband as well."

Livingston paused, his bushy brows drawing together in a frown. "And what have you heard?" he asked.

"Only that you are an astute businessman, and that you have advised the Kidds on many occasions." She looked earnestly up at him, her blue-green eyes wide with admiration.

"Yes, we have had some, er, business together," he said, looking uncomfortable, and began to move away.

"You are a friend of Lord Richard Coote, the earl?" Wynn said, delaying him by laying a hand on his sleeve.

He frowned, nodded, and cleared his throat, looking ill at ease.

Wynn gazed into the smoky room where Bellomont sat. "Such a commanding person. I have wanted to meet him all evening." She turned her back on Gerald and gazed innocently at Livingston, and continued, "Do you think the lord governor would deign to speak to an ignorant girl like me?"

Raising an eyebrow, Livingston looked toward Bellomont who was sitting glaring in displeasure at his wife's antics. It might be an opportune moment to distract him with a young woman, Livingston decided. Perhaps Wynn could forestall an outburst of Bellomont's choleric temper. For the rumors floating about suggested that the governor had not only backed a voyage that had failed, but had actually sponsored pirates. This financial loss, compounded with his wife's extravagances, was considered to be contributing to his ill health, and none of his companions quite knew where they stood with him just now. It might not hurt Livingston's relationship with the governor if he procured the man some slight entertainment, he calculated.

Livingston touched Wynn on the elbow. "Perhaps you would like to meet him now. He seems to have a free moment." Indeed, the room had cleared, and

Bellomont was alone save for two men who were carrying on their own discussion at the table nearest to him. He was just taking a pinch of snuff as Livingston guided Wynn into the room, leaving Gerald to toy with his watch and chain.

"What is it, Livingston?" Bellomont grunted as they came near. He was still fumbling with the snuffbox and ignored Wynn completely.

Livingston coughed. "This young lady, sir, has asked to meet you."

Bellomont glared at Livingston, but his gaze softened as it fell on Wynn. She was conscious of the carmine tint to his nose as Livingston pushed her forward.

"May I present Miss Wynn Cox, lately of London."

She curtsied deeply, lowering her eyes. "Your Lordship," she said.

"Well," Bellomont said, when she had risen, "what is it you want?"

Wynn put her hand to her breast and, fluttering her lashes, said, "I merely wished to meet such an exalted person as yourself."

Bellomont grunted again. "Livingston, get her a stool to sit on." Then to Wynn, "Would you like some punch, my dear? Livingston, send in another bowl." Livingston left to do the governor's bidding.

"So," he said, fluttering a hand, "why is it you think I am so exalted a personage?"

Wynn stared at the flabby old man, willing her nervousness to abate. She found her voice. "To be honored as you are by the appointment to the governorship. To have control over the lives of so many people. Surely you must be a wise and important person. But tell me, sir, is it not lonely to be above people so?"

Bellomont gazed at her speculatively, as Wynn looked at him more openly. Just then his wife's pealing laughter reached them from the room across the hall. Wynn leaned closer to the governor, affecting intimacy.

"I would very much like to know such a great man as yourself," she said, leaning toward him and swallowing hard as Bellomont stared at her, taking in her rounded breasts, small waist and the dainty ankle she exposed beneath her fawn-colored satin gown.

He leaned toward her, lifting one of her curls. "Supposing I were to allow you to know me better?" he asked, his eyes greedy. "What would you want in return for the pleasure of your company?" Suddenly he dropped the curl. "However, I'm not a complete fool, my dear. You may be impressed with my power, but it's only because you want something from me." He reached over and pinched her arm, and at his touch, she couldn't help but flinch.

She glanced away. "Of course," she began, "it would be flattering if you repaid my, my gesture toward you with a favor." She swallowed hard, shutting her eyes. If it came to it, could she force herself to go through with his demands — if it meant Robert's life?

"We would have to see first if you pleased me, hmmm?" Bellomont said.

"I would please you, sir," she said, struggling to keep the tremor out of her voice.

"Well, then." He sat back and sniffed through his nose as if they were near the conclusion of an attractive business deal. "What is it you want from me?"

"It's about the *Adventure Galley*, sir," Wynn said in a small, tight voice.

"What?" he boomed at her, glaring so fiercely she could barely confront him.

"I beg you, sir, for a fair judgment of Captain Kidd and his crew when they return with their booty for the Crown. You may have heard rumors of piratical acts, but I assure you, if you give them a chance to explain their motives they can clear their names."

He glowered at her. "And how would you know anything of this moot topic? Surely a young woman of your breeding does not go offering herself to a man in my position on behalf of a privateer she has no acquaintance with? I had not heard that Captain Kidd had a mistress." He gazed at her shrewdly. "But perhaps it is someone else," he said, his lips twisting scornfully.

She dropped her eyes. "It is someone else," she said.

"Ah yes. I begin to see. What man sails with Captain Kidd who holds your heart?" He frowned again. "And you think that by offering up your flesh you can save your lover's neck? For shame. You'll do no such thing. Your young man, whoever he may be, has broken the law, along with Captain Kidd, and they will hang for it if they do not right themselves soon. There will be nothing I can do if I have to hand the lot of them over to the king.

"Don't mistake me," he continued. "I had high hopes for this venture. But Captain Kidd has let us all down."

"Surely there is a reason," Wynn said, dropping all pretense of being a possible mistress as she made one last appeal. "My fiancé, Robert Lamley, is Captain Kidd's first mate, and most loyal to the king."

"Bah," said Bellomont. "He has done nothing to show his loyalty. Forget him, miss. Marry an honest citizen and give up all thoughts of pirates."

Wynn sucked in her breath and stood, her tears of anger splashing into the candle flame, making it waver in front of Bellomont's face.

"You must reconsider," she stammered. "They'll prove themselves yet to the Crown." And she stumbled from the room.

She did not know where to go. Surely not back to the dancing room. A group of merry-makers stood around the eating table. She did not want to shoulder past them, so she fled to the end of the hallway and up the stairs. She sat down on the top floor, burying her head in her hands and wiping her tears away with the hem of her skirt. She was angry that she had failed, and embarrassed about the way she tried, but it was for Robert's sake.

Slowly her sobs subsided and she drew in deep breaths. Gradually she became aware of muffled voices behind her, coming from a room off to her right. She remembered seeing her brother and the girl come up here earlier. She wanted to find her brother now, and so she crept up to the door and put her eye to the keyhole before she realized what she was doing.

James, his clothing undone and his trousers lowered, knelt over the girl, who reclined before him, her hair spread over the pillow behind her, her skirt raised, and her legs spread apart under him. James bent down to her unlaced bodice and kissed her large upturned breasts, and the girl caressed his shaggy blond head with her hands, moaning as he moved his mouth over her. Then he lowered his buttocks, placing his fingers at the opening where her legs met. He massaged her there as she writhed, her moans increasing.

"Please, please, now," she cried raggedly, as he guided his member into her body. He raised his head to look at her face as he thrust his hips toward her. He fell on her as they gripped each other about the torso. The movements acquired a rhythm, and Wynn's mouth went dry as she felt a trembling at the same place in her body that the couple before her had joined themselves. She did not know how long she stared at them before James's thrusts began to move faster and faster. Then he threw back his head and cried out. He shuddered and collapsed on the girl, who bit into his shoulder.

Wynn, flushed and trembling, turned her back to the door, thinking of Robert's scintillating touch on her skin. Smoothing her skirts, she realized she didn't want to be discovered spying on her own brother. She pulled herself up, patting her curls into place, and after several deep breaths, walked to the stairs, using the newel post to steady herself.

The sounds from the room behind her indicated that James and the girl, having finished their coupling, had begun to fix their clothing, so she hurried to the bottom of the stairs. No one was in the hallway, so she walked to the punch bowl and filled a glass, badly needing a drink to cool her throat, which was raw from her earlier sobbing.

In a few moments, whistling to himself, James descended the stairs alone. Out of the corner of her eye, she saw him hitch up the waistband of his trousers under his coat. When she turned toward him, he was smiling. It took him a moment to focus on her, but when he did, his smile widened. Wynn blushed scarlet, but could not resist his good-humored look.

"Hello, Brother," she said. Then she set her glass down. "I've a need for some fresh air. Would you be good enough to take me home?"

"Wouldn't mind some fresh air myself," he said, brushing the hair off his forehead. Wynn led the way downstairs, avoiding the gazes of the other company in the tavern. Outside, she stood for a moment under the oaken sign that proclaimed the identity of the White Rose. James caught up to her and offered his arm, inhaling a deep breath of fresh air as they stepped into the cobbled street.

Wynn looked straight ahead, glad for the night air to cool her damp skin. The stuffy rooms of the tavern and her newfound sensuality, combined with the erotic act she had accidentally witnessed, had left her moist with perspiration. Her cheeks were hot as she wondered if she would ever confide in her brother that she had witnessed his sexual congress.

Chapter Ten

When Wynn had ushered Livingston into Sarah's study he had said little to her, perhaps disappointed at the outcome of his attempts to assuage Bellomont with the young woman's company. Some time later, she heard him taking his leave, and came downstairs just as Sarah turned from the front door, her face pale, her head held rigidly.

"What is it?" asked Wynn, following Sarah into the parlor.

"He wrote a letter to William a few weeks ago," said Sarah. "He tried to warn him of the impending danger."

"Yes?"

"There was also a letter sent from Lord Bellomont, dated the same day as his own, but he has learned from reliable sources that both letters were stolen. He fears that William and Robert have no notion of what awaits them when they return."

Sarah stood before the mantle, her hands clasped in the folds of her skirt. "The brigantine *Joanna* is being sent to Madagascar to catch pirates — among them," her voice faltered — "William and Robert."

"Oh no," Wynn whispered. Then to Sarah, "What else did he say?"

Sarah straightened her shoulders, shook her head, her dark curls falling over her collarbone, exposed by the neckline of her dress. "Nothing, only that the arrest papers have already been issued." Then she turned away as if she did not wish to discuss it any further.

"Sarah, we've got to help them."

To Wynn's dismay, she saw a look of stoic resolve on Sarah's face. "No, Wynn. I'm afraid we must bear up to this. It was perhaps fated from the beginning."

"Fate?" cried Wynn in disbelief. "Surely you do not believe that?"

But Sarah was resolute. "I do not know what I believe." She turned to gaze out the window at the seagulls swooping down on their prey, swimming just under the surface of the water. "I will stand by William no matter what, of course. But surely you can see there are factors at work here that a mere woman cannot influence. I have asked Livingston to do his best on William's behalf. Since Livingston has put money into the enterprise, he has something to gain by a promising outcome. I have also sought audience with Governor Bellomont. But the man is impervious." She gazed with sympathy at her young cousin. "You are young, and I am sorry this had to happen. But I'm afraid it is in God's hands." Sarah laid a hand on Wynn's arm and then retreated from the room.

"No," Wynn whispered, her arm cold where Sarah had touched her. "God may turn his back on them, but surely I cannot."

Sarah kept to herself, receiving no visitors, and if Wynn had not been so worried about Robert, she would have been concerned for Sarah's state of mind. But in her heart, she knew that Sarah must face her fate alone.

For if Captain Kidd's fate was sealed, Robert Lamley's was not.

He was not the captain; he had simply obeyed orders and fought a mutinous crew, Wynn reasoned, so perhaps there was still a chance for him. But she knew that something must be done soon if she were to avert disaster, for even if the people of New York would think little of the affair one way or the other, Wynn knew the political winds that blew across the sea from England would work against Robert. And there were Bellomont's feelings of outrage to be taken into account as well.

Legally, a privateer was a privately owned armed vessel, which in time of war had a commission from the government to commit acts of war on vessels of the king's enemies. Such had been the case when the *Adventure Galley* had set sail. A pirate, on the other hand, was one who committed robbery or other acts of violence on the sea without having any authority and independent from any organized government or political society. How Robert and William could be construed pirates even now seemed far-fetched.

Wynn chafed for action, even if Sarah did not. She was not her father's daughter if she could not turn a desperate situation to her favor. It was that spirit that had seen her family through many a stormy circumstance and had brought her to the New World. And so one balmy day, as the sun glinted off the water, she walked boldly up to the skipper of the *Joanna*, bound for Madagascar.

A heavyset man with a salt-and-pepper beard, he did not seem difficult to approach. Wearing a long-waisted bodice that fell about the hips over a plain skirt and a hood that covered her hair, which was combed flat on top with curls at the side, Wynn appeared a woman of substantial means, one well able to pay her passage. She mustered her courage and stepped through the crowd on the pier and up to the captain, who was reviewing a list of supplies submitted to him for approval by the ship's steward.

"Captain Shaw, I believe?" she asked.

"Yes, what is it?" he answered gruffly, a man with far too much on his mind to be bothered with a woman's queries.

"You are bound, I believe, to the Indian Ocean?"

"I am." He took his eyes off the list and eyed her curiously.

"I wish to book passage on your ship."

Captain Shaw paused a moment as his eyes flitted over her person, and she drew herself up, lifting her chin an inch or two. Then he threw back his head and laughed.

"This ship can take no passengers, and anyway, Madagascar is no place for a lady." Then his face became serious, and he looked at her more closely. "What do you want there anyhow?" His voice was deep, gravelly, but not unkind.

"That is my business," she said stiffly. "I should think a captain would care only that he got paid, and I assure you, I can pay."

"It's not the money I'm worried about," he replied, rubbing his brow with the back of his hand. "As I said, the case is closed. We take no one on board who doesn't work." And with that he turned aside.

"I can work," said Wynn, catching his blue coat sleeve to keep him from leaving.

"What would you do on a brigantine such as this?" he asked in derision. She had expected some difficulty when she had decided to present herself, so this challenge did not take her aback.

"I can write and do figures," she said.

Indeed, this caught the captain off guard. Even though he could write and read well himself, the audacity of the offer intrigued him. These were strange times, and life did not always follow conventional patterns either here in New York or in the Far East where he was heading. The idea that a ship's captain should have a secretary, and a woman at that, was enough to at least make him hesitate.

Wynn turned her blue eyes and innocent face up to his, unaware that she was triggering urgings in the man that could be dangerous to her on the voyage she wanted to take. Captain Shaw was not a particularly lecherous man, but the sight of a pretty young woman offering to work for him on a long voyage where there would be no other women brought licentious thoughts to his mind.

Then he frowned at her. She didn't look the sort of woman to want that sort of business arrangement. Perhaps she didn't realize the risks she took. "Look here," he finally said. "A woman doesn't sail on a privateer, no matter what she says she can do. If I took you on as my secretary, why, the crew would laugh me right off the bowsprit and rape you after."

Wynn felt her hopes ebbing, and in spite of his words, meant to shock her, she hung onto what might be her only chance to get to Robert. "I wouldn't be afraid of the crew if you were there to protect me," she said resolutely.

"My dear lady, you don't know what you're asking. You wouldn't even be safe from me," he said, leering at her in an unmistakable manner.

Words stuck in her throat. She knew that any other passenger ships sailing to Madagascar would make stops in England and along the coast of Africa. By the time she reached her destination, Robert might be gone. She needed a ship that was heading directly to Madagascar, and this one was.

She had already considered what the price might be, and she was prepared to lose her honor if it meant saving Robert's life. Her virtue was worth sacrificing if only she could be with him again, and warn him of Bellomont's displeasure. If Robert chose never to return home she would be able to escape with him. She realized that there were other misfortunes that could also lie ahead of her: She might never see her home or family again, or ever be able, once more, to live in a civilized society.

"No matter what your young man is worth to you, you're better off at home," the captain continued.

She caught her breath.

"You wonder how I know?" he asked.

She nodded.

"I have no doubt you're running after a young man, because only passion would make a woman so crazy she'd give up everything to be at his side. And the poor devil probably isn't even worth it." He turned away, leaving her standing on the dock.

As Wynn watched him walk away she felt anger rising in her and she whispered to the *Joanna*, lying at anchor. "You'll not leave without me, that I promise." And she left the dock, a contingent plan in mind.

She found Gerald Portman at the Sign of the Three Pigeons where his offices were located in Petticoat Lane, a block from the Exchange. She knew she would have to be careful about what she revealed to him. Still, aside from the slim possibility that her brother might help her, Gerald was her only hope. And she doubted her brother's ability to help. He would be too worried about her safety, and besides, there was little he could do except loan her some of his clothes, for she had determined to stow away on the ship.

She entered the front door of Gerald's office and shut the door behind her, its bell tinkling overhead. The clerk looked up, saw it was Wynn, and went to fetch Gerald.

"My dear," said Gerald, coming out to the front. "What brings you here? Come in, come in." And he led her to his private office and shut the door. "Please sit down," he said, drawing up a chair.

"Now," he said when she was seated, "what did you

wish to see me about?" For he knew she would not trouble herself to come all the way to see him on just a social visit.

"I'm afraid I have a favor to ask, Gerald."

"What is it, my dear? You know I will do anything to help you if I can."

"I'm afraid I need to borrow a sum of money."

Gerald drew his brows together. "Is your family in need? Surely, Sarah . . ." He let the sentence drift off.

"Well, no, it isn't exactly that." She bit her lip. *He mustn't refuse her, he simply mustn't.* "It has to do with a personal problem," she said.

"What is the problem?"

"I'm afraid I can't tell you — you'll just have to trust me that it's important." Asking for money embarrassed her, but she knew she'd have to have it in case she was caught, so she could bribe the captain or any crew member who might discover her.

Looking at Gerald beseechingly, she leaned forward to take his hand. "Gerald, if you've ever cared for me, please help me now. This matters more to me than anything. I will repay you, I promise."

Gerald's heart contracted as he looked at the desperation in her eyes and felt the clasp of her hand on his. "Do your parents know of this?" he asked gravely.

"No," she admitted. "I'm afraid they wouldn't approve."

"I see," said Gerald. He cleared his throat, gently drawing his hand away. "Does this have anything to do with Robert Lamley?" He had heard the most recent rumors about the dubious voyage of the *Adventure Galley*, and he was aware of the consequences the crew might face on their return home. He could only suppose that the loan Wynn wanted was going to help Robert in some way, though how, he could not guess.

"Yes," she said in answer to his question about

Robert, forcing herself not to shrink from his gaze. "I want to help him. I cannot tell you how, I can only beg you to aid me. You are my last hope."

Gerald sat quietly, fighting the urge to stand, turn his back on her and say no. But he knew that if he refused her he would lose her affection forever. As it was, if he helped her, he might lose the money, but she would still think fondly of him. And if Robert were hanged or imprisoned, she might still turn to him. This hope was enough to make him give in.

"I think the money could be had." It pained him to say it, and he avoided her eyes as he asked, "How much do you need?"

"Could you give me," she hesitated, "fifty pounds?" She dared not ask for more, and it seemed enough to bribe passage and pay for food if necessary.

He swallowed, fingering his watch and chain. "Very well," he said. If she had asked him for a thousand pounds, or indeed of all his assets, he doubted he could have refused her. Perhaps he was weak to feel this way, but when he looked at her bright blue eyes, and her burnished hair, his heart palpitated. He could not deny his love for her, even though it was unrequited, and he reflected that if they had lived in England, where marriages were often made for convenience rather than love, he might have married her.

Indeed, he thought her father paid far too little attention to her, for no one, it seemed, but himself seemed to try to stop her from loving Robert Lamley.

He went to his safe and, turning his back to her momentarily, opened the door. He extracted the sum she wanted from the safe and, folding the pound notes in his hand, turned and handed them to her. She kissed him gratefully on the cheek and gave his hand a little squeeze. He closed his eyes, pain and love mingling in him. To have her so close and yet know she would never be his was hard to bear.

After she left, Gerald sat at his desk and stared out

the window for a long time, trying to face the fact that he was alone. There would be no young bright thing to enliven his life. She would go to that man she loved. He only hoped that Robert could live up to her love for him.

He realized, with a sense of alarm, that he would probably never marry now. He had not married in his youth, because it had been hard enough to carve out a life here in the New World without worrying about taking care of a family. Besides, there had been fewer young women here to choose from then.

He squeezed his eyes shut. It was too late now. There would be no one to comfort him in his old age, which was closer than he ever dared admit before. No one would have him, or at least no one he loved.

He opened his eyes and gazed out the window at the people passing down the street in and out of the sunlight. He realized, with a stab of pain in his chest, that he was more miserable than he had ever been before.

If he could not have Wynn Cox for a wife, he ought to look elsewhere. But the thought frightened him. He was too old to embark on that sort of thing. It had been easy to court Wynn. He was friendly with Sarah, and his friendship for Wynn had grown naturally out of his visits to the Kidd household. But where would he look now? Fear paralyzed him. It was too late for love. He would never be loved. He opened his mouth but did not utter the cry that gathered in his chest. He shuddered with the realization that he had never given voice to this kind of despair. The need for love now seemed so overwhelming it almost decimated him.

Wynn left Gerald's office without a backward glance, although she knew what giving her this money must have cost him. She knew what feelings struggled inside Gerald, but she had to steel herself against her sympathy for him. She had always been honest with him, never letting him think she could give him her heart. If Gerald

Portman had never loved another woman, it was not Wynn's fault. She did not mean to be cruel, but he must find his own way without her.

She took a deep breath as she hastened along Broad Street toward the gate in the old wall that led from Broadway out toward the burying ground. She had the money. She was almost free. Now it only remained for her to see her brother.

She had considered simply taking the clothes and leaving a note, but she couldn't bear to do that to James. She had to say good-bye.

Then she slowed her pace as a cart rattled past. What if he prevented her from going? Would he do that? What if he told their parents and they prevented her from leaving? But no, she was a grown woman now, and besides, James would never betray her. She knew his loyalty to her would come first, just as it always had. But still, no one would knowingly allow her to embark on such a dangerous venture. Even James might try to stop her.

She slowed her steps even more as she approached the city gate, but the curious glances she noticed from some of the women on their way to market brought her to her senses, and she hurried on. James would simply have to understand, she told herself.

Once past the salt meadow, she could see the clapboard house, which was now nearly complete. Once the shingled roof was on, her family could move from the small cramped brick house in town to this new one with its large kitchen and hall.

"Hey," she called as she neared the house. James and Clarence, the youth she had danced with at the assembly, were working on the walls.

"Did you bring us lunch?" James yelled to her from his perch on the second story.

"Why no, is it lunch time?" she asked, looking about her.

James leapt down and came toward her, the perspiration sticking to his white shirt, open at the neck to reveal the tan he was getting from being outside so much.

To think she might never see him again! A lump formed in her throat. Then a new fear assailed her. If she told him what she was going to do, her parents and Sarah would accuse James of complicity if he knew about it and didn't stop her. She hadn't thought of that. She had no right to make him take the blame for something she had decided to do.

She was staring at him oddly. He stopped chattering. "What's wrong, Sis?" he asked.

"Ah, nothing. That is, I just came to see if you wanted anything."

James frowned at her. She was certainly acting strangely. "But you didn't bring us anything to eat, did you?"

"Well no, I didn't." She swallowed. "James, I'm going to do some mending this afternoon. Do your breeches need repairing?" asked Wynn, her cheeks coloring. Why was she blushing? he wondered. Hadn't she sewn his linens and breeches since he was eleven years old?

"None of my breeches need mending just now. Why do you ask?"

"Oh" — she swung her skirt back and forth nervously — "what with all the work you've been doing, I thought you might have torn some of them."

He regarded her suspiciously, but let the subject drop.

"Come on, Clarence." He waved to him to come down the ladder. "We'll have to go to Mother's kitchen if we're to get anything to eat. My sister would let us starve."

James walked along beside her slowly, waiting for Clarence to catch up. Finally he spoke. "Why did you come from that direction? You usually come here from the other gate."

Knots formed in her stomach. "I was in town. I went to see Gerald," she said truthfully.

"I didn't know you were so fond of our neighbor," he said, his voice teasing.

She tossed her head. "I had to take him a letter from Sarah."

Because of that strange level of communication that flows between persons who have come from the same womb, James knew there was something on Wynn's mind. However, he also knew she wasn't ready to talk about it. She would tell him when she wanted to and not before. It was probably more bad news about Robert Lamley's voyage, he surmised. He was annoyed that she had allowed herself to get so wrapped up in that situation and he rued the day she had decided to marry a sailor, for James shared her belief that a sailor's life was hardly a stable one.

They walked along the lanes that led through the plots of land being set aside for new homes. The growth of the town northward was so rapid that Wynn could imagine the day when the entire tip of the island, from the battery up past Collect Pond, would be populated. Her heart contracted at the thought that she might never see this land again, but perhaps, she fervently hoped, things would yet come right for her and Robert.

They had now reached the town and walked along Wall Street, which was unpaved, skirting the refuse at the side of the road. Turning down King Street, they approached the Coxes' temporary home, a little house, squeezed tightly next to its neighbors. Although she wasn't prepared to face her parents, she knew she would have to make her peace with them before she left home — maybe forever.

She clutched James's hand suddenly as he led the way up the steps. "James," she said.

"Yes?" he asked, looking down into the face he knew better than his own.

Her heart pounded in her throat. She wanted so badly to confide in him. But she closed her eyes and shook her head.

"Nothing," she replied.

Chapter Eleven

Filled with guilt, Wynn followed James up the steps. Clarence had announced that he was meeting some friends at a nearby coffee house, so they had waved him on his way.

She walked through the large hall to the kitchen at the back of the house where a long trestle table with joined stools sat in the center of the room. Pots and cooking utensils hung from iron hoods in front of the fireplace, where Emily Cox, Wynn's mother, was preparing a dinner of salted shad. For a moment Wynn stood in the entranceway, quietly watching her mother, who was dressed in a homespun gown with a high, wide collar and calico apron. She saw that although time had left its marks on her mother's face, her cheeks were still pink, and her blue eyes as clear as Wynn's. The softspoken Emily Cox had the strength to bear difficult times. She wouldn't be a settler in the New World if that weren't so, for there was no room for weak persons on its soil.

Wynn took off her hood and tippet and donned an

apron to help. She kept her hands busy to avoid looking at her mother as Emily Cox brought pewter plates from the cupboard at the side of the room and placed them on the table.

"How is Mistress Sarah today?" she asked of her daughter.

"She keeps to herself, I fear," said Wynn, glad to deflect the conversation from herself, even if the topic were something very close to what was on her mind.

Emily set the pewter around the table. "A charming woman, Sarah. But it's a shame about her husband. I fear for her if the gossip is true. Oh, not that Captain Kidd wouldn't be welcome here among his old neighbors. Fine man, they say. But the lords justices accuse him of awful deeds, it seems."

Wynn didn't dare look up. "They do say that," was all she managed.

Just then James came into the room and reached for the porcelain bowl full of freshly picked apples. Wynn glanced up, and the magnetism of his gaze held hers for a moment. Then she hastily looked away.

What's the use? she thought. James would know she was hiding something. He always knew. She put her hand on his arm as she passed him on the way to the cupboard. If he knew she had a secret, she hoped to convey to him that he must keep it to himself for the present. In the instant that she looked at him she felt an understanding pass between them. She let go of his sleeve and moved on to help with the shad.

Now that she was resolved to leave Manhattan Island and seek out her love, she did not know how she could remain another minute in this room. Her heart pounded in her chest, and her flesh tingled. She would not be able to eat much, yet it was important that she appear normal. Taking her place beside James, she smoothed her apron and folded her hands, waiting for her father to come in.

She heard the scrape of her father's footsteps in the entryway, and then joined them.

"Ah, late I am again, I see," he said as she placed his flat-crowned boater hat on the carved chest. His long hair fell straight to his shoulders, and he was dressed in a loose coat open over a waistcoat and bib cravat. Cotton ribbed stockings rose above brown leather shoes with silver buckles.

"Hello, Father," James said as the older man pulled a straight-backed chair toward the table and settled himself onto the rush seat.

The family bowed their heads as Jonathan Cox led them in noontime grace. ". . . and we thank Thee for the many opportunities You have given us in this New World," her father said in an accent that revealed the Scots blood from his mother's side. "And watch over our cousin Sarah in her present hardship. Guide her husband, the captain, on his dangerous voyage."

And Robert too, thought Wynn.

"And may justice and mercy be with us all. Amen."

"Amen," they all chorused.

He raised his head, his benevolent eyes shining on his beloved family. Wynn pulled her head up slowly, the muscles in the back of her neck tense. At once James began to speak to his father about the building of the house.

She had almost forgotten to listen to their chatter, when she was suddenly addressed.

"Wynn, do you think you'll be able to help your mother with the flower garden as well as the vegetable garden?"

"Oh, oh yes, of course." It wouldn't do to appear absentminded, even though they already considered her a dreamer, what with her books and other pastimes considered unsuitable for women. She tried, however, not to appear any more distracted than usual.

"We'll be able to move in by September. Of course,

you'll have to walk farther to Sarah's, won't you, dear?" asked her mother.

"Yes, that is so," she said, forcing out the words. Somehow she got through the meal, afterward helping to clear away the dishes, and any uneaten food. She put any food that would keep back in the pantry, and threw the rest into the street for the hogs that roamed about eating scraps.

The two men left — James to work on the house, and her father to make his rounds of Sarah's property, and Wynn was finally alone with her mother.

"Mother," she said as the older woman sat down to peel some potatoes at the same table where they had just taken their meal.

"Yes, dear?"

"I believe I'll do some mending this afternoon. Where are the linens that need sewing?"

"In my sewing basket upstairs. You may work here with me if you like."

"Yes, Mother."

She hurried up the narrow stairway to the bedrooms on the second floor. In her parents' room she located the basket sitting on the trunk that still held many of the clothes they'd brought over from England. Sitting on the feather bed, she lifted them out. There were several linen shirts, and she picked two of James's that would serve her purpose. Then she found some coarse stockings and rolled them in the shirt. She had to hurry now. Her mother would wonder what was taking her so long.

She tiptoed to her bedroom and stuffed the clothing under her feather bed. Then she whisked into James's room next door and lifted open his trunk, biting her lip as she tried to keep the hinges from creaking. She rummaged through his clothes, finally finding some kersey breeches that would fit her after a few adjustments had been made. Then she went once more to her parents' room, and, placing the breeches under the linens in the basket, took it up and went downstairs.

In the kitchen, her mother still sat peeling potatoes. Wynn took a seat beside her so that she wouldn't have to face her directly, and pulled out some linen to work on. She threaded a needle and applied herself to the task of mending shirts, darning stockings and repairing whatever she could find. Then, concealing them below the table in her lap, she took the breeches from the bottom of the basket and began to sew tucks into the waist. She and James had often compared their measurements as they were growing up, and though she knew her hips were more rounded and would fill out James's breeches, her waist was narrower, and the breeches would not stay up without some tucks and a belt.

They passed the afternoon pleasantly, occasionally making light conversation. Most of the time, however, they were silent, the ticking of the tall clock in the hall the only intrusion on their thoughts.

As the sun sank lower in the sky, Wynn's mother turned to the chore of preparing a cold supper for the evening meal, a big meal having been served in the middle of the day. The languorous afternoon she had spent had put Wynn into a more relaxed mood, and when James came in she smiled at his banter during supper. Afterward James and Jonathan retired to the front stoop where Jonathan lit a pipe, Wynn and her mother joining them after they had cleared away the dishes.

Wynn sat on the top step, her knees against her father's back, gazing out over the placid street at the pink and orange sunset over the Hudson River. She felt so thankful for the peace and beauty of the scene that she wondered, for a moment, if she were a fool to consider leaving. She felt enormous gratitude for the life provided for both her and her family in the New World. But with a stab of pain, she realized that she could never be totally fulfilled in her new life without Robert. With a sense of grief she realized she was no longer the young girl who could depend on her family to provide her with everything she needed. She had become a grown woman, and she must remain firm in her resolve to leave, for unless she did, she was certain she would never see Robert again.

James lounged next to her on the top step, observing her from under the blond hair that fell across his brow. He leaned comfortably on one elbow, his legs sprawled on the steps below him. He stared at his sister intently, and when she returned his look with a half smile, he raised an eyebrow questioningly, and then grinned widely.

In that moment, Wynn knew he had read her thoughts, and as if to prove it, he spoke.

"Father," he said, his eyes still on his sister's face. "I believe when the house is finished, I would like to go to sea."

Wynn's eyes widened and she held her breath.

"What's that, James?" asked Jonathan with a chuckle, waving his pipe in an arc. "Wasn't our voyage from England enough for you?"

Wynn knew he referred to the cramped quarters and tossing and pitching of the ship that had brought them from England.

"As a passenger, yes," said James, determined to pursue the idea. "But for a sailor, ah, what a life that could be. Imagine, Father, I'd see not only this beautiful land, up and down the coast from Boston to St. Augustine, but I'd sail to the Far East as well."

Wanting to shake him, Wynn pressed her lips together. She knew he was challenging her and if she had any doubts about what she was going to do, he would now force her to confront them.

But they had played this game before, and she was not about to be weakened in her resolve. She lifted her chin. "I agree, Father. James should learn all about ships. Why, some of the wealthiest merchants are sailing captains. Take our Captain Kidd and Robert Lamley, before ill luck befell them," she said, meeting James's gaze straight on.

Jonathan nodded. "James is a grown man now. I would not oppose it. It's time you started on a trade, son. The house is nearly finished. If you're serious about going to sea, perhaps next month I'll acquaint myself with some merchants that put into port here. I caution you though," he said. "It's a hard life. You think you labor over that house, but you wait 'til you're standing aloft on a footrope furling a sail, and that at a good clip at sea, not while standing in port."

James laughed. "I'm strong enough, and I'm not afraid of work. I'll be a good sailor, you'll see."

Jonathan drew his bushy eyebrows together. "I'd hoped to speak to Captain Kidd about you when he returned from his voyage. Now that doesn't look likely. "No," he continued. "I'll have to find another captain." Again James looked at Wynn with a mischievous glimmer in his eye.

She frowned. Surely James wasn't plotting something diabolical on his own. She had known him to set traps for her and tease her into revealing herself, but surely if he knew she was planning something important, he wouldn't dare slip her up.

She tossed her head and looked at the darkening sky. Neighbors on other stoops were going in, and so the Coxes too rose. Her mother went to the hearth and stirred the coals a little, for she and Jonathan would sit up for a while, she with her needlework and he with his pipe and a book. As Wynn bade them good night, her heart contracted and a lump arose in her throat. But the *Joanna* sailed tomorrow. It was tonight or never.

"Good night, Mother," she said, hoping her mother did not hear the catch in her voice. She bent to kiss her mother's cheek. Was it her imagination, or was her mother's cheek a little cold?

Then she leaned down to her father. "Good night, Papa," she said, brushing his mustache with her lips.

He patted her hand. "Sleep well, little one."

She turned to leave, the muscles in her face frozen. She walked, then when she was up the stairs, ran the few steps to her bedroom and fell onto her bed, hiccoughing sobs. But resolve hardened her, and finally she sat up and wiped away the tears. Gazing around the tiny room, she thought again of James's odd behavior and wondered what he was up to. But there was no time to dwell on that. He could not stop her now that her mind was made up and her things ready.

She undressed, folded her gown and laid it in her trunk. Then she pulled on James's shirt and breeches, tying the breeches with a cord at the waist. The tucks had worked wonderfully, for the breeches fit her very well. She smiled at herself in the small mirror next to her highboy. Then she opened her trunk again, extracting a pair of sturdy leather shoes that laced up the ankles. She also had a cap that had belonged to either her brother or father at one time but had found its way into her trunk. She packed everything she planned to take in a small portmanteau. Then she scrawled a note to her parents, asking for their forgiveness and love, blew out the candle, and lay down on her bed.

Excitement throbbed in her veins. Gone were any feelings of regret, for Robert awaited her, and she was full of hope. She closed her eyes, but only to sleep for a short time. When it was pitch black outside, she would arise and steal out. In the darkness she heard the thumps and murmurs of the rest of the family as they went to bed. Lights passed her door, then candles were blown out, and she slept.

A few hours later, Wynn stirred, her eyes flying open at the sound of a door creaking.

She let several minutes pass. Then, quietly, she pulled the covers aside and her bare feet touched the hardwood floor. Again, she strained her ears for any sound that would tell her whether someone was awake. But none came. She pulled on the woolen stockings quietly, left the note on her highboy, and then, picking up the portmanteau and placing the cap on her head, she tiptoed out.

Her heart was racing so hard it was difficult to believe that no one else could hear the deafening sound it made in her temples. At the head of the stairs, she placed a hand on the balustrade. Carefully she lowered herself to the first step, avoiding the boards she knew creaked. By the time she reached the bottom, she could almost breathe. Now for the front door. If only the dogs wouldn't wake up and bark.

She trod softly across the entryway, portmanteau in hand. Then she placed her fingers on the bolt, her hands as cold as the metal. Struggling, she pulled the bolt aside. Then she opened the door just wide enough to slip through. Once outside, she realized there was no way to bolt it from that side.

"You'll just have to leave it open," came a whisper behind her.

She gasped, turned, and faced James. He covered her mouth with his hand to stifle her involuntary cry.

"Shhh," he said. "I'm going with you."

She struggled to speak, but he kept his hand firmly over her mouth, gripping her arm with his other hand.

"Shut up," he whispered. His voice sounded almost angry, but then he gave her a sardonic grin. "I climbed out the window, myself."

She sighed, and seeing that she was once again in control of herself, he took his hand away from her mouth. Then he jerked his head toward the street, indicating that if they were going to talk, it had best be done elsewhere than at the door of their parents' house.

She followed him down the steps, and he led her to the corner, where the street lantern had gone out, and it was relatively dark.

"There's no time to explain," he said with a twinkle in his eye. "I told you I was going to sea."

"But I didn't know you meant now."

"Why not? You're going."

"James, you're mad."

"I'm not. You heard Father. He approves. He'll approve even more when he learns I've gone to protect you."

"You told them?"

"Yes. In a note. I didn't want them to worry."

"James," she nearly choked. Then she wanted to laugh. She had always thought her brother clever. But this time he had outdone himself. "Oh James. I wanted to tell you, but I thought you'd worry about me."

"I know. That's how I figured it out. I knew I couldn't stop you. You're too crazy in love with that friend of Captain Kidd. So I figured the next best thing was to go along, make sure nothing happened to you. I'm just going to become a sailor a little sooner than I'd thought."

"But what about the house?"

"Father and the hired men can finish it. And I'm sure Sarah Kidd will do anything she can to help Mother. So you see, it's all taken care of."

"Oh, James." Her eyes glistened. A great wave of joy passed through her as she realized she wasn't going to embark on the perilous journey alone, and she threw her arms around his neck.

He allowed her a brief hug and then removed her arms from his neck. "Come on, we have to go aboard."

"Oh." Her heart fell. Now came the difficult part.

"How will we sneak on board?"

"Oh, don't worry," he laughed softly. "You don't have to stow away. You're my brother. I've already signed us on as apprentices. I saw the captain and convinced him of our competence." James flexed a muscle in his arm. "I showed him these."

She couldn't help smiling as she thought of her brother disarming the skeptical Captain Shaw.

"Come on. Before we get to the docks I have to cut your hair."

"What?"

"Well, you can't hide it under that cap all the time, not when you're working. Don't worry, we won't cut it all off, just the curls. It just has to be the same length as mine. Then you'll look more like my brother."

They hurried down the street and turned a corner into a vacant lot. Standing in the shadow of an old shed, James pulled a pair of shears from his pack. "Now stand still," he ordered her.

Wynn shut her eyes. She hated to sacrifice the curls, and she shivered momentarily as she wondered if she would appear ugly to Robert. But she clenched her jaw. After all, the disguise would help her reach him. When James was finished, he handed her a serge cloak he had carried on his arm.

"Here, you'll need this to keep the sea spray off you." Then he grinned as he placed the cap back on her head, shoving it to a cocky angle. "Now let's go," he said, "before the night watchman comes this way."

At the docks men moved about in the darkness, for when a ship was leaving, the preparations had to done before daylight. As they approached the lantern light of the wharf, Wynn's nerve momentarily deserted her, but James walked resolutely ahead, and she hurried to catch up.

The *Joanna*'s masts swayed above them, the glow

from the lanterns casting an eerie light on the officers who paced the deck. But James did not hesitate. He marched to the gangplank.

"Who goes there?" called a sailor from aboard the ship.

"James Cox and his brother, John," said James. "Request permission to board."

"Come ahead," the man said.

Wynn swallowed hard as James led her up the gangplank, and she felt it sway under her feet. One step sideways and she knew she would fall into the icy water.

When they reached the top, the sailor held a lantern over his manifest. "Here ye be. James and John Cox, apprentices. You spoke to Master Shaw."

Wynn gripped her bag tighter as she contemplated confronting Captain Shaw, the man she had asked for passage. Fear struck her heart as she imagined what he might do if he recognized her.

"This way," said the sailor who had allowed them to board, and she was almost left standing on the gangplank as her brother moved off with the other man.

She caught up and the sailor led them below decks. As they passed the captain's cabin, she caught a glimpse inside. Polished wood and brass made an elegant roomy cabin for Master Shaw. But the captain was not in his quarters.

Below, on another deck, the sailor showed them where to stow their gear. "You can sling your hammocks here," he said.

She swallowed again. The thought of sleeping with all these men frightened her. She glanced at James, who gave her a reassuring grin.

"I'm Mr. Larson," the sailor said. "The paper says this is your first voyage, so you'll need to learn the ropes."

"That's right," said James. "What should we do first?"

"Can ye scrub?"

"Aye," said James.

"Then put on these and come with me. You'll swab the deck."

They dressed in the heavy woolen trousers provided them, then went on deck. By now there was enough dawn light to see by. Wynn stayed near James, scrubbing the deck until her fingers, knees and back ached. By the time the sun was high overhead, she didn't think she could move another inch.

"I'm about done in," said James, standing behind her and wiping his brow. She climbed to her feet and followed his gaze out over the town.

The sun glinted off tile roofs, and seagulls squealed and soared around them. The only time she had gazed on the town thus was when she'd arrived. How strange! It had only been a year ago that the unknown world awaited her. How could she have foreseen that she would be leaving again to face a much greater unknown so soon. She pressed her lips together, afraid to say anything that would betray her emotion.

She and James went to fetch clean water from the barrels that had been rolled up the gangplank. Shouts around them told them they were about to cast off.

"Let her fall," the captain shouted, his order repeated by the bosun, and Wynn watched breathlessly as the sails unfurled.

Men flew aloft and the ship picked up speed. Wynn felt a catch in her throat as the small town at the tip of Manhattan Island shrank before her gaze. Soon they passed the other islands in the harbor, and she grabbed her bucket and tried to stay out of the way of the bustling sailors.

She knew she would have to learn all the sailors' cries, and how to handle the lines. She would have to learn to be useful and develop the strength of a real sailor, for she didn't dare risk letting Captain Shaw know she had sneaked aboard his ship after all. She shuddered as she remembered his leering words, "You wouldn't even be safe from me."

As the *Joanna* glided through the narrows and out to sea, Mr. Larson found James and John again and delivered some elementary instructions in sailing. Wynn watched as James set about winning the man's confidence. A ruddy-complected fellow, he was an inch or two shorter than her brother, but with slightly broader shoulders, a man strong enough to protect them if they should need his help, Wynn realized.

They ate with the men in the mess, and Wynn remained silent, speaking in a low gruff voice only when spoken to. She played dumb, even to accepting the cutting remarks James threw in her direction. He wanted the others to know he was the smarter of the two, the one to be dealt with, but that he protected his younger, more ignorant brother.

Her ears colored at the obscene jokes the sailors told, but she kept her cap low over her eyes so that she would not betray her discomfort.

By the end of the first day, she was tired and sore, and when she collapsed in her hammock, she was thankful just to close her eyes. From the semidarkness, lighted only by faint moonlight coming through the portholes, came the melancholy tune of a harmonica.

"G'night, John," came the mirthful voice beside her. She would have punched him in the stomach, but she didn't have the strength.

Chapter Twelve

As the days passed, Wynn grew even more thankful that James was aboard, for she was sure she would not have survived otherwise. He protected her unobtrusively, standing nearby when she had to undress, and taking on half of her work so that she could gradually strengthen her body. She picked up the sailors' jargon quickly, and James drilled her on it when they took their meals. Mr. Larson showed her knots and splices, but she preferred to stay on deck while James climbed in the rigging. She knew she didn't have the strength to perch on the yard and haul up the sail by the yard ropes and bunting.

In spite of her best efforts to become a fit sailor, she would often have to grit her teeth to fight off the pain of blisters and aching limbs. Desperation would have driven her to give up and go to the captain, risking her fate. But James's presence helped her hang onto her resolve for as long as possible. Yet she knew that before they reached the Indian Ocean, she would have to find another solution. If she had stowed away, other dangers might have beset her, but she wouldn't have been so agonizingly tired from performing a man's work.

One day, her lids drooping, she had nearly dozed off when a passing sailor bumped into her. "Watch yerself, mate," said the man as he carried a large keg across the deck.

She looked up into the hot sun and raised a hand to her burnt face. Though she kept as much of herself covered as she could, her face and neck had taken a beating from the sun's rays and her peeling skin was tender to the touch. And they were still in the cooler northern hemisphere. She couldn't imagine how she would endure the heat when they finally reached the tropics.

She began to consider the alternatives. They were now far out at sea and would not put into port again until they reached the West Indies. If she revealed herself to the captain, perhaps she could convince him to either take her money for passage or let her do some woman's work. If so, her hands, blistered and red from hauling lines, would have time to heal. James was fast learning to be an able seaman and reveled in it. For him it was a great joke that his brother John was a woman. But she wondered how he would take the taunts of the other seamen if she revealed herself to the captain, for surely he would not keep it a secret.

Wearily she stood and returned to her station. Just then her foot slipped on the slick deck and she tripped. "Oh!" she cried as she lost her balance and her head bounced off the metal fastenings of a nearby keg. Her hip hit the deck, and tears sprang to her eyes. A rough arm pulled her to her feet, but the knock on the head had made her dizzy. Her eyes continued to water, and her vision blurred.

"You all right, mate?" It was Mr. Larson. Suddenly her lip trembled. She wanted to lean on a strong shoulder just for once. She felt wretched in her disguise.

Grief and frustration flooded through her and she wanted to cry. She rubbed her eyes with her hands, but her vision refused to clear. Dizziness assailed her, and with a little cry, she reached out toward Mr. Larson. Voices swam around her and images wavered in and out. Then everything went dark.

As if from a long distance, she heard her brother's voice. "Stand back, mates," he said, kneeling beside her. Another man's hand was fumbling with her collar, and James knocked it away, but not before her shirt front was ripped open to her breast.

"Blimy," the man said. "It's a woman."

James covered her, and she fought the darkness threatening to descend on her again.

"Damn," said another man. "We only thought to help him breathe."

James muttered a curse, then lifted her up and she fell against him, her mind swimming in and out of pools of consciousness.

"It's the sun," another sailor said. "Better get her below."

As James carried her below, she finally gave way to the swoon that had begun, once again, to envelop her.

She awoke to find herself lying in a cozy bed with feather comforters. Her forehead felt damp, and she pushed back the covers to discover that someone had dressed her in a clean shirt, and she wore no breeches. A hand drew a damp cloth across her brow. As her mind fought to clear, she became aware of voices and the gentle movements of the ship.

"Sis, you all right?" James hovered above her, laying a hand on her head.

She mumbled a reply.

"You had quite a nasty knock on the head," he said, smiling down at her.

"Where am I?" She blinked, looking upward at the dark mahogany surroundings. She sensed another presence in the room. Her mind held onto the notion that the shirt she wore wasn't hers, and, more than the injury, she began to fear the consequences of her fainting spell. But at the same time she wanted to plunge deeper among the soft comforters on the wide bed and rest her strained muscles and aching head. Even in the fog that shrouded her brain, she realized the captain must know she was a woman.

"You're in the great cabin," said James, his mouth quirking into a grin. "When you fell, some of the well-meaning deckhands tried to strip away your shirt so you could get some air, and they, er ah . . ." his face colored, "They discovered you were a female."

"Oh," was all she could reply.

"Anyway, take it easy. The ship's doctor looked at you and said you had nothing worse than bruises. He put a salve on your hands too, for the rope burns, and bandaged them."

"What about the captain?"

"Oh, he's all right. A lot of bluster at first. Said he'd set us both ashore at the first port we come to, but I doubt he'll do it. I've been using my persuasive powers on him, and you can always do a little charming yourself." He winked at her.

Wynn tried to sit up. Just then Captain Shaw walked into the cabin and stood behind James, his feet apart and his face glaring down at her. His severe look made Wynn want to fall back into the pillows, but she made an effort to remain sitting.

He cleared his throat and addressed James. "If your sister" — he twisted the word "sister" sarcastically — "is up to it, I'd like a few words with her alone."

James locked gazes with Wynn as if to reassure her, then turned to the captain. "It's all right, sir. She's coming round. Please don't be too hard on her, sir. If there's any punishment to be dealt, you can punish me.

My sister is just a foolish girl. And she'll pay for her passage."

Wynn wondered how James knew she had passage money, but she didn't question him in the captain's presence.

As Captain Shaw approached Wynn, James saluted and moved back several feet, but made no move to leave the cabin.

"Now," the captain began. "Just what did you hope to accomplish by sneaking on board my ship?"

"I didn't sneak on. I signed on," she said with as much spunk as she could muster. She knew that she would have to match wits with him if she were to be allowed the privileges she wanted on board this ship. "And I believe you know where I am going, Captain," she said. "I asked you for passage."

"Yes, I remember you. Odd that I didn't spot you among the crew. But then again there are a hundred men on board. I don't know all their names, only their faces." He looked her over, his eyes brazenly wandering over her body. Although the shirt covered her to her collarbone, only opening to reveal her sunburned throat, she pulled the coverlet further up around her.

"So, you are still running to Madagascar on some pretended errand of love. I am surprised at your brother. I would have bound and gagged a sister of mine who wanted to go to sea for any reason. This is no place for a woman."

"James let me come because he knew he couldn't stop me." She raised her chin in a gesture of defiance. "He only came along to protect me." She emphasized her last words, making sure the captain would get her meaning.

The captain still glowered at her. "I should hang you overboard by your heels, and your brother too, for that matter."

"You wouldn't do that, would you Captain?" she said, reaching toward his arm. He looked down at her bandaged hand, then lifted it, staring at her fingers. When he looked back into her eyes, she could see the lust in his face, overpowering the anger.

She shrank inwardly, but held his gaze with her own determined one.

"There is one way you could pay for your passage," he growled in his gravelly voice. "I told you of it when you stood on the quay that day. You know what I speak of." And his eyes seemed to pierce the covers she held to her breast with one hand.

"Captain," James interrupted, taking a step forward, "surely, you would not sully my sister's honor."

The captain's eyes never left her face, though his voice betrayed his irritation at James's presence. "She has sullied her own honor by sneaking aboard this vessel."

"She is not a criminal. As she said herself, she signed on for duty."

"Duties she cannot carry out," answered Captain Shaw sharply. "She is not fit to climb ropes. I'm surprised she was able to do anything at all. What does a woman know about running a ship?"

Wynn grimaced. "I have learned much," she said.

"Damn it," Captain Shaw grunted, releasing her hand, "I will not tarnish your honor, whatever it's worth, not unless you ask for it." The lustful look receded slightly as he cupped her chin in his hand. "But I can see in your eyes that you do not ask for it, at least not from me."

Wynn looked down, her strength beginning to ebb. "No," she said. Then she lay back and shut her eyes. The long days of hot sun and the raw wounds on her hands made her want nothing more than to sleep. Her body desperately needed healing.

"I'll do anything else you say, Captain, and I'll pay for my passage in money," she said and drifted off to sleep.

When she awoke, she was alone. Through the cabin portholes she could see that the sky was dark, and a lantern swung above the captain's table, which was bolted to the floor. A gnawing in her stomach reminded her she hadn't eaten since early the morning before her fall, and she wasn't sure how many days might have intervened since then. Now she wanted food. She sat up and placed her feet on the cabin deck.

Just then the ship rolled with a wave and Wynn lost her balance. The ship rolled again and outside she heard the howl of a fierce wind. Above, voices were giving orders to stand by. A storm was approaching.

She righted herself and stood, holding onto the back of the captain's chair. Where were her clothes? She saw them lying in a heap on the floor and stumbled toward them. Then, with another roll of the ship, she grabbed the clothing and fell back toward the bed. She struggled into the breeches and stockings, tucking in the shirt she had slept in. Just as she found her shoes, the cabin door swung open, and Wynn could hear the men running about as they prepared to ride out the storm.

"Lee fore brace!" the mate shouted. She had learned this meant the wind was heading. She trembled, a new excitement gripping her. This was what she had heard Robert talk of so often — man challenging an angry sea. Now every seaman's ability would be tested. They would pit their skills along with the strength of the sturdy ship against the storm to see who would win.

No longer caring who saw her, for she was no longer dissembling, she crept up the ladder to the upper deck. Holding onto the hatchway, she watched as a great wave approached. She could not even guess its height, except that it looked to her to be as tall as the tallest mast. The ship met the wave head on, and when the wave broke, the *Joanna* slid down the back of it. Wynn dared not move as she saw the men pull lines. The masts strained, and she heard a deafening crack and watched with horror as the topgallant tipped toward the deck.

Just then the first mate caught sight of her and yelled something to the captain, who stood on the quarterdeck. She could not hear his shouts above the building storm, but saw a sailor approach her, as the rain pelted down in her face.

He cupped his hands and yelled, "Get below. Captain's orders!"

Wynn nodded and plunged toward the ladder. She would have fallen into the dark interior of the ship as it pitched her forward, but strong arms suddenly caught her.

"Take hold!" the sailor shouted, and she grabbed for the top rung, her feet catching on the rungs below. Holding on tightly, she looked up at the sailor who shouted for her to get below and strap herself in.

She scrambled downward and fought her way along the swaying passage to the cabin, swinging the door shut and hurling herself toward the bed, which was built solidly into the wall. There she strapped herself in and clung to the side of the bed as the storm raged.

Fear clutched at her. This was no adventure, no game to be won; this was life and death and if a man survived it seemed as much a matter of luck as skill. Robert must have been mad to have been so obsessed with this monster sea. Then she wondered with a sick heart if the sea would take her life just as it had taken the life of the woman he had loved all those years ago.

For hours she held on as the ship creaked and pitched in the storm. When a particularly thunderous crash threatened to throw her clear of the bed, despite the straps, she heard the men's cries become even more anguished. She chafed to find James, but she knew she'd be no good on deck. She might even cause someone more danger by being in the way. She would have to hang on in the cabin until she heard something from the captain.

She lost all sense of time as the thunder and crash of waves whirled the tiny ship in a watery inferno throughout the night. Her knuckles white from holding on so tightly, Wynn finally noticed that the ship was no longer throwing her from side to side in the bunk. Instead, the ship was gently riding up and down, and waves no longer crashed against the hull. A gray sky lit the stern portholes, and Wynn knew it was day.

The door of the cabin opened, and the captain entered. His uniform was drenched, and he flung himself in his chair, moaning wearily. Wynn struggled to her feet. Obviously she ought to get out of the man's cabin now. He would need his bed.

"Excuse me, sir," said Wynn.

He lifted his head, looking at her with bloodshot eyes. "Oh, you," was all he said.

"Is there something I can do?"

He grunted. "You can stay here for now."

"My brother?"

"Hmmm? Oh, him. He's all right." The captain put his head wearily in his hands. Wynn felt sorry for the man. His ship had been nearly broken in half, and he had great burdens to carry. She realized that she and James had only made things worse for him and she was thankful he had not thrown them overboard.

"Captain," she said. "My brother James, where is he?"

The man looked at her wearily. "On deck where he should be. We've a mast to repair."

Wynn found that she could walk steadily, and she headed for the door and the ladder to go up. On deck she saw that the topgallant had broken, and the men were untangling lines and mending sails. But the ship had held against the demon storm, and their course was now clear. A fresh breeze blew across Wynn's brow, and she took a gulp of air.

"Lay in," came the order for men aloft to move in toward the mast.

Then she saw James on the fo'c'sle deck and when he looked her way, she waved. He waved back, grinning, and she could tell that he was actually enjoying what he was doing. His muscles strained as he leaned on a line, and she could see that he would not have time to talk to her. But she knew he would be relieved to find she was all right. She walked a little on deck, stretching her cramped muscles.

The sun rose over a blue sea, and the aftermath of the storm was surprisingly peaceful, as if heaven had spent itself. The battle was over, and Wynn could see that the men had enjoyed winning it.

Just then Mr. Larson found her. She smiled at him in embarrassment, then looked down. He did not seem disgruntled and she thought she saw a smile tug at his lips, although he did his best to maintain a sober expression.

"You fared all right during the storm then?" asked Mr. Larson.

"Yes, and you?"

"Aye. She blow'd up fast, she did. And we shipped water, but we didn't founder."

"I admire your skill," she said. "I'm afraid I wouldn't have known what to do."

"The captain got her before the wind. It was nip and tuck there for a while, the lee pump bein' all the while under water, but we managed."

Wynn nodded, absorbing what he said. Her exposure to sailors' jargon while she was posing as a boy stood her in good stead now. She walked to the railing and leaned out, her hair flying behind her as the *Joanna* slipped along in the sea. She sighed, feeling compassion and admiration for the men who had kept the ship under sail all through the storm. And now they were on course again. She was headed for Robert. A smile broke over her face as the sky lightened. She was glad to be rid of her disguise, and a new sense of freedom pervaded her.

As the weeks passed, Wynn was kept busy working in the galley, peeling potatoes and stirring huge cauldrons of soups and stews for the mess.

She now slept in the first mate's cabin. It was small compared to the great cabin but at least she had privacy. The mate was disgruntled about giving up his quarters but didn't hold a grudge. She was subject to catcalls from the rest of the crew, but the men kept their distance since both her brother and the captain kept a protective eye on her.

The captain granted leave wherever they put into port for wood, water and provisions. Then Wynn got a chance to walk on land again, and, safely escorted by her brother, watched as the dark-skinned natives in the island ports traded their trinkets with the seamen and dark-eyed women flaunted themselves in front of the handsome sailors. Interesting though these stops were, as they neared the equator, Wynn was eager to be on her way, for she was well aware of the miles that still lay between herself and Robert.

At night the silvery moon threw its light over the dark water as the ship glided on with billowing sails. She learned something of the night skies, favoring the cooling breezes of the night after they rounded the Cape of Good Hope and set a north-northwesterly course into the eastern seas.

Here the South Atlantic rollers collided violently with

the Agulhas Current, and the ship rode waves building at times to heights of seventy feet, the smoke off the bow attesting to undersea volcanos. At sunset the ship knifed through a fiery red ocean with an orange ceiling of clouds overhead. The black shapes of nearby islands were outlined against the sky, and Wynn stood in awe of the mysterious waters before her.

Now flotsam and jetsam bumped the sides of the ship as they approached Madagascar. In the day, fleecy clouds hovered over an emerald sea that turned sapphire-blue at evening, and gulls dove past the ship's billowing sails, hunting for fish to eat. Excitement built as the ship prepared to drop anchor, and Captain Shaw stood on the quarterdeck, his glass to his eye. It was here they hoped to meet up with Captain Kidd and the *Adventure Galley*. It was here, too, that Wynn prayed that she would be reunited with her beloved.

The evening before they would put into port was quiet, as Wynn cleaned the galley after the last meal of the day while the surly cook played cards with a group of boisterous men in the mess.

James wandered in and heaved himself onto a keg of flour. "Hi, Sis," he said.

She whirled around. "James," she said, wiping the grease off her forehead. He pulled out his pocketknife to do some carving.

"What are you making?" she asked.

He winked. "I don't know. Some trinket to trade to the natives."

"In exchange for what?"

He smiled slyly and Wynn flushed, remembering James's exploits on the night of the dance assembly at home.

Noticing her embarrassment, James guffawed. "Oh, don't worry, Sis. I can take care of myself." Then he became more serious. "Come to think of it, you'd better stick to me if you leave the ship. It'd be dangerous for you to go anywhere here alone."

She sighed. "I suppose you're right. Being a woman is sometimes such a nuisance."

"But," James kidded her, "where would we poor men be without women?"

She blushed, thinking of her journey's purpose. For she could not deny her need for a man, a special man, who waited for her, she hoped, here in Madagascar. Her heart quickened at the thought.

But she had no time to ruminate, for shouts of excitement on deck told them they were coming up to St. Mary's Island, set like a jewel off the eastern coast of Madagascar. Wynn finished her tasks, then followed her brother topside. Dusk had descended on the bluish ridge of distant land, and the dark water was smooth and clear, stretching to the mainland. At the south end of St. Mary's, a circular lagoon was protected by narrows, doubly fortified by the adjacent coastline of the mainland. The port glimmered ahead now as lanterns burned against the emerald vegetation that rose luxuriously up steep hills, and the red-tiled roofs and white minarets caught the last rays of a dying sun. Long sloping beaches invited respite for weary sailors.

Other vessels sailed to and from the port, which was much smaller than New York. Still, pinnaces and sloops, with their rigging worn and weathered, were anchored beside Moorish ships displacing one to two hundred tons. Smaller ships found shelter in bays and inlets that appeared to snake inland.

Wynn gazed at the stark rigging and rounded hulls they approached. With a chill she realized that one of the larger ships bore a name that sounded familiar. She leaned forward and squinted to get a better view in the fading light. The bow was turned away from her as the ship rode at anchor, but she was almost sure she read the name correctly.

With a cry, she looked around for the captain. What would he do now? For she was sure she had spied the *Quedah Merchant*, the prize Drago Calicut had spoken of.

Chapter Thirteen

Wynn scrubbed herself in fresh water and put on a clean ruffled shirt she had bought in Capetown. Then she donned a clean pair of breeches and shoes with bright buckles that Mr. Larson had given her. All her thoughts were concentrated on Robert, and her hands shook as she dressed herself in anticipation of actually seeing him here.

She combed her hair and tied it at the back of her neck with a velvet ribbon, for although it had grown out, it still lacked its curls. Then she set a cap low on her head. She and James agreed that she would be safer in this pirate haven if she maintained her male disguise. She laughed to herself as she got dressed for her night on the town, never having dreamed before this voyage that she would ever appear thus.

James, who had gone ahead, returned with news of the *Quedah Merchant*. It was indeed moored here, laden with treasure, it was rumored, and the *Adventure Galley* was storm-damaged and could sail no further. So much he had learned from other sailors on the quay. Now he was about to accompany Captain Shaw and would come back for Wynn as soon as he felt it was safe for her to come ashore.

Putting the *Joanna* under guard, Captain Shaw then went ashore to seek out Kidd and Lamley. Wynn had to restrain herself from running after him and creating a scene, for she knew that would only endanger their position. She wanted to find Robert before Captain Shaw got to him with his arrest papers, but she waited and readied herself until James returned for her.

James and Robert had never met, and she wondered briefly what they would think of one another. Not that it mattered. For all her loyalty to her brother, she loved Robert more. Now that she had come this far, nothing would stop her from being with him.

Then a stab of doubt assailed her. What if he were angry that she had come? His letters had been full of love and regret, but those were written some months ago. What if his mind had changed?

"Oh, Robert, please don't turn from me now," she whispered.

"Are you ready, Sis?" James knocked and entered her small cabin, surveying his sister. "Well, I've escorted you out on an evening before, but never dressed like this," he teased.

She ignored his taunt and asked, "What news?"

"I followed Captain Shaw as far as I could. He's gone aboard the *Adventure Galley*."

She gasped. "Then he might arrest them now." A knot formed in her stomach.

James shook his head. "Hard to tell if Robert's with him. They say Kidd has locked himself in his cabin."

As they climbed on deck, a fresh breeze cooled their faces and from the shore they could hear the beat of drums, music and voices floating over the water as the pirates fraternized with the natives. Her earlier nervousness about walking the streets of such a notorious port had disappeared because of her larger concern for Robert and William.

"This could be our ruin," she whispered to James. "It all depends on William's reception of Captain Shaw." And who was to say if he had allies among the pirates who frequented this port? The *Joanna* could easily be overrun and all of them taken prisoner. But Captain Shaw did not seem worried about that, as he had sailed confidently into the harbor to bring the *Adventure Galley* officers home. Wynn glanced warily at the sailors on watch. Pistols and knives gleamed in the moonlight and she shivered at the thought of the violence that could result if all did not go well.

James helped her climb overboard into the shallop that would take them ashore. "I only pray they are not arrested before we reach them," he said.

She trembled as they glided to shore and climbed out onto a wooden quay. They made their way among crates and boxes toward the village. Once they set foot on the fertile red soil of the island, the lights and noise from the village grew louder. Dark-skinned natives offered dried fruit, used shoes, curative herbs and magic amulets, anxious to help the sailors spend their money. A woman in a colorful print material wrapped tightly around her shiny skin swayed by a group of sailors who were having a smoke under a lantern. One of the men put an arm around her and walked away with her into the darkness.

Other women with laughing black eyes and flowers behind their ears threw seductive glances at the men. A wave of jealousy assailed Wynn. Had Robert been seduced by one of these exotic native women? Surely his virility would have forced him to seek an outlet for his sexual appetites by now. The thought sickened her, but she followed James resolutely into the town.

"Watch out for pickpockets," James said in a low

voice, glancing at the beggars and other dark figures with gleaming eyes that watched from corners of the shacks they passed. In the bazaar men gathered in thatched huts to drink or stood in groups, bargaining with vendors for tobacco. Pieces of eight passed from pale hands to dark ones, and the street was alive with activity. The cries of hucksters vied with the squawks of the many birds fluttering in their cages as they complained to passers-by.

Wynn's heart beat faster, and her eyes darted to every tall man with black hair. But each time the head turned and the face revealed a countenance other than Robert's.

Nudging her, James pointed to a large man with bushy whiskers and mustache who was dressed in a silver brocade coat with a silver-hilted sword at his waist. Although gentlemanly white ruffles showed at his neck and wrists, the scar on his face, only partially hidden by the facial hair, betrayed his true profession. As he removed his tri-cornered feathered hat to scratch his matted hair, James leaned down to whisper in Wynn's ear, "That's Whisking Clark," he said. "I've seen him in New York."

Wynn tilted her head to eye her brother. "When did you have a chance to identify pirates in New York?" she asked.

He gave her a wry smile. There were several escapades in that town his sister did not know about yet.

They turned off the main thoroughfare and walked toward the beach. Wynn could smell the sweet fruits that grew on the island. Bananas, plantains, coconuts, oranges, lemons, and pineapples made this a paradise for sailors fearing scurvy on long voyages.

As they neared the harbor again they began to discern the shapes of the vessels moored there. They walked toward a Dutch sloop, repainted and disguised as a pirate vessel, and as they passed its bow, another, larger shape came into view, anchored farther out in the water.

"That's it, I'm almost sure," said Wynn, stepping onto the quay. There the magnificent Moorish ship, the *Quedah Merchant*, rode at anchor, a dark hulk against darker waters and pale night sky. She caught her breath. "I've never seen a ship so large."

"Five hundred tons, she is," said James. They could see lights in the great cabin and made out silhouettes of two men moving about, though they couldn't identify them at this distance.

Their eyes pierced the darkness, and they walked to the end of the wharf, where it seemed no one else was about. "We might as well go back," James said.

But Wynn tensed. At the end of the quay, leaning against a wooden rail with his foot on a crate, was a solitary figure she would recognize anywhere, even in the dark. She clutched James's sleeve. "It's Robert," she said, pointing to the man who was leaning on the railing staring out to sea. Even now she could sense the strain that must be torturing him. "Leave me now," she whispered urgently.

James hesitated. If it were Robert, then he could safely leave her, but what if she were mistaken? "Are you sure?" he asked in a whisper.

Wynn nodded and, releasing her brother's sleeve, walked toward the tall, muscular figure leaning at the end of the pier, not waiting to find out if James stayed or left. She took several deep breaths and was about to call out, when her voice stuck in her throat. As she stood trembling, looking at Robert's rigid back, an idea came to her. Why not determine her reception before she revealed herself? She was dressed as a young man and her hat hid her face. Why not pretend to be a young sailor, just long enough to get her bearings? Robert had always had the upper hand with her before. Why not take this one little chance? Already amusement and irony, combined with the relief she felt at seeing him safe and whole, were enough to give her the courage to carry out the small deception.

She lifted her shoulders and lowered her chin, making sure the cap was fastened tightly on her head. She took a few scuffling steps toward him, then leaned on the railing a few feet distant and let out a sigh.

Robert half turned, sensing the new presence, and saw the young man in the sailor's cap. He shifted his weight and glanced at the newcomer. He didn't mind passing the time with whoever it was to take his mind off his worries.

Panic rose in her. She did not know what to say, or whether her voice, even when lowered, would give her away. She rubbed her brow with her sleeve and sighed again.

"Warm night," Robert said, turning completely around so that his back was to the rail and he rested on his elbows. Wynn winced at the sight of his face. His lips were drawn and the worry lines about his eyes were deeper than before.

"Aye," she said in a low-pitched voice. "What ship?" she ventured.

Robert tipped his head in the direction of the huge Moorish vessel and said, "The *Quedah Merchant* now. Aye, but we've had bad luck. Our first ship, the *Adventure Galley*, is seaworn. We'll burn her for her iron more than likely." Then, in a chilling tone, he said, "And when we do, part of myself will go up with her."

Wynn was silent for a moment and then asked, "Have you sailed far?"

"More than twenty thousand miles," he said with a sigh. Then his tone turned bitter. "And for nothing. You?" he asked.

She swallowed. If she risked naming any ship in the harbor except the one she had arrived on, Robert might know she was lying, for how would she know how long these ships had been here? She would have to tell him the truth.

"The *Joanna*," she said. "Supply ship," she added, hoping that would satisfy his curiosity, for she knew that in addition to the piracy in these parts, many enterprising captains made fortunes selling provisions to the pirates.

But Robert was not much interested in her ship, seeming to have more need to talk himself. "Privateers we were," said Robert, throwing a splinter from the railing into the water.

"Aye," said Wynn, as if that explained everything.

"Would that I had never left New York," he said.

Wynn's heart stopped beating for a second. "Aye," she said again. "That be yer home?"

"It is." He lowered his voice. "But I'm afraid I may never see it again."

Fear pounded in her. "Why not?" she asked.

"There're orders for our arrest now. My captain, not having any luck with privateering, succumbed to a mutinous crew and took prizes that make him a pirate captain. I fear there's no turning back."

"Then ye be a pirate too?" asked Wynn, her success so far at her dissimulation making her bolder.

He shrugged. "Not if we can clear ourselves and the twelve men left to us. The rest of the crew deserted to that cutthroat pirate Robert Culliford."

"Oh I've heard of Culliford before," said Wynn. "What will ye do now?"

"Sail with Captain Kidd," he said bitterly. "He's my friend and he needs me now. But my life will be ruined if he's arrested for a pirate and me with him."

Wynn dared to lean closer and take on a conspiratorial tone, "Then why don't ye become a real pirate? Take prizes, rich booty?"

He glowered at the dark ahead of him. "It's not in my

blood, nor Captain Kidd's. He has a family, and I have . . ." his voice drifted off. Then he spoke again in a stronger tone. "I have a family too, and property," he added, as if to explain.

"That be in New York?"

"Yes." He clamped his mouth shut, and Wynn frowned. He wasn't saying what she wanted to hear.

She turned to the water so he couldn't see her face and asked, "You have a woman?"

Robert let out a long breath. He did not speak for a moment.

"Aye. I have," he finally said, his voice angry, and she wondered if he would continue on. "But what's love worth if I never see her again?"

Her heart pounded in her ears, and it was all she could do to keep from throwing herself at his feet, but she waited until her voice would sound even again before she spoke.

"She be in New York then?" she asked.

He nodded. "As far away from here as she could be." He shrugged and gave a bitter laugh. "At least that's how it seems to me. I never thought I'd be tied to a woman again, but I have to say it's happened. I tried not to let her wrap herself around my heart, but she has. I never saw eyes so innocent, yet with a silent yearning to be loved," he said. Then he stopped and looked directly at Wynn. " 'Course you're too young to know about love. You bedded a woman yet?" he asked, a trace of teasing in his voice.

His gaze seemed to penetrate her pretense, but she tried to laugh. She knew the embarrassment in her laugh would suit her guise as a young man perhaps looking to bed a woman for the first time.

To her relief, Robert looked out to sea again. "This woman," he said through almost gritted teeth, "made me forget all other women, and I've never even bedded her yet." He sounded so angry, it made Wynn want to laugh. Then he shrugged and flung himself away from the rail, his boots scraping on the wharf as he took two steps away.

"Ah, what's the use?" he said. "I've no word she still loves me. She'll not want to wait for a sailing man who's bound to be hanged. And better for her if she doesn't."

Wynn could maintain the disguise no longer. She faced him and removed her hat. "Robert," she said in her own voice, "I do love you, and I've sailed twelve thousand miles to tell you so."

Robert stood as still as a stone looking at her, his jaw clenching and his black eyes blazing. His arms froze at his sides, and for a moment she feared the shock was too great. But then he moved. Stepping toward her, he clutched her shoulders in his powerful grip.

She wrenched her neck backward to look into his anguished face. For a moment neither of them breathed. Finally, when she thought she would die for lack of breath, she managed to whisper his name again.

"Robert," she said and turned her head to place her cheek against the hard chest beneath his white shirt. His body relaxed a trace, but he lifted her chin in his hand so he could look her in the eye again.

"I can't believe this," he growled, and at first she thought she had only made him angry.

"I'm sorry," she gasped, but his hand became more gentle, and he smoothed her cheek with his palm. He shook his head in disbelief.

"You little minx," he muttered. "How on earth did you find me here?" Then he pushed her back a step so he could look at her attire. "And what is the meaning of that outfit?"

Wynn wanted to laugh and cry at the same time. "Oh Robert, it really is me, and I've risked life and limb and my brother's, too, just to find you."

"Your brother brought you here? How?" he demanded.

She did laugh then. "Don't look so horror-stricken. I tried to get passage on the *Joanna*, only I couldn't, so I tried to stow away, only James wouldn't let me. So we signed on. Oh dear," she gulped. She doubted what she was saying would make any sense.

Robert shut his eyes and pulled her to him, encircling her with his arms. As they swayed together, she could hear his heart beating and tears of relief spilled down her cheeks as she drank in the scent and feel of him.

He held her tightly, too overcome to speak as she pulled him as close to herself as she could. "It's been so long," she whispered.

Then a growing desire spread through her. He lowered his face to her hair and ears, tasting her, moving his hands slowly over her body. She met his explorations with her own, holding nothing back. She tilted her head to kiss his lips, encircling his neck with her arms. She clung to him as his hands explored every inch of her, as if he wanted to assure himself that she was whole and that he had all of her.

He slid his hands over her breasts, down her sides, and cupped her buttocks. Then suddenly he backed away, laughing. She looked puzzled.

"We'd better seek cover," he said with a sardonic lift of the eyebrow. "If anyone saw two sailors doing this, they would not understand."

She smiled as desire lit up her eyes. "Yes," she breathed.

He took her arm and guided her down the pier to the hard-packed soil beyond. Then he pulled her along the shore in the direction of some trees. There dense foliage hid a small clearing of soft grass, and Robert pulled her to him as he leaned against the trunk of a large tree. He pulled her shirt out of her breeches and sought her bare back with his hands. Then he took her mouth once again, his tongue delving insistently. One hand slid down to her buttocks, pulling her against him so that she could feel the burgeoning of his loins.

She gasped as the tremor deep within her began, and breathing jerkily, he unfastened the rest of her clothing. Her head swam in the sensations that enveloped her, but she did not protest his rush to satisfy his passion. She understood his need and the frustrations he had lived with all these months, for they were no less her own.

Gently he lowered her body to the ground and laid her on the trousers she had shed. "Beautiful, my love," he whispered, his tongue darting over the tips of her breasts, causing her a spasm of delight. His fingers massaged her stomach and her silky thighs, and she kissed his face and his hair as he opened the front of his shirt and lowered his breeches.

As her hands roamed over his hard body, she realized that never had she known such pleasure. After all the waiting her passion was intensified beyond anything she had ever expected. Robert, too, seemed to be drinking in his fulfillment.

"Touch me, my love," he whispered, his tongue darting in and out of her ear. And he wrapped her hand around his throbbing member. She moaned with pleasure as again his tongue plunged the depths of her eager mouth.

He spread her legs and sought her opening, massaging her gently. "I can't wait any longer," he said huskily. "I want you, Wynn."

For a moment he hesitated. He whispered in her ear. "This may hurt you, my love. I'll try to ease the pain."

She breathed heavily. "I do not care about the pain," she said, pulling him closer to her.

He was in her then, and as he pushed against her, she felt her flesh tear. Her cry was muffled in her throat as he placed his mouth on hers. He lay still for a moment, until her flesh numbed. When he felt her relax, he began the slow movements that would build his desire to uncontrollable ecstasy.

She moaned under him, sensing his need, forgetting her pain as she helped him release. He breathed heavily, moving against her. She felt him move in her, and soon she matched his rhythm, seeking the warm fulfillment that was to be hers.

Their bodies moved together until Robert began to jerk faster. He threw his chin up and let out a fierce growl. She clutched him, wrapping her legs around him as her own passion built to fever pitch, every nerve in her body obeying his commands. Then he gave one mighty thrust and slumped against her, his hips still moving, eliciting the last drops of passion. Her body swam in pleasure as she held him tightly. Never did she want him to remove himself from her. She had fought for her love and now she wanted nothing to take it from her.

They lay together breathing in their delight and satisfaction with each other. Then as their breathing became normal, Wynn gently moved her fingers over his naked back, his shirt still open to her breasts. She was content to have him drink her in.

Finally, when limbs and bones began to complain of their position, Robert eased himself onto his elbows and began to pull away. She looked hungrily into his eyes, and he kissed her cheeks and nose.

"Don't worry, my pet," he whispered. "We'll have this and better whenever you want. Now that I've got you, I'll never let you out of my sight again. I promise." His warm look dwelled on her for a moment, and then a look of fear stole into his eyes. He did not speak of the ugly doubt that circumstances beyond him might force them apart, for he did not want to think of it.

He got to his knees, and closed his trousers as she began to reach for her clothes. But his hand stopped her. "No, let me look at you that way," he said. His eyes devoured her naked flesh in the darkness. "You're beautiful, my love."

Her lips curved in a smile as her skin tingled from his gaze and from the ocean breeze that drifted over her. Finally, he lifted her to her knees and clasped her against him, caressing her skin with his hands. He held her gently, and when his hands found her hair, he chuckled.

"Did you cut off your curls so you could travel incognito?" he teased.

"James cut them off," she said.

"Ah, the enterprising James. And where is your brother now?"

"Oh, I had forgotten about him. I do not know." She smiled mischievously at Robert.

"Perhaps we should go and see if he has gotten into trouble. A young man, his first time at sea, could be taken advantage of, especially in a port like this." They rose, and she dressed and smoothed her hair. Then she turned about in front of him.

"Do you think I look fit?" she asked.

His merry eyes lit with passion again as he caught her in his grasp and molested her mouth with his own. When he released her he said, "You look fit enough for me, and that is all that matters." And he spanked her bottom with his broad flat hand, making her laugh as they walked through the tall grass.

They sauntered into the village and she kept near him, though she did her best to affect the walk of a man, and Robert refrained from touching her. At the end of the main street, a fight had broken out. Feathers strewn about were evidence of a cockfight, and evidently the losing owner was not satisfied with the results.

Robert and Wynn stood at some distance as she scanned the cheering crowd for James. She saw him on the edge of the crowd, but his attention had been distracted by a dark-skinned native beauty who passed by the crowd of men. She had caught James's eye and was engaged in luring him into the shadows of the thatch-roofed hut.

James had turned from the cockfight, tipped his hat back over his brow, and was smiling at the woman. She languorously swayed her hips and ran her finger across the cloth wrapping her bosom. She moistened her lips, then gestured to him as to how much her delights would cost.

"There he is," said Wynn. "James," she called. He turned his head, and the woman, seeing the other party, ran away. James straightened, eyeing the dark man standing beside his sister, before he walked toward them.

"You must be Robert Lamley," James said. Then he winked at his sister. "I can tell by the glow in her cheeks."

Robert stepped forward and gripped the younger man's hand. He was taller than James by about two inches. As the two men sized each other up, Wynn thought she glimpsed approval in her brother's eyes.

"What is your ship called?" asked Robert.

"The *Joanna*," James said. "But we must talk. Captain Shaw is here for your arrest."

They walked together back toward the docks as James and Wynn told Robert briefly of their voyage and of Captain Shaw's mission.

"It is as I thought," said Robert. "Still, perhaps we can negotiate with him. William is anxious to go home. Almost as anxious as I was," he smiled grimly, "before tonight." He pulled Wynn toward him and kissed her ear.

"I must speak to William, but I dare not take you with me. It is dangerous. He has locked himself in his cabin against the crew who deserted to Culliford. They threaten to burn the ship unless he swears allegiance to Culliford."

"Who is this Culliford?" asked James.

"A notorious pirate captain. He knew William in the East Indies, stole his ship, the *Blessed William*, years ago, and William came here to arrest him on the power of his privateering commission." Robert shook his head. "But the crew laughed at him, and most of them left the ship. Those few who are left guard the *Adventure Galley* against the others, and William has passed out small arms and pistols and barricaded his cabin with bales of goods. I must see how things lie."

He turned to Wynn. "Stay with your brother." Then, looking meaningfully at the younger man. "Do not take your eyes off her," he said and turned to hail the small boat that would take him out to the *Adventure Galley*.

Brother and sister shrank back into the shadows while Robert stepped into the shallop to go out to the ship. Suddenly, Wynn stiffened. What if Captain Shaw was waiting on the ship to arrest him? She started forward, but James held her back.

"No. He knows best," her brother said as they watched the shallop slip through the water.

Finally they saw Robert climb the rope ladder to the upper deck. The sailors on watch recognized him and let him go aft. He knocked on the cabin door, and after some moments they saw it open and he passed through. From the lights in the stern windows they saw William and Robert, their heads bowed in conversation. She held her breath as she watched. Captain Shaw must not yet have attempted to arrest them.

She looked enquiringly at James, but he shook his head. Still, Robert did not come back for them, so James and his sister sat down on the dock to wait.

Chapter Fourteen

Neither James nor Wynn saw the darkly clad figures that slipped over the railings of the *Adventure Galley* a little while after Robert entered William's cabin. The quiet lap of oars on the lee side of the ship blended in with the night sounds of the harbor, and so gave no cause for alarm.

Tom Perkins leaned against the bulkhead in the bow of the ship. At his feet lay a piece of ivory he had been carving. He did not hear the soft tread of soles that slipped up behind him, nor the unfurling of a bandanna in the hands of one of his erstwhile shipmates. But he was roused from his musings as the man behind him slid along the bulkhead just inches from him.

"Wh—," but the word was choked off by the bandanna that went round his mouth and was tied tightly behind his head. He struggled, but the hard butt of a pistol smashed the back of his skull, and unconsciousness came as he hit the deck with a soft grunt.

The stealthy pirate signaled to a companion who had

hid in the shadows near the watch. Catlike, he sprang forward and stuffed a rag into his victim's mouth at the same time his shiny blade entered the other man's ribs. Blood ran over the deck, filling the cracks between the oaken planks. Another man, and then another was felled in such a manner until all four who stood watch had either left this life or lay unconscious on the deck. When all was secure, the pirate, now at the wheel, gave a signal, and a longboat slipped out from the shadows of a sloop behind which she had been waiting.

Six men pulled the oars while, in the stern of the longboat, a small wiry man with black knee boots, brown serge trousers, and a wide black belt with a large gold buckle sat. He wore a red silk blouse opened at the neck. But more than the costume, it was the face that arrested attention. He had a long hooked nose, thin lips, and was missing a front tooth. His skin was dark and leathery from the sun, his eyes small with a habitual squint, and he wore a paisley silk scarf wrapped around his short dark hair with a knot over his right ear, the tails hanging down over his right shoulder.

He leaned forward in the stern, his eyes intent on the ship ahead, as his men pulled up to the port side of the ship, away from St. Mary's docks. A man on the upper deck threw down a rope ladder; there was a soft thump against the hull and then the crew in the longboat caught it. Culliford placed one foot in the ladder and then climbed it, the oarsman holding it until he scrambled over the railing. Then he waved an arm and the longboat cast off.

"No trouble, Cap'n," whispered one of the pirates. "They're all ready to meet their maker, and Captain Kidd's locked up sweet as you please in that cabin. We'll starve 'em out if nothin' else," chortled the pirate who made the report.

But Culliford silenced him. "I don't want him starved. He's no use to me dead. He'll swear allegiance

to Robert Culliford afore he leaves this ship, he will."
And the wiry pirate scowled at his men. Although shorter than most of them, he had a way of looking at a man that struck fear into his heart.

"And the other one?" he hissed.

" 'E joined Cap'n Kidd a few minutes ago. Saw 'em come aboard and Kidd let him in his cabin. Been talkin' in there some time, they have."

Culliford gave a low growl as he said, "Robert Lamley, is it?"

"Aye, and he's armed," volunteered one of the men.

"We'll take 'em both at once then. Be done with it. Then, me mateys, they'll turn over this heap a timbers we stands on an' that Moorish hulk," Culliford said with a gleam in his eye. For he knew of the treasure-laden *Quedah Merchant* that floated nearby. He rubbed his chin as he gestured for the men to draw near.

"Position yourselves around the cabin," he directed. "I'll shout for Kidd to come out and talk. Course, he'll be covered by his mate." He had not planned for the mate to be aboard, but a slight adjustment of his plans was all that was necessary to take this added obstacle into account.

"But I'll get Kidd in me hands one way or t'other, so no one, Lamley nor the rest of the crew on that other ship, will make a move lest Captain Kidd's throat be cut." Liking the plan, he grinned mirthlessly, revealing the gap in his teeth. "Now move quietly, me lads. We don't want to give the alarm, not till I'm ready." And they moved aft, skirting the cannon.

When the men were in position, Culliford pulled the pearl-handled wheel lock pistol from his belt and pointed it at the door to the great cabin. He unsheathed a dagger that was strapped to his boot, and with a high-pitched yell that ripped through the quiet night and sent shivers down the backs of his own crew, he threw the dagger so that the blade split the timbers of the door.

"Captain Kidd. Yer surrounded. Come out of there and surrender to Captain Culliford. You've nothing to do locked up in that cabin. Yer crew's left you and you can't sail yer prize home without one. Swear allegiance to Robert Culliford, and yer life'll be spared. Ye kin sail with me, and we'll share yer prize. Yer life's forfeit at home, so what have ye to lose?"

Inside the cabin, Robert spun on one heel to face the cabin door that had taken the dagger. Bales of goods were piled next to the door and the cabin windows had been boarded up.

"What the devil?" cursed Robert as he unsheathed his sword. Behind him William, his eyes bloodshot from lack of sleep, rose to his feet, grabbing up the pistol that lay primed and charged on the table before him.

"It's that monster Culliford again," he said. "The man'll be the death of me," he muttered into his beard.

"Well he won't be the death of me," swore Robert. He yelled, "What do you want, Culliford?" His voice boomed through the wood so that it reached Culliford's ears.

"Mr. Lamley," called Culliford, "it's yer captain I want. Unless ye think ye can talk some sense into 'im. The tropics've addled 'is brain. I fear he's no match for the likes of me, not without a crew to back him. And most've them've come to me."

"And what would you have him do?" called Robert, knowing the answer, but playing for time.

"He'll have my ships, that's what," said Kidd, coming from behind the table, pistols in hand. "And me with them."

"Come out," called Culliford. "I just want to talk to ye."

Robert thought quickly. He was tempted to blow a hole through the door and take Culliford in the same explosion. But it was not likely he was alone. He would have men to cover him, and the men on watch must have been overtaken. That meant he and William were alone facing Culliford, and they would have to fight their way out of the cabin. Thank God, he thought, Wynn and her brother were safely on shore.

But the choice was made for them as smoke seeped under the door, and they heard Culliford's cackle. The pirate knew that the hold was empty, that Kidd's deserting crew had carried away great guns, powder, shot, sails, cable and whatever else they pleased so that there was little loss to burning Kidd out of his cabin.

"Smoke," said Robert, laying the sword aside to extract a large handkerchief from his pocket and tie it around his nose and mouth. William did the same. "He would burn us out," said Robert as he again armed himself with two pistols stuck in his belt and his sword in hand.

"We'd best surrender," said Kidd, the fight gone out of him. But he picked up his pistols halfheartedly, as if from force of habit.

Robert winced to see his friend so demoralized. He was no longer the self-assured man Robert had once respected. The loss of his crew and lack of prizes had chipped away at William's decisiveness. But if his superior had lost his will to defend himself, Robert had not, and he was not about to surrender to the accursed Culliford.

The smoke was thicker now, and Robert knocked the bales of goods aside as William faced the door, his pistols ready. Then, as Robert yanked open the door, William fired both shots, the reports sending him reeling back a step. A cry was heard, but Robert did not wait to find out if Culliford had been wounded. He and William bolted through the smoke even as flames licked their feet, for the deck had caught fire.

The air sang with the downward rush of a blade as Robert leapt aside and then lunged with his own sword, wounding his assailant in the shoulder. As he withdrew his sword, he heard scuffling behind him and turned to see William and Culliford circling each other, hate gleaming in their eyes, tear-filled from the smoke. Culliford still called taunts to William, but Robert had no time to watch them as two more threats appeared. He took a blow on his shoulder from behind. At the same time, a shot rang out next to his head, but he had already turned and leapt toward the man who had hit him with the butt of his pistol. The man tossed the empty pistol aside and took a knife from his belt.

Robert took cover behind a cask and aimed at the man who had tried to shoot him. The man was reloading, but Robert's fire blew his opponent's hand away before he had time to finish his task. He drew his sword in time to ward off the man approaching with the knife.

By now cries rang out in the night, and the men on board the *Quedah Merchant* had clambered into their longboat and were climbing up the ladder to the *Adventure Galley* to help. The ship was overrun with pirates and Kidd's small crew in hand-to-hand combat, even as flames climbed the rigging, and the red and orange tongues licked at the night sky.

Kidd and Culliford had spent their shot and were engaged in sword play that carried them aft. The wiry pirate had backed William up the ladder to the fo'c'sle deck, and, with a swift downward slice, Kidd's sword took a piece of the other man's ear. The pirate howled as William climbed the ladder and crouched by the foremast. As he gazed over his burning ship, the red and orange flames illuminating other ships in the harbor, fierce anger took hold of him, shaking him out of the apathy he'd been victim of these last months. Suddenly all the cruelty of fate turning against him ceased to seem an Act of God against which he had no recourse. Instead he now saw it as a work of evil he could stave off with his own hands.

A paisley bandanna was now visible at the top of the

ladder as Culliford, his pain enraging him, followed Kidd up to the fo'c'sle deck. Every nerve in William's body was primed to rid him of his enemy, and with the superhuman strength that comes from intense emotion, Kidd leapt at Culliford, knocking him backward on the ladder. The pirate's cry and Kidd's bloodcurdling yell pierced the chaos that filled the harbor, and those on shore watching in horror as the ship burned, heard the unearthly sound.

The flames had swept the rigging, and the sound of splintering wood caused the men to halt their fighting to look up. Above them the mainmast tilted slowly and began to fall as men dove overboard to avoid being incinerated. Robert looked up and saw that the slowly falling mast and her spars were aimed straight for the two grappling captains on the fo'c'sle deck.

"William!" he called through the din, his hands cupped around his mouth. "Jump!" And as the blazing mast fell, he dove from the railing.

He swam underwater, as far away from the ship as he could before regaining the surface. Other sailors had done the same, placing as much distance between them and the sinking inferno as they could, for the *Adventure Galley* was about to go down.

Robert shook the water from his face, trying to spot William. He saw men swimming off to his left, and he took several powerful strokes in that direction. But he found neither Kidd nor Culliford. The ship was now a mass of fire. When she sank she would pull all those nearby with her into the smoldering, watery depths, and even as Robert swam he could feel the currents from the sinking ship tug at him. But he fought against them and he had now swum far enough that he could reach the *Quedah Merchant*'s moorings.

"Master Lamley!" came a cry from on board, and Samuel Bradley tossed him a line. It was a miracle that the *Quedah Merchant* had not caught any sparks, but the wind was blowing away from her, and so she was safe from conflagration. Robert fastened the line around his waist, still trying to pierce the dark waters around him for any sign of his captain.

"Have you seen William?" he called to Samuel, who scanned the waters from the deck above him.

"No sign," answered Samuel, who had been left to watch the Moorish vessel. Robert made his way to the rope ladder that dropped before him and swung to and from the curved hull of the ship like a hanged man. He grasped the ladder rungs and pulled himself up and over the railing.

"Thank God, Robert," came Samuel's voice when Robert set foot on deck. "What of the captain?" he asked, as Robert peeled away his shirt and shook the water from his head.

"Couldn't see him. I shouted for him to jump. He was with Culliford."

Both men turned to watch the burning ship as her bow pointed skyward. She gave a great shudder as the flaming spars flew off into the water, and then she sank, bow last, with a great hiss, as water rushed in after her. Wreckage floated everywhere, bumping the hull of the *Quedah Merchant* as Robert and Samuel began pulling up some of the crew members who had made it to the larger ship, but there was no sign of William or Culliford anywhere. Finally, when the night was at its very darkest, just before dawn, all the men who had been rescued were on deck where they were binding their wounds. Meanwhile, Culliford's pirates had picked up their own men and rowed away in the longboat.

As Robert strode the deck, doing what he could for the pitiful remnants of his crew, a feeling like a hideous cold claw wrapped itself around his heart. He sought out Samuel. "I've got to go ashore," he said.

"But Culliford could be out there, and there's his crew to deal with," Samuel protested. "They'll not be happy that their plans went awry. If they hoped to gain a ship, she's gone now. They'll be for this one next. For here's where the real treasure lies."

"I know that, and we'll have to hold them off the best we can, but I've got to find William. And —" He cleared his throat. "— another ship's come in. The *Joanna*, out from New York."

"I've seen her," said Samuel as he continued to wrap a man's leg with torn linen.

"Your sister's cousin, Wynn Cox, was aboard with her brother, James, a sailor." Robert shook his head at the ironic horror of the last hour. "I don't know where they are now. She was expecting me to send for them, and though her brother's a strong enough lad, they could've run into trouble."

"Blimy," said Samuel. "Mistress Wynn in this port?"

Robert allowed himself to smile briefly. "Well, you wouldn't recognize her if you saw her. I didn't. She and her brother signed on as able seamen."

"She signed on as a *man*!"

"She was found out eventually. Luckily she wasn't raped by the captain."

"That'd be Captain Shaw," said Samuel. "I know him. He's an honorable man, from what I know."

"Aye," said Robert. But he would hate to trust a man under the influence of the southern seas after seeing its results on William. Hastily changing into dry clothing, he armed himself with a cutlass and a pistol with dry powder. Then he went to one of the longboats lashed to the main deck. Two of the men came forward to help him lower the boat over the side, and when it was down, Robert hoisted himself into it.

"Send word," called Samuel.

"Aye," answered Robert. "Keep watch." There hadn't been enough men to send any with him. A dim light now paled the darkness as Robert rowed silently through the harbor now strewn with parts of the *Adventure Galley*. Men worked to clear the wreckage away from their ships, and Robert's course took him up the beach, some distance away from the quays. When his boat scraped bottom, he leapt out into knee-deep water and hauled her ashore, pulling her onto the sand as far as he could and unshipping the oars.

This business finished, he checked his weapons and looked about. An angry curse forming on his lips, he clenched his fist. Why did God want him to suffer so? Why had the sea meant nothing but loss and torture for him? But as he tramped along the shore, scanning the shallows, his anger turned to self-pity. It was his own fault for coming on this voyage. But then if he hadn't, William might have been strung up by his own men. Even now, he might be dead. He prayed that he would not find William's body washed ashore.

Wynn and James had rushed to the end of the quay when they heard the shouting on board the *Adventure Galley*, watching in horror as the torches were lit and the cabin set afire. Spying a boat tied to the quay, they rushed over to it, frantically fumbling at its moorings.

"We've no arms," James yelled to Wynn. "You stay here." But she had already stepped into the small boat, seized an oar and pushed them away from the quay. James rowed toward the burning ship. But as the rigging went up in flames, he lifted the oars, pausing to think. He knew that if the ship sank, they would be pulled under too, but they could pick up survivors if they didn't get too close.

"Why have you stopped?" called Wynn from the stern, "Go on!" At that moment the mainmast splintered and fell, and through the din they heard Robert's call to jump. Sailors leapt from the blazing inferno, and James began to row toward them. Holding an oar out to the nearest sailor who bobbed to the surface, James saw it was Richard Barlicorn, Kidd's servant.

As soon as he was in the boat, he said, "For God's sake, try to save the captain. He went over the side the same time as I did."

Wynn searched the waters, desperately praying they would find Robert as well.

"Over there, that's the captain!" said Barlicorn, and James began to row toward a man who was swimming over to them.

"It's William," said Wynn when as they were close enough to make him out, and soon they had him safely in the boat. Then they picked up two other survivors and made for shore.

"Where's Robert?" Wynn asked William as soon as he had recovered from his exertions in the water. She feared the worst.

William shook his head. "He jumped."

Hope mingled with the fear that gripped her. "Then he made it?"

"Can't say," said William. "Let us hope so."

They came to shore and clambered out. "You're hurt," Wynn said, noticing the blood running down from William's shoulder. Wincing as he moved his arm, he shook his head. "Only a flesh wound. See to the men first."

"We'll have to get them to land," she said, and she thought of the clearing where she had gone with Robert. At least they could lie down on the grass while she and James cleaned the wounds and bound them. "Is there a doctor in the village?" she ventured.

William shrugged. "If they walk in fear of Culliford, they'll be afraid to come and tend our men. But I'll send a man to the village to see." As Richard Barlicorn was not hurt badly, he volunteered to go for the doctor.

Wynn bound William's arm with a piece torn from

his shirt, and after she and James had done what they could to alleviate the pain of the sailors' wounds, James started back to the boat. "I'll see about the other men," he said.

But William stopped him. "Not now. You'd be sucked under." And they walked to the beach to see the *Adventure Galley* give a last great shudder, tip her bow skyward then sink into the harbor waters.

"At least I can help the ones who've made it to shore," said James, running toward the water. As William watched the *Adventure Galley* go down, Wynn sensed his desolation. She laid a hand on his arm. "At least the *Quedah Merchant*'s still safe, isn't she?"

He shrugged. "She may be for now, but Culliford'll be after her."

"It was Robert Culliford then," she said.

"It was," answered William. "Though if he's about, he's minus a piece of ear.

"I have to get back to the *Quedah Merchant*," he said. "I had hoped to take home what's left of her spoils to satisfy my owners."

"Did Robert tell you of the arrest orders?"

"Aye, he did. It is my hope that I can convince Captain Shaw of my innocence and show him the goods which belong to the owners. I have promised to take them in, and so perhaps Captain Shaw will allow us to sail home on our own."

Poor William, thought Wynn, but she couldn't help but think he had brought some of his problems on himself, and endangered Robert by involving him in his foolhardy mission.

"Do you think Robert might have made it to the *Quedah Merchant*?"

"It's likely," said William.

"Then I'll come with you," said Wynn.

He turned her proposal over in his mind, and then

said, "Best to stay here with the men where you'll be safe. Culliford might be waiting for me."

Damn Culliford! What did she care about him? But she saw it was useless to argue with William. "You'll make sure to send word then?" she asked.

"Aye. That I'll do."

"But what if Robert's wounded?"

William paused. He seemed to take his mind off his own troubles long enough to feel sympathy for her. "Don't worry. He'll be all right. Culliford was with me, and none of the other scum is any match for your Robert."

Behind them, the moans of some of the wounded men reminded her of their discomfort, and seeing that William would not allow her to accompany him, she turned to tend to their needs. James returned with a few straggling men, and Kidd took count of the men still left to him.

Tom Perkins was found drowned, and Wynn could see the remorse in the eyes of the captain who had led his men into such danger. Then he left them and took a small boat out to his one remaining ship. Wynn watched him go, praying that soon she would have news of Robert.

The doctor fetched by Richard Barlicorn set about his work hastily. It was obvious that he didn't want to be caught on the wrong side of things, for by now the entire village was aware of Captain Culliford's malice toward Kidd's crew, and fear kept most of the villagers from offering any help. The doctor dressed the wounds, set a broken arm, and then hurried away.

The men lay, albeit uncomfortably, in the grass as dawn pushed the night away. But the pale morning light did little to assuage Wynn's fears. Surely Robert ought to have sent word to her by now. Unless he was hurt — or worse. She fought to keep her mind from conjuring up a picture of his inert form floating out to sea.

James lay on the grass, his head propped on one hand. "I'm done out," he said to his sister. "You be all right for a while, if I shut my eyes?"

"Yes, James, you sleep."

"You should too," he said, stretching out, his eyelids drooping.

She nodded and tried to make herself comfortable nearby, tossing about for a short while, fretting about Robert.

She must have nodded off, for when she opened her eyes, the sun had risen well past the horizon, and morning light was full upon them. She shook the fatigue from her head and sat up. To her right, James snored. She stood, brushing the grass from her damp clothing. She gave James a hasty glance. Surely a few moments away from the men wouldn't hurt. Robert might be looking for them, and since this patch of ground was so sheltered from the beach, it would be a good idea to step out and see if there were any sign of him.

As she walked toward the clump of low bushes that separated them from the open shore, she thought she heard the rustle of an animal in the undergrowth, but as she passed through a thicket of prickly shrubs, she could see nothing. She walked farther out toward the shoreline, squinting into the sun. Then her heart lifted and she began to run, for in the distance she could see Robert striding in her direction.

Just as she opened her mouth to call to him, a hand was clapped over her mouth, and she was yanked back toward the bushes at the edge of the beach. Unsheathing his sword, Robert lunged toward them, but stopped when he saw the glint of the knife blade pressed against Wynn's throat.

"Stand back, Lamley," her captor called out. "This little lady is no sailor, in spite of her disguise."

"Let her go, Culliford," Robert called to the pirate. "Take me instead."

But Culliford dragged her toward the trees. "I think not. She will be more help than you would be in persuading Captain Kidd to surrender."

"What do you want then?" asked Robert, grimly clutching his sword, but, afraid to endanger Wynn, he made no move forward.

"I'll speak to your captain about that," said Culliford.

"He'll never capitulate to you, Culliford, so you can forget it."

"We'll see about that," Culliford said, pressing the blade into Wynn's throat. She screamed as she felt it bite into her flesh and Robert rushed forward, coming to a halt only when Culliford once more shouted a warning.

Wynn stood frozen, the pain searing her, afraid to move because of the conflict she could see in Robert's face as both love for her and the desire for vengeance on Culliford flashed in his dark eyes.

The moment of tension was broken by Culliford's men calling from down the shore. James, hands bound behind him and his mouth gagged with a handkerchief, was being propelled by two of Culliford's men toward a longboat that was pulled up on the beach. He struggled with them, but to no avail.

"Thought you were safe, eh?" Culliford sneered. "But sleeping men, and wounded ones at that, are no match for a half hundred of mine." He laughed loudly. "My two hundred against your twelve," he called to Robert, and he yanked Wynn toward the longboat.

"The Moorish treasure will be mine yet," he called gleefully to Robert. "Tell Captain Kidd I've got the girl."

Robert stood, his sword raised in one hand, his pistol in the other. But two more pirates stood near a second longboat, their pistols aimed for his head. One of them fired, and Robert dropped his weapons, grabbing his left arm with his right hand. Forcing Wynn into the boat, the pirates held her as Culliford tied her hands and placed a scarf over her mouth to prevent her from screaming. Then she was bundled into the bottom of the boat, Culliford jumped in and the two longboats pushed off.

What had happened to the wounded men, she was afraid to think, but then she saw them being led along the beach, hands tied behind them. The men limping along made a pitiful sight, but at least they were being taken prisoner, she thought, not being murdered. She saw Robert raise his pistol with his good hand and take aim, but he dared not shoot, for fear he would hit Wynn or her brother in the other boat.

Tears streamed down her face as they made for the harbor. How cruel fate was! To be reunited with her Robert only to be once again wrenched away from him. She glared at the pirate who sat in the bow of the boat. If she could get her hands on a sword, she would gladly run him through, she thought. In the other boat her brother, bound and gagged, now slumped forward as if he had been knocked unconscious.

Swearing, Robert lowered his pistol and shoved it into his belt. Once the boats were out of sight, he turned and headed for the quay. He knew he could never fight Culliford alone, and he needed whatever help he could get. He also knew the rest of the populace would not fight against Culliford, for this was the sort of place where everyone turned a deaf ear and a blind eye to trouble. And in sheer numbers Culliford had the advantage. They would be hard pressed to fight against him with the few men now left on board the *Quedah Merchant*. The rest had been either taken prisoner or tempted away by the spoils of piracy. If it would guarantee Wynn's freedom, Robert would prevail upon

William to give up the *Quedah Merchant*'s treasure to Culliford but he knew better than to trust Culliford to stand by his word.

Robert dared not allow himself to think what Culliford might do to Wynn before he could get to her. The outrage that flooded him was enough to make him want to kill the insidious pirate if he got his hands on him. He strode to where he'd left his boat and with his good arm pushed it into the water, then made for the ship where William and Samuel held their beleaguered crew.

Chapter Fifteen

As the longboats pulled alongside Culliford's ship, the *Mocha Frigate*, Wynn's hands were freed and she was roughly pushed toward the ladder and made to climb. Once on board, she was taken to the hold where the pirates bound her to a post, making sure her gag was fast. Crowded between barrels of provisions, rigging and ammunition, she was left alone in the dark. She clenched her jaw, trying not to panic. The glimmer of light from above and the sound of footsteps announced the arrival of company.

Then she saw a burly pirate with a gold ring in his left ear carrying James into the hold. He was still tied up and his head lolled forward as if he were unconscious. Then the pirates left them, shutting out the light.

Wynn tried to make a sound through the gag, which bit into her mouth, but her cries were muffled. James moaned slightly, and she wriggled in her bonds, trying to get free. She thought of Robert, standing on the shore, helpless against the pirates. She knew Culliford had left Robert on the beach in order to send William the message that he wanted the *Quedah Merchant* as well as William's submission. If the pirates had captured Robert instead, at least they would be together now, she thought as tears of frustration and grief rolled down her cheeks.

Leaning forward, Wynn tried to rub the ropes that bound her wrists against the timber she was tied to, but the movement only chafed her wrists more. And, when she strained at the gag, she bruised the corners of her mouth. Finally giving up, she slumped against the splintery wood as she felt the ship get under way. Where were they going now? Sobs choked her. If Culliford put out to sea, she would never see Robert again.

She cried silently for a few moments, the darkness adding to her fear. Finally exhaustion overtook her, and, giving in to the darkness and the gentle rocking of the ship, she fell into a doze.

How long they sailed, she did not know, but James's moans as he awoke made her jerk her head up. She heard the creak of a hinge, and then the hatch was opened and three grimy pirates climbed down. One of them carried a bowl of soup. Wynn roused herself at the smell of the food, although the odor coming to her was not an especially appealing one. But if the pirates intended to feed them, they would have to be untied, and she would have a chance to speak to her brother.

The man with the bowl placed it in front of James, and a stocky man with a bushy brown beard prodded Wynn's shoulder with the tip of his sword. He was so dirty that when he came near, she wrinkled her nose at the odor emanating from him.

"You don't get to eat with your brother, lady," said the pirate. "Captain Culliford wants to see you in his cabin."

When her hands and mouth were freed and she first tried to stand, she found that her legs had gone to sleep. "Oh!" she cried, as she stumbled. The sword tip prodded her again, making her jump.

"I'm coming," she snapped at the man, who laughed at her discomfort. She limped toward the ladder and climbed first to the orlop deck, then the gun deck, and finally to the upper deck where the great cabin sat aft. The man pushed her in the direction of the cabin door.

Although fatigue and hunger contributed to her despair, she tried to marshall her thoughts. If she could overcome her anger and fear enough to reason with Culliford, perhaps there was hope yet. She could at least ascertain what he wanted and find out where he was taking them.

The door opened, she was shoved inside, and then the door slammed shut behind her. Culliford sat, taking his ease, at the far end of the cabin on a velvet-covered daybed. He was eating grapes from a silver bowl and sipping a liquid that looked like claret, and reminded Wynn of her acute thirst.

But she forced her eyes away from the food and drink to look around her. The cabin contained all the normal necessities of life that she had remarked in Captain Shaw's cabin, along with certain luxurious items. An ebony-inlaid chest stood next to an armoire gilded with figures of animals and trees, and the hangings over the large captain's bed were of shiny gold damask.

"You like my cabin?" asked Culliford with satisfied glee. He motioned her to come forward. "Come here. Don't be afraid."

She doubted her safety with this evil man, but she straightened her stance and faced him, deciding that she would try to be civil in order to bargain for time. She bit back the insults and curses she longed to throw at him, and spoke as genteelly as she could. As she raised her head to speak, she glanced into a gilt-edged mirror hanging above the ebony chest, and was dismayed at her disheveled appearance.

"You wanted to see me," she said with a set to her chin.

Culliford pretended to be examining a grape between his fingers.

"You have a liking for fine things," he finally said, giving her a sidelong glance.

She did not answer, but stared at him defiantly.

He popped the grape into his mouth and swallowed. "I saw your eyes when you entered my little cabin. So much the better for me," he said, rising and circling her. Lifting a strand of her limp tangled hair, he felt the texture as if inspecting some material he might buy, and then let it fall. She shuddered inwardly at his touch but remained rigid.

He stopped in front of her, and she noticed now how short he was, for his eyes were on a level with her own. She thought with some satisfaction that in hand-to-hand combat he would be no match for Robert.

Below the paisley bandanna that covered his dark curling hair, he wore a bandage that completely covered his right ear, and she remembered that William had said he had cut away part of it. If he tried to touch her again, she had only to grab for the wounded ear to make him feel pain, she thought.

"I have no interest in either you or your ship," she said.

"Cleaned up and dressed properly, you just might do," he said, ignoring her comment. She saw the avarice in his beady eyes as his long thin fingers reached across her toward the armoire. Unfastening the latch, he threw open the doors and revealed a woman's wardrobe of silks, satins, taffeta, lace and velvet.

Wynn's eyes widened in surprise. Culliford grabbed her by the arm and jerked her toward the armoire, where he extracted some folds of crimson velvet edged in gold lace and touched its plush softness to her cheek.

She frowned, and the pirate laughed. "Perhaps this would be too warm in the present climate. Ah, yes, you would be more comfortable in this." And he extracted a filmy negligee of diaphanous material with puffed sleeves and a plunging neckline. He held it up, considering how it would look on her.

"Very good," he said, and he laid the negligee on the back of the captain's chair. He then stepped to the door and called for a servant to bring a bath. "Surely you would like a bath and a change of clothes," he said, leering at her.

She snorted at him. "If you think I will bathe in front of you, you are mistaken."

"I am under no such delusion. I am a patient man, miss. I am not in the mood to force my attentions upon you, if that is what you think. I merely wish to make you as comfortable as possible, for you should consider yourself my guest."

"If I am your guest, then why will you not let me go?"

"Ah, that is a matter between Captain Kidd and myself." He frowned at her.

"But surely I have nothing to do with Captain Kidd's affairs."

"Ah," he said, pointing a finger at her. "I think you do. At least you claim the heart of someone close to Captain Kidd. And your lover can influence the captain. So you see . . ." He let the sentence dangle.

"Do not worry," he said, walking to the door. "You shall have your privacy. But please, make use of the water and soap. You are not a pleasant sight, and I like pretty things around me."

She clenched her fists, glaring at him as he made his exit. The servant brought the water in a wooden tub and set it before her.

Now that she was alone, the idea of a bath was truly tempting. She had not had a proper wash in some time. She approached the water doubtfully, then decided she would take the chance. Keeping her back to the door, she stripped. The feel of the water on her naked flesh brought a sigh to her lips. She slid into the tub, the refreshing water up to her chin, and she rubbed the soap over her skin. She dared not dally, and when her hair and body were as clean as she could make them, she reached for the towel the servant had left on the chair. She wrapped it around her and stepped out.

Then she considered what to wear. Her old clothes were so filthy she did not want to put them back on. But she would certainly not put on the flimsy gown Culliford had suggested. He would take it as a gesture of submission. Instead she walked to the armoire. Perhaps there was something more practical she could wear.

She ran her hands across the fine fabrics, finding nothing suitable. But at the far end of the armoire, she found several pairs of men's breeches and cambric shirts with ruffles on the front. This was what she would wear, she decided with a sardonic grin. She had already grown accustomed to men's clothing, and she would not give Culliford the satisfaction of seeing her dressed in his collection of finery.

She fastened the trousers, which fit her well, for Culliford's small frame was nearly the same size as hers. However, the shirt sleeves were too long, and she had to push them up toward her elbows. She toweled her hair dry and combed it with her fingers, letting it fall naturally around her head.

When Culliford returned, he took one glance at her and then threw back his head in a mirthless laugh. "Ah, my little minx, I see you have not chosen the gown. But your practical attire is perhaps better considering what is in store for you."

She raised her eyebrows in curiosity, but she did not speak.

"You would not perhaps like walking two days and climbing hills on foot clad in such flimsy material and with sandals on your feet. Still, the male attire does not entirely hide your comeliness."

"Two days' walk?" she said.

He smiled his evil smile. "Where did you think we were going? To England? No, my dear. We're going to my little hideaway where I will lay my plans to snare the eminent Captain Kidd."

"He will not be interested in your plans."

"But, as I have said, his first mate, the man he so depends on now, will be interested. And besides, you are related to the captain's wife. I do not think he will turn his back on so near a relative, and I am confident that Robert Lamley would not let him."

"They may have no choice. Your plans may be useless. Captain Shaw of the *Joanna* has arrived with orders for their arrest. They have probably already left St. Mary's." She hoped that by saying it she had not put herself in worse stead, for she would hate Culliford to think he had her all to himself, that there was no hope for a rescue.

"Oh, so I've heard," he said. "The orders for our friend the captain are being talked about throughout England's commonwealth, are they not?" He smiled in derision. "But perhaps I can show you something to take your mind off your concerns . . . ."

"I cannot imagine being interested in anything you have to show me."

"Nevertheless." He turned and kicked open a heavy chest that sat at the foot of the bed. She could not stifle a gasp. In the chest lay gold necklaces studded with amber and coral, pieces of Arabian and Christian gold, melted bars of silver.

He opened another chest in which lay scarlet, green, sapphire, and blue Indian silks. "Perhaps some of these things could be yours if you wished to cooperate with me."

Hatred mounted in her. "I would never lower myself to become mistress of a pirate captain," she spit at him.

He caught her wrists and pulled her to him, forcing her to face him. "A fiery little cat you are. Well, so much the better. Besides, you are already the mistress of a pirate, or didn't you know it?"

His grasp repulsed her, and she spat out her words. "My fiancé is no pirate," she said. "And I am disgusted at your conceit that you could tempt me with your ill-gotten goods. You are not the sort of man a woman could feel anything for besides."

With a grunt of disgust, he threw her from him. Dizziness threatened to overtake her, but she squeezed her eyes shut and steadied herself against the back of the captain's chair.

He slammed the chests shut with a laugh. "We shall see. But now we have very nearly reached our destination and must prepare to disembark. I am sorry to have to bruise your lovely mouth, but I must stop you from being tempted to make trouble." And he pulled out his handkerchief and shook it free before winding it to use as a gag.

"And do not think," he continued, "that the native tribes will take any pity on you. On the contrary. They are quite familiar with slavery in these parts and think nothing of it. In fact," he said in a more menacing tone, "should you cause me any trouble, I might consider making a gift of you to one of the Sakalava kings on the other side of the island. He is fond of white skin." And he took her chin between two fingers, gloating at her.

She could not think of a fitting epithet for him and so thrust her chin up haughtily. In spite of her anger and fear, she had to think logically. Perhaps there would be a means of escape, and if she could communicate with her brother, they could think of how to get away.

As he led her onto the deck, she tried to determine their location. They had anchored in a sandy bay, and now she could see several long canoes paddled by brown-skinned natives coming in their direction. When they came nearer the ship, she could see the canoes had been hollowed out of tree trunks and were about three feet deep. The natives propelled the canoes with spade-shaped paddles, which they used facing forward.

Wynn was forced to climb down the rope ladder that the pirates flung over the side of the ship; and when she stepped into the canoe, she sat down quickly. Culliford followed. She glanced upward, but James was nowhere to be seen.

As the canoes made for shore, she could see that they were headed for a river that cut through thick vegetation that covered the steep hills around the bay.

The natives chanted as they dug their paddles into the water, and she wondered how they had come to serve Culliford. With every stroke, she was going farther and farther away from Robert, and in order to keep herself from giving way to the feeling of desolation that threatened to overtake her, she tried to memorize her surroundings in case she needed to find her way out again.

In the distance a dull roar made her wonder if they were near a waterfall. As they paddled upriver, she saw that they were in a deep gorge cut into the rose-colored granite that was visible where the thick tropical forest did not grow. Rapids began to batter the canoe, and when they rounded a curve they were in sight of rushing falls. The natives pulled the canoes onto the muddy shore where some trees had been cleared away, and Wynn stepped out.

"I'm afraid you'll have to walk from here," said Culliford as he alighted behind her.

"Where?" she asked, for all around them was the dense forest, the sound of the cascading falls drumming in their ears.

"You'll see," he said, and then motioned for the bearers to move. They had loaded Culliford's belongings from another canoe onto stretchers made of bamboo poles lashed across with rush fiber. The men lifted the poles to their shoulders and set out through the forest.

Something scurried out of the undergrowth and ran down to the water, and Wynn was startled to see an ugly animal that very much resembled the pigs that roamed the streets of New York.

Culliford laughed. "It's a river hog, my dear," he said, nudging her forward. They set out on a small dirt path that led upriver. Ferns covered damp hollows and climbed up the trunks of trees to nestle in the crevices and forks of branches, while overhead the spreading crowns of the fan palm and the branching heads of the pandanus with its long tough serrated leaves shaded them from the strong sunlight.

She glanced up once at the call of a bold crow with a large white clerical type of collar and white breast perched on the limb of a teak tree. The nearby sound of wailing made her skin prickle, and as she ducked under a branch, a small glossy brown animal with the face of a fox and large expressive round eyes darted down the end of a branch to stare at her.

She started, but the affectionate look of the animal and its thick soft-looking fur made her curious. The animal was agile, its bushy tail flitting in the air behind it, and must be the lemur she had heard was indigenous to the island. Then the lemur uttered another long melancholy cry and skittered away up the tree branch.

After walking for what must have been a mile, the novelty of the jungle and Wynn's desire to mark their path was overcome by her fatigue. She was hungry and the thought of being alone with the scurrilous pirate and the brown-skinned natives caused her new anxiety. Her body ached and her apathy was such that she could have crouched down on the dirt and stayed there, but Culliford pressed them on.

The path became rocky and steep, and though other creatures darted through the underbrush at the approach of humans, Wynn ceased to care about them. However, in spite of her utter dejection, her eye was caught by the colorful birds that inhabited the river valley — the diving duck of brown plumage and rose-colored beak, the white egret, the heron, and the slaty black parrot that called insults to them as they passed.

As the day wore on, the humidity became stifling. The echo of the falls had been left behind as they climbed higher on the twisting path. Wynn began to despair of ever finding her way out again. Even if she managed to get back to the mouth of the river, she would need a canoe. She could not speak the native tongue, and she had no money to bribe the natives.

They trudged on until her feet and back were nothing but a mass of solid pain, and her arms bled from the scratches of thorny branches that tore through her shirt. Darkness surrounded them, and she assumed that it was because they had travelled deeper into the forest, but when she looked overhead she saw that light no longer peeked through the thick branches and long prickly leaves. She did not know when the natives had lit the torches made of dry grass fixed to the end of bamboos, but it was by their light alone that they now traveled up the hillside.

"Oh," Wynn grunted as she stubbed her toe on a rock protruding from the red soil. Suddenly the fatigue from the day's walk and the lack of food were too much, and she fell into the dirt, unable to move. Although she was afraid Culliford would abuse her or make one of the natives prick her with his spear, she was unable to rouse herself.

"I can't go on," she whispered, ashamed to show weakness, but unable to get up. Voices swam above her as the dust choked her nostrils, and then darkness enshrouded her.

When she came to, daylight was visible above her head, and she lay on a woven straw mat. The torches stood in a semicircle around a small clearing where meat was roasting. At the smell of food, she struggled to sit up. A native dressed in a sacklike garment made of some kind of woven fiber brought her a earthen bowl full of rice. The man had light olive skin, a long straight nose, and the thin lips and high cheekbones that spoke of his Malagasy ancestry.

She nodded her thanks and hungrily gulped down the rice. The same man then brought her a bowl of fruit — pears divested of their spiny covering, and mangoes so luscious they made her mouth water. She tried to look into the man's eyes, but he kept his eyes lowered. Again a wave of hopelessness passed over her as she realized she was alone without friends in a hostile country.

Culliford's approach added to her ill humor. "Feeling better now?" he said.

"I hardly expect you to care much about my comfort," she said.

"On the contrary, my dear. I am trying to make you as comfortable as possible. Damaged goods are no advantage in a negotiation, are they now? I am only sorry that until we reach my stronghold, there is little comfort to be had in these surroundings. However, when we reach my little castle, you will have every luxury you could desire."

She did not answer, but he ordered the bearers to bring her a drink.

"Try this," he said, handing her a flask.

"What is it?"

"Bomboo. A drink of sugar, limes and water, nothing more."

She tasted it hesitantly, and finding it thirst-quenching, swallowed it down.

"There is a stream down there," he said with a glint in his eye, "where you may bathe if you wish. Rakotas will take you."

A native now approached. He had an erect bearing, slightly oblique dark brown eyes and a high, intelligent-looking forehead. On his head was a turban. His chest was bare save for a necklace of crocodile teeth, and there was a brass band around his upper arm. He wore a sarong of scarlet-colored coarse cloth, and his feet were bare but for a brass wire ring on one toe.

"Rakotas is my Hova servant. He was born into slavery because of his parents' debts to the Hova chieftain. But I purchased him."

Rakotas said something in his native language, which sounded soft and musical to Wynn's ears. Something in the slave's proud bearing struck a chord in her, and she was able to smile at him as he planted his long spear of ebony wood into the ground and nodded to her. In spite of the threatening weapon, Wynn took a liking to him.

But then she admonished herself. She must be so delirious and desperate that she sought friendship and sympathy in these hostile surroundings where there was none. But she would at least let him lead her to the water where she could wash her face and as much of her skin as was possible without disrobing.

The tall servant held the branches aside for her as she half slid, half scrambled down the rocky reedy path to the small stream. Large dark blue cuckoos rose in a flurry as her passage disturbed their rest. Ever present were the lemurs crouched above her and leaping from branch to branch.

Rakotas stood with his straight back to her as Wynn dipped her hand into the refreshing water and cooled her parched face and throat. When she was finished, she stumbled back up the bank to where the party had broken camp and were ready to depart. The sun was now pushing back the early morning darkness, and the torches were extinguished.

She groaned at the thought of another day's walk, but she fell in line. At least Culliford left her hands and mouth free, assured she had enough sense not to try to escape into this tangled forest. Now the hills rose steeply, and basalt and granite outcroppings formed steps for them to climb the almost vertical mountains. Still the dense foliage did not recede, and clinging to the hills were tall hardwood trees that rose to considerable heights. A careless misstep would have plunged them to their deaths over precipitous clefts in the hillsides that fell to churning rapids and cataracts far below. Once a wildcat with his handsome stripes crouched above them, but sprang away as they came near.

When she thought her bleeding hands and feet would take her no further, they came out on a level cliff. The sudden parting of trees caused her to look up, and she gasped. For above them, rising atop the dense foliage, was a reddish fortress. The pirate stronghold was built of solid stone and thick beams cut from the hardwood trees of the forest. Dark veins of the hard granite rock revealed quartz that glinted in the sun. It perched on a cliff that fell sharply into the jungle below them, and it looked as if there was no approach other than the path they followed. The place seemed impregnable from below.

As they climbed nearer, she could see the long rolling moorlike hills behind the castle. They were covered with coarse dry grass and lava beds and were separated from the stronghold by a deep gorge that lay to the south. Directly below was the tangled forest which tumbled over the steep slopes, and made her feel truly isolated.

They passed through a wooden gate and then walked across a wooden bridge with a rope railing. The height made Wynn dizzy. Once on the other side, it was only a few steps to the large wooden door which swung open. The natives set their bundles down in the small courtyard, but Wynn, Culliford and some of the pirates who had accompanied them followed Rakotas to another door, which he opened. They stepped into a dark interior.

After adjusting her eyes to the darkness she could see several passageways leading off from the large earthen-floored room with windows so small that only a little light was able to pass through. Culliford spoke to his men, and many of them disappeared down the passageway to their left. Two guards stood next to a door to which Culliford gestured.

When the door opened, Wynn was startled to see a bright, stone-paved courtyard. Blinking in the light, she crossed the courtyard and passed through an arched entryway into a room which made her gasp in surprise. The room, with its hardwood floor and beamed ceiling, was luxuriously furnished. Cushions were scattered around a low teakwood table on which sat a silver tea service and silver bowls laden with exotic tropical fruit. How had they managed to carry the furniture and objets d'art up the steep rocky path through the jungle? she wondered.

"Welcome to my humble dwelling," said Culliford.

He snapped his fingers, and a native woman appeared, her long straight black hair hanging down her back. A cloth of soft green cotton was wrapped around her body and over one shoulder. She approached and bowed to the ground.

"This is Renisoa. Follow her and she will see to your needs. After you have refreshed yourself, perhaps you will join me for some food."

"I don't suppose I have a choice," said Wynn with irritation. And she followed Renisoa through a well-lit corridor into another wing of the odd fortress in which Culliford apparently enjoyed his ill-gotten wealth. Despite her fatigue, she couldn't help but notice the woven hangings and carved idols that decorated the walls and corners of every room through which they passed. They were in sharp contrast to the heavy European furniture upholstered with velvet cushions and tassles of gold. At least the place would offer some comfort, Wynn thought, compared with the jungle floor. But what comfort could there ever be until she was once more restored to the arms of her lover? A sob escaped her as she envisioned his face.

Tears were streaming down her cheeks as Renisoa opened a door that led to a moderately sized room with woven mats covering the walls. "You stay here," the woman said in English.

Chapter Sixteen

When Robert boarded the *Quedah Merchant* the day Culliford took Wynn away, he found William standing on deck and sharing out some more of the spoils with the men. Bales of silks, muslins and various goods were being counted by Samuel and divided into shares, each share being represented by three or four bales and an odd assortment of other goods.

"They've already taken forty pounds of plate and all our provisions from the other ship," he said as Robert approached. "I might as well pay these men what I can from the spoils, and we'll buy provisions with some of the rest. There'll still be enough left to show for the voyage once we put into port at home."

Robert frowned. What William said was true. The men were hard-pressed on so long a voyage with no pay, and it was an act of faith to pay the men something. Legally, the booty belonged to the Crown. But he couldn't think for long about what William was planning to do with the goods. There were more pressing matters.

"That cur Culliford's captured Wynn and her brother," he announced to Kidd and the crew. "We've got to save them."

William looked up from his counting. "Are you sure? But they were with the wounded men."

"Culliford's crew surrounded them. He's probably taken them to his stronghold above Antongil Bay. They've got a head start on us, but if we leave now, we can get to them before they're holed up in that place."

"Look around you, man," said Kidd. "They outnumber us ten to one. And it looks like you're bleeding to death under that rag you've got wrapped around your wrist."

"It's only a flesh wound," said Robert, wincing as he moved his arm.

"How do you propose we go after them, and you wounded? And we can't leave this ship unguarded." Kidd sat down on a bolt of muslin. "A fine kettle of fish, this is."

"Boat approaching," called the watch. Kidd stood and stepped to the railing. "Who goes there?"

"In the King's name, Captain Shaw of the *Joanna*," came the answer. "Request permission to come aboard."

Robert narrowed his gaze. So it was to be the arrest. "Not now," he muttered to himself, clenching his fists.

"Do you want us to hold them off, sir?" asked Abel Owens, the cook, who now doubled as a seaman.

But Kidd, who had never heard of the arrest orders, raised a hand and shook his head. "Nay, let 'em come. We're innocent."

"We can ask for their help to fight Culliford," said Robert.

"Aye," said William. Then he called to the men in the boat, "Permission granted."

Captain Shaw and three of his men came aboard. William and Robert stood before him, as Shaw, eyeing them, cleared his throat. His glance lingered for a moment on Robert, who noticed his curiosity. This was the man Wynn had tricked. Robert frowned as he met the man's stare and then his face cleared as he remembered that the man had behaved decently and Robert need not fight him over Wynn's honor.

Shaw drew himself erect, faced William, unfolded a piece of paper he had in his breast pocket and read from it. "By the authority vested in me I am ordered to pursue and apprehend Captain William Kidd and his first mate, Robert Lamley, and their accomplices whenever they shall arrive," he read. "And likewise secure his ships and all the effects therein, it being their excellencies' the lords justices' intentions that right be done to those who have been injured and robbed by the said Kidd and that he and his associates be prosecuted with the utmost rigor of the law." He lowered the paper. "What have you to say for yourselves?"

"If you have orders to arrest us, then so be it," said William. "But I have been greatly wronged, which I shall prove to their excellencies upon my imminent return to England. I have no quarrel with you, sir, that the ship you stand on is the king's property. As you can see for yourself, though, my crew has deserted and my log has been burned. Nevertheless, I am servant of our dread sovereign, William the Third, and I stand ready to obey his command."

Captain Shaw shifted his weight uncomfortably. In truth, he felt sorry for Captain Kidd, who seemed much more a victim of ill luck than a pirate.

"Perhaps we can ask your help in return for our cooperation," Robert spoke up.

Shaw eyed him curiously.

"There are real pirates in this realm that the king and lords justices would be most pleased to apprehend. I speak in particular of Robert Culliford, who burned our ship and has abducted my fiancée and her brother, relatives of Captain William Kidd's wife. I know where the pirate's stronghold is, and I believe we can overcome them."

Captain Shaw muttered a curse. "You are asking me to ignore my orders and offer my services to the very men I have been sent here to arrest — to go chasing after a girl and her mad brother whom I should have punished anyway? And you want me to put my life at risk while I am doing it!"

"I am asking that, yes, sir," Robert said with a small smile.

Silently Robert watched Captain Shaw, as he stood quietly contemplating the situation. The sun burned down on them, and the air was still laden with the smoke from the night's conflagration. Samuel and the rest of the small crew leaned against the bulwark awaiting orders while the waves gently slapped the hull below them.

Narrowing his eyes, Shaw weighed the alternatives. "Culliford, you say?"

"Aye," said Robert. "The man's wanted in England, I'll warrant. He's half a day ahead of us now, and he'll leave the bay guarded in any case. The best way to them is to sail to the north part of the island. From Diego Bay we climb the hills and cross the moors. It's possible to come upon his hideout from behind."

"How do you know of this?"

"I'm no friend of Culliford's, if that's what you are insinuating. But the sailors in the village, whose tongues are loosened with rum, often give more information than they realize."

"We could pay your expenses, Captain," said William.

"With what? The king's booty?"

William kept silent as Shaw went on. "Supposing we take this Culliford, how do I know you'll come with me afterward?"

"Leave some of your men with the *Quedah Merchant*," said Robert. "That way even if we fail to return, you can take the ship in."

"I'm not sayin' yes, mind you," said Captain Shaw. "And I'll not place my men in unnecessary danger. I made it clear it was you I came for, and so far the pirates have not bothered us. But it might be a service to the Crown to bring in Culliford as well. If you helped, it might, er, help mitigate your charges."

Robert nodded. Such Acts of Grace for pirates who either surrendered by a certain date or turned king's evidence in order to help convict another criminal were often extended to those who had broken the law. Although William remained obdurate about his innocence, Robert was no longer convinced he would be considered innocent by the authorities. If, along with rescuing Wynn, they captured Culliford as well, it could greatly help their circumstances in England.

Aloud he said, "If we're going to swing at the end of a rope in England, we might as well risk our skins saving innocent people who've been abducted through no wrongdoing of their own."

"All right," Captain Shaw finally said. "I'll leave twenty men here to guard your ship. You come to my cabin and we'll discuss it." He turned and called to the rest of the party, and some of his men came on board. Then Robert and William descended with Captain Shaw into the boat to return to the *Joanna*.

James's head throbbed violently and he winced as he turned on the straw mat. A hand moved a moist cloth over his forehead, and then something was placed between his lips. He felt a cool fruity liquid seep between his lips, and he drank thirstily.

Where was he? The last he remembered was waking up in the dark hold of the ship. But after that everything went black again. Was he still in the hold? The darkness seemed to confirm it, but he didn't feel the rocking of the ship. Could he be on solid ground? And beneath his shirt he could feel the prickles of some kind of straw mat against his back.

Then a voice uttered words that sounded like "Keep still," but the voice had a floating, fluid sound, and he realized that whoever was with him spoke English with a heavy accent he had never heard before.

"Where?" he began, but two cool fingers were pressed to his lips.

"Do not speak," came the voice, which he now recognized was a woman's. He tried to adjust his eyes to the darkness, and from a crack of sunlight that came into the far side of the room around what looked like a bamboo screen, he now focused on a woman kneeling by him. She was nearly as dark as the shadows that surrounded them, but he could see that she had black hair that fell straight down in front of her.

He blinked his eyes and stared at her. She wore a band of gold around her forehead and around her throat. Then James lay his head back and closed his eyes again. He must be dreaming. But when he inhaled, the sweet scent of perfume wafted over his nostrils.

"Do you feel better?" asked the woman.

He grunted. "Where am I?"

"You remember nothing?" came the low melodious voice.

"I remember being tied up in the ship; then, oh yes, I was given something to eat; then," he rolled his head from side to side, "nothing."

She brushed her fingers across his cheek. "You were drugged. The bearers brought you up the mountain in a palanquin."

He grunted again. He did remember dreaming that he heard a waterfall and then crying sound, like a person or an animal in distress. Then it all began to come back to him. "Culliford?" he asked. "I am his prisoner?"

It seemed to him the woman's eyes sparkled. "That is right."

He turned his head to look at her. "Who are you? And where is my sister?"

"Ha," said the woman, moving her arm so that a bracelet she wore jangled near him. "If your sister is that skinny pale white woman who came here dressed as a man, she is probably with my master. He has taken a liking to her."

James tried to rouse himself, but she put a hand on his chest and pressed him back onto the mat. "Do not worry. He will not hurt her. Besides using her for his own amusement, he wishes to keep her as a hostage. He does not harm his hostages. For then they are of no use to him to exchange for the riches he is so greedy for."

"Oh," he said, falling back onto the mat. Never before had he felt so weak, and even if his sister had been in some danger, he did not think he could get up to try to help her. The soporific drug must not have completely worn off.

White teeth gleamed against red lips. "And you will be my hostage."

"What?"

She jangled her bracelet again. "For as long as your sister keeps the master occupied, I have nothing to do. He is not thinking of me. Do you know what I speak of?"

He tried to turn his head to look into her eyes. "You?"

"I was Culliford's mistress." She curled her lip. "Now he has no use for me." Her black eyes flamed with anger as she told James her story. "My father was a Hova king, and Culliford paid my family much gold for me."

"But surely if you were a king's daughter, your family would not sell you?"

"I am the younger daughter. There was no one worthy of me, and my family was greatly in need of money. Our villages have fallen upon many hard times. So I was sold."

"I see," said James. He didn't, but he was in too much pain to think it over.

"Here," she said. "Drink this." And she lifted a bowl to his lips and poured more of the fruity liquid into his mouth. "I have dressed your wounds. You will heal. And then . . ." She smiled suggestively and ran her hands over his face and down his chest.

In spite of his weak condition, James felt a slight arousal in his loins. He looked at the graceful arm, the high cheekbones, the aquiline nose and the curved lips. But then he frowned. Evidently, in spite of the slave princess's ministrations, they were in a tight spot.

"We must get out of here," he mumbled, half to himself. "Our friends — oh," he groaned as pain shot through his head.

"Shhh," she said. "I must go. I will return."

"My sister . . ."

Her mouth twisted in derision. "Do not worry about your sister."

And she was gone.

Princess Andriva parted the damask curtains that led to the inner chamber of Culliford's bedroom. She crossed the soft Persian carpet to the velvet-covered, mahogany daybed on which her master reclined.

"You sent for me?" she asked, as she bowed to touch her forehead to his feet.

He reached for a handful of her black hair and pulled her closer, looking into her liquid brown eyes.

"What do you wish, my master?"

"Hmph," he growled, then pushed her away. "I wanted to warn you," he said.

She gazed at him, a question in her eyes.

"I have heard that you have expressed interest in a certain yellow-headed prisoner."

"A prisoner?"

He grabbed her hair again, this time jerking her head backward. "You know what prisoner I am talking about. The one the bearers brought up the mountain last night. Do not take too much interest in him, do you understand?"

She lowered her eyes, her long dark lashes quivering. "Master, you know that I do not look at any other man. He is nothing compared to my loyalty to you. I am your servant. And you possess my heart."

He leaned back, seemingly more satisfied. "I know the attraction that lion-haired men have for you, even though you try to hide it from me. But do not let your secret cravings get the better of you. I have special plans for the two prisoners, and I do not want anyone to interfere with them until I am ready."

Andriva raised her head proudly. "And you, my master? Do you not also have a weakness for white skin and eyes blue like the sea upon which you sail?"

His eyes flickered for a moment, and his lip curled as he reached for her. She moved closer, holding his eyes with her own. "I too may look at blue eyes, but there are no eyes with the power of yours, master."

He trailed a finger across her chin. "Yes, that is as it should be." Then he lowered his hand and motioned her to leave him. "Leave me now; I must think."

After sleeping most of the next day, Wynn submitted to the ministrations of the serving woman, Renisoa. She had bathed in scented water and now wore a light blue silken lamba, loose folds of material wound around her body and across one arm. Renisoa had brushed her hair and let it fluff out from her head, as it was not long enough to braid. Then she put a single orchid over Wynn's right ear.

Breathing in the refreshing scent from the perfume Renisoa sprinkled over her, Wynn made her wants known by gestures as the serving woman spoke little English. As the sun sank over the moors behind them, Renisoa beckoned Wynn to follow her.

She steeled herself for what she imagined was going to be an interview with Culliford, but her skin felt clammy with fear as she followed her serving woman through the stone-paved corridors of the stronghold. She cast about her for a weapon or a possible exit, but she had no way to conceal anything very large on her person, and all the doors were guarded by villainous-looking pirates or half-naked Malagasy carrying spears and shields.

As they turned a corner and approached a heavy teakwood door, she saw an olive-skinned woman with long shiny black hair slip through the door and close it behind her. Her arms were bare except for gold bracelets, and she wore gold at her throat and across her forehead. She paused as Wynn approached, and Wynn shivered at the woman's malevolent stare. She uttered a few words in Malagasy to Renisoa, and then she disappeared down a dark corridor.

Wynn stepped into an airy room. Bamboo shades had been raised to allow the breezes to waft across it, and the walls were hung with damask. Cushions were thrown about the corners, and Culliford sat before a table laden with silver bowls of grapes, guavas, and a carafe.

"Ah," he said. "You look refreshed." His eyes wandered over her figure, which the lamba covered modestly except for the shoulders.

She frowned under his gaze as he lifted a piece of fruit. "Come, you must be hungry. May I tempt you with a slice of orange?"

She did not answer but walked forward and selected her own piece of fruit, a pear, which she bit into. In truth, she was starving, not having eaten since Renisoa had brought her some rice and tea at midday. She sat down in a mahogany chair opposite him, avoiding his eyes and concentrating on the food.

The door opened and two natives entered, placed trays of steaming food before them and then left. She breathed in the odor of curry, and her stomach growled.

Culliford laughed. "I hope you enjoy your repast," he said as he poured a goblet full of wine and offered it to her.

She refused it, wanting to keep her head clear, but she ate all the food on her plate, the spicy curry making her eyes water. Finally, revived by the food, she sat back studying the man opposite her. He clapped his hands and several natives entered from the balcony. They carried musical instruments made from the strong outer fiber of bamboo stretched over hardwood bows. The musicians sat down and began playing the stringed instruments, and Wynn was surprised at the pleasing sound — like the tones from a guitar.

Culliford took another sip of wine. She noticed that his lids drooped and his words were slurred. "And so, do you not find your surroundings pleasing?" he asked.

"I do not find anything at all pleasing about my present circumstances," she said. "It is never pleasing to find oneself a prisoner."

"But you must not think of yourself in that way," he

countered. "Have I not said that you are my guest? Are you not provided with everything you need for your comfort?"

"What does comfort matter if I am forced to remain here away from my . . . friends," she said. "And what have you done with my brother?"

"If I said you could leave, where would you go? You yourself have pointed out that your friends, as you call them, are not waiting for you. You are miles from any port, surrounded by jungle. Are you not better off here with me for the moment?"

She ignored his question. "How long do you intend to keep me here?"

"Ha," he said. "Until the notorious Captain Kidd sees things my way and offers to ransom you with his Moorish prize and serve under me."

"Why should you want him to serve with you?"

"He is an able captain, for all his foolish mistakes on this voyage of his. He knows these waters, and I can use his knowledge."

It was on the tip of her tongue to ask that if William would serve Culliford, mightn't he free Robert and herself? But then she realized with shame that Robert would never desert his captain, and she herself could never ask William to make such a sacrifice. It was only her love for Robert that drove her to such desperate thoughts.

Instead she said, "You waste your time, sir. The booty he has possession of belongs to the Crown, and he'll not surrender it. Besides, I am nothing to him but a poor relation. Do you think he'll risk his reputation and his life for the likes of me? Think again, Captain."

Culliford studied her, rubbing his chin. "He is a man of honor. I've no doubt he'll seek me out to avenge the death of his first mate."

Wynn stared at him, not fully absorbing his words at first. When she did, the color drained from her face. "You're lying," she said.

Culliford looked at her with mock sympathy. "I am sorry I had to tell you."

"No," she said. She stood, clenching her hands. "You lie. He was standing on the beach. You only hit him in the shoulder."

But Culliford shook his head. "My men followed him when he tried to reach his boat after that. They put an end to him. A pity, I am sure, even though the man was on the wrong side of things."

"But you said on the ship . . ."

"I did not know then. It was later that my men reported to me."

"Then they could be mistaken." Robert couldn't be dead, she thought fiercely. Her mind simply refused to take it in. She had seen him raise his arm, then one of the pirates had fired. He had dropped his pistol, but he had not fallen, he had only grabbed his arm with the other hand. Even though tears blurred her vision her mind kept insisting Culliford was lying.

Through her tears, she saw Culliford yawn and then walk over to the cushions that lay at the edge of a Persion rug. He slumped down on them and lazily patted the cushion beside him.

"Come now. I will do what I can to make you forget him." And his eyelids drooped as his hand fell limp. The musicians seemed to know when their presence was no longer wanted and moved silently through the door by the balcony. Culliford mumbled something, his eyes closed. Finally his head lolled to one side and he slept.

Puzzled, Wynn knelt and examined him. He was sound asleep. She looked toward the table, and her eye fell on the empty wine goblet. She walked over to it and lifted it to her nostrils. She could smell nothing, but she knew that it would have been possible to disguise a drug. But who would have done this?

Then, a picture of the olive-skinned woman with the gold bracelets came into her mind. She remembered the flashing dark eyes filled with hatred. Now she realized what she had seen in the woman's eyes. Jealousy. She sat down on the mahogany chair, sighing at her reprieve. Apparently Culliford had a native mistress who had a possessive streak.

She wiped away her tears, shut her eyes, and uttered a prayer for Robert's life. It was not possible that he was dead, she thought, for she would feel it if he were. Pulling herself up, she tiptoed to the door. She would try to find out if James were here, and together they might be able to devise a way to escape.

Andriva hurried down the twisting passageway to the prisoners' quarters. She had bribed the guards to keep James in a room where she could reach him instead of in the dungeon, which stank of death.

When she entered his room, he was sitting up on his mat. She saw that he had eaten the food she had sent and partaken of the wine, and she was pleased for it meant he was recovering.

Now she would have her revenge. She sent the guards outside and shut the door behind them. They would not bother her, nor would Culliford, for she had drugged his wine.

"You are better?" she asked James in her silky singsong voice.

He looked at her with interest. "I am better," he answered as she came and sat next to him, placing her hand on his forehead. Grabbing her hand, he kissed the palm of it, and she threw back her head, her dark hair falling in ripples over her olive shoulders as she laughed deep in her throat.

"Tell me," he said, "how did you learn English?"

She gave him a teasing look. "Other white men came to our village before Culliford. One found he liked the life among our people. He taught me certain things." James was sure the man had taught her more than English.

She slipped her little finger between his teeth as she moved to stretch her legs out on the mat next to him. He reached around her waist, his hands caressing her through the loose folds of her lamba. And she gazed upward, her dark eyes glittering as he rolled her onto her back. As his hand traveled up the silky skin of her arm, he lowered his mouth to hers, running his tongue over her white teeth, and then she parted them to take a tiny nip at his tongue.

Already, his groin bulged with desire as she moved her hips under him, and he lifted his head to gaze at the satiny skin showing where the folds of material covering her had loosened. He placed a hand on one of her breasts even as her dextrous fingers tugged at his waist and she ran her fingers under his shirt, gingerly touching his back. He slipped a thumb into the soft material to lower it over her silky mounds, and she arched her head back, her black hair spreading around her in a fan. The cloth loosened further, and with a shake of her shoulders, the lamba fell away, revealing ripe breasts tipped with dark nipples.

He took one of them in his mouth as she plunged a hand into his breeches, reaching for his groin. He unfastened the buttons on his pants, giving her access to his erect organ. Then he applied his mouth to her breasts again as she writhed, pushing her breasts up to him. She pulled his breeches lower, and he shrugged out of them, lying naked on top of her. Then she rolled over so that she straddled him. Her lamba had fallen to her hips and he caught a glimpse of her navel between her slightly protruding hip bones. He caressed the curve of her thighs, finally cupping his hand between her legs as she lay atop him, her breasts crushed against his chest.

Then she lifted her hips slightly so that he could move his hand inside her lamba to touch her moist center with the tips of his fingers. Breathing in the scent of her, he massaged her, causing her to moan in excitement. Then she reached for his organ with her hands and, sitting upright, placed him inside her. Her long black hair covered her breasts except for the pointed tips that pierced the dark tresses.

Groaning with the pleasure of her movements as she swayed above him, James reached for her shoulders, bringing her face toward him so their mouths met in hurried excitement. Then, frenzied, she began to quiver, and he thrust his hips upward again and again, as she pushed against his shaft. She clawed at his shoulders with her long nails while he held her to him, thrusting more quickly and deeply, his passion building, perspiration breaking out over his skin in the airless room.

Then with one final thrust, he spent himself, crying out in pleasure. She panted against him as she exhaled sharply. For a moment she clung to him, and then she rolled to the side.

He felt light-headed after the exertion, for he was still not completely recovered from his wounds. His hand moved once over the breast that fell against him, and then he slept, unaware of the satisfied look she gave him. She had gotten what she desired and, at the same time, had succeeded in preventing Culliford from touching the white woman. The thought pleased her.

Muttering in her native tongue, she gathered her lamba about her. She was not yet finished with Culliford, who would live to regret the day he bought her for a slave, she vowed.

Chapter Seventeen

Wynn came to the end of a corridor where three steps led down to another passageway. She knew it would not be long before someone noticed she had slipped away, so she needed to make the best of her opportunity. She reasoned that if James had been brought to the castle, he was probably being kept in some wing away from her quarters to prevent them from communicating.

But as she came to the end of the passage and turned, she came face to face with two natives standing with their arms crossed and their backs against a large door. Their spears and shields leaned against the wall.

A swarthy man in sailor's garb roused himself from his squatting position in the corner. "Well, what's the little lady doin' this far from her chambers?"

Wynn tried to think of a quick explanation. But she decided it was better to tell a half-truth in hopes that her punishment would be lighter if she were honest. "I was trying to find my way back to my quarters. Captain Culliford fell asleep and neglected to provide me with an escort."

The pirate grabbed her elbow in a manner that made her wince. He led her back the way she had come, but not before the door opened behind the two native guards, and, to Wynn's surprise, Culliford's mistress slipped out. She glanced past the woman in the soft lamba through the opening before the door closed.

James lay, to all appearances, sleeping on a straw mat. One arm was thrown over his head and his torso was bare. Only a piece of linen covered his form from the hips down. Wynn looked quickly at the woman who had emerged from the room. The fiery black eyes which stared back at Wynn seemed less antagonistic, although the expression was still haughty. Wynn flushed at the implications.

"My brother," she said to the woman, not knowing whether or not she spoke English. "Is he all right?"

The woman studied her for a long moment before she answered. Then she held her head erect, looking through slightly lowered lids as she said in a melodious, accented voice, "His wounds are healing." Then she spoke sharply to the pirate who held Wynn by the elbow.

"Take her away. She is not allowed in this quarter." Then the woman went in the other direction, and the pirate led Wynn back through the dark corridors toward her room. They passed many heavy doors, and Wynn still wondered which might offer escape. She wondered, too, at the comment that there was only one approach to the stronghold. There must be a way across the gorge to the moors behind them. But then, she realized with discouragement, she was probably so desperate she was grasping at straws. One thing at least, James was here, and he was alive.

Still, she had no way to get a message to him, and there was no guarantee that they could get out. Roughly twisting her arm, the pirate shoved her into her room, shutting the door, and bolting it from the outside.

After some time Renisoa appeared with a goblet of wine, which Wynn again refused, remembering the sleeping draught that must have found its way into Culliford's drink. After the serving girl left, Wynn paced the small room, kicking a cushion across the floor in frustration.

Oh Robert, she thought in desperation, *where are you?* And she lay down on her mat to try to rest. From the jungle came a cacophony of sounds. The lemurs cried, and there was a steady beat of drums from a distant village. Finally, physical and emotional exhaustion overtook her, and she slept deeply.

The sun was a round shimmering disk rising over the tinted water as the *Joanna* rounded Madagascar's northern tip. Although they had left under cover of darkness, Robert did not underestimate Culliford's cleverness, and they had stayed well out to sea in order to avoid any spies he might have posted. Finally they came to the Bay of Diego, a large natural harbor cut into the northern coast of Madagascar. Here, where ships put in on the main route to India, the *Joanna* would anchor, and the men designated to go ashore would provision themselves for the march into the mountainous hinterland.

Robert scanned the sandy beaches, where the low-spreading foliage was punctuated by the tall, graceful filao tree with its fine leaves. The fan palms cast their shade along the shores, and the air was heavy with gathering moisture. Soon the rains would break, and with them the monsoons would reverse direction. If they could get away from here, the blessed winds would blow them around the Cape and into the Atlantic. He turned from where he stood on the quarterdeck and watched as Captain Shaw tipped his ensign to a merchantman. Even though he and William were technically under arrest, they had sworn on their honor not to try to outrun Captain Shaw in return for his help to try to capture Culliford and rescue Wynn and James.

William hoped the venture would win back some of their lost prestige so that the lords justices would look with favor on them when they arrived home. But their honor mattered little to Robert at the moment. He was merely intent on reaching Culliford, for he dared not dwell for long on what ravages the cur might be inflicting upon his beloved.

Wynn was sure that Andriva's jealousy of Culliford would help to protect her virtue. As she lay on her straw mat listening to the jungle sounds she began to formulate an idea. When she had glimpsed her brother lying half-naked in his quarters after the mysterious woman departed, she had guessed what had taken place in his room. She was no longer a naive girl and the thought brought a smile to her lips. Women had always fancied James, commenting on his angelic looks even when he was a young boy, and Wynn had no doubt that he took advantage of his ability to twist women around his little finger.

If Culliford's mistress was attracted to him, she might be the key to their escape. For if they were to escape, they would need help. Wynn suspected the woman hated her because Wynn posed a threat to her position with Culliford. But if she could show her she had no desire to remain with the pirate, perhaps she could persuade the woman to help them.

But escape to where? They would have to get down the mountains, and then they would need a boat. Even if they made their way back to St. Mary's, it was doubtful that Robert and William would still be there. But Wynn refused to consider the possible dangers they might have to face between here and their salvation. The only alternative was to stay, and that was unthinkable.

Culliford had said he planned to use her as a hostage, but she doubted William would ever surrender to the pirate. He was already on shaky ground in the eyes of his backers, and such a move would be his doom. James and she would have to get out of this situation by themselves, and then try to send word to Robert and William.

Wynn sat up and put her feet on the cool stone floor. She must get Renisoa to take her to Culliford's mistress. Perhaps she could even send a note to James, for he probably did not even know she was here. Surely if the woman had enough power in this pirate's den to administer sleeping draughts and visit prisoners unhindered, she could lead them out of the stronghold and safely down to the bay. And they would pay her later for the help. If Wynn was right, the beautiful native woman would not say no to the promise of gold and jewels, fine silks and spices.

Crossing the room, Wynn knocked on the door and called out Renisoa's name. Although the native guard on the other side grunted, she did not know if Renisoa had heard her or not.

Andriva meticulously braided her hair, and with the help of a slave carefully wound it around her head. Then she wrapped a wine-colored silk lamba around her body. Humming to herself, she then replaced the gold bracelets on her arms. She felt sated with sexual pleasure, but sweeter even than her physical satisfaction was the thought of her revenge.

She suspected that for some time Culliford had been growing tired of her. No longer did she have the power over him that she had once had. No longer did he bring her ivory combs, blood-red rubies or perfumes from India. He had been restless of late, desiring new horizons, and now he had the white woman. Whether he had decided to keep Andriva or not, she did not know, but one thing she swore: She would not stand by and become a serving woman to the favored mistress. Nor would she be unceremoniously handed back to her tribe. And such were the only alternatives for a Hova princess slave who had fallen from favor.

Andriva picked up a long silver dagger, the metal gleaming in the moonlight that spilled into the room from the high windows facing over the sharp cliff of the gorge to the west of the stronghold. She smiled as she ran her finger carefully along the sharp blade, and then she laughed — a low throaty sound meant for no one's ears but her own. She waved an arc in the air with the dagger, vowing that the sharp metal would soon cut into white skin.

There was a soft knock on her door. She turned as her slave opened the door and Renisoa entered, bowing her head to the ground in front of the favored mistress.

"What is it?" Andriva asked in Malagasy.

"The white woman," answered Renisoa. "She wishes to see you. I did not know if you would come."

Andriva curled her lip in a satisfied smile. She placed the blade on the low table in front of her, her finger lingering on its point.

"That is good. You did well to come to me. I will see her tomorrow night." She knew what the white woman wanted to ask of her, and it would be well to make her wait.

The day passed slowly for Wynn. Renisoa took her out to a balcony for some air at midday, but she refused to respond to Wynn's pleas for help. Again in the evening

Wynn prepared to dine with Culliford. She was certain he would be angry that he had missed his opportunity the previous evening, and she feared the consequences. She thought of James. When she had tried to persuade Renisoa to take him a message, she had only gazed steadily at Wynn as if she did not understand. When Wynn had asked her if she had taken her message to the beautiful native woman they had seen in the corridor, she had been met with equally dubious looks, and after hours of getting no answer at all, Wynn wanted to cry from frustration.

Sometimes Wynn suspected that her waiting woman knew more English than she let on, but then she berated herself for thinking that Renisoa would ever be willing to risk being killed because she had helped the prisoners. She had probably never known any other world but the island, and why would she want to give up her position in Culliford's household for the harder life in the jungle? Wynn decided she would never be able to deduce the type of mind that lay behind Renisoa's modest countenance.

Now she tried to think of some measure to prevent the inevitable confrontation with Culliford, but she could think of none. She had to resign herself to the fact that she would, indeed, be forced to see him.

She turned around as the door opened and, to her surprise, two bearers carried in a tray of food and placed it before her on a low table. She understood by their gestures that it was meant for her. They had just left when she looked up to see Culliford's native mistress standing inside the door. Wynn had not heard her enter.

Andriva spoke in the same melodious tone of voice Wynn had become accustomed to in the Malagasy speech of Renisoa. But this woman's voice had a sharper tone to it, and she evidently still considered Wynn an opponent. She had to make this woman understand that they were both on the same side, that they both wanted the same thing.

"You wanted to see the princess Andriva," she said, moving with a silent step farther into the room. "Why?"

Wynn stepped forward to meet her and spoke in a low voice. She did not know if she could trust this woman who called herself by the strange-sounding name, but she had to take the risk.

"I want your help," she said. "I can pay you."

Andriva held her head high, and Wynn could see by her bearing that this woman was not a common slave. "What could you pay me with? What could you possibly possess that I do not already have?"

Wynn maintained her gaze, matching the other woman's haughty tone with one of confidence. "If you will help us get to our ship, you will be rewarded from the treasure that rides in the hold."

"Treasure?" Andriva's eyes became round, and she eyed Wynn curiously. Still, her proud attitude wore on Wynn's patience. She wanted to shake the straight squared shoulders and make the woman cooperate. She had no time for this queenly conversation, but she reminded herself that to be insistent would ruin any chance she had. She had to appeal to this woman's desires, and she hoped fervently that the noble princess was as greedy as she was jealous of her position as the pirate's favorite.

But to Wynn's surprise Andriva narrowed her eyes and said, "I might help you. But if I do, I will go with you. For if I am caught, do you know what Culliford would do to me?" And she gestured with her fingers across her throat. "He gives no mercy to traitors."

"But why would you want to leave him?" asked Wynn, puzzled.

"Because he no longer favors me. My fate here is

worse than death. I would be made to serve another mistress such as yourself." And she spat upon the floor, causing Wynn to step back, startled at her vehemence.

"But where will you go?"

Now Andriva drew herself up. "My father was a Hova chieftain. He used to rule this side of the island." Then her tone filled with bitterness. "Then the pirates overran the hills, demanding tribute from my father and other tribes. My father offered me to Culliford and I was forced to serve him."

She flung her dark hair back over her shoulders. "I was treated well at first. He gave me pretty things and I ruled the household. He was pleased that I knew some of his language and he made me practice it. He treated me well, until now." And she turned her flashing eyes on Wynn.

Wynn pretended not to understand her meaning and asked, "What has happened now?"

"He is no longer satisfied with his little kingdom. He wants more. He makes plans to subdue the Sakalava kings on the western shores of the island. He seeks more wealth, more power." She narrowed her eyes. "More women. No longer will I rule."

Wynn nodded, her pulse racing. She had not thought it would be so easy to obtain Andriva's help, but the woman's dissatisfaction was working to her benefit. Then her eyes widened as Andriva lifted the silver dagger from the folds of her lamba. Frightened, Wynn stepped back, thinking the woman meant to use the weapon on her.

But then she saw the gleam of relish in the other woman's eyes as she brought the blade up before her eyes. "I will use this," she said, "on him."

Chills ran down Wynn's spine even though she knew she herself might be forced to plunge such a weapon into Culliford if it meant saving her own skin. She was grateful that Andriva's hatred was turned toward the unsuspecting pirate captain and not herself.

"If he no longer desires me for his paramour, I will see that he has no one else."

Wynn swallowed as she contemplated the gleam in Andriva's eyes. The woman must be half mad, she thought, still not totally reassured that she would not turn the blade on her at the slightest provocation.

Finding her voice, she asked, "When will we leave this place?"

Andriva hid the blade in the folds of her lamba once more and whispered harshly, "Tomorrow night. I will come for you."

"My brother?"

Wynn did not miss the triumphant look that passed over Andriva's face as she said, "Do not worry about your brother. He will be waiting for you." And she disappeared, closing the door behind her.

Wynn pounded her fist on the bolted door, but she was still a prisoner. She pressed her forehead to the back of the door and sighed. How could she trust the vengeful woman? And yet, what choice did she have?

She turned back to the steaming dish of rice that waited on the table, deciding that she might as well eat, for once in the jungle, even with Andriva's knowledge of the country, they could not depend on finding nourishing food. Supposing Andriva wanted only to get rid of them and left them in the forest on their own? Forcing this frightening thought out of her mind, she swallowed the nourishing food.

Culliford did not send for her, and after she had eaten her fill, she was left alone. She examined the room for another way out, but there was none. The high small windows looked down on a sheer wall of rock that dropped for at least forty feet to the dense foliage that grew out of the steep hills below.

The long night stretched interminably, filled with thoughts that crowded into her mind. She thought of Robert's face, his touch, but such memories made her cry softly to herself. She was sure he was not dead, but he might be hurt, and it tortured her that she could not now be with him to take care of him. Still Culliford's words about his death caused an ugly doubt that threatened to overwhelm her.

More than once she sat up, thinking she heard voices or footsteps. But the sounds, quickly mixed with the jungle noises, were muffled. Once she thought she heard the sharp report of a rifle, but then she decided it was only the sudden beat of a ceremonial drum in a distant village. Finally, toward dawn, she slept.

When she awoke, light was streaming through the tiny windows. She had dreamed that she was on the ship, and the windows were the portholes letting in the morning light and salt spray. But then she felt the itchy mat beneath her, and her heart filled with the desolation she was becoming accustomed to. She wondered suddenly if Culliford kept other prisoners locked away in these dark rooms that reminded her so much of the hold of a ship.

When Renisoa came, she plied the woman with questions, but she was met with the same stoic glances. Not wanting to arouse the woman's suspicion, she fell silent as the woman brushed her hair.

The day crawled forward, and Wynn, with nothing to occupy her, tried to identify the sounds that came to her through the closed door. When she grew tired of that, she tried to imagine how Robert and William might plan a rescue. But would they know where Culliford had brought James and her? She gave a sob as she thought that they might now be sailing around the Cape. But surely they could not have departed, for the monsoons had not yet begun.

Sometimes the sky was so leaden it appeared that gathering rains would soon break. But the air remained heavy, and it did not rain.

She longed for darkness, while, at the same time, she feared it. What if Andriva did not keep her word? What if she had only raised her hopes in order to laugh at Wynn's disappointment?

When Renisoa brought her food at midday, Wynn had to force herself to eat, even though she told herself she needed the sustenance. But her stomach remained knotted with anxiety.

The hours passed, and Wynn paced the floor nervously. How late would Andriva come? Would Wynn have to see Culliford first? Surely Andriva would prevent that if she could. Then a chill passed down Wynn's spine as she remembered what Andriva planned to do with the dagger. Perhaps she would carry out her revenge before she came for them.

The sun had lowered when the door opened. Wynn had lain down on the mat to stare apathetically at the ceiling, and now she turned her head to see someone enter clothed in a dark brown lamba with a hood that covered most of her face. Wynn sat up, suddenly realizing that the torture of waiting was finally over.

"Put this on," said Andriva in a hoarse whisper, handing Wynn a garment similar to the one she wore.

Wynn got up and hastily donned the clothing over her light lamba. Then Andriva handed her some soft leather shoes. "The walking will be difficult," she said.

When Wynn was dressed, they walked to the door, where Andriva peered out. She whispered, "Follow me. We must move quickly, and once we are out of the fortress we cannot come back. When they discover our absence, we will be followed."

"The guards?" Wynn asked, remembering the men in front of James's quarters.

"They have been bribed."

Wynn saw the dagger gleam in Andriva's hands, and the sight of the weapon made her tremble. The dagger, which ought to bring comfort, still frightened Wynn as she envisioned it being turned against her. If only Andriva was telling the truth.

She followed Andriva quickly along the dark passageways lit by torches angling out from the walls. She held the cloth of her garment in her hands to avoid tripping on the rough stone floors. Finally they turned in the passageway and descended three steps, and Wynn thought she recognized the door to James's room. But the guards were not at their stations. She experienced a glimmer of relief, as she realized that perhaps the native woman spoke the truth.

Andriva unlocked the door, motioned Wynn in and then passed through. It took a moment for her eyes to adjust to the semidarkness, but in the moonlight spilling from the tiny windows set into the high stone walls, she saw a figure move, and then James threw a hood back from his head and laughed.

"James," she whispered as he came forward to squeeze her arms. "I was so worried."

"Me too, Sis," he said with obvious relief in his voice. Then he held her away from him to look at her, and Wynn saw the old familiar twinkle in his eye.

But Andriva hurried them along. "Come," she said. James pulled the hood up to cover his blond hair, and when Andriva motioned to them, they slipped into the corridor. In a few steps they came to a door that led into a courtyard, and, crossing that, they passed through another door, which Andriva opened with a key.

Wynn held her breath as they hurried along a passage that seemed to slope downward for some distance. Finally they came to an outer door. This too was locked, but the resourceful Hova princess possessed the key for this door as well.

They no sooner closed the door behind them, than a

cry went up from within the compound. Wynn's heart lurched. They had been missed.

"Hurry," said Andriva. "Down this path." She led the way through some thick underbrush down a steep, narrow, rocky path. They hurried on, yanking their cloaks away from the barbed branches that grabbed at them. Wynn slipped and cried out as her head hit a rock, and she felt her arm twist beneath her. James helped her up as Andriva called for them to hurry, and soon they were making better progress.

Once when Wynn glanced back, she could see torches wavering on the slopes above them. She could hear orders being shouted, and even though they were in Malagasy, she could tell from their tone that there was confusion as to which direction the fugitives had taken.

"Stop," hissed Andriva, and they drew up behind her. She parted some branches, and Wynn gasped.

"Good God," said James as they gazed into the yawning depths of a bottomless gorge. On the other side, the bright moonlight lit the rolling moors.

"How do we get across?" said James.

"There." Andriva pointed farther to the left to a rope bridge swinging in the moonlight.

"Great Heavens," James swore, and Wynn felt her stomach lurch into her throat.

"They will think we've taken it, but we will go this way," Andriva hissed to them, and she plunged into the depths of the jungle again.

Wynn cast another glance at the bridge to the moorlands before she followed James and Andriva. For a brief moment, she thought she saw someone moving out on the bridge. But then James whispered, "Hurry Wynn," and she followed.

They knelt in a deep recess, completely covered by branches and long spiky leaves, where they could see the torches of the pirates and their native guides winding a trail down the mountain toward the gorge. Shouts echoed across the cavernous gorge as both pirates and natives followed in confused pursuit.

"Do not move," whispered Andriva. From the hollow where they hunched, they could see nothing except an occasional flare of light between the leaves, but they were well hidden. Wynn nestled against a large tree root with James crouched in front of her, his head covered with the dark hood. Indeed it was so dark that if she had not known of her companions' presence, she would have thought she was alone.

Now she heard the thrashing of branches as the pursuers came nearer. Finally she heard Culliford's voice raised, as natives cut a path ever closer.

Her heart hammered as she heard them pass only a few feet from them to take the bridge. Mightn't the natives know of this hideout? If Andriva knew of it, it stood to reason that others knew as well.

But the pirates took to the bridge, and then the sound of a pistol shattered the night. A hideous cry came from a man who had been hit, and Wynn shut her eyes, feeling as if she herself had taken the pistol's ball. She clutched James's shoulder. The man's horrible scream faded away as if he were falling into the gorge, and then for a moment all was quiet.

Then lights flared from the direction of the bridge, and there were more pistol reports, and after several seconds Wynn came to the same realization that James voiced.

"Someone's firing from the other side," he whispered.

Cries and yells now came from across the gorge, and Wynn leaned forward to hear better. From the sounds, she deduced that most of the pirates had been either on the bridge or had reached the other side by the time the firing had started. The natives had run back to this side to take cover.

Before they could ponder what had happened, Andriva said, "Now, while they are fighting, we must move quickly." And she roused them to pass through the branches she held aside and take a jagged rocky path into the depths of the jungle. Wynn lost all sense of time as she doggedly followed Andriva. Finally they came to a stream, the moonlight glancing off the silver rushing water.

The current was so strong, Wynn wondered how they would get across, but Andriva pointed to some stepping stones. Lifting her garments, she stepped across, waiting on the opposite bank as Wynn prepared to follow her.

A shot rang out above them, and Andriva screamed, her dagger clattering onto the rocks as she fell face-downward into the water.

Wynn gasped as James made across the rocks to the other side, lifted Andriva's lifeless form and then dropped it back into the water. Then he retrieved the dagger. Wynn did not want to be left alone on this side of the stream with the pirates above her, for they had obviously discovered their trail. Pulling up the hem of her clothing she ran across on the stones as James crouched on the opposite bank waiting for her, the dagger clasped in his right hand.

"Run!" he said as she reached the bank and fled past him.

Chapter Eighteen

Wynn and James tore into the jungle, blind fear propelling them onward. Wynn had no time to grieve at the horror of Andriva's death, for primitive instincts for survival drove her forward. Branches tore at them as they left behind the sounds of shouts and shots ringing out, until total darkness surrounded them once again.

Finally James came to a stop, Wynn bumping up against him. "Listen," he said.

At first she could hear nothing but the sound of her own heart pounding in her ears, but gradually her breathing subsided, and she stood quietly, straining to hear in the darkness. She heard nothing. "Why aren't they following?" she asked in a hushed voice.

"Don't know." She could hear James's heavy breathing beside her.

"Andriva?"

"The ball from the pistol killed her."

Wynn could not sort out her emotions. Violent death was horrible, certainly, but as she hardly knew the woman she found it difficult to feel anything but incredulity at the events surrounding them. Then she remembered the intimacies that James must have had with the woman, and she tried to make out his face in the darkness.

"I'm sorry," she said.

But he shook his head and let the branch he had pushed aside fall back into place. "Nothing to be done now," he said.

"But surely we can bury her," Wynn suggested.

"Too dangerous. Her own people will find her."

"She was a chieftain's daughter," she said. "A princess."

"Yes." But his voice betrayed no emotion. "We've got to think of ourselves now. Can't stay here. We're still too close."

The jungle closed in all around them. Then another thought struck her.

"Who fired from the other side of the gorge, I wonder?" she asked.

"I've been wondering that myself," said James.

"You don't suppose —?" she began.

But he interrupted her. "Seems unlikely, and yet . . ."

"James, if it is Robert, we can't leave now."

"What can we do? We can't just walk back in there. What good would the two of us be against their numbers? No, it's better if we can get back to civilization and then find out what's happened. We can't be sure if it was Robert or William or anyone else we know. Culliford has many enemies. It could even have been some of the island tribes."

"With pistols?"

"Well, you have a point there. But we can't go back now."

"Then where will we go?"

"I don't know any more than you do. But it's best to

try to find the water. If we make our way downhill, we'll come to a river valley eventually. Then we can follow its course to the bay."

The very thought that Robert might be in the pirate stronghold rooted her to the spot, but she knew that what James said made sense. They had no way of knowing if their friends had fought their way to the pirate's fortification only to find out that she and James had escaped. If their friends had taken over the stronghold, it would be safe to return. But if not, if they were prisoners . . . . But she could not let herself think along those lines — the irony of fate would drive her mad.

James moved forward, thrashing branches aside, as Wynn followed reluctantly. They traveled through thick underbrush, and she tried not to think of the wild creatures all around them that might not like being disturbed. They made slow progress in the dark — James cutting away some of the undergrowth with the dagger — until finally the foliage around them thinned out and they came to a clearing.

"Where are we?" she whispered.

"I don't know."

Across a flat area of ground, there seemed to be a sharp rise, and the top of the ridge was outlined against the moonlit sky. Here the forest receded, but what lay beyond the ridge, they did not know.

They moved forward hesitantly, then James said, "We'll keep to the edge and circle around. There seems to be some kind of hut over there. I don't know if anyone's about."

Wynn trembled, fearing that they might have come upon a village. If they stumbled into a native dwelling, they had no way of knowing what kind of reception to expect. Or worse, what if this were one of Culliford's outposts?

They made their way through the waist-high grass, then came closer to what looked like a stone structure built into the side of the hill. Now Wynn could see that there appeared to be several tall pillars in front of the structure, like tall dead trees shorn of branches and leaves.

She held back a little as James went to see if anyone was inside. "There's no one here," he said when he came back to where she stood. "I think we can stay here for the night."

"What is it?"

"Can't say." He picked up a smooth white horn that looked like it had come from a bullock. "It might be a ceremonial place."

Wynn hesitated, but she supposed she ought to be glad they had found any shelter at all. She followed James between the tall pole-like trees and through a small doorway. Two flat stones had been erected and another laid across the top to form the door.

"Wait here," he said as he felt his way forward into the gloomy interior. His hand came to a shelf that protruded from the wall, and then his hands touched the folds of some sort of cotton cloth. There seemed to be several large parcels wrapped and lying on the shelves. He was careful not to let his hands roam too far for fear of reaching into a nest of some insect or animal that had made its home here. But as he tentatively felt along the length of the folds, he ascertained that they seemed to be about five feet long. Suddenly his hand froze on the rounded shape at the end of the wrapped figure, and the hair on the back of his neck stood on end.

"Good Lord!" he exclaimed, and hastily retreated to where Wynn stood, just inside the entrance. Just then the moon came out from behind a cloud and illuminated skulls grinning down on them from the top of the poles they had passed under.

Wynn clapped her hand over her mouth to stifle the scream that rose in her throat.

"We can't stay here," said James as he led her out

onto the hard-packed dirt in front of the vault. "It's a burial place. If the natives found us here, they would kill us for defiling a sacred place."

Wynn shook with terror as she followed James back around the clearing. Now sheer panic overcame her as they plunged back into the forest. Tears stung at her eyes and thorns scraped her arms. Alone in the forest, where could they go? No place seemed safe between the wild animals who were surely unused to humans interfering in their domain, natives who might or might not be friendly, and pirates who would cut their throats if they were caught.

James led her downhill, and soon they could hear a river in the distance. They paused to catch their breath, and Wynn thought she could hear the roar of the waterfall she remembered. But no, they could not be near enough. That was a day's journey away, and in which direction, she had no idea.

Overhead, between the thick branches, the sky was black. Where they had seen stars before, clouds now covered the sky.

"It's thundering," James said, and Wynn remembered it was nearly time for the monsoons. Already the air held moisture, and it would not be long before the clouds broke.

They made their way downhill until they came to a hollow near the aerial roots of a pandanus tree. A few steps from them was a small brook. They drank their fill and then tried to make themselves as comfortable as possible against the coiling roots in the soft ground.

Sleep was long in coming. Though she agreed with James that it would have been foolhardy to return to the pirate stronghold, she had the feeling that Robert had been on his way to rescue them, and that they had missed each other in the darkness. She tried to pray, but she could not seem to communicate with a deity that could deal out such a cruel fate. But it was not the deity's fault, she thought as she fell into an uncomfortable doze: humans lived with the blunders of their own making.

Through the night, they huddled beneath the roots of the tree, and awaking from a cramped sleep to gray skies, they were thankful at least for daylight to see by.

They searched about for something edible. James picked some fruit, while Wynn washed and drank again from the stream. They breakfasted on guavas and pears, shorn of their prickly skins with the dagger, their only weapon.

Now the hills rose steeply all around them, and Wynn found her fortitude waning.

"We'll follow the stream," James said. "It will lead us out."

She resigned herself to following him, though with every step she was filled with dread at the idea that she might be moving farther and farther away from Robert.

They walked all that day and spent the night in a hollow next to the stream. The next day the stream joined a fast-flowing river. True to James's predictions, after following the river for most of that day, they came to a place where more light pierced the long prickly leaves and spreading branches above them. The soil below was red and rocky, and then quite suddenly they were on a path that led out to a rocky beach. They were at sea level.

"Oh, James, the bay," said Wynn, pushing her damp hair away from her forehead and blinking in the sunlight. Before them stretched blue water, and they stood for some moments just staring at it. Then she looked back at the steep hills they had descended — the hills that hid Culliford's stronghold.

They followed the curve of land toward the mouth of the bay, traveling cautiously, keeping near the trees, which at some places came right up to the water's edge. By now, in spite of the bananas they had eaten for their breakfast, Wynn felt hungry and tired. The humidity rose, and now even the air seemed to be pressing down on them. She did not know how long they walked that morning, and she was about to beg for a rest when James stopped suddenly, and she stumbled toward him. Then she looked up to see what had made him come up short. Following his gaze, she drew in her breath. For at the mouth of the bay to which they had now come, an East Indiaman floated with furled sails. She seemed for a moment like a specter of their imagination.

But James spoke through clenched teeth. "It's the *Mocha Frigate*, Culliford's ship."

Wynn opened her mouth to form the word "How," when out of the trees ahead of them sprang three bearded pirates. James had readied his dagger, but now more men appeared behind them, and one clapped a dirty hand over Wynn's mouth, preventing her from screaming. Realizing that struggle would be futile, she allowed them to propel her along the pebbly beach. It took three men to disarm James, but now his hands were tied behind him and the dagger tucked into one of the pirate's belts.

"Thought you'd get away, did you?" said the burly man who pushed Wynn into a boat that had pulled up. "Couldn't escape from Master Culliford though," he said with a self-satisfied laugh. She watched the shoreline recede as the boat was rowed out to the *Mocha Frigate*. Wynn tried to chew the rag that bound her mouth, but even if she got free, what then? Her head slumped forward. Evidently Robert and William had not succeeded in gaining the pirate's stronghold. If she had felt desolate locked away in that stronghold, a numbing apathy now seized her as they approached the pirate ship. She had never felt this hopeless. And now she had to admit that Robert must either be dead or taken prisoner by Captain Shaw.

The boat pulled alongside, and a rope ladder was tossed down. Her hands were freed so she could climb aboard, and she thought with discouragement of the many ships she had sailed on since she had left her home in England. Of all of them, this one inspired the most dislike.

She climbed the ladder, and as she stepped over the gangway, she looked into the black eyes of Robert Culliford, a man she hated worse than death. She choked down the bile that rose in her throat at the sight of him. Then she was pushed in the direction of the fo'c'sle deck and soon her brother followed her. They were lashed on opposite sides of the foremast. She could not see James, as the ropes pinned her shoulders and she could barely turn her head.

"Well, my friends," said Culliford. "I see you did not like my hospitality."

Wynn glowered at him over the handkerchief that covered her mouth. Culliford went on. "A brave pair you are, I will admit, to find your way through the hostile jungle. But, ah, yes, I had forgotten you had a guide. A pity she tired of her position with me." Here he stopped pacing in front of them and moved close to Wynn, his gaze burning with hatred. But she lifted her chin defiantly.

"You are probably asking yourselves how I got here before you," the pirate said. He gave a cruel laugh. "You did not come by the most direct route, of course. Had you paddled from the source of the river, you would have reached here before now. Nevertheless you reached here sooner than I would have expected. Much sooner."

"However," he said, his hands on his hips, "you have all fallen into my hands quite nicely." Then he gave them an angry look. "In spite of a foolish attempt to surprise me on the bridge two nights ago, I have taken several prisoners, who, now that they see their friends in my hands also, will surely understand the futility of holding out against me any longer."

As he spoke, Wynn was conscious of a growing feeling of dread. Prisoners? Then someone *had* tried to rescue them.

Laughing harshly, Culliford motioned to his men to bring out the prisoners. "I have something I believe you will want to see."

Again fear and anger coursed through Wynn as the door to Culliford's cabin was opened and William Kidd was roughly led out. Behind him came Captain Shaw, Hugh Parrot, Gabriel Loft, and others of Kidd's crew. A cry rose in her throat, but was muffled by the gag. If the two captains had come to this pass, what then of Robert? If only she could speak to them.

Culliford strode over to the prisoners and looked them up and down. William looked haggard and thin, and Wynn's heart went out to the poor man who had suffered first at the hands of the greedy Whig syndicate that had sent him on this voyage, then an unruly crew, made mutinous from misfortune, and now his enemy, this pirate captain. Poor William. He seemed a doomed man. Her eyes traveled searchingly over Captain Shaw, whose clothes were not so shabby as William's, and who looked considerably disgruntled. He had not planned for things to end this way. When he met her eyes it was with anger, and Wynn shrank against the mast, for she knew she had contributed to his troubles.

Her eyes searched the group of prisoners, but Robert was not among them.

"You see what trouble your friends have gotten themselves into for your benefit?" Culliford continued to taunt them. "It was your welfare they were trying to preserve by their arduous journey over the moors. Or am I to assume it was my company they sought?"

Culliford narrowed his wily eyes as he studied their faces. "Somehow I expected a more joyous reunion," he said, "although you are not in much of a position to celebrate." Then he returned to stand before Wynn. "I believe I see how it is, though. You miss your beloved

Robert Lamley, who foolishly tried to stop me at St. Mary's. I have told you he is dead."

She looked past him at William, who raised his head, and she saw him move it ever so slightly to indicate that Culliford was lying. She tried to still the wild beating of her heart. Perhaps Culliford thought Robert was dead, but she could see in William's eyes that he was not.

As William's men stared dejectedly at the deck, Culliford's crew took up their stations, some with cat-o'-nine-tails in their hands. Through the tears that ran from her eyes, she watched as Culliford turned to face Kidd.

"Well, what do you say, Captain? Your rescue was to no avail. I have the remnants of your crew before me. Now all that remains is to take your ship."

"It is the king's ship you speak of," said William valiantly, but Wynn could see the effort it cost him.

"But soon to be mine," said Culliford. "What say you, Captain Kidd? Would it not be better for you to now swear allegiance to Captain Culliford and join me on the high seas to improve your wealth?"

Kidd did not answer, but his own crew members who had deserted him for Culliford at St. Mary's now laughed derisively at him. In spite of her own misery, it pained Wynn to see him thus humiliated.

"We'd rather fire ten shots at you than one at the pirates you came to chase," jeered one sailor sitting on the edge of the quarterdeck.

"Well," said Culliford, striding proudly before Kidd. "You see how it is. My crew and my guns have already swelled at your expense."

Kidd averted his gaze from the pirate, well aware that Culliford had seized twenty of his guns from the *Adventure Galley* and that Culliford's crew now numbered at least a hundred and forty.

"And now the *Quedah Merchant* rides at anchor,"

Culliford continued. "But I'll let you keep a fair share of the booty if you'll yield the ship to me."

William looked at Wynn and James tied to the mast, and at his men in irons. There was little he could do. "What would you have me do then?" he said.

"Aha," said Culliford. He unsheathed his sword with a flourish. "Kneel," he commanded.

William hesitated, and Culliford pointed the tip of the sword at William's chest and repeated his order. "Kneel."

William went down on one knee.

"Now swear!" yelled Culliford, a man now drunk with power.

"What shall I swear?" asked William.

"You will swear allegiance to me," said the pirate.

"So I swear then," said Kidd.

The sword tip came up to William's chin. "Is that an oath that I can believe comes in all sincerity? I give you ten seconds to come up with a better oath, one that will please me."

"I swear that I will do as you say. That I will never attempt to molest you or your men in any way."

"What else?"

Again William hesitated, gathering his thoughts. Finally he spoke, and a chill ran down Wynn's spine as he said, "Before I would do you any harm, I would have my soul fry in hell fire."

Wynn trembled at the strong words, which seemed to placate Culliford, who withdrew his sword. "Your capitulation pleases me," he said. "Now you may rise and we will drink to your oath in my cabin."

Kidd stood, and the man behind him shoved him in the direction of the great cabin. The other pirates fell to their tasks, and the prisoners were chained to the deck.

Wynn expected that they would be thrown into the hold, but she soon discovered why they had been left on deck. The sun was a far worse torture than the darkness of the hold, and soon thirst burned her throat and the ropes scraped at her skin through her torn clothing. She tried in vain to speak to James, but her mouth was too firmly gagged.

The heat of the day gave way to the warm evening breezes as the *Mocha Frigate* headed south. Darkness fell and the stars appeared only to be hidden and then peek through the clouds that formed and reformed in the sky, as the men on watch paced the deck.

She had been asleep for some time when a movement awoke her. Her head throbbed from overexposure to the sun, and now tears of frustration dried on her burning eyes as she tried to move her swollen tongue. She looked about her at the blurry shadows and then closed her eyes again in hopes that sleep would numb her. But the movement near her caused her to open her eyes again. This time it was closer. Was some pirate going to take advantage of the darkness and cut her down so he could use her for his own pleasure? The thought frightened her, and her nerves came alive. She strained to turn her head.

"Ssst," came a sound, and then she saw someone crouched behind a coil of line at her feet. "It's me."

She breathed in sharply as the shadow became a figure, and then she saw it was James. She tried to wriggle around to see how he had gotten free, but she still could not move.

James moved toward her, keeping to the shadows. "Don't make a sound. I'll cut you down." Then he loosened the gag and worked the ropes free. She sank to the deck and whispered, "James, how did you get free?"

"I learned a few things about these knots on the *Joanna*," he said.

"Bless you, James, we are saved."

"Not quite, but I have a plan. Follow me, and keep to the shadows."

Freed of their bonds, James and Wynn sneaked aft where he handed her a long sharp knife. "Use this if you need to."

She grasped the knife tightly as they crept along through the waist of the ship, where she took cover behind a crate while James crouched in wait for the watch to come his way. When he passed James sprang, covering the man's mouth with one hand to prevent his outcry as the cold steel entered his ribs. James lowered the man's body to the deck and extracted a pistol from his belt.

They pressed on toward the great cabin. Carefully, they sneaked up to one of the cabin windows, left open to catch whatever breeze possible. Inside Culliford and William were looking at a map, while Captain Shaw sat to one side, looking like he'd like to slit both their throats. James motioned to her and they sank into the shadows of the bulkhead.

"Have they any arms?" she asked.

James shook his head. "None that I can see."

"How can we —" she began, but James's gesture silenced her, for overhead they could hear the footsteps of the man on watch. She steeled her resolve. If they were to overtake Culliford they would have to get weapons to the two captains with him. Then they would stand a better chance. It stood to reason that if they took the pirate captain the crew would change loyalties quickly enough if they were promised booty.

Wynn and James now crept toward the ladder while above them the watch stood looking out to sea. James crawled silently up the ladder to the quarterdeck. Crouching in the shadows, he crept up to the unsuspecting pirate as Wynn followed up the ladder, her knife ready. James leapt up and raised his pistol butt. There was a whoosh of air, and then a sharp knock on the man's skull that made him groan and lurch to his knees.

James started toward the man, but halted, frozen. Wynn followed the direction of his gaze and the blood rushed in her veins. In the distance she saw a ship moving toward them, its billowing sails illuminated by the silvery moonlight.

"Look," she whispered, pointing.

"Quickly," said James, "Release our men," and he gave her instructions. She crept down from the quarterdeck to do as she was bid, and came upon the men, all slumped forward as she had been. Rousing them, she warned them to be quiet as she cut them free of their ropes and slit the knots of their gags.

"It's Miss Wynn," said Hugh Parrot when she had untied him.

"Hush," she said. "Help the others." She handed him James's knife. The other men murmured their thanks as Wynn passed on James's orders, and soon they stole away to their assigned positions.

As she crept forward, she saw that James now stood on the quarterdeck. She squinted into the darkness as a pale sky now pushed the night toward morning. Suddenly her mouth went dry and her heart hammered. For as the ship came closer, she saw that it was the *Quedah Merchant*. But how? What crew had been left to sail her?

The fast approach of the large ship threw her into confusion. Still Culliford's crew slept, unaware of the approach of the big ship, as there was now no watch to warn them. James ran up the Union Jack to half-mast as a signal that a small body of men on board meant to overthrow the pirates, and Wynn prayed fervently that whoever commanded the *Quedah Merchant* meant to help them.

Wynn followed her brother down the ladder and whispered that all their men were in position. Cautioning her to take cover, he then aimed his pistol at the cabin door.

Suddenly from below, a great cry arose as someone finally spotted the *Quedah Merchant*. There was a burst of flame from the other ship, and with a roar a cannonball fired across the *Mocha Frigate*'s bow. James shot the fastenings off the cabin door, quickly jumping aside as Culliford returned fire. Wynn threw William the pistol they had taken from the watchman and then tossed a knife to Captain Shaw.

Now Culliford's men swarmed up through the hatchway, but Kidd's men were waiting for them, and soon the erstwhile prisoners had seized enough arms from the surprised pirates to put up a fight in earnest. Meanwhile the *Quedah Merchant* had drawn alongside, and its sailors jumped to their aid. Wynn looked up and uttered a cry of joy as she saw Robert leap from the *Quedah Merchant* onto the deck of the *Mocha Frigate*.

"Robert," she cried, but she doubted he heard her above the din of battle in which he was soon engaged.

Noticing a second pirate approaching Robert from behind, Wynn ran toward him, clutching her knife. Robert fired point-blank at his assailant, but before he could turn, the man behind him raised a sword.

Wynn screamed and lunged at the man, her knife thrusting into his ribs, just as he slashed downward. His weapon fell to the deck, missing Robert's shoulder by just a few inches.

"Take cover," Robert yelled at her, and was soon lost in the smoke of the battle.

What with the force already on board the *Mocha Frigate*, and Robert's contingent of men, the fighting was now nearly even, and most of Culliford's crew were cut down as they came up from the hold before they could even raise a weapon. As the pirates slipped and fell in their own blood, Wynn strained to see what was happening. She caught a glimpse of William clashing swords with Culliford while Captain Shaw covered him from the other side, and once she saw James engaged near the railing hand-to-hand. The other man was bigger than James, and he bent James backward until she thought his back would break. But Robert spotted them and in one mighty leap reached James's side and slashed his assailant in the ribs.

Finally the fighting was over, the pirates surrendering to Robert's stronger force. As the smoke began to clear Wynn could see that Culliford had been bound hand and foot, and his mouth gagged. Then she saw Robert stagger toward her, and she rushed to him.

"Robert," she sobbed as she reached for him. Then, afraid she would hurt him, she asked, "Are you hurt?"

He shook his head tiredly. "Only a scratch here and there." Then he took her in his arms and held her close to him. She didn't mind the sweat and blood, she was so thankful to see him safe.

"It's over," he said, his head sagging, and only then did she realize the great fatigue he must be suffering. He leaned on her shoulder as she guided him toward the cabin.

When they had counted their losses and buried the dead at sea, Captain Shaw left a crew to man the *Mocha Frigate*. With Captain Shaw officially in charge, they sailed for St. Mary's, where he would then board his own ship. Since they had captured Culliford, he would allow Kidd and Lamley to sail the *Quedah Merchant* home under his escort. There would now be a fair wind to blow them around the Cape, and in the hold of the Moorish ship was a rich hoard of merchandise — gold and pieces of eight with which to please Kidd's backers.

They stocked provisions for the voyage, for even with the monsoons behind them they would be at least two months at sea. At last, Wynn thought, she would be able to spend time with Robert. And with a grateful heart she set about the task of nursing the bedraggled crew.

Chapter Nineteen

With Robert, James, William, and Samuel Bradley, Wynn sat in the great cabin of the *Quedah Merchant*, sipping Madeira in celebration of their deliverance. Culliford had been put in irons on board Captain Shaw's ship, the *Joanna*, but the party was a somber one, as they began to discuss their predicament.

Wynn watched her lover's face, which was creased with lines of worry. "Now that you're with us, you are still in danger," he said to Wynn, setting his decanter on the polished wood table that was bolted to the floor. "You'll be accused of conspiring with pirates."

Captain Kidd nodded in agreement. His appearance had improved, Wynn thought, since he'd had a chance to clean himself up, trim his beard and don new clothes. Now that his crew had been bolstered with men from Shaw's ship, he was almost his old self again.

"Even if we clear ourselves at home," he said, "you'd be better off sailing with Shaw."

Wynn looked into Robert's eyes. "I will not leave my

fiancé," she said. "Or my cousin's husband." She turned to William, trusting that this reminder of their relationship would surely influence him to let her stay on board.

Kidd grunted noncommittally and leaned back, clenching his pipe between his teeth. From where he'd been leaning on the cabin door, James pushed himself forward. "I'll have to sail with Shaw," he said, "since I signed on with him."

William nodded, taking the pipe from his mouth. "There's no need to keep you here. Your parents and my wife would cut my throat if they thought I'd dragged you into this." Then he stood and began pacing the cabin.

"Surely now our backers in London will help us," he said. "Bellomont gave his word."

Wynn could see the muscles tighten in Robert's jaw. "Two of our backers are now lords justices," he said, "and they have ordered your arrest. William, don't you see? There will be no help from that quarter. And the king may turn to our ruing now." He glowered at the empty glass that stood in front of him.

"I can explain everything," said William. "And the booty from the *Quedah Merchant* should adequately satisfy my financial obligations."

Still Robert argued. He said moodily, "She wasn't a pirate ship, and you know it."

Kidd averted his gaze, looking out the cabin windows. "She was Moorish."

"Hah!" Robert exclaimed. "You still think that will rectify the matter. I tell you, William, you will find no sympathy. Just because she was not a Christian ship did not give you the right to take her."

"Robert," Kidd said in a tone of voice that made Wynn look up at him quickly. "We have been over this before. She showed French passes. My men would not settle for less. They were starving."

Wynn wished fervently she could accept William's argument but the fear that gnawed at her heart made her more inclined to listen to Robert.

"What will we do next?" she asked William.

"Sail for New York, of course. I've been away too long."

"I thought your orders were to proceed to Boston with the goods taken," James said, as he poured himself another glass of wine.

"So they are," said Kidd, "but I am not sure of my reception there. I have a plan."

"The treasure?" asked Wynn. Robert raised an eyebrow as she went on. "Surely you will do as you say, show the treasure to the governor as property of the Crown, and he will clear you and Robert." She reached for Robert's hand. "It must be so. And Sarah has been so worried."

It was the first mention of Sarah's name, and silence fell. As Wynn looked at William she saw the pain in his eyes.

"I must go home to Sarah," he said, his eyes moist. James and Robert looked away, embarrassed at his show of emotion, but Wynn rose and approached him, placing her hand gently on his arm, trying to offer him the comfort that Sarah would want him to have. He took her hand in his own and shut his eyes.

"How is Sarah?" he asked.

"She misses you," said Wynn, a catch in her throat. "Other than that she is well." Wynn felt suddenly filled with compassion for this man. She herself was just learning to be loved the way she knew William and Sarah loved each other, and their devotion touched her. Robert moved to stand behind her, and she eased away from the captain, turning as Robert held her against his chest. She no longer cared who saw them as his lips touched her hair and his hands pressed her gently to him.

James cleared his throat. "I'll be going now," he said.

William stood and shook his hand. "I owe you a great debt. You *and* your sister," he said, a twinkle returning to his eye. "I pray both our journeys home are safe."

"Good luck, sir," said James to the captain. Then he turned to Robert. "You'll take good care of my sister, I hope," he said, and the two men shook hands firmly. She held back her tears as she saw Robert look gravely into her brother's eyes.

"Thank you," Robert said solemnly, "for what you've done. You've no need to worry about your sister."

"It's you I should thank," said James. "You saved my life."

"As you would have done for me," said Robert.

Wynn followed James out on deck to say good-bye. They walked to the railing, and he looked at her flushed face, taking in the new serenity that showed in her eyes.

"You love him very much," he said.

Wynn smiled. "Why, Brother, you sound so serious. Of course I love him." She tossed her hair over her shoulder, pressing quivering lips together.

"It's just that you're my only sister, Wynn, and you know how close we've been." He kicked the deck, and she reached out to hug him.

"I know," she sniffled, emotion suddenly filling her. "But I do love him." She sighed and released James, who looked away, embarrassed.

"It'll happen to you someday," she teased him.

"Ah, Sis," he said, hugging her again.

"Go on now," she said. "You'll be late."

"Take care, Sis," he said, his voice husky as he released her and walked toward the gangplank, turning to wave. Then he was gone.

She returned to the cabin where the men were still discussing their plans. Robert put his arm around her shoulders as she heaved a sigh, thinking that Captain Shaw, at any rate, would be glad to be rid of her.

Robert turned to William. "I'll surrender my quarters to Wynn," he said. "I'll sling a hammock on the gun deck."

William nodded, and Wynn knew that propriety would have to be observed, for after all, she was the captain's relation by marriage.

"Good night, Cousin," said William. "I'm sorry your welcome aboard this ship wasn't a more pleasant one."

She bid him good night, then Robert prodded her along through the passage that led to the first mate's quarters. A small bed was bolted to the wall, and a trunk and writing table decorated with Moorish designs made up the rest of the furniture. The porthole opened onto a darkening sky.

Robert pulled her to him. "In such a cabin I lived all these many months without you," he said, "thinking I'd never see you again."

She wound her arms around his neck and he breathed deeply as he joined her mouth with his. For a long time they merely clung together, drawing strength from one another. Then he nibbled at her ear, but before she could respond, he pulled away to look at her face.

"Not yet, my sweet. I want you above all things, but I am still troubled by our discussion with William. Come walk with me on deck. The night air will clear my mind." Then he crushed her to him. "Oh God, Wynn, you don't know how good it is just to be able to talk to you. To tell you of the things I have feared. I can't talk to William anymore. I used to think he had sound judgment, but after this voyage, I've begun to doubt him." He sighed and loosened his hold on her.

"But who am I to bore you with all this. You haven't been with us; you probably don't understand what I am talking about."

"But I do," she protested. "We've had more news in New York than you know, and Drago Calicut told me of your deserters and how you took this ship."

"So you did meet Drago?"

"I did. We met in the Boar's Head Tavern, and I paid him five shillings for his story. He said you'd paid him five as well."

A twinkle lit Robert's eyes as he said, "So I did, so I did. My money wasn't wasted after all. And I do apologize. I am so distracted by your luscious body that I forget about your ingenious mind." He laughed and squeezed her waist.

Wynn blushed and said, "Let's take that walk on deck. Fresh air would do us both some good." Then, in a more serious tone, she said, "I feel sorry for William. And I fear for you, Robert. I had forgotten we were still in a great deal of danger."

He put his arms around her, probing her ear with his tongue. His sensuous touch brought a flow of blood to the surface of her skin and she craved more caresses, but Robert whispered, "We have all night, my pet."

She looked at him questioningly. "But you said you were to sleep on the gun deck."

"Who said anything about sleeping?" he chuckled. Then he opened the door and led the way on deck.

The ship was quiet. The men on watch saluted Robert and followed Wynn with their eyes. She stared at the tall naked masts against the deep velvet sky. Tomorrow the men would climb aloft and the voyage would get under way. Now the ship gently rocked in the dark water under the glistening half-moon, the *Joanna* anchored to starboard.

"We'll be on this ship for months," she said, relishing the thought of all the time she could spend with Robert when he was not on duty.

He looked at the ship with a critical eye. "She's really too worn out to sail all the way home," he said. "Too big to hide and too barnacled and seaworn to outsail another ship if we're chased."

"Why would we be chased?" asked Wynn.

He shrugged his shoulders, looking pensive.

"I don't understand," she persisted. "You've got evidence to clear yourselves with, and besides, the *Joanna* is escorting us."

Robert rested one elbow on the railing, his chin on his fist. "Yes," he said. "But what if we become separated from the *Joanna*?"

"Robert," she pulled his shoulder so that he had to turn and face her. "What do you mean?" His tone of voice had made her suspicious. "You're not planning to try to outrun Captain Shaw, are you?"

Robert's gaze roamed over her face as he half smiled. "It's not for you to worry about," he said as he lowered his mouth to kiss her lips.

She swayed against him, forgetting her question, parting her lips as his tongue teased her. The heat of desire climbed upward in her body, and she moaned softly as he moved his mouth from hers to taste her earlobes and neck. His fingers unbuttoned the top button of the ruffled shirt she wore, and his hand cupped her breast as his mouth moved even lower. She sank against his taut body as he raised his head to kiss her hair.

"My sweet," he said, "I cannot wait any longer. I want you now." And he led her to her quarters.

Once inside the first mate's cabin he closed the door, then unbuttoned his shirt. As he did so, Wynn pressed the palms of her hands on his strong tanned chest, her fingers playing with the hard male nipples. He unfastened her trousers, letting them fall. Then he rid himself of his own trousers, and they finally both stood nude, gazing at each other in the pale moonlight that came in through the porthole. She thrilled at the sight of his manly physique, every muscle attesting to the hard work he did. She slid her hands lovingly over the smooth, taut skin, then stared with embarrassment at the protruding instrument of his desire. As he had the first time they made love, he took her hand and wrapped it around his organ, then he touched her lightly with his fingertips.

Little shivers darted over her skin wherever his fingers caressed. He drew circles on her shoulders, her rising breasts, made rings around her nipples. Then he outlined her waist and hips, finally plunging his fingers into the core of her desire. Her excitement caused her to massage him harder, until he lifted her onto the bed and lay beside her. Still, he did not want to rush their lovemaking. Now that there was time to caress and enjoy each other, he gazed at every part of her body as if he wanted to memorize every fine detail.

Wynn looked shyly back. She was overwhelmed to be with a man this way, yet Robert made her feel so safe that she was not afraid to let him know of her own desire. When she looked at him, it seemed to excite him even more. His love tool stood hard in her hand. His fingers moved to the centre of her pleasure and ripples of sensation such as she had never known coursed through her until she thought she would lose all control. She had felt warm in his embrace before, but never in all her dreams had she imagined that the intimacies between a man and a woman could bring such heightened sensations. There were no words for it. She simply lay there, exuding passion and taking as much as Robert gave.

Finally, when the foreplay built to an almost unbearable intensity, he moved on top of her. Using his tongue to tease her flesh, he began with her earlobes, then her neck, her breasts, her waist, stopping to explore her delicate navel, then he trailed down to the soft cushion around her sexuality. There, he explored with his tongue where his fingers had been, as Wynn lay with her legs apart in wonderment at this new lesson in love. She caressed his shaggy head, maneuvering it to heighten her own pleasure.

He increased the speed with which he teased her with his tongue, causing a slow thunderous trembling in her loins. She was near the bursting point and lifted her legs as the sensation began to build.

She gasped and cried out, not knowing what to do with this maddening sensation. And as Robert sensed what was about to happen to her, he quickly raised himself and replaced his tongue with his maleness, heavy with desire. Then as she continued the upward climb toward her erotic explosion, he joined her with his own rhythmic thrusts.

She could hold out no longer. Her body writhed as she cried out. Still, as the explosions came, one after the other, Robert thrust into her. Finally he moved with a speed she thought would tear her flesh, but she clung for dear life to his strong shoulders. At last he spent himself, and after a few final thrusts, he lay against her. Still she held him, and she lowered her hands to hold his buttocks tightly. So delicious was this new pleasure that she wished to keep it inside her as long as it would last. After several moments, he turned his head toward her.

"Oh, Robert," she said softly, after she had found her voice. "Is it always like this?"

He laughed huskily. "It is not like this with just anyone, my dear. But you and I have something special, I will admit." And he pulled away from her to lie on his side behind her, stretching his full length against her and running his hand over her midriff.

"I have never known love so sweet," he whispered in her ear.

She glowed, then curled herself against him to feel as

much of his skin against her back as she could. Love was sweet indeed, she thought as languor began to shroud her. Now that she had found it, she would never give it up.

Robert held her until he too was overcome with drowsiness, and slept, more deeply than he had for many months.

Just before dawn, Robert extracted himself from their tangled limbs and softly rose. He dressed, then covered Wynn, bending for a final kiss before stealing away to the crew's quarters. Soon they would be married, and he could have all he wanted of her, which, he thought, could never be enough.

Wynn slept on until the sound of tramping feet above her told her the crew was up and about. She stretched luxuriously as the sun shone through the little porthole, and the ship gently rocked her. She sighed. If this was how life would be aboard ship with Robert, she didn't think she would half mind his going to sea.

But then she realized she was being silly. She remembered the horrors of the fighting she had been through. Of course their delightful dreamy night of love was not typical of shipboard life. And indeed, she had no idea what the future held. With these less pleasant thoughts, she rose and picked up the clothing that was strewn about.

When she was again presentable, she went on deck. Some hundred yards distant, the *Joanna* followed them, sails trimmed.

"How would you like to see some of the treasure?" Robert said after greeting her.

"You mean the king's booty?" she asked, a trace of asperity in her voice.

"Of course." He winked at her. Then she followed him below decks, blinking her eyes to accustom herself to the semidarkness. In the hold, shafts of light from the portholes illuminated the chests that stood among crates, kegs and spare parts for the ship. Robert threw back the lid of a large chest.

Wynn was astounded. She had never seen such jewels, even in Culliford's cabin. Arabian gold coins, so bright that even in the dark hold their magnificence shone; rubies, agates, amethysts set in the finest metals. Then he threw open another trunk. Here was gold cloth, such as a king might wear; silk so fine it felt like a soft cocoon; rich brocades; gold and silver lace. Amazed, Wynn ran her hands over the sensuous prizes. No wonder Culliford had coveted this ship. She looked at Robert, thinking that if ever a man were tempted to turn pirate, such treasure might do it.

"What about the rightful owners?" she asked in a quiet voice.

Robert frowned as he, too, studied the treasure. "The king is the rightful owner now. When William found out this ship was led by an English captain, he suggested turning it over to its owners, but the crew forced his hand."

"But that crew is gone. Most of them deserted to Culliford, and the English captain has run away too."

Robert shrugged. "You are right. And William is counting on this treasure to square his agreement with his backers. Otherwise there is nothing, and he will lose twenty thousand pounds as the Articles of Agreement require if there is no booty."

"Then the booty must go to the Crown. Otherwise . . ."

"We will be ruined," Robert said. He looked away. "I'm just not sure of the outcome."

"What do you mean?"

He kicked the lid shut on the valuable gems. "I don't know. I try to see it as William must. When you've got a good reputation and you stand for something in a community, when you've been called on by your king, and you fail, what have you got left?"

He glanced at her. "I know what you'll say. You've got your loved ones." He pulled her close to him and massaged the back of her neck. "If your loved ones look up to you and respect you for the success you've become, I can understand wanting to live up to it. But how will they feel if you lose everything? If you fail?"

"Robert, don't say such things. You know I'd stand by you no matter what happened, and I'm sure Sarah would do the same for William. Please don't make it sound so grim."

It was true. She would live in poverty with Robert rather than live without him. What did those material comforts matter? Then she thought about Sarah and her fine clothes, her little daughter and their comfortable house. She wondered if Sarah would feel the same way. Wynn had always assumed so. After all, wasn't that what love and marriage meant? A commitment no matter what came?

Robert kissed her hair and forehead softly. Then he kissed her mouth and they clung together hungrily. He pressed her against him and she could feel his desire. She was helpless to resist as his hands sought the soft curves of her body. But then he lifted his head and inhaled deeply.

"No, no, my sweet, not here, not now." He pulled away from her and looked into her face. "There's work to be done." He lowered his face for one last lingering kiss, then he turned and led her out of the hold. As they went, she glanced one last time at the treasure.

In the next few days they met with several storms, and in one of them their ship became separated from the *Joanna*. Kidd had sworn that if that should happen, after stopping in New York to see his wife, he would continue directly on to Boston and turn himself in to Governor Bellomont. So when they saw no more of

Captain Shaw's ship Wynn was not unduly alarmed. Her only fear was for her brother's safety. But Robert convinced her of the lad's resilience, and she had to be content with the thought that he could now take care of himself.

They had been sailing for nearly two months when Samuel took sick, and William thought it best to put him in a doctor's care ashore. They approached the West Indies and put in at Anguilla, but when the governor refused to let them come ashore because of their arrest, they sailed on to St. Thomas. As at Anguilla, the Danish governor was afraid to allow the crew to come ashore for if English ships came for them, and the governor protected them, the English would close the harbor, he informed them. But because of Samuel's illness he allowed him ashore to receive medical attention, and so the party saw Samuel safely into the governor's care.

From St. Thomas they sailed on to the Mona Passage and from there to the Delaware Cape, some fourteen hundred miles further. Kidd gave orders to put in at Hore Kill on the coast of Delaware so they could take on food and water and gather news. Wynn stood close to Robert as the gangplank was lowered, thankful they would once again set foot in the colonies. Robert held her arm.

"Watch your step in this place," he said. "Keep by me. Pirates haunt these parts."

"But my dear Robert, you are accused of piracy yourself," she said. But when she looked into his cold eyes, she regretted her teasing.

At Hore Kill, the news was the same — because they were wanted for piracy they could not linger here. They were told that the *Joanna* had put into port two weeks before and then continued up the coast, news which relieved Wynn about her brother's well-being.

The *Quedah Merchant* cast off again and traveled along the wild New Jersey coast, where Wynn was reminded of her voyage to the New World. How little she knew then that she would pass this way again and under such circumstances. A wave of nostalgia swept over her, and suddenly she longed to see New York and home.

It was after a squall had blown them farther out into the ocean than they had planned that Wynn first began to question William's moves. For when they came to the lower reaches of the Hudson, they did not make for New York. Instead, William set out into the Atlantic again, rounded the tip of Long Island, and sailed into Oyster Bay.

Chapter Twenty

The *Quedah Merchant* drifted slowly around its anchor in Long Island Sound, as, unable to sleep, Wynn paced the deck. She pulled her cloak around her and watched the land take shape as the first gray light of dawn illuminated the darkness.

Late the night before, William had gone ashore and sent word that he had arrived home. Many questions plagued Wynn. If he was so sure of his reception in New York, why did he not sail into New York Harbor? Why this secrecy? In spite of the fact that they had lost the *Joanna*, they were officially under the arrest of Captain Shaw, and the orders were to sail directly to Boston after stopping in New York for William to see his wife. So why had they stopped here at the eastern tip of Long Island?

Wynn also began to feel that her presence was becoming a burden to Robert. He seemed more and more preoccupied, and she felt him withdrawing from her. She hoped this was only because he was worried about the business at hand. But the thought gnawed at her that now he had spent his passion, perhaps he was finding her a nuisance.

Perhaps joining Robert on this voyage had been a mistake after all. Naturally he had been excited when he had first seen her, and passionate, both evidence of his needs. But what of a deeper, more enduring love? He had seemed almost cool these past few nights. They had made love, but not with the fire and eagerness they had first shared. Her heart turned cold when she contemplated that perhaps he did not really love her as much as he had said. Perhaps he had deceived himself.

She shivered in the November chill. Robert came on deck to relieve the watch. He nodded to her from the quarterdeck, but she deemed it best not to intrude on his thoughts. Feeling the chill, she decided to go to the galley to see if there was coffee. She was about to move forward when she glanced at Robert and saw that he was standing rigidly, watching as, from the west, around the tip of Long Island, came a sloop. It was still quite far off, but Robert lowered his glass and descended to report the news to the great cabin.

Wynn found a pot of boiling coffee in the galley. They were fortunate that Abel Owens, the cook from the *Adventure Galley*, still traveled with them. She was sipping a cup of coffee, enjoying the warmth, when she felt the *Quedah Merchant* bump against another ship, presumably the one she had seen from on deck. She went back on deck to watch Robert give orders for the passengers on the sloop to come aboard the *Quedah Merchant*.

Then Wynn quickened her steps as she saw the graceful Sarah Kidd, accompanied by her small daughter, cross the gangplank from the sloop. She was escorted by a man of medium height who wore a heavy cloak. William stepped forward to embrace his wife, and Wynn waited only a moment before calling out the other woman's name and running forward.

Stepping out of her husband's embrace, as William picked up his daughter, Sarah turned toward Wynn with open arms.

"Cousin," said Sarah, as she kissed Wynn on the cheek. As Wynn hugged Sarah, she could feel how thin she had become. Sarah's tear-stained cheeks showed how relieved she was to be with her husband again.

"How are you, Cousin?" asked Wynn through her own tears. "How good it is to see you."

"I am well," said Sarah. "And I'm glad you are safe. Your parents have been distracted with worry."

Wynn lowered her gaze. "I feared that, yet I had no choice."

Sarah's face showed compassion for her young cousin. "I know," she said softly. Then she turned back to William, who took her by the arm and led her to his cabin. As Wynn met Robert's eyes, a similar scene flashed before her — that of the Kidd family embracing on the dock when William returned from his voyage to England. She remembered with feeling the way she and Robert had been drawn together that first time, so overcome were they by the other couple's emotions.

But now Robert did not come to her. She tried to tell herself it was because their own bond had been established, and no reaffirmation of it was needed. But she would have gained much comfort from Robert's strong arm about her, and she felt bereaved. When she glanced at his face and saw the anxiety that filled it, she wanted to go to him, but then he turned and began speaking to the man who had accompanied Sarah.

William returned on deck and motioned for the other man to follow him to his cabin. Wynn and Robert were left standing alone on deck, and when he finally turned toward her, he reached for her and she went into his arms. But as he held her, she could sense his tension. After breathing in her softness for a few moments, he seemed to steel himself against her and gently pulled away. She looked searchingly into his face, but his forced smile told her nothing.

"We should join the others," he said. "The man with Sarah is Mr. James Emmot, a lawyer, and he will have news that will be important to us." His mouth returned to its rigid set, and the anxiety returned to his face. "It may concern you."

Suddenly she felt cold with apprehension: Robert was going to send her away from the ship. With leaden limbs she followed him into the captain's cabin.

Inside, William and James Emmot were engaged in conversation, while Sarah sat calmly listening. Even after several months of separation from her husband, Sarah still managed to emanate a serenity that startled Wynn. Suddenly Wynn envied Sarah her ability to accept whatever came her way.

She sat next to Sarah and glanced at Robert, who had concentrated his gaze on James Emmot, who was dressed in a dark blue, slightly waisted coat and flared shirt, with ruffled shirt sleeves emerging out of large buttoned cuffs. He had cast his Brandenburg overcoat and fringed gloves on a chair.

"Wynn Cox," said William, "this is James Emmot, an old friend of mine. He is a vestryman at Trinity Church and a lawyer." Mr. Emmot bowed over her hand briefly.

"Emmot has been advising us to use caution in dealing with Bellomont," William informed Robert.

"I knew it," said Robert. "That man is not to be trusted." The blood rose in Robert's face, and Wynn could sense the anger that lay just below the surface. Her memory of the governor and her own feeble attempts to intervene for the officers of the *Adventure Galley* also came to mind, making her blush.

"Mr. Emmot will act as my intermediary," said

William. "The men want assurances that they will be fairly treated when we arrive in Boston. I must know which way the land lies."

Robert glowered. "You *know* which way the land lies. The Tories are in Parliament making mincemeat of our noble backers. Surely they will use you as a scapegoat, William, and me along with you. I do not understand why you fail to see it."

The set of the captain's chin told Wynn that he felt differently. "No doubt they will wonder at the rumors that have circulated, but when they are made to realize the hardships we have undergone to preserve the ship, and that I never did anything contrary to the king's commission, surely we will get a fair hearing."

Robert shrugged disgustedly. "Bah," he said. "They will not listen, for now they must save their own skins. Bellomont most of all. He is responsible for ridding the sea of piracy, and he will take whatever action he must to make it seem he is doing so. He will use you, my friend. I am willing to wager the entire contents of this ship on that."

For a moment no one spoke, and the tension that filled the cabin made it seem very small indeed. Then Sarah spoke.

"Perhaps Mr. Emmot can persuade Governor Bellomont to be lenient. At least he will find out Lord Bellomont's position on the matter when he sees him."

"I shall send along my two French passes," said William. "They are evidence that I acted in good faith when I took the *November* and the *Quedah Merchant*. He'll see that I acted in the best interests of the king."

"But what reasons has he to believe you any more than the false stories that he may have already heard?" asked Robert.

Sarah fidgeted in her seat, and realizing that she

wished to leave the men to their discussion, Wynn laid a hand on Sarah's arm and said, "Would you like me to accompany you on deck?"

"Of course," said Sarah, rising. They left the men to their interview and went on deck. By now broad daylight shone on Long Island Sound's blue water, which reflected brightly against the green trees and yellow fields stretching out beyond the dunes.

"You are going to have to make a choice, Wynn dear," said Sarah, her violet eyes clear.

"What choice is there that I have not already made?" asked Wynn.

"You have reason to fear for Robert's life," Sarah said, coming straight to the point. "You have been away, you do not hear the gossip, feel the attitudes that seem to drift on the wind, even from as far away as Boston."

"But what can I do?" asked Wynn.

"Your family would want you to leave Robert, go home and forget about this unfortunate affair. After a period of time, you can start life anew."

"I cannot leave Robert any more than you can leave your husband. Surely you understand that."

"If you love Robert as I do William, then I understand. But I pity you as well." She looked off into the distance, and, as if she had repeated these thoughts to herself a dozen times a day these past months, said, "William and I have shared time together. We have had happiness."

Then she turned to Wynn. "But you and Robert are just at the beginning. Is it well to love only for a little time and then have your heart broken by matters you have no control over? Is it not better to break off with Robert before it is too late?"

"I have already loved Robert, and I do not have a choice," Wynn said, and then, embarrassed, dropped her gaze.

Sarah took her hands, and when Wynn looked up, she saw the tears that glistened in her cousin's eyes. "Then you have known happiness," she said.

Thankful that Sarah understood and did not condemn her, Wynn nodded. "Yes."

"Of course Robert will not desert William," Sarah continued.

"No, he would never do that. He is a loyal man."

"He is also a good man." The two women stood silently in their shared grief and understanding as the sun began to warm the deck.

"But Sarah, all is not lost yet. William's evidence may still save them."

Sarah shrugged, sighing deeply. "Yes, it might."

"I admit I have been worried," Wynn said. "Robert has seemed more distant the past few days. Perhaps he resents my presence here. Perhaps I am making things harder for him."

Sarah assessed this information. "Yes, of course it is harder for him. He looks at you and knows he is in imminent danger of losing you through the circumstances he finds himself in. And he can do nothing." Then, with obvious effort, she added, "Even about things that may not be his fault."

So Sarah knew something of how Robert must feel — that it was William's bad judgment that had gotten them into their present predicament.

"I know what you are saying. That he thinks if he is to hang, he would not suffer as much if he did not have someone to lose." She was surprised she could utter these words so calmly, but she went on. "Oh, Sarah, I simply cannot believe it will come to that. It must not!"

Sarah looked out over the water. "It may," she said.

Wynn knew that her cousin was not making it easy for her, because Sarah felt that Wynn needed to hear the truth, needed to confront the dire possibilities and make a choice based on harsh reality, rather than on the heart's emotions. After her talk with Sarah, Wynn could never claim ignorance. With full knowledge she would be committing herself to a dangerous love, and she might eventually have nothing to show for it, not even a husband.

"Thank you for your advice, Sarah," she said. "But I know what I must do. If Robert wants me here, I'll stay by his side. I'm aware that there may be no time for a wedding until this matter is finished, but if he needs me, I'll stay with him, just as you will surely stay by William."

Sarah inclined her head, acknowledging her cousin's acceptance of her role. Wynn left Sarah to her thoughts and went forward to see if she could be of some help in the galley. They were running the ship with such a small crew that Wynn found plenty of work to do. Cooking in the galley was nothing like preparing meals in a kitchen at home, but she had by now become accustomed to the tiny surroundings, huge utensils, and crude methods.

William and Robert stayed with James Emmot throughout the morning. When Wynn took the captain some coffee, she found him drafting a letter a letter to Governor Bellomont, stating his position and offering the French passes as evidence of his good intentions. Emmot would deliver the letter to Bellomont as Kidd's emissary.

The rest of the day time hung heavily on Wynn's hands, and she wished she had more work to do. Robert's lack of attention continued to irritate her, and Sarah was uncommunicative, so Wynn kept to herself. At last, the sun crept toward the western horizon, and Wynn changed into one of the dresses that Sarah had brought for her.

As she pulled on the plush gown with its thick silk pile, she realized how used she had become to broadcloth trousers and cambric shirts. As the plush met her skin, she looked lovingly at Robert's cambric shirt tossed on the bunk beside her. How soft the shirt seemed by comparison to this dress with all its folds and stays.

She found the others in the captain's cabin where they were about to sit down to dinner. Robert continued to brood, avoiding her gaze throughout the meal and concentrating on his glass of Burgundy instead. When he did glance at her, he seemed to look through, and not at her. The others discussed the voyage, but it had ceased to matter to her.

She wished she could leave the table, but there was nowhere to go save her cabin on the deck, and for the first time in all these months, she chafed against the confinement on board a ship. She had not minded, when she had Robert's comfort, but when he ignored her for so long, she could hardly stand it. Perhaps Sarah was right. Perhaps she should leave the ship. She seemed to be more of a burden than anything else. Perhaps he even wanted to ask her to leave but could not find the words.

Finding the cabin too oppressive, she finally excused herself. "If you will all excuse me," she said as she stood, "I believe I'll take some fresh air."

The men stood, scraping back their chairs. "Of course, Cousin," said William. "I'm afraid our dinner conversation hasn't been very stimulating."

"Don't worry about me, Captain," she said. "I only wish I had more to contribute to your discussion."

Wynn was looking over the bow of the ship when she heard Robert's tread behind her. She did not turn as she felt his strong hands grasp her shoulders lightly, but she closed her eyes as a slight tremor passed through her.

He pulled her against his chest and breathed into her hair. She did not speak, no longer knowing what he wanted from her, but she swayed against him as the motion of the ship rocked them.

Finally she drew herself up and turned in his arms to

face him. She had to find out. She had to know if she should take this opportunity to tear herself from him. She tried to speak, but the words choked her.

Robert stared down at her blue eyes and exhaled a long slow breath. "What is wrong? You do not look well."

"Robert," she managed to get out, "I fear my presence here is no longer a help to you. I feel I should leave this ship. I believe I will go back to New York."

He frowned, his face filling with an emotion she could not place. She flinched, remembering his anger the day he hit her as they had walked along the quay by Sarah's house. But she knew in her heart he would never strike her now, and she was surprised that the memory brought back such a strong feeling of fear.

He turned away from her, the muscles in his neck tense. "If that is what you wish," he said.

"It is not what I wish, it is what I . . . that is, I don't know what you want me to do anymore." A sob escaped her as she leaned on the railing, one hand covering her face. She felt foolish, crying in front of him, but being so near him released emotions she had carefully controlled for the last several days. Seeing her distress, he turned partially toward her. "I only want your happiness," he said, taking her in his arms, this time holding her tightly against him.

She fingered the ruffles on the front of his shirt. "I thought perhaps you had tired of me," she said, all of her frustration and self-doubt pouring out. "I didn't want to cause you more problems. I thought, perhaps, I should go ashore for that reason."

He smoothed her tangled hair with one hand. "My poor little love," he said. "Of course I want you. It is I who have been chastising myself for having dragged you into an affair that you should have nothing to do with."

"But Robert," she said, turning her tear-stained face up toward him. "I thought the captain had plans to clear himself and the crew. Surely Lord Bellomont and the king will realize you did only what you could do under the circumstances."

He kissed away her tears, and the feel of him against her eased her pain. She clung to him, desiring that he never let go of her. Here in his arms was home. She knew then without a doubt that she would never leave him of her own volition. He would have to throw her into the sea to make her loosen her grasp on him.

He sighed and then cradled her head against his chest as he stared into the darkening evening. "If only it were that easy," he said. "Perhaps William did not always do what he should have done."

"How do you mean?"

"The view of truth and right and wrong differs the world over. Many times over I have asked myself what I would have done had I been in command. And I never come up with the same answers twice. It is a hard thing, Wynn. I do know that our Captain Kidd did not begin this voyage auspiciously. Then when he lost his crew at the Nore and they were replaced with pirate sympathizers from New York, perhaps he lost some of his nerve. He did not sail boldly for Madagascar's eastern coast when we first arrived there. He seemed to wait to ambush them when they left that island. Only things did not work as he had planned. Ill luck, I call it."

"Ill luck?" she asked, frowning. She was so relieved that Robert had not cast her out that she had a hard time concentrating on all he now said.

"But Robert, surely it will help if you act now with certainty. What does this James Emmot advise?"

"He is a lawyer, and he advises caution. We sail at midnight to carry Mr. Emmot to Stonington, Connecticut. From there he will go to Boston to negotiate for us."

"What will we do then?"

"We will wait, my pet," he said, looking down into

her innocent face. She raised her hand to smooth his brow. Then she caressed his cheek. He caught her hand in his and kissed it.

"Oh, Robert, if you still love me, please don't shut me off. I want to share in this as well. Surely you know that."

He quirked his lips in a smile of surrender, and slowly the love returned to his eyes. He bent to kiss her.

She returned his kiss eagerly. The hunger and passion were still there, but tempered with more giving than taking now, full of reassuring and caring. For some time they held each other as the doubt and anxiety of the last few days was transmuted to a new unity of spirit. She would not let go of him until she knew their feelings were again one in purpose.

"Are you sure you want me, Robert?" she finally whispered.

He sighed into her hair, which blew about them in the breeze. "I was always sure I needed you. Only the old doubt began to haunt me. I felt I had no right to bring you into this kind of life. I may not survive this ordeal, and then where would you be left? You would know that I loved you, but you would have nothing to show for it."

"Sarah made me realize that as well. She pointed out that I had to make a choice."

"And?"

She breathed into his shirt. "I think you know what I decided."

"Yes," he said, holding her and kissing her lovingly. "We have both chosen, for better or for worse."

Chapter Twenty-one

Six days passed after James Emmot left the little party. When he finally returned he brought with him a letter from Lord Bellomont to Captain Kidd. Also accompanying him was Bellomont's emissary, Duncan Campbell, a bookseller and the postmaster of Boston.

They all now sat with Campbell in the captain's cabin much as they had the first night Emmot had arrived. A lighthearted young man, dressed a la mode, with ruddy cheeks and lively gestures, Campbell treated every argument with so much assurance of its validity that Wynn could not really tell whose side he was on.

While listening to Campbell, Wynn began to realize the sensation they were causing wherever the story of Captain Kidd's voyage circulated. For the first time in her life she found herself the center of gossip that must be traveling from Delaware to Boston and possibly to London. The thought was appalling.

She walked over to the stern window to look out. She was beginning to feel anxious to be on land again. She had thought more and more about her parents the past few days. She was so close to home and yet so distant from them. She had written, assuring them that all was well, and that she and Robert would visit them as soon as possible. She hoped to be married at home, but even as she wrote it, she knew she said that more for her parents' sake than for her own. She also knew that, as captain of the ship, William could marry them, but he had such weighty matters on his mind now that she felt it was the wrong time to bring it up. And it would make her father happy if she were married by a priest. They would wait until they reached Boston, though Wynn knew it was doubtful there were any Catholics there. Because Robert's family was Protestant, perhaps her parents would not mind if she were married by a Protestant clergyman, and it mattered little to Wynn who it was who married them. Only their commitment to each other seemed important to her now.

The captain poured more wine for his guests, and for the second time the letter from Lord Bellomont was read aloud, this time by William. When the letter was first delivered, Duncan Campbell had read it out loud to William and Robert at the captain's request. Now William read it to the others, pausing to take a drink of wine or to comment on the letter's contents. He seemed alternately pleased and disgruntled by what he read. " 'Mr. Emmot came to me last Tuesday night late, telling me he came from you, but was shy of telling me where he parted from you. He proposed to me that I would grant you a pardon: I answered that I have never granted one yet; and that I had set myself a rule, not to grant a pardon to anybody whatever without the king's express leave or command.' "

"You see," Robert interjected. "He places the burden on the king's shoulders."

William waved him into silence and continued. " 'He told me you declared and protested your innocence; that you owned there were two ships taken; but that your men did it violently against your will; and had used you barbarously by imprisoning you and treating you ill most part of the voyage, and often attempting to murder you.' "

Wynn shuddered at these words. Robert had not spoken of physical violence on the voyage, but she knew he must have had to use force to defend the captain. She looked at Sarah, seated across the table, stoically listening as William continued the letter: " '. . . two French passes taken on board the two ships which your men rifled; and I am apt to believe they will be a good article to justify you, if the late peace were not, by the treaty between England and France, to operate in that part of the world at the time the hostility was committed, as I am almost confident it was not to do!' " England and France were no longer at war, but this news had not traveled to that portion of the globe where the *Adventure Galley* had sailed and looted for the Crown. William read on: " 'Mr. Emmot also told me you had about the value of forty thousand pounds in the ship with you.' "

Wynn's skin prickled at the memory of the silky gleaming cloth, silver and gold lace, and the radiant jewels. Then she shook off the vision and once more listened to Captain Kidd as he intoned Bellomont's words. To her, the letter sounded pompous and full of double meanings. What was the author of the letter really trying to say?

The captain read the next part more slowly: " '. . . he told me that you showed a great sense of honor and justice in professing, with many asseverations, your settled and serious design all along to do honor to your commission and never to do the least thing contrary to your duty and allegiance to the king: And this I have to say in your defense, that several persons at New York, who I can bring to evidence if there be occasion, did tell me that by several advices from Madagascar and that part of the world, they were informed of your men's revolting from you in one place; which I am pretty sure they said was at Madagascar; and that others of them compelled you, much against your will, to take and rifle two ships.' "

William stopped, drank from his tankard, then gestured to the others. "You see, there are already witnesses to the mutiny."

Wynn saw Robert's cold stare, as if he wished to say something to William but could not find the words.

"Who are these men who would come to your defense?" asked Sarah.

"No matter," said William. "The word spread, and those who know the truth will say so." He set the tankard on the table.

Robert crossed the cabin, and for a moment all attention turned toward him.

"Do not be so hasty to believe Bellomont," he said. "This may be merely an inducement to come to port."

"Come, Robert," said the captain. "This letter is his document. See how he assures us of fair treatment: 'I have advised with His Majesty's council and shewed them this letter this afternoon; and they are of the opinion, that if your case be so clear as you (or Mr. Emmot for you) have said, then you may safely come hither; and I make no manner of doubt but to obtain the king's pardon for you and those few men you have left, who, I understand, have been faithful to you and refused as well as you to dishonor the commission you had from England.

" 'I assure you on my word and honor, I will perform nicely what I have now promised: Though this I declare beforehand, that whatever treasure or goods you bring hither I will not meddle with the least bit of them; but they shall be left with such trusty persons as the council shall advise until I receive orders from England how they shall be disposed of. Mr. Campbell will satisfy you that this that I have now writ is the sense of the council and of your humble servant, Bellomont.' "

All were silent until Robert spoke up. "He does not promise anything. Only if we can *prove* our innocence will we obtain the king's pardon."

"Governor Bellomont means well, I assure you," said Duncan Campbell. No one acknowledged him, so he continued. "He adjures you to cooperate because of your dangerous position."

"I will write a reply," said Captain Kidd.

"Words, words," said Robert. "I fear they will not save us. We will be hanged for pirates yet," he murmured, speaking more to himself than to anyone in particular.

William chose to ignore him. "Mr. Campbell will carry our reply to the governor," he said.

"And my own memorial of all I have seen and heard," said Campbell, trying to impress the company. Wynn found herself impatient with this intruder, who seemed the type of man who could try to make friends in high places and ingratiate himself into the best social circles.

As if Campbell's remark had ended the discussion, Sarah rose. The gentlemen took the hint and made ready to go to their quarters. Robert said good night to Sarah and William. Then he strode over to Wynn, taking her hand and leading her out, straight to the first mate's cabin. There, he shut the door and removed his coat.

He reached for her, and she went to him, feeling the rigid hold of his tense muscles. He rubbed her neck and stroked her body, and Wynn could feel his need, not of passion, but of an outlet for what he was living through. In discord with the man who had led him to this dilemma, yet forced by friendship and loyalty to obey him, Robert was torn apart in mind and soul. She gently pressed her body against his, hoping to ease his tension. When he bent his face to her, she parted her lips, becoming a vessel for his fierce expression.

They divested themselves of their clothing, and Wynn fell into the bunk beside him. Silently and deliberately they made love, Wynn responding to his every move, her perceptions made more acute by her desire to comfort, to please, to be one with this man.

After their passion had reached its pinnacle and slowly descended to peaceful surrender, Robert moved beside her and lay on his back, his arm thrown behind his head, his eyes open.

Wynn turned on her side, raising her hand to trace the line of his cheek and jaw. "What will William say to Lord Bellomont?" she asked tentatively.

Robert took a breath. "He will deny the rumors and false stories that have been reported of us, and explain why he was fearful of going into the harbor." He turned his face to look at her. "He's wrong though. Damn him. He should have sailed right into Boston and shown Bellomont those French passes. He is losing his reputation. Why does he plead that the ships were taken violently and against his will in one breath and then turn and hand over French passes? If they were French ships, then it was his duty to take them. He did not need a mutiny to make him do it. Bellomont may not find the French passes especially efficacious evidence."

Wynn raised herself on an elbow. "Well, were they taken against his will? Robert, you were there. Was it mutiny or not?"

His eyes took on a hard look and he raised his hand to cup her cheek. "The less said the better. If you were, God forbid, called on a witness stand, I would not want you to perjure yourself."

She felt the blood drain out of her. "Do you think I could be called as a witness?"

"I don't know. I hope not, but it is possible, likely

even, since you sailed with us from Madagascar. So you see why it has tormented me that I let you sail with us." He pulled her down next to him. "It was my own greed. I could not bear to let you sail with Shaw."

She smiled ruefully. "I doubt Captain Shaw would have let me on his ship again in any case. So you see, you had no choice."

Late that same night, Captain Kidd sat in his cabin, thoughtfully twisting his pen. He had tried to scratch out his letter to Bellomont, but with little success. Somehow, he could not get his thoughts organized. Then an idea struck him. If he could get someone else to do the writing while he thought about the lines to be put down, it would be a great help.

He suddenly snapped his fingers — of course! His cousin was aboard, and she could write while he dictated. He moved toward his cabin door. He hated to wake her, and there was something else that bothered him as well. He was not unaware of where his first mate was spending most of his nights, and he didn't want to embarrass the two lovers if, when he knocked, they were in the midst of intimacies. He frowned, deciding he would have to take the risk. He needed her secretarial skills.

Approaching the first mate's cabin, William cleared his throat loudly. Then he knocked firmly on the door.

Inside the cabin, Robert sat up, but Wynn restrained him. "Who is it?" she called out.

"It's the captain, miss. I wonder if you might help me on this matter of the letter to Lord Bellomont. I cannot seem to get my hand and my brain to agree. Perhaps if I dictate the letter you could put it down for me, if you would be so kind."

Wynn threw back the covers. "Of course, Captain. I'll be right there."

"Take your time," said William, and Wynn and Robert listened to his receding footsteps. Then she slipped out of bed and reached for her dress. Robert grinned at her from the narrow bunk.

"Such a pity," he murmured, a gleam in his eye.

"What?"

"That you have to cover that beauty with women's rags."

"Well, you wouldn't want me to appear before our dear captain naked, would you?" Robert slapped her bottom as she scurried out the door.

He had been right in telling Wynn what Captain Kidd would say in his reply to Bellomont. For he told of the ninety men who deserted him for Captain Culliford of the *Mocha Frigate*, and how these men committed acts of piracy. He went on to say he had no doubt that he and the few men left to him could explain their innocence, otherwise they would have no need to return to these parts of the world; he was here because of his owners' interests. He told who was on board now and how they had stood by him, particularly Robert Lamley, the first mate; but his men would not come to Boston until they were assured they would not be molested.

Wynn listened intently and copied it all down, pausing to clarify a point where she did not think it would read well. There was only an hour left 'til dawn by the time she blotted the paper and bid the captain good night. She left it for him to read over, made her way back to her quarters, and fell thankfully into the hard bunk. She had become so used to life at sea she wondered if she would ever be able to fall asleep on land without this gentle rocking to put her to sleep. But then she dreamed of being in a soft bed with Robert next to her, and she pulled the coarse blanket up to her chin and fell asleep.

By the time she rose and dressed the next day, the ship was moving.

Chapter Twenty-two

At Gardiner's Island they put in and traded some of the gold they carried with the lord of the island, John Gardiner, in return for provisions. Kidd had sent Duncan Campbell on ahead with a letter to Bellomont and it was not just the blustery wind that made Wynn shiver as they rounded the cape and made for Boston.

Their dire circumstances erased the normal curiosity she would have had about the New England seacoast and Boston Harbor. For it was in this part of the New World the wily Earl of Bellomont now resided and carried out the office of governor of New England and New York. His purpose was to rid the seas of piracy and he was apparently doing everything he could to that end. Sarah said that he had fought those in New York who had vested interests in piracy, and he had forced merchants who were fostering the Red Sea trade to cease their operations.

But Wynn could not help but suspect duplicity in Bellomont's character, and she dreaded seeing him again after having made such a spectacle of herself at their first meeting. She hoped fervently that she could avoid the man, for his letter to William had made her feel anxious.

And so, instead of joyfully hailing the throbbing harbor town as they prepared to land, Wynn had the uneasy feeling that they were sailing into a trap.

She had come to believe, more and more, that all of their problems were William's fault and she had formed a sad opinion of the captain's character. Although a man of wealth and reputation, he had crumbled before the obstacles he had faced and become a mere pawn for his backers. As Robert had told her, he had simply not been able to say no to the king. And look where it had gotten him. As she contemplated the possible cost to Robert because of his loyalty to his captain, sweat broke out on her forehead despite the chill in the air. She leaned against the bulkhead as the ship sailed up the narrow, twisting channel that connected Boston with the ocean. The harbor with its shacks along the wharf blurred before her in the mist. Steadying herself as the ship rolled in the choppy surf, she felt her way along the railing to her cabin, for she wanted to be out of the crew's way as they prepared to drop anchor. On her way back, she met Sarah, who was cloaked against the heavy weather, and she gestured for Wynn to follow her to the great cabin. There they seated themselves on chairs which were heavy enough not to be tossed about by the waves.

Although Wynn's hands felt clammy, she knew she was not ill. Fear was passing through her, and with it, strange premonitions. "Oh Sarah," she said, her straw-colored hair falling around her face as she threw back the hood of her cloak. "I fear the most awful things. Must we go to Boston? I wish we could turn around and go home, really home, to New York."

Sarah took her cold hands as Wynn tried to explain

her feelings. "I do fear this place, Sarah, and I cannot tell you why."

Sarah raised a dark eyebrow. "No matter what we fear, we must not show it, Wynn," she reminded her cousin, and Wynn sank back in the chair. It was true. Although she had felt a moment of weakness, she knew that Robert would need to see only her strength.

"I know. William and Robert are strong men, but fate has given them very little assurance, and they need us. I am sorry, Sarah. I will not speak of it again."

Sarah's face had a pallor that Wynn did not like. She looked away, saying, "Is it fate, or is it . . ." But she did not finish her thought.

Wynn kept quiet her own thoughts. She wanted to throw the blame for their ill fortune on William, but she could not insult her cousin. Surely though, Sarah knew her husband had made several blunders which had led to this impasse. But Wynn's expression must have betrayed her thoughts, because Sarah seemed to have read them.

"Or was it my husband who led us into this?" she said with more fortitude than she had been able to summon a moment ago.

Wynn wanted to say something reassuring, but the words would not form.

In an offhanded manner, Sarah continued, "My first husband was a sailing man, and so were my own father and brother. I do not profess to know their business, but I confess that these are strange affairs. The sea is a hard mistress." She gave a little shrug. "The only one I have ever fought, and for that I should be grateful. But still, she weaves her spell.

"I knew this commission was dangerous, even mad. Imagine the poorly manned *Adventure Galley* setting out against the legions of pirates who swarm the Indian seas. I would never speak against my husband, but I've had many a month to consider what happened when they sailed to Madagascar that dreadful day. I think my husband lost his nerve."

Wynn was shocked to hear Sarah confess that she, too, had contemplated the facts and come to the same conclusion as Wynn. Sarah's husband was no rash buccaneer, but the owner of a merchant fleet who had been singled out for bravery while fighting in the East Indies. Truly it must have been a difficult position, as Sarah must understand. If he had feared the results of the voyage, commissioned from the Whig lords and the king, couldn't he have just refused?

Wynn looked sympathetically at Sarah. The lines around her dark eyes and the droop of her sensual lips betrayed the strain she had been under. Wynn wondered if she too was showing signs of wear. She brushed her palm over her windblown hair. Would Robert ever see her with curls again, and dressed in frills?

With a sudden longing she thought of her parents' new home, Sarah's graceful house and the stimulating people in New York. She even thought of Gerald Portman, whom she had not considered these many months. For a fleeting instant she thought of the comfortable life she would be leading right now if she had accepted his offer. She hunched her shoulders and rubbed her arms. It might be a long and dreadful time before she ever saw that cozy life again.

But when she thought of Robert, she remembered his tangy skin against hers, the promises they had made to one another at night after passion-filled embraces. She knew she could never again be happy with those old comforts if she couldn't share them with Robert. No, whatever his fate was going to be, she must suffer it with him.

The crew dropped anchor, and the passengers prepared to disembark. Boston's small wood, brick and stone dwellings housed its six thousand residents between Copp's Hill in the North End, Fort Hill in the

South End, and the steep slopes of Beacon Hill in the west. Warehouses and wharves fringed the waterfront, overlooking a forest of masts and wooded islands in the harbor, while merchantmen, fishing boats and even boats from Maine crowded the waters. The hubbub on the docks as sailors, dock workers, ship builders and shipmasters shouted orders, was evidence of the colonial town's thriving trade. But the excitement of being in a new town was lost on Wynn as they stepped into the skiff that would take them to the dock.

Boston had survived several fires, rebellion, drought, famine and disease. Here there were no aristocrats, no royalty to control local affairs, no land barons, and merchants were among the most respected citizens. It was a strong community, but Wynn felt isolated from it, for she feared Boston's sense of justice was not going to apply to them.

Duncan Campbell stood on the dock to meet them. He was dressed in fine brocade, cambric, and high-heeled shoes with bright buckles, and he carried one of the most decorative tri-cornered hats Wynn had ever seen. He led them through the clatter along the docks to a carriage, his servants fetching along their luggage. A fellow Scotsman of Captain Kidd's, he had kindly offered lodging to the little party at his house. But for all the man's gallantry, Wynn did not feel safe in his hands.

As they settled themselves in the carriage, Wynn peered out at the winding streets of Boston. Like New York, signs swinging from brackets indicated the trades carried on in the brick and stone houses. She only wished she were seeing Boston on a more auspicious occasion. Its crooked streets, alleys and lanes could have held much to explore, had things been different. Most of the houses seemed small and dark, no more than three stories high, and most people traveled on foot.

The carriage jolted over the uneven streets and came to a stop in front of a handsome three-story brick house. The carriage door opened, and Robert helped her to the ground. They were ushered into the parlor.

Here comfortable wing chairs, a settee upholstered in rose damask, delft tiles surrounding the fireplace and raised paneled walls attested to the Campbells' fine living. An ornamental mirror hung in the hallway over bannister-backed side chairs, padded with crimson and gold cushions secured to the legs with gold tassels.

A small woman dressed in taffeta covered with lace, her hair styled in a myriad of ringlets, came into the parlor, and Duncan Campbell introduced her as his wife, Miriam. She offered her hand to the guests and then summoned a servant to bring refreshments.

William clapped Campbell on the back, saying, "My friend and countryman, what shall we do to express our appreciation?"

"No trouble, sir," exclaimed their host as he poured wine from a silver carafe. "My rank as postmaster offers me a chance to be of service to you on the governor's behalf, and my wife thrives on entertaining, don't you, Miriam?"

As Wynn was handed a goblet, she turned her eyes toward the small lady presiding over the refreshments. Her refined manners and dress made Wynn suddenly self-conscious about her tattered appearance. At least now that they were on land, perhaps she would be able to send for some of her clothes.

"It is our pleasure to entertain such a *celebrated* party," said Miriam, and Wynn noticed the way her voice lingered on the word *celebrated*. The wine suddenly felt dry in her throat, for she was sure that they were providing not only entertainment for Mrs. Campbell, but a spectacle for gossip, as well. Surely the postmaster was in the best position to frank out the latest news to all parts. Wynn felt hypocritical standing in this circle, making polite conversation when she really wanted to give these Bostonians a piece of her mind. At the moment she would be glad to have escaped anywhere with Robert. She couldn't care less about his loyalty to Captain Kidd. If William had gotten them into this mess, as Sarah and the others seemed to agree, then let him get himself out of it. Robert didn't need to play the fool any longer, even if the captain was related to Wynn by marriage. What mattered reputation if happiness was the cost?

But, looking at Robert, she remembered that he too was being held responsible for acts of piracy, for he was an officer of the ship. If he ran away from the law now, he could never return. And where would they go? She had left England to come to America. If they fled America, they could never go to any country England ruled. It struck her that they really belonged nowhere, and it brought a sick feeling to her stomach.

None too soon, Mrs. Campbell offered to show them their rooms. "My dear," she said, following Wynn into her room, the curiosity evident in her voice, "I have heard the amazing tale of how you left your home with your brother to seek out your fiancé to warn him of the threat to his life. I am truly astonished that a woman as fair as you would leave everything behind for such an adventure. I didn't mean to imply anything," Miriam quickly added, as Wynn stared coldly at her and remained silent. "I only meant that surely you are without your usual things, and that until you can send for your wardrobe, I would be much obliged if you picked some clothing to suit you from this closet." And she opened doors to reveal a sumptuous collection of gowns. Wynn's eyes widened as she gazed upon the fine fabrics.

She had been away from genteel living for so long that she had forgotten what it was like to care about her appearance. Now as she caught her reflection in an ornamented looking glass, she realized how bedraggled she looked beside the neat, well-dressed Miriam Campbell.

"Thank you," she said, regretting her asperity toward her hostess. "I believe I will freshen up and change. I appreciate your offer. And could I ask you a favor?" She blushed.

"Of course, you must make this your home until your, uh, little difficulty is settled. I understand you are to be married."

"Yes, though goodness knows when," Wynn sighed. "I wonder if something could be done with my hair? You see, I had to cut it off when I — " she felt suddenly sheepish explaining all this to Miriam Campbell. "Well, I cut my hair, that is, my brother did, when we ran away to sea, and I haven't been near a curling iron since."

Suddenly she laughed. It was true, she was an adventurer. Why not enjoy telling the story? If Miriam Campbell was going to gossip about her, she might as well have the truth of the matter. From the look on the woman's face, Wynn could tell she had captured her interest.

"Of course," said Miriam. "I'll send my maid Heidi." She left the room, a look of satisfaction on her face. Wynn decided that she was probably rushing out to tell her friends that pirates and wayward women were staying under her roof, and there was nothing she could do about it, for they were here to see the governor.

Wynn took her time with her toilette, and with the maid's help, she bathed and dressed. A pair of cutting shears and a curling iron took care of the unruly tresses, now grown out to an odd length. Her toilette completed, Wynn was pleased with what she saw in the mirror. The long-sleeved brown velvet gown with ecru lace adorning the bodice and wrists flattered her sun- and windburned complexion. Just seeing herself thus gave her new hope. Surely this misunderstanding with the governor would end, life would return to normal, and she and Robert would be married. She shivered a little, contemplating the joys of conjugal life.

When Wynn went down for dinner, the men were deep in conversation. But her appearance on the stairway made them all turn to look at her. Sentences were left unfinished as she descended the stairway, her fingers gliding along the smooth handrail of the balustrade. Robert stepped forward and offered her his arm. She felt her flesh quiver as she tucked her hand into his elbow and saw the look of hunger in his eyes. The time spent primping had been worth the effort.

"You are ravishing," he said in a low voice, escorting her to the dining room where the others were gathering. The other gentlemen bowed as she passed them, and she thought she saw a twinkle in William's eyes. Duncan Campbell could not resist teasing her.

"Can this be the young lady who went to sea to be with her beloved?" he said.

"Sir, I beg you," Robert began, but realizing that his temper was rising, Wynn interposed.

"It's all right, Robert. The disguise was the hardest part," she said in a bandying tone, and the men laughed. She felt Robert relax, but he remained close by her, ready to pounce on any man who came too close.

Sarah joined them, and the men complimented her dress made of a lavender material, which brought out the color of her eyes. But her face still held that trace of sadness that Wynn had seen in her ever since Captain Kidd had sailed away. It was a pity to see her beauty marred by such heavy cares, Wynn thought, realizing that she was no longer jealous of Sarah's beauty, so secure was she now in Robert's love. Indeed Robert's eyes almost never left her, roving from her blue eyes to the clever arrangement of her hair, down her graceful throat and over her bare shoulders to her breasts, which sloped outward under the velvet garment.

Wynn felt a thrill at his gaze, and she flushed, thinking of his hands gently lowering her gown so that he could admire her tender breasts, which were his to gaze upon. She noticed that he was drinking more wine than usual, and she could feel that he was also thinking similar thoughts. It was with an effort that he turned to the conversation at hand.

"I hope you are prepared to see Bellomont tomorrow," he said to William. "It was clever of him to delay seeing us today and wait until he is sitting in council tomorrow."

William waved aside what he considered to be a triviality. "No matter. I sent his wife a few jewels and a thousand pounds in gold sewn up in a green silk bag," he said.

"Husband!" said Sarah. "If you persist in showering everyone with so many gifts, there will be nothing left for the king."

The others at the table laughed nervously. Remembering the treasure on board the ship, Wynn thought cynically that there was more than enough to go around, and he would not run out. She also knew that the political climate was somewhat immoral in any case; that officials of all stations cheated and stole from the government.

Robert had also told her of the cruelty meted out by captains of most naval and merchant ships. Piracy was a reaction to the hard life to which seamen were subjected. In the midst of all this cruelty and corruption, it seemed to her that Robert and William were truthful individuals. But then perhaps that was the difficulty. If the governor was unscrupulous, how could they please him? Evidently William had thought that a gift would help to sway him.

"When will you go to see the governor?" she asked Robert.

"Tomorrow," he grumbled. "But do not worry about it."

"But I shall worry," she said, almost to herself. "And I wish I could be with you."

Robert looked at her tenderly. "My love, that is kind of you, but you could do nothing. We will handle this affair, and then," he intoned, determination returning to his voice, "we shall be married."

He turned to the others and broke through the buzzing conversation, lifting his glass. "Pour your glasses full, ladies and gentlemen. I would like to make a toast to my fiancée, this ravishing lady on my left, whom I cannot keep my eyes from tonight."

Wynn blushed and looked down, embarrassed by Robert's salutation. The chairs scraped back, and the men stood. She looked up to see Sarah smiling at her and Miriam Campbell gazing at her with something like envy on her face.

The men drank to her health. Then the captain spoke. "To the couple's health and happiness," he said, and Duncan Campbell said, "Hear, hear." They drank again. Then the ladies joined in with their lilting voices, and Robert sat down.

He was drinking too much, Wynn thought, which led her to believe that he was more worried than he would admit about tomorrow's interview. She finished her meal and then rose with the ladies to leave the men to their port. She hoped Robert would not have too much of it, as she followed their hostess out.

In the drawing room, she refused the offer of a cordial and took coffee instead. As Sarah complimented Miriam on the running of her home, Wynn's mind wandered back to Robert's plight. She knew that if they had remained in southern waters, they could have evaded the coming confrontation indefinitely. But of course William couldn't have stayed there forever, apart from

Sarah and their little daughter, who was now safely asleep upstairs.

She was aware of Miriam Campbell interrupting her thoughts. "I daresay you must be excited at the prospect of marrying such a handsome gentleman."

"Of course," said Wynn, unsure as to where this conversation was going to lead.

Miriam giggled. "My dear, I'll never forget my wedding night." Her tone was suggestive, and Wynn looked away. She couldn't very well admit she had already experienced amorous delights with Robert. Polite society would be outraged.

A pang of guilt threatened her. If they had remained in surroundings like these, she wondered if she would have allowed Robert any bold advances. But in the heat of the tropics, in so desperate a situation, it had seemed natural to give herself to him. She felt her face redden and hoped that Miriam assumed she was simply shy about the subject of marriage. Sarah knew better, but her discretion would prevent her from making any slips.

"Of course you know what is expected of you?" Miriam continued. "Your cousin will have helped you with these matters."

At this point Sarah came to the rescue. "Why yes. Wynn and I have had an intimate conversation. I am sure she will be quite happy on her wedding night."

Just then the drawing room door opened, and the men entered. Behind them there was a commotion in the hallway. The butler had answered the front door, and after an exchange with someone outside, he accepted a green silk bag which he brought into the drawing room. Wynn saw Sarah's hand flutter to her heart.

"Damn," said Robert.

The butler cleared his throat. "The parcel is from Lady Bellomont. She returns it to you, sir." He brought the bag forward, and William took it with trembling hands. Then Wynn understood. It was the gift, or rather the bribe, that William had sent to Bellomont. This was certainly a bad omen, Wynn thought, putting a hand on Robert's arm, but he only turned away, running his other hand through his hair in silent protest at this latest gesture by his foolish friend.

"I believe I'll have that cordial now," Wynn said to Miriam, for she knew she would need its soporific effect after she had retired to bed.

Richard, Earl of Bellomont, sat in council in his house, at an elaborate table which nearly filled the end of the council chambers. He leaned back in his upholstered arm chair with its elegantly carved Spanish feet, watching Robert and Captain Kidd as they strode across the geometric-patterned floor. Robert studied the severe faces beneath their powdered periwigs on either side of Bellomont, his eyes finally coming to rest on the yellow-faced earl, who wore a robe impressively ringed with silver fox and gold and silver brocade. So, thought Robert, finally I meet the man who was responsible for this ill-fated voyage and who now controls our fate. William stepped forward, sweeping his tri-cornered hat in front of him as he bowed. "Greetings, Lord Bellomont," he said.

As Bellomont leaned forward, Robert noticed that one foot rested on a velvet-cushioned hassock, and he remembered that the man suffered from severe gout.

"Mr. Kidd," said Bellomont with a heavy frown, "forgo the niceties. Your account of the voyage — have you got it?"

"My Lord Bellomont," said Kidd. "You know that my log was burned when my crew mutinied at St. Mary's in Madagascar. I have only my word and that of my first mate, Mr. Lamley, for what has occurred. But I assure you we can provide you with the details necessary to answer any and all questions you may have."

"You have until five o'clock tomorrow to prepare and produce a detailed account of your movements since leaving England," Bellomont said, glowering.

"Lord Bellomont!" protested the captain. "That's not nearly enough time."

Then Bellomont turned his wily eyes on Robert. "Your friend can help you."

Robert felt his skin prickle in dislike of this man. William went on with his inexorable protestations of innocence, but Bellomont waved them aside.

"I trust you have an inventory."

Kidd reached into his coat and extracted a paper which he unfolded and handed to Bellomont. "Here, sir, is the extent of the goods aboard our ship."

Bellomont adjusted his monocle and read the list. "One thousand one hundred eleven troy ounces of gold; two thousand three hundred fifty-three ounces of silver, seventeen and three-eighths ounces of jewels or precious stones, fifty-seven bags of sugar, forty-one bales of merchandise and seventeen pieces of canvas."

"And what else has leaked away between the East Indies and here?"

Robert could restrain himself no longer. "Sir, if that is an accusation, I assure you . . ."

"Silence, Mr. Lamley!" Bellomont interrupted him. "You need not defend your friend's egregious behavior. Mr. Kidd took the liberty of sending my wife a thousand pounds in gold dust and ingots yesterday, which I ordered her to return. That gold is property of the Crown."

Robert felt the blood rise in his face. Among officials who often bribed one another, a gift of that sort was common enough, and he resented Bellomont's hypocritical treatment of the man he had ordered off to an impossible commission at sea. He was about to speak again, when William stayed him.

"Lord Bellomont misunderstands my gesture," he

said. "I merely wished to demonstrate the quality of treasure we had to present for your reckoning."

"Bah," said Bellomont. He stood, awkwardly leaning on the polished table which reflected his image. "Prepare a narrative of your voyage with accurate details and come here with it tomorrow at five o'clock. I suggest you leave now as you have much work to do."

William turned to Robert. "Come," he said in a voice brooking no dissent. They took their leave, their footsteps echoing with a hollow ring as they made their way out of the chambers and down the winding staircase with its intricately carved balustrade to the hallway below. Robert resented the opulence of the cherry-colored silk and scarlet and silver brocade hangings in the hall. Though it was Bellomont's wife, Kate, who insisted on such ostentatious decoration, Robert suspected that all this wealth had not come honestly. Not that he approved of William's bribe, but he still resented Bellomont's churlish piousness. As they descended the red freestone steps from the porch to the courtyard, William mopped the sweat from his brow.

"I have a thirst, Robert. Let us take refreshment at the Blue Anchor Tavern. It's not far."

Robert ignored the comment. "Do you really expect him to pardon us?"

"The king has allowed him power to issue pardon if he so wishes."

"But he is timid of using it. His letter said he had made himself a rule never to pardon piracy without the king's express leave and command."

"Come, Robert, let us forget this for a while. A drop of rum would do me good."

"William, be sensible. We have work to do. He has demanded a full report."

"Calm yourself, Robert. There's enough time for that after we have quenched our thirst."

"I'm warning you, William. If you don't write that

narrative, I will. I was there. I can say what these eyes saw, and what these ears heard. Perhaps I'd do a better job. I'd tell the truth, and what I think of the king's stinking commission!"

"Robert, my man. You get yourself too riled. You know how things are. Bellomont may howl, but he'll come through. And besides, Livingston and the owners will settle up with us."

"Livingston, ha! He'll probably ask to be released from the bond he entered into as your guarantor."

"If he does, I doubt Bellomont will let him out of it. No, it's too late for that now. He'll have to stand behind us."

Robert reluctantly followed him into the street and to the Blue Anchor Tavern. He would have to make sure his friend did not drink too much, for he must get started on the narrative that very day.

While the men were away, Wynn nervously paced the drawing room. She had tried to write a letter to her family, but there was nothing she really wanted to say. Then she had sat thinking of James and wondering when she would see him again, for apparently the *Joanna* had made it safely to port.

It was near evening when she woke with a start. She had fallen asleep in the upholstered chair by the fireplace, where Heidi had lit a fire. A hand shook her by the shoulder, and she looked up to find Robert standing beside her.

"Oh, Robert!" she cried as she rose and threw herself into his arms. "What a horrible long day. You've been gone for so long."

He pressed his cheek against hers, but when she looked at his face, she saw the worry written on it.

"What is it? What's wrong?" she asked, fear paralyzing her.

"It's William," he said, turning from her and shaking his head. "Bellomont instructed him to write a narrative of the voyage to replace the log that was burnt. But he will not do it. I can no longer understand him. He speaks with confidence, and yet he will take no action to save himself."

Wynn looked at Robert thoughtfully. "Perhaps," she said slowly, "he has given up."

Robert raised his head and stared at an oil painting of one of the Campbell ancestors looking down at them from the wall. "Yes, I fear that may be the case," he said.

"Oh, Robert," she said, "we can't let him give up — we must not."

He turned toward her. "You are right, but I cannot make him do anything."

"Robert, I have an idea. Remember on the ship how he dictated the letter to me, and I wrote it down? Perhaps I could help him. Perhaps if he narrated the voyage I could write it for him."

Robert considered her proposal. "Yes," he finally said. "It might just work. Good. We'll go to him at once."

"It must be near suppertime. Perhaps we could mention it at the table."

"No, I'll go to him now. You're a godsend, my little one. He'll have to agree." And she thought she saw a flicker of hope in Robert's eyes as he left her.

William agreed, and after supper, Wynn settled down in Duncan Campbell's study to write down William's narration of the voyage. "A Narrative of the Voyage of Captain William Kidd, Commander of the *Adventure Galley* from London to the East Indies," she began. The document, she realized, would be the only record of the voyage, and she encouraged William to be as accurate as his memory would allow.

Near midnight, her hand began to cramp, and she had

to stop William, who was scratching his head trying to remember the date the ship had met up with the Portuguese man-of-war.

"Captain," she said. "I fear I cannot go on. My hand is cramped, and I cannot push it across the page. Let us rest and continue in the morning."

"Yes, yes," said William. "It is difficult to remember all this anyway. It's easy when you have your log to depend on, but working from memory alone is most difficult. One memory is attracted to another that is similar, and trying to recall everything in sequence is like unraveling a ball of yarn."

He raised his hands in a gesture of perplexity. "Go on," he said, motioning her from the room. "I'll just finish this glass of port, then to bed with me."

"Good night then, Captain."

"Good night."

She closed the door softly behind her then tiptoed to the stairs. She wondered if Robert had gone up yet. Then she heard a stirring in the parlor and crossed the hall to go in. Robert shifted himself from an uncomfortable-looking position in the Turkey-worked settee where he had evidently been sleeping. She crept up to him, but sensing her presence, he sat up.

She went to him. "Robert, you needn't have waited up."

He reached for her, pulling her down onto his lap. "I'll be the judge of my needs," he growled into her ear, making her laugh. "And the work?"

She chuckled. "It was a struggle, but we got started."

"It isn't finished?"

"No, it isn't. We'll finish tomorrow, when my hand and his brain are rested."

"No matter. You should be getting to bed," he whispered, brushing his lips against her hair. He held her close and kissed her long and lingeringly. Then he nuzzled her shoulder, and she turned her cheek against his dark shiny hair.

"I'd like to take you to bed, my little dove, but I'm afraid I can't do that in this house. Scandal would fly. I'll have to be satisfied with escorting you to the bedroom door and wishing you pleasant dreams."

She sighed and allowed him to lead her across the room to the stairs. Taking a candle from the hall, she preceded him up, and at the top of the stairs turned left toward her room. At the door they stopped and he leaned one hand on the door frame and looked down at her sleepy face. He brushed his fingers across her smooth cheeks.

"Good night, my love," he said and kissed her once more, gently. Wynn found it hard to let him go. She somehow feared that this would be the last night they would be together. Her feelings perplexed her, for he gave no evidence that such would be the case, but gently opened the door. She went in, closing it regretfully behind her.

She looked at the four-poster bed with its ruffled valance, the curtains drawn back. She would find little comfort in that bed, even if it was softer and roomier than the ship bunk. Nevertheless, she struggled out of her clothes and climbed in between the covers. More tired than she had thought, she fell asleep quickly.

The next day William delayed working on his report until afternoon. When Wynn saw Robert, he was appalled at this news of William's further procrastination. Behind closed doors, she could hear him arguing with William. She passed on, not wanting an idle servant to think she was eavesdropping, and sat down on a settee, running her hand nervously over its needlework, waiting for one of the men to emerge from the study.

Later that afternoon Wynn was standing at the casement window looking out to the street, trying to decide whether or not to go out and have a look around the town. The house was getting on her nerves, and William had locked himself in the study. She was beginning to feel like a caged animal, with nothing to do, and just as she had decided that fresh air would raise her spirits, she saw William go down the steps and turn into the street. She was so intent on watching him, she did not hear Robert's footsteps behind her on the carpet.

"If you want to know where he's gone, I'll tell you," he said as she turned to him with a start. "He's no doubt gone to the Blue Anchor Tavern."

Wynn noticed the strained lines on his brow and the disapproval in his voice. But then his look softened as he looked at her. "Come sit beside me, my love, and make me forget these hideous things." And he led her to the settee.

"Robert," she said, suddenly sick and tired of the tension between her beloved and the captain, "if you and William disagree, why do you try so hard to make him see your point of view?" She nestled her cheek against his shoulder. "Why can't we just leave him to his fate? Surely if he is arrested, there is nothing you can do."

"What would you have me do? Run away, desert him as the others have? Don't you think I haven't considered it? I could take you to a tropical island somewhere. But it wouldn't work. William's fate is my fate. My family has a good name. It will go down in the annals of history that I sailed with Captain Kidd. And what about you, my love? If you ran away with me, you would be branded a pirate's woman, and you'd have to live on a ship."

"Oh, Robert, I don't care where I live as long as it's with you."

He caressed her cheeks. "I know you mean that, sweetheart. But you'd soon tire of that kind of life. You're made for gowns like this one, houses like this one, and perhaps children."

Then he leaned back and sighed. "I might as well go after him and try to shake him out of his languor. He's gone to the tavern, I'm sure. And after he drinks he's even less clear-headed than before."

"Why doesn't he want to finish the narrative?"

"I don't know," said Robert. "Perhaps because his own thoughts on the matters are so unclear that he is afraid to commit himself."

"But he's said time and again that you are all innocent; that the crew was mutinous — and he does have the French passes."

Robert's eyes took on the hard look that Wynn had seen so often in the past. "But that is the problem. If the crew had been truly mutinous, then he would not need to defend himself with the French passes. If they were really French ships, then it was his duty to capture them, and he need not rely on the excuse of the mutinous crew. But he is afraid to give up either argument for fear the other won't work, thereby weakening our position."

"It sounds impossible." She shook her head.

Robert stood, and she stood with him, impulsively gripping his arms. Each time he left her, she felt that she would never see him again. If only she could control her feelings of panic. She was certain it did Robert no good to see her this way. He gently pulled away.

"I must go, my love. Once this job is done, we'll have plenty of time together, I promise you." He kissed her gently on the forehead and turned to leave. She stood alone in the deepening shadows, jumping when the door shut with finality.

Chapter Twenty-three

In the dim light of the Blue Anchor Tavern, Robert stood looking at the patrons, but William was not among them. He approached the landlord, a brisk and jolly-looking man with bushy side whiskers, leaning on his frame bar, behind which punch bowls, decanters, flip glasses and mugs were all stored on shelves. "Say, friend, was Captain Kidd in here today?" Robert interrupted the man's lively conversation with a ruddy-looking customer.

"Let's see . . . Captain Kidd. Yes he was. He had a few pints, then he left."

"Did he say where he was going?"

The landlord scratched his chin. "No, no he didn't."

"Many thanks," said Robert, turning to leave. If Kidd wasn't at the tavern, then where was he? An uncomfortable feeling started Robert's stomach churning as he instinctively headed in the direction of Governor Bellomont's house. He didn't know why Kidd would have gone there, since the narrative of the voyage wasn't finished, but it was the only place Robert could think of to look. He hurried along the winding streets, and as he rounded the corner that brought him in view of the governor's mansion, he uttered a curse. Kidd was on the porch steps, his sword drawn, surrounded by the police.

Robert rushed into the melee, shouting at William, and a surprised policeman aimed his pistol at him. Robert slammed a fist into him, and with a well-placed boot, knocked the pistol away from him, grabbed it, and rushed up the steps.

Kidd had succeeded in wounding one man, and as Robert joined him, he rushed into the house. Seeing the danger they were in, Robert held his pistol on the angry policemen and followed William into the house. After he had caught his breath, anger began to boil in him.

"What the devil — ?" but he turned to discover that William had disappeared. Robert tramped up the winding staircase to the council chambers, and there, standing before a shocked governor and council, still brandishing his sword, was William, uttering unintelligible curses and threats.

With a signal from Bellomont, more policemen surrounded them. Realizing that they would be hanged for sure if they killed anyone here, Robert was about to surrender his pistol when Bellomont spoke.

"I must perforce put you both under arrest," he said.

"What charge?" Robert shouted, enraged at both William and the governor.

Unruffled, Bellomont answered, "Piracy." Then he turned to Kidd. "And a charge of murder for you as well."

Kidd began to struggle, his face red, more from truculence than drink, Robert thought, but three policemen pinned his arms on the governor's table and disarmed him.

"This is unfair," protested Kidd, but the governor waved a hand.

"You, sir, have provided the evidence by your execrable behavior. I am without patience. Perhaps in jail you can see your way clear to provide the narrative I require."

"This is an outrage!" Kidd continued, his voice slurred. "Livingston will agree. I demand that word be sent to my backers."

"Livingston has already been to see me," said the governor. "He tried to weasel out of our agreement, but of course I would not let him. I am impatient at your attempts to juggle and embezzle the cargo. I am delivering up the jewels you sent to my wife in addition to the ingots and gold dust she returned to you. I am also preparing a full report to the backers in London, so rest assured they will be informed."

"Sir," interrupted Robert, realizing this might be the last chance to palliate what the governor considered to be their crimes. "Since you have our inventory, you cannot accuse us of stealing the goods."

"Just so," Bellomont continued. "And neither of you will escape me now. I have orders signed by myself and the council to arrest both you and the seven others of your crew who were with you, and throw you into Stone Prison."

"But sir," said Robert, controlling his anger, for he knew that William's gracelessness and stubbornness had gotten them into this spot, "how can we adequately prepare our report from prison? Would it not be better to continue work in our own quarters? Surely the discomforts of prison will not help our memories any."

Bellomont slammed his fist onto the polished wood table so hard his periwig jumped. "You have not been able to produce the report I require. Perhaps a little seclusion will do you good. You will not be distracted by the nearness of the Blue Anchor Tavern."

Robert glared at Kidd. As much as he loved his friend, he was furious at Kidd's indolence with regard to writing the required narrative. And Bellomont was, at least, right about one thing — Kidd's attitude didn't help.

"Take them away," Bellomont commanded.

A policeman gave William a shove, and Robert, looking disdainfully at the officer who motioned with his pistol, stepped ahead of him, not waiting to be manhandled.

Robert's head throbbed violently, and he grimaced with pain as a vision of Wynn flashed before his eyes. It would kill her to know he was going to prison. Just as they approached the double oak doors that led to the porch downstairs, a policeman barked out an order for them to halt.

"Governor Bellomont has a message," he said.

Robert turned and glowered at the man, while William stood silently. "Well?"

"The French passes. He will keep them for you until the trial." Robert frowned. There was something about this he didn't like. Then the guards surrounded the two men and nudged them down the steps.

When Robert failed to return before dinner, Wynn began to worry and sent for a servant to see if there had been any messages, but there were none. She found Sarah in the drawing room, sitting in a silver brocade wing chair, winding a ball of yarn, and staring absently into space.

Just then the servant returned. "Excuse me, ladies," said the maid, curtseying. "Mrs. Campbell wants to know how many for dinner."

Sarah put down her yarn. "Why, I don't know. I don't know where they . . ." But her sentence was interrupted by a loud knocking on the door, distracting the maid, who turned to see if there was someone to answer it. The butler appeared and opened the door, and after a few moments he entered the drawing room, followed by a page.

The butler bowed. "A messenger from Governor Bellomont." He withdrew, casting a look of opprobrium at the maid, who was peering over the boy's shoulder. Both servants left the room as the young messenger held out a rolled-up letter. Sarah rose and took it.

"It's got the governor's seal."

But before Sarah could break the seal, the young page spoke, sounding exceedingly grown up. "The governor says to inform you he has arrested Captain Kidd and Mr. Robert Lamley, and that he has had them taken to Stone Prison. The letter explains the orders."

"Prison," said Sarah, staring dumbly at the boy.

Wynn felt her knees grow weak, and then the room began to whirl around her and everything went black.

When she returned to consciousness she discovered she was lying in a bed. "Miss Wynn," said a voice beside her. Trying to decide whether the voice was male or female, she felt a hand brush a damp cloth over her forehead. Then her vision cleared, and she saw the maid, Heidi, hovering over her with a concerned look on her face.

"Oh," said Wynn as she felt the ache in her head. Then it all came back. She struggled to sit up, but Heidi tried to dissuade her.

"Don't try to get up; you took a nasty fall. I'll get Miss Miriam." Wynn did not protest, and in a moment the maid returned with Miriam Campbell. Her hostess looked pale, but whether it was because of concern for Wynn or because she did not know what to do with an incapacitated guest, Wynn did not know.

"My dear," said Miriam. "Are you feeling better?"

Wynn's throat felt dry, but she tried to speak. "I think so. What happened?"

"You hit your head on the corner of a side table, my dear. You gave us quite a scare."

"Robert? Where is he?" Wynn clutched at Miriam's arm. "Did they really take them to prison?"

Miriam looked uncomfortable. "I'm afraid they did."

Wynn fell back into the pillows, a pain clutching her heart as if someone had run a knife through her. "Where's Sarah?"

"She's still in her room, resting. It was quite a shock, I am sure."

"I must go to her," said Wynn, trying to rise. But Miriam tried to restrain her.

"You mustn't. Your head."

But Wynn pushed aside the covers. "I'm quite all right," she insisted. She would not have this woman hovering over her. "It's just a bruise. I'm quite over the faint now." She sat up and pushed her way past Miriam, who stood open-mouthed, not knowing what to do. Wynn ignored her and made her way to the hall. There she leaned against the wall. She did feel a trifle unsteady, but she had to find Sarah.

Pushing open Sarah's door, she peered in. Sarah was sitting at a small writing table with her hands folded. Her face was pinched, but she was not crying. Wynn walked slowly toward her, and the two women stared at each other, dry-eyed.

"Whatever are we to do?" murmured Wynn, sinking onto the bed. Sarah looked at her strangely.

"Do? I doubt there is anything we can do."

A sob choked Wynn's response. She could not cry in front of Miriam, but here with the cousin she had come to love like a sister, she let herself go. Her shoulders heaved, and she lay facedown on the bed, clutching the embroidered linen and squeezing it in a ball.

"It can't be," she moaned. She felt the cushions beside her sink as Sarah sat down beside her and reached to comfort her. Wynn had sought Sarah out to comfort her, but now it seemed it was Wynn herself who needed the solace.

Robert was in prison. She couldn't stand the thought. She gasped for breath and wiped her eyes and nose on the handkerchief Sarah provided her.

"I've got to see him," she said.

"When the time comes," said Sarah.

"No, no. How can you say that? I must go to him now."

Sarah sighed. "We will see them if we can."

"Sarah, how can you remain so calm?" Wynn sniffled into the handkerchief. "You always seem so ready to accept tragedy. How can you face danger like that?"

"Is there any other way to face it?" There was a hard edge to Sarah's voice, but it remained level. Wynn didn't know how Sarah managed to keep her feelings all inside her like that. For surely she was as pained about William's imprisonment as Wynn was about Robert's. She looked at Sarah through watery eyes and shivered. She would rather be able to pour out her misery, she thought, than keep it trapped inside her. She was frightened by the glazed look in Sarah's eyes. It couldn't be good for her to repress her grief.

Then gradually, as if coming back from a great distance, Sarah focused on her cousin.

"Wash your face, Wynn," she said. "We will go see Governor Bellomont."

Wynn sat up. "Do you mean that?"

"Yes, hurry now."

Wynn ran to sponge her face and fetch her cloak, anxious to take advantage of Sarah's decision to act.

She met her in the hallway downstairs, and they hurried out the door. In the narrow winding streets, it was quicker to go on foot than by carriage. They turned into a broader street, which was paved with cobblestones brought up from the beach. Soon they spied the governor's courtyard, its green lawn and two tall oak trees flanking the paved walk up to the massive red stone entrance with its oak doors. A servant answered their ring.

"Mrs. Sarah Kidd and Miss Wynn Cox to see Lord Bellomont," said Sarah. The servant asked them to wait in the hall.

After a moment they were ushered into the library, where the governor sat alone. They barely noticed the richly panelled room, handsomely appointed with silk curtains and silver plate. Marble sculptures and inlaid side tables stood beside Italian chairs. Wynn looked straight ahead at the man who sat behind a large mahogany desk. A servant closed the doors behind them, and they approached him.

"Forgive me if I do not rise, ladies. I am ill with the gout." He grimaced as if to emphasize his discomfort.

"Sir, you have confined my husband to prison," Sarah began. A struggle went on in Wynn. She would have tried to charm the man if it had not been for her grief and anger as well as her embarrassment about the way she had acted at their previous meeting.

"I am aware of what I have done," he said, nodding to Sarah.

"This is my cousin, Miss Wynn Cox," Sarah went on, "engaged to marry Robert Lamley."

"Yes," said Bellomont sarcastically. "We have met."

Wynn could not allow his tone of voice to put her off. "When may we see them, sir?"

He raised an eyebrow. "You may see them when *I* am satisfied they have produced a narrative of the unfortunate voyage of the *Adventure Galley* and accounted for all the treasure taken during that voyage."

"But sir," protested Sarah. "I'm sure everything will be accounted for, including the treasure."

"I've seen it with my very eyes," added Wynn.

"The treasure, ladies," said Bellomont, his face changing shades from yellow through red to purple, "is most likely scattered from the southern seas to the tip of New York state. In fact your husband seems to have dispersed it in so many places that I really cannot be sure where it all is. He even sought to bribe me with presents to my wife."

"I'm sure he did not intend —" said Sarah, but he cut her off.

"If your husband has any scruples left, madam," he said and turned to Wynn, "or if that scoundrel with him has any, let them demonstrate their intelligence by writing a detailed account of their voyage. It will be read, and then we'll see which side of the law they stand on."

Sarah stood, her shoulders slumping in despair, but Wynn stepped forward. "Lord Bellomont," she said, leveling her gaze at him. "I had begun writing Captain Kidd's narrative as he dictated it to me in Duncan Campbell's study. I can bring it to you."

"Hmph," he replied. "I don't care if he's begun it, I want to see it finished."

"But . . ."

He cut her off. "The captain spent the better part of the afternoon drinking, then he charged in here like the cutthroat pirate he is, followed by that reprobate first mate of his."

"Sir," Wynn implored, but he raised a hand to stop her.

"It is unfortunate, miss, that you have gotten involved with this bunch of pirates. If Mrs. Kidd had any scruples, she would advise you to return to your parents at once and forget Robert Lamley, for he is doomed.

Even if he does well by himself at the trial, his reputation will be tainted and he'll probably go away to sea again. You were mistaken when you tried to intercede on his behalf when you met me in New York. You are still mistaken. He does not deserve you. Only a woman uncaring of her reputation would continue in this manner."

Wynn realized her arguments on behalf of the narrative were futile, but she wasn't going to allow this miserable gouty old man to keep her out of the prison where Robert was being held.

"I demand to be taken to my fiancé at once," she said.

"Wynn," Sarah said, trying to stop her.

But she lifted her chin defiantly. "When may I see him?"

Bellomont glowered at her. "Bah. Go home where you belong. I'll speak to the council and send word."

Seeing that Wynn was about to inveigh against him, Sarah pulled her by the arm. "Thank you, Your Excellency," said Sarah, pushing Wynn toward the door.

Outside, she whispered to Wynn. "You shouldn't have said you'd seen the treasure."

"Why not? They'll find out I was on board. Does that make me a pirate too?"

"I hope not," said Sarah. "In heaven's name, I hope not."

They returned home silently. In the Campbells' house, Wynn told Heidi she would have a tray in her room. She wasn't at all hungry, and she certainly didn't feel like eating in front of the garrulous Campbells.

How the evening passed, Wynn didn't know. She ate a little soup, then lay on her bed fully clothed, trying to think of a way to see Robert. For she would go mad if she had to wait.

She also tried to remember something she'd noticed at Bellomont's house. It was something he'd done as they were talking, but at the time she'd been too distraught to pay attention. Now going over the scene in her mind's eye, she tried to remember what it was Bellomont had done.

Finally, it came back to her. The French passes. Robert had shown them to her on the ship, and she was sure she had seen Bellomont slip something that looked just like them into a drawer while she and Sarah were there. Then she remembered that William had sent them to Bellomont with his letter. Evidently the governor had them in his possession.

They were important evidence. Could Bellomont be trusted with them? She knew that William counted on him to prove their innocence, but Robert believed that if they were to be proven innocent, they would have to rely on their own persuasive powers. She pondered these matters before drifting off to sleep.

The next day Wynn rose early, dressed in a plain linen dress and put her hair under a cornet. Then she went downstairs and slipped by the dining room, for she did not want anyone to know where she was going.

It was the first time she had walked alone on the streets of Boston, and she felt suddenly oppressed, thinking of the witchcraft hysteria that had spread from Salem to the other coastal towns in this area only seven years ago. For an instant she almost believed she could hear the poor women's cries as she hurried toward the gaol.

After asking directions, she had no trouble finding the crudely constructed wooden edifice. As Wynn approached the doors she cringed at the thought that Robert was inside this awful place, thrown together with common criminals, lunatics and other misfits of society, and she knew she would do anything to obtain his freedom.

She knocked on the heavy door, and it was opened by a guard with scraggly black hair, who wore a skimpy doublet and short, loose breeches. He had a gun, bayonet and a cutlass, which hung from his belt.

"I want to see one of the prisoners," she said.

He shrugged and walked away, passing through another door, leaving her in a small damp alcove with little light. In a moment he returned with a stern-faced man in a gray uniform. Wynn felt no great sympathy emanating from him.

"I am the prison keeper, madam. I understand you wish to see a prisoner?"

Wynn swallowed her fears. "Yes," she said. "Mr. Robert Lamley. He is confined with Captain William Kidd, I believe."

The man rubbed his close-clipped beard and looked her over, determining whether or not he ought to let her in to see the prisoner.

"The captain you speak of is in solitary confinement, but your Mr. Lamley, he's here. Any relation?" he asked.

"What?"

"Are you any relation to the prisoner?"

"Well," she stammered, "we're engaged to be married."

"Oh, I see." The prison keeper nodded. "Well, I don't have any orders that he can't have a visitor. Captain Kidd's another story. Governor says no one is to see him. I suppose it's all right. Come with me."

Her relief was tremendous. She followed, her flesh shrinking at the idea of being in a jail, as he led the way down a dark passage, but she summoned her courage for Robert's sake.

The prison keeper unlocked one heavy door after another until they arrived at a long row of dark cells. Finally they stopped at the end of the passage, and the prison keeper rattled the gate of the dark little cubicle.

At first Wynn didn't see him. But then Robert emerged from the shadows and stood in the one ray of gray light that came in from a small window high overhead. She gripped the cold bars that separated them. They froze her hands, but she hardly noticed, as Robert stepped forward, his boots scuffing on the dirt floor. She could see that his face was thinner already and that lines had deepened in his brow.

"Oh, Robert," she said as he reached the bars and took her cold hands in his.

His voice sounded strained to the breaking point when he spoke, but he attempted a smile for Wynn's sake. "My love, you shouldn't have come," he said.

She turned her head sideways to lay her cheek against his hands gripping the cold bars. How she hated the evil bars of iron that kept him from her.

"What will happen now?" she asked in a whisper.

"I fear the worst and hope for the best," he said. Some of the strength seemed to return to his voice. "There's an old saying, 'He who goes to sea for pastime would go to hell for pleasure.' You see where it's got us."

She winced. She had always thought something of that sort, but now was no time to throw Robert's battle with the sea into his face. "What will you do?" she asked, fighting the tears that threatened.

"Hmph. Await Bellomont's pleasure, I suppose. I have not even been able to talk to William. He's in irons in solitary confinement."

"How awful. Poor Sarah."

"Listen to me, Wynn." He turned her chin to face him. "You shouldn't be involved in this. Go home to New York. Your parents will never forgive me as it is."

Tears now streamed down her face. "They would if we were married," she said.

A look of pain seared through his eyes. "I had foolishly hoped we would have matters settled by now. I thought we would be on our way home to a glorious wedding."

"But we aren't," she said. "It isn't that easy. The governor and the Tories and the king are not ready to forgive you. Well, I don't want to wait any longer. They may put you on trial. They may send you away. I don't want you to go away, Robert, not before I am your wife. I want to marry you now."

"I know, my sweet. I want us to be married more than anything else in the world."

"Then marry me now!"

He frowned quizzically. "What? Marry you in gaol? Don't be foolish."

"But you can. We could find a clergyman to seal our vows."

"Are you mad?" The words were an accusation, but his eyes became alive with tumultuous emotions — confusion, hope, love and doubt shone from them. She was surprised at her boldness, but she was certain that she wanted to marry him — to ask a blessing on their immutable love.

An unfortunate turn of affairs had interrupted their plans, but looking into his eyes, she knew her love would strengthen her, so she could do battle with fate if need be.

"My dearest one, I know you love me. But you would be left in penury if I cannot manage to escape this latest disgrace. I could not leave you a widow."

She could see the effort these words cost him, but she was resolute. "Better to be a wife than left with nothing. If I am to be a widow, I'll face that when it comes." She softened her voice. "But Robert, that won't happen. They can't hang you for piracy, they wouldn't do that."

"No, not here. Piracy's not a hanging offence in Massachusetts. But Bellomont has orders to send us to England."

"To England!" she echoed. How far away that seemed. "I don't care. I want to marry you now."

"Here?" he asked, still unbelieving.

"Yes! I know we can get a clergyman. Duncan Campbell will help us. Sarah will help. Oh, Robert," she said, kissing his fingers, "I know we can do it. I love you so." Her words rushed over each other as he reached for her, caressing her through the iron bars.

"I love you, my dearest. I love you with all my heart," he said, his voice breaking. "If you want to be married, then we'll be married. I only curse the day I brought you to this."

"Do not say any more," she pleaded, "for I *bless* the day I met you."

The shuffling of the prison keeper reminded them that they were not alone. Wynn swallowed and brushed away her tears. "I'll find a clergyman and then I'll come back. I'll bring Sarah too," she said.

"If it's not too hard on her to come here. Wynn," he said solemnly. "I fear things will not go well for Sarah and William."

"How can it be any worse for them?" she said.

"As captain of the unlucky voyage, he is bound to get the worst of it."

"Oh dear," she said, a new dread filling her heart.

"Go now, dearest, and see to things. My brave girl," he said and kissed her fingers.

She nodded, taking in his strong features, scarred with the suffering of the last months. But a new light seemed to emanate from him, and it lifted her heart that she had brought him happiness. Then she remembered she wanted to speak to him about the French passes. There wasn't much time. She lowered her voice.

"Robert, did William send Bellomont the French passes?"

"Yes," he said, bending closer to hear her. "Though I advised him not to."

She nodded. "I think I know where they are. He had them when Sarah and I went to see him."

Robert knit his brows and uttered a curse. "We should never have given them up."

The guard interrupted them then, so there was no time for a reply. She turned, picking up her skirts, and hurried along the corridor, neither looking to the right nor the left at the poor souls reaching out to her.

Once out in the light, she rubbed her eyes. Though the winter day was gray and rain threatened, the daylight burned her eyes compared to the darkness of the gaol. She hurried along the streets back to the Campbells' neighborhood and up to the house.

Inside, a tomblike atmosphere pervaded. Wynn ran up the stairs in search of Sarah. She found her in her room on the second floor sitting at her dressing table slowly brushing her hair.

"Sarah," said Wynn, rushing in and sitting on a wing chair to catch her breath. "I've seen Robert."

Sarah turned to her, a look of hope briefly replacing the pain in her eyes as her husband's name formed on her lips.

But Wynn shook her head. "I didn't see William. They've been separated." Then she laid her hands on Sarah's dressing table. "Sarah, I'm going to marry Robert."

Sarah's eyes held Wynn's, a look of bewilderment in them.

"I'm going to marry him *now*, while he's in gaol."

Sarah blinked, and it took her some time to react. "Are you sure this is what you want?" she finally asked.

Wynn nodded. "Yes. I want to be able to stand by him as his wife, nothing less."

"Then you must do it."

"You will come with me?"

Sarah hesitated for only a moment, then said, "Yes, I will come."

"Then I must find a clergyman to perform the marriage." She knew her family would have preferred a priest, but since Boston was a Puritan town, and Robert was a Protestant, a minister would do.

"All right," said Sarah, brushing her hair back, and standing. Wynn's plans gave her something to do, far better than sitting doing nothing while both men languished in prison.

Wynn consulted Miriam Campbell, who, though surprised at the idea, did not issue a judgment. She said her husband could help with the arrangements, though it might take some time. Wynn urged her to make things happen as quickly as possible, though she understood that certain preparations had to be made before the actual ceremony. They would dispense with the details of dowry and jointure, for there was no time for that, and, in any case, only her present feeling mattered. Money for her future was of little importance.

When she couldn't visit Robert, she sent him messages of love and hope. Meanwhile, she laid her own plans, of which she told Robert nothing. After appealing to the governor, Sarah was finally allowed to visit William, and each time she returned from one of those visits her face seemed older, more ashen.

Wynn found that there was nothing she could say to comfort her friend. Rather, they sat silently together in the parlor, dark from lack of sunlight and dank from lack of human warmth.

At long last the marriage was sanctioned. On a gloomy day, with only a little more sun than they had been having for the last week, Wynn, accompanied by Sarah, the clergyman and the prison keeper, made her way through the awful corridors of the gaol once more to where Robert awaited them.

As she saw him, her heart went out to him. He came to the bars that separated them, looked at her with love in his eyes and kissed her trembling fingers, which she held against his warm lips. They gazed at one another, their hearts aching with pain and love as the minister performed the ceremony. Wynn hardly heard the words. When it came time for Robert to put his hand on the prayer book, the words stuck in his throat. "With all my worldly goods I thee endow," he finally said, his face a mask of pain. For what had he of worldly goods?

After they had exchanged vows, with Sarah and the prison keeper as witnesses, they were left alone for a few moments. Wynn felt content to simply hold Robert's hand against her face.

"I am your wife now," she said softly. "Surely there can be no greater happiness than this."

"You are my wife, and I desire you above all things," he said in a voice trembling with emotion.

"Soon we will be together," she said. "I know it."

"How can you know it when these iron bars and these oaken walls confine me?"

"You will be free. Justice will be done. I know, Robert, I am sure of it."

"I wish I could believe you. You don't know how often I've considered making an escape. But that would only endanger you more."

"I've thought of that too, Robert." She sighed. "And I would gladly run away with you. But you would be dishonored and your life would always be in danger."

"I don't care about danger for myself, only for you."

"And I care about you. No, we must wait and see what justice will bring. Surely there will be enough evidence to clear you if you are brought to trial."

She shut her eyes as conflict tore at her heart. No, she did not want Robert to try to escape, and to live forever more with a tainted reputation. And she had a plan. She had thought of a way to sneak into Bellomont's house. She would steal the French passes.

Chapter Twenty-four

The air turned frigid, and though Christmas approached, the season had little meaning for Wynn. Each visit to the gaol left her with a feeling of constriction, as if a cold hand were wrapped around her heart. She longed to visit her family in New York, but she dared not be away from Boston for even the few days it would take to make the journey, for fear of what might transpire between Bellomont and the king. The governor had received orders to send all pirates in his custody to London to be tried, though as yet he had not carried out these orders.

When she walked home from visiting the gaol, Wynn often took the route that led past Bellomont's household. She would walk slowly past, studying the house. Early mornings as well, she would rise before dawn and make her way through the streets with those vendors carrying fresh bread or fresh fish to the houses. With her hood pulled over her face, she would stand, watching who came and went from the governor's mansion as the house came to life in the mornings before the governor rose.

Now she had a plan. This morning she rose from bed, pulled from her closet a simple homespun dress and long apron that covered the skirt, covered her head with a cornet with a cotton ruffle that came about her cheeks, drew on a plain woolen cloak against the cold, and slipped out of the house, taking a wicker basket she'd hidden behind her door.

As she approached the governor's mansion, she slowed her pace. Then from around a corner came what she was waiting for: a horse-drawn wagon full of fresh-smelling loaves of bread. As the wagon drew up to Bellomont's house, she hurried around behind it.

"Good morning," she called out to the driver.

He didn't speak but stared at Wynn, who had woken him from his early morning reverie. She took advantage of his silence to hurry on with her chatter. "Cook asked for two extra loaves this morning. There's a dinner, you know, guests and all. She sent me to help you carry. Now, if you'll just pick out two of the freshest for the extras," and she gossiped on as the man slowly got down and started to unload fresh loaves of bread into the basket Wynn held out for him. When he was finished, she thanked him nicely and put a coin in his hand. Then she stood on the brick sidewalk and watched him drive down the street.

She made her way around the house to the kitchen entrance. It was still so early there was no one about. She summoned her courage, pulled the cornet forward to hide more of her face, and approached the door. Her heart pounded in her chest as the person she had been waiting for appeared. A large woman, her hair piled under a kerchief and an apron tied around her large waist, opened the door. This was Cook. She paused for a moment on the top step, yawning, then she started down the steps, muttering to herself.

Wynn was within speaking distance now, and she called out a chipper "Good morning, ma'am."

The woman turned to her, then seeing the bread she held up, returned the "Good morning."

"Brought these for you. Wagon's gone on," Wynn said, offering the basket to the woman, who started to take it. Then she seemed to have a second thought.

"Just set 'em inside, would ye? I've got to wake up that lazy stable boy. He'll have to groom the horses."

"Surely," said Wynn, waiting for the woman to pass her on the steps and amble toward the stable at the back of the house. She could not believe her luck. The door to the kitchen was open before her.

She hastened inside and crossed the large kitchen, setting the basket on the huge table in the center of the room where meals were prepared. Looking quickly about her, she passed through the opposite door to a hallway. By the time Cook returned, she would see the basket and assume the baker's assistant had put it on the table and left. But by that time, Wynn would be deep in the house.

She made her way tentatively along the still dark hallway. From having been inside the house once and from watching it since then, she tried to reconstruct the layout of the house. She knew that the kitchen was at the back of the house and that the library was on the second floor. If she followed this corridor she would eventually come to the front entrance. Then she would follow the staircase up and turn right.

She came to a corridor that branched off, and from the marble floor, she knew she was in the right part of the house. Out of the darkness before her loomed a heavy oak door, with an oval mirror to the left of it. If only she could avoid discovery. If she were caught now, everything would be ruined. She dared not even contemplate what recourse Bellomont might take if he caught her in his study rifling his drawers. But she could not imagine him rising this early. At least she had seen no sign that he was an early riser on all the mornings she had watched the house.

She climbed the stairs. It was still quiet — too early for any activity in the front part of the house. She held her breath as she pushed on the double oak doors, but they gave way, and she went in. There, at the far end of the room, was the mahogany desk before which she and Sarah had stood that day. The drawer must have been the center one. Of course, since then he might have placed the passes somewhere else, but she had to try here first. She crept forward on tiptoe to the long polished desk.

There was the drawer and she reached toward it, careful not to stumble or knock anything over in the dim light. Brass knobs protruded from the front, and she grasped one and pulled, but the drawer did not give. Although she had told herself it would probably be locked she felt utterly dejected, and her heart seemed to plunge to the pit of her stomach.

Often there was a way to open a desk drawer even without the key, she told herself — a catch or spring hidden from the eye but responsive to the touch. She ran her fingers along the bottom of the drawer but discovered nothing.

She knelt. Adjusting her eyes to the dim light, she ran her fingers along the side of the drawer, locating the runners from which it was suspended. Then she drew in a quick breath as she felt a short peg at the back. It stuck out on the left side of the drawer, but there was nothing similar on the right side. Closing her eyes, she pushed.

Gently she pulled the drawer by the knobs. It came open. The drawer must have been built with this catch in case the owner accidentally lost his key. She breathed a sigh of relief and realized she had been holding her breath for several seconds. She looked down into the drawer. There, lying half hidden by some other papers, were the French passes, bearing the coat of arms of the French East India Company in their lower left corners.

She had not a moment to lose. She tucked the passes into her pocket, slid the drawer shut until she heard it latch, and then hurried across the room.

Now what should she do? She had concentrated her planning on gaining entrance to Bellomont's house, not on how to get out. Now her instincts told her to go downstairs and out the front of the house rather than the back, for Cook would see her. She only hoped it was still too early for any of the other staff to be in that part of the house.

She slipped down the stairs, finally coming to the front entrance. As she passed beneath the foyer archway in front of the entrance, she again held her breath. She peered at the doors. She could see light coming through the crack between them, and she could see nothing to indicate they were locked.

She pushed. They gave, and she breathed again. She passed through as quietly as she could and then began to run down the steps and along the walk. She desperately wanted to flee from the house as quickly as possible. She had the passes, and she would use them to save Robert if need be. But she slowed down and began to walk. It would not do to be seen running from the governor's house. She prayed that no one would wake up and decide to look out the window just then.

At the end of the walk, she turned into the street and ran all the way back to Duncan Campbell's house. No one was up yet, and she entered and made her way safely to her room, where she lay down with her eyes open for the next two hours until she heard the household begin to stir.

The transportation orders finally came through and William Kidd, Robert Lamley, and the seven seamen who had also been arrested were ushered from their cells and put into a coach that would take them overland to New York. There they would board the H.M.S. *Advice*.

Sarah and Wynn were home when the news came. A small boy delivered a handwritten note from Governor Bellomont addressed to Mrs. William Kidd and Mrs. Robert Lamley.

"It's got the governor's seal on it, I see," said Sarah, handing the folded piece of paper to Wynn.

Her heart pounded. For a fleeting moment, she wondered if it might contain good news. Perhaps someone had spoken out for the prisoners. But even as she tore it open she knew she was probably wrong. So small a piece of paper could contain nothing so hopeful. As she scanned it, her heart contracted and her face lost its color.

"What is it?" asked Sarah, steadying herself as she read Wynn's face. Wynn read aloud: " '. . . taken from this place to New York and placed aboard the H.M.S. *Advice*, for transportation to London at the king's orders.' Oh, Sarah, he is sending them abroad."

"When are they going?"

Wynn hastily consulted the letter, then slowly raised her head, letting her hands fall to her lap, "They've gone. He says they left before dawn this morning."

Sarah pressed her hands together.

"Sarah, we can still see them in New York if we leave now."

For a moment Sarah looked blank, and Wynn feared that her dazed mood would return and render her incapable of action. But her eyes remained bright. "Yes," she said, nodding. "We must leave immediately."

"Perhaps we can get a coach," said Wynn, "or maybe a ship. You stay here and pack and I'll see about transportation."

They sprang into action. Wynn hurried out into the brisk air and ran to the docks. No ship was leaving that would put in at New York, but she found a coach. Then she hurried back to the Campbells' house and up to her room. She pulled out the portmanteau she had carried on shipboard and began to stuff it with her belongings. She also packed a small trunk that had arrived from her mother when Wynn had written that she and Robert were married and that she would remain in Boston until she knew his fate.

Sarah was busy in her room, and when the women had their things ready, Sarah went to see Miriam Campbell who, although taken aback at the hasty leave-taking, understood it was probably for the best. Wynn thought the woman must be relieved to see them go. Duncan Campbell had stood by them because of his bond with William as a fellow Scotsman, but the burden of being associated with men who were being accused of piracy could have done nothing to enhance the Campbells' situation in this Puritan town.

In a few hours Wynn found herself seated close to Sarah and her daughter in a coach bound for New York. She had dressed warmly, for frost covered the ground, and they had rugs over their laps to offset the chill. The coach, carrying four other passengers and the mail, set out on the Boston Post Road at a brisk pace. Heavy curtains, drawn over the windows to help keep out the cold, darkened the interior.

They knew they would not overtake the prisoners, but they hoped to reach New York before the men set sail for England. And then what? Wynn jerked herself out of her reverie. So far she had determined only to get home to New York. To see her family, to sleep in her own bed, and to be near Robert. But now she realized that if she wanted to remain near him, she too would have to go to England.

"Sarah," she began, peeking out of her fur hood at her cousin who quietly met her gaze. The other passengers seemed oblivious to them, but Wynn hated to say anything too personal.

"We, that is, I," she licked her lips. Her mouth felt cold and dry. "I think we should go to England."

Sarah turned to face forward once more. After a moment her lips parted slightly, as if to reply, but she then firmly closed her lips and stared ahead. Wynn said no more. It was not the right time to discuss it further.

Their journey was a hard one, for the rutted road was frozen, and the driver was pushing the horses to move as fast as they could. Although it had been some years since there had been an Indian attack along this road, old fears were not easily forgotten. Once they had to disembark and walk while the coachman and the footman pushed the coach out of a deep hole. They were lucky not to have broken the axle. They spent one night in hard beds in a Rhode Island inn and one night in Hartford, where they changed horses.

In spite of the jolting of the carriage and the strain she was under, Wynn managed to doze off once in a while. Once, near the end of their journey, she awoke to see that Sarah had raised a curtain and was staring out.

"Look," said Sarah, pointing to some bare trees that leaned over a small road leading off the main byway.

"What is it?" None of the scenery looked at all familiar to Wynn.

"We're near the farm," said Sarah. And from the warmth in her voice, Wynn knew how much Sarah had missed her home. When she turned back to Wynn, color had appeared in her cheeks, and her eyelashes were glistening.

"The farm," Wynn said softly, a bittersweet emotion filling her heart as she remembered her time with Robert there. She remembered, blushing, how Robert had laid his hands on her as they lay on the blanket in the warm sun; how he had pressed his thigh against her leg, and how wanton it had made her feel.

She was married to him now, and he had bedded her. She lifted the rug and glanced down at the thin gold ring that encircled her left ring finger. Then she covered her hand again with the thick rug. Married, yet hardly the way she had imagined. They had no home yet, no freedom, no . . . Tears sprang to her eyes, and she forced herself to put these depressing thoughts out of her mind. Somehow, they would come through this and then they would be happy.

She still possessed the French passes. At first she had expected Bellomont to notice they were missing, but if he had, she had not heard of it. His silence about the passes confirmed her suspicion that he intended to suppress them at the trial. If that were the case then she had done right to steal them, for they might be needed as evidence.

The coach jolted over the last hill and finally the town was sighted. Now houses sprang out of the woods on their left and right, and here and there a shanty with a family of blacks attested to the slaves and freed slaves that were so common here. She thought about Judson, and how she had almost gotten to know him as a fellow human being on that same picnic she had been remembering earlier. That seemed so long ago now.

They were coming into town; the houses were closer together, and Wynn strained unsuccessfully to get a glimpse of her family's house. They passed through the Queen Street Gate, now standing alone where the old wall had finally been torn down, and as they made their way down the Strand, they passed Sarah's house and then on to the coffee house, where the passengers wearily got down.

Wynn unfolded her stiff body and stepped into the sunlight, blinking her eyes and trying to focus on her surroundings. New York! How long she had been away! Perhaps it seemed so long because of the great distance she had traveled in her own experience, she reflected. The streets seemed the same, muddy from some recent rain, although there had been no snow here yet. Few people were about in the brisk wind that blew off the water, but the door to the coffee house opened and closed as passengers from the coach and patrons from inside passed through, some with letters, which the coach had brought.

"We can walk from here," Sarah said. "I'll send Judson for the luggage." Wynn nodded and followed her. They made their way down Broadway and up the Strand. As they passed the harbor, Wynn strained to see if the H.M.S. *Advice* were visible, but she saw no sign of a ship by that name. Finally they pulled themselves up the steps that led to Sarah's brick house, and the door was flung open and Elizabeth bobbed out to greet them, her eyes wide in disbelief.

"Mistress Sarah, and oh, Miss Wynn. I can't believe it. You didn't send word you were coming." She curtsied, then led them in, smoothing her dress and looking around distractedly. "Nothing is ready. Oh dear me. If only I'd known."

"Calm yourself, Elizabeth," said Sarah. "It's all right. We didn't know ourselves we were coming. But when we heard that my husband and Mr. Lamley were being sent here to go aboard a ship to England, we thought it would be faster to travel here than to send a message. Where's Judson?"

"Oh, he's in back, ma'am. He'll be awfully glad to see you. Shall I get him?"

"Please send him to the coffee house for our luggage. Wynn will be wanting to go on home." Then she turned to her cousin. "Go to your family, my dear. I'll send word when I've heard some news."

Wynn kissed her on the cheek then turned back to the door. She wanted to see her family, of course, but right now her mind was on Robert. She must discover when the *Advice* was leaving so she could make her plans.

She went out into the blustery weather again. Once on the street she turned her face northward to make her way to her family's new house. She wondered about the reception she would be given. They would be surprised to see her, but, she hoped, they would also be very relieved. They wouldn't be happy that she wouldn't be staying long, she reflected. And they might try to dissuade her from following Robert to England.

She turned into the road to the house, pulling her cloak tighter around her, for the wind coming off the water had a sting to it. She blinked her eyes as she hurried along. She was just about to climb the steps leading up to the front door of the new house, now completed and rising three stories with a shingled roof, when she heard a familiar yell from down the road.

"James!" she called, running down the road to meet him. "I thought you would be at sea."

He picked her up, whooped and spun her around. When he set her down, he clasped her in a bear hug. "God Almighty, if it isn't my little sister," he said, laughing. "The *Joanna*'s put in for the winter, but I'll be signing on a coastal ship as soon as I can. Where'd you come from?" he asked, pulling her by the arm toward the house.

"I'll explain everything," she said breathlessly. "Give me a chance."

"Mother and Father will be glad to see you."

She stopped as they reached the steps. "Will they? Are they still angry with me?"

He grinned. "Not really. I did a good job of persuading them you were in good hands. They just want your happiness, Wynn, you know that."

"Yes, I'm grateful for that." When they reached the top step he turned to face her, his expression sober. "What's hapened to Robert?" he asked.

"He's here," she said, her cheerfulness draining from her. "In irons, aboard the H.M.S. *Advice*, bound for England."

"Oh God," murmured James. His clear blue eyes

filled with compassion, then he placed his arm around her in a protective gesture. "Come inside."

The tears sliding down her soft cheeks, Wynn's mother enfolded her daughter in her arms and insisted on seeing to Wynn's every need. Finally Jonathan came in.

"Father," she cried, a lump forming in her throat when he came into the kitchen.

Seeing his daughter before him brought a light to his eyes, and though he hesitated a moment, remembering the pain she had also caused him, he opened his arms to embrace her, he was so thankful to see her.

As the women prepared dinner, Wynn told her story, passing rapidly over the details of her flight from their house, in order not to wound her parents. Nor did she mention anything about England. She did not bring up Robert's present plight until they were through dinner and sampling her mother's apple pie and fresh coffee made with chicory.

They had fallen silent after a long story James had told about his adventures on the *Joanna*. In the spring, James planned to go back to the East.

"Who knows?" he said, sticking out his chest. "Perhaps I'll sign up for a great exploration that establishes a new trade route." Then he looked guiltily at Wynn and lowered his eyes. She would not want to be reminded about the East just now.

But Wynn laid a hand on her brother's arm. "Of course you will, James."

"I'm sorry, Sis. I know you don't want to hear about this now."

"It's all right." Then she uttered the thought she had been harboring. "James, you might be able to help me. You would be better equipped than I to seek out the *Advice* and see," she lowered her voice self consciously, "if Robert is on it." She clenched her hands together in her lap. Being at home was a welcome respite, but the enormity of her problems prevented her from experiencing the joy she should have had at this reunion. How would she see Robert? How would she get to London? She had no money and didn't know if Robert could arrange to send her any, and she was too proud to ask her parents for help.

Her mother smoothed her daughter's hair. "You need some rest, Wynn dear. You are right. James or your father can go to the ship, and you will stay with us until your husband sends word."

Wynn nodded, not trusting herself to speak. When she looked up at her understanding family, she could barely see them through the tears that streamed down her face. "Thank you," she finally got out as she rose to go to her room.

Upstairs, she sat down on the soft bed with the comforter on it. She ran her hand over the smooth surface and laid her head on a pillow. The house felt so warm, so comfortable, while outside the wind battered at the sturdy walls. She could hear howling as the wind found an opening somewhere above her in the roof and tried to sneak through whatever small passage it had found. How lovely it would be to stay here. But as she looked around her, she realized that this was no longer her room.

Nor was the room she had occupied in Sarah's house hers. Indeed, she was no longer a part of any household. And the house she had grown up in on the other side of the ocean didn't belong to her family anymore. The fact was, she really had no home she could call her own. A small tear slipped down the side of her nose and onto the pillow. She couldn't go back. It was too late now. She must follow Robert no matter where it led her.

There was a knock on her door, and she lifted her head. "Who is it?"

James pushed open the door enough to look in. "It's me, Sis. May I come in?"

"Of course." She sat up, propping the pillow behind her and spreading out her skirt. "I'm so glad you're here, James," she said, reaching in her pocket for a handkerchief.

He sat down on the maple turned stool near the bed and took one of her hands in his and patted it. "Me too," he said.

For a moment they just smiled sadly at each other.

"It isn't like it used to be, is it?" James said.

"You mean the house?"

"Everything," he said. "Our lives."

"Yes, I was just thinking that."

"We've moved on."

"Yes." She bit her lip. She was leaving her family behind. But for what kind of future?

"When do you think you'll get a ship?" she asked.

He shrugged. "There are plenty of sloops going up and down the coast. I don't know. What about you?"

"Me?"

"You'll go to England, won't you?"

"Yes," she said.

"For Robert's trial."

"I have to be with him."

James's gaze wavered. "I know that, all right. It's just that you've grown up all of a sudden. You're a married woman now."

She grinned. "You've grown up too."

He looked embarrassed and studied his hands. "Yes, I guess so." Then he looked at her again. "You want me to find him for you?"

"Yes, James." She sat closer to him now, her eyes pleading with him.

"All right, Sis. I'll do as you say."

"Thank you." Then she embraced him, and he held her briefly.

"You called me 'little sister' when you saw me," she said, her chin on his shoulder.

"I guess we've been through so much together that I've come to think of you as my little sister instead of my older one."

"I know. Funny, isn't it? You're a very special brother, James." He squeezed her tightly once more.

"You're special too. That's why I don't want you to get hurt."

"Don't worry about me so much," she said.

"Well," he said, standing. "I'll go see what I can find out."

He kissed her on the forehead. Then she lay back down again to watch him leave, shut her eyes, and eventually slept.

The next morning, a cold bright sun shone in her window. It was still early, and it seemed as if no one else was up, so she went downstairs to stir up the hearth. Then she busied herself making breakfast. At last she was joined by her mother, and then the men came down to partake of the generous meal. James left to go to the *Advice*, and Jonathan had business to attend to. So after helping her mother clear the dishes, Wynn decided to visit Sarah. Perhaps she had heard something.

Wynn donned her cloak and hurried to Sarah's, where Elizabeth let her in and offered her coffee. "Miss Sarah's at the table. I'm sure she'll be happy to see you."

"Hello, Cousin," said Sarah, rising to kiss her. She had groomed herself and looked refreshed after the hard journey they had shared. "How is your family?"

"They're well, and they have asked after you."

Sarah smiled gently. "I am well. Indeed much better than before."

Wynn looked at her quizzically. "Why is that?"

"I think because I am home."

"But what about —" Wynn stopped herself before she spoke William's name. "I'm sorry," she said instead. "I shouldn't pry."

"My dear Wynn, do you not think we have shared enough to be frank with each other? If you have an observation to make, I beg you to make it."

"But it was impertinent of me. I was just going to ask how you could find home a welcome without William here."

Sarah eyed her more seriously. "I have been asking myself that. And you may be surprised to hear what I have to say, Wynn. But as you know, I have had many months to think about this."

She paused and Wynn watched her, not daring to break in on her thoughts. Sarah stood and walked to the cupboard, where she ran her fingers lightly around a china platter with a delicate design hand-painted on it. Then she turned around and wrapped her hands around the polished wood of a chair back.

"I love my husband," she began. "And I would do anything for him. He has given me —" she gestured around the room "— all this and so much more." Her eyes were warm and Wynn felt her heart beat quickly as Sarah revealed her innermost thoughts. She nodded encouragement to her friend.

"I have always been faithful to him, and I always will be, as long —" she paused to swallow "— as he lives," she finished.

Wynn raised an eyebrow, but Sarah hurried on. "I saw William last night, Wynn. He is held prisoner in a cabin on board the *Advice*. But he is comfortable."

Wynn leaned forward but Sarah guessed what she was about to ask and went on. "He is not allowed to speak to the other prisoners, who are . . . they are in irons, my dear."

Again Wynn felt the cold steel hand wrap around her heart.

"I shall not go to England," Sarah said, and Wynn began to understand what she was leading up to. Her body turned ice-cold, and her heart felt like lead.

"You would stay here?"

Sarah sat down again. "Yes, let me explain. William is, well, he is still hopeful. But I have talked to other people who know of these affairs. I have had a sort of premonition, and I have become resigned to my fate.

"I said before that I would do anything for my husband." Then she looked Wynn right in the eyes. "But I will not watch him hang."

With a sharp intake of breath Wynn sat up straight, staring at Sarah. "But you do not know that he will hang."

Sarah continued, her gaze level, the violet eyes now penetrating. "Why else is he being transported to England?"

"Because," said Wynn, "the king has ordered him to stand trial there. His commission was from King William the Third."

"I believe it is more than that," said Sarah calmly. "The noble backers of the *Adventure Galley* enterprise are now being compromised. Privateering ventures are private business arrangements. Yet Lord Somers granted the royal seal sanctioning this voyage. Some are saying he knew beforehand that it was a piratical venture. The lords justices need a scapegoat, Wynn. They must pin the blame on someone. I think William will be convicted." Her calmness now crumbling, she leaned forward, putting her head in her hands.

Wynn was too shocked to move. She did not know whether she should comfort her friend or leave her to her grief. She felt confused. She had wanted to discuss Robert's plight as well. If William were to hang, would Robert hang with him? It was too awful to contemplate. And she hated to burden her friend with her own problems, so dreadful was Sarah's certainty of her husband's fate.

After a few moments of silence, Wynn rose to leave. She needed to get away from Sarah and try to gather her thoughts enough to understand what she had said, but Sarah prevented her from leaving so soon.

"Wait," Sarah mumbled after she had dabbed her face with a handkerchief. "You shouldn't let my feelings determine your decisions, Wynn. It may very well be that Robert is not in danger."

Wynn sat back down. "What do you mean? He backed William in all his decisions."

"He merely followed orders."

There was a stony silence. Wynn tried to concentrate on the meaning of this. Yes, Robert had followed orders as was the law of the sea. But if William was a pirate, did that not mean that Robert was a pirate as well? Of course, he could have led a mutiny against Kidd and kept the ship to its purpose. But he would never have fought against his friend, William, and the crew might not have gone along with him, in any case. It was a complex issue, but Wynn did see that since Robert had not been captain of the ship, his situation would be a different one to judge.

"Are you saying that you will stay here, but that I should go to the trial?" Wynn asked.

Sarah raised her eyes to Wynn's. "Robert would need you. Especially if he is let go. Then you could —" Sarah choked slightly "— be together."

Wynn felt forlorn. She knew she had to go to England, but she had been hoping for Sarah's company, at least. Now she would be alone.

"Sarah, are you sure you won't go?" It still seemed incredible to her that Sarah would desert her husband in his hour of need.

But Sarah, reading her thoughts, interpreted this for her. "I have spoken to William. It is what he wants. He would not have me humiliated if things go badly. If his luck turns for the better then he will return to me. He will be happier if I stay safely at home. So we have agreed."

Trying to assimilate all that Sarah had said, Wynn sat for a while with Sarah in a compassionate silence. Surely she had never shared so much with another woman. Finally she made ready to take her leave.

"Sarah, I pray that Providence shines on both our husbands. I will try to offer William what consolation I can if I see him in England."

Sarah took Wynn's hand. "Oh yes, that would mean so much to me. You must go for both of us, Wynn. Then perhaps —" Sarah managed a little smile "— Providence will be good to us after all."

Wynn hugged Sarah and left as, blinking back her tears, she began to confront the enormity of her burden.

Chapter Twenty-five

In the five-hundred-year-old Newgate Prison vice and corruption were rampant. Living in overcrowded and verminous conditions, the prisoners were forced to pay the gaolers for their food and the smallest conveniences. And it was in this place of horror that Robert and William awaited trial.

The House of Commons ordered all papers in connection with the *Adventure Galley* syndicate to be laid before them by the admiralty. Just before the trial it was discovered that the French passes Kidd had surrendered to Bellomont in Boston were missing.

William Kidd was no longer a well man, and the cold dampness and filth of Newgate only contributed to his deterioration. The men had been kept in a dark cell and the lack of proper warm clothing and exercise had also weakened them.

Nor was their mental state helped by the denial for several months of pen and paper as well as visitors. Finally, just before their trial, they were allowed to exercise in the prison yard where they moved slowly, blinded by the daylight after months of darkness, their feet frozen by the contact with the cold cement where the soles of their boots had worn through.

Wynn had now been in London awaiting the trial for several weeks. She had made the voyage alone, and although her mother wept to think of her leaving so soon after returning to the family circle, she understood Wynn's devotion to her husband. In London, Verity Conway, a family friend, welcomed Wynn. The Conway house was not too far from the Old Bailey, where the trial was to take place, and Verity, who had thought she would never see Wynn again, offered her a room for as long as she wished to stay.

Unable to see Robert, Wynn had spent her days trying to talk to the authorities so she could ascertain her husband's condition. The prisoners were not granted counsel of any kind until the day before the trial, and indeed were denied any means of preparation for the moment when they would stand in the dock. Wynn had not even been sure she would be able to get in to watch the proceedings, but at last she had managed to get permission.

On the day of the opening proceedings, Wynn and Verity found seats in the back of the gallery on a hard bench. They had come early enough to watch the court assemble. Even though it was still winter, perspiration moistened Wynn's clothing. As she leaned against the hard wooden back of the bench, her bones seemed to come into direct contact with the wood, and she realized how thin she must have become. It seemed that she sat there for several hours, but in reality it was only a fraction of that time before the jury assembled.

There were nine accused prisoners from the *Adventure Galley*. They could not give evidence except by asking questions and giving explanations in response to the queries of the judge or counsel for the Crown.

Now the jury filed in, and the seventeen men were sworn in. All appeared to be men of means, dressed conservatively in well-tailored coats and waistcoats, most wearing full-crowned hats or broad-brimmed hats trimmed with feathers. An ornate silver oar, symbol of the admiralty court's jurisdiction over crimes on the high seas, lay on a table in front of the judges. Wynn had tried to learn who the judges were and Verity, who now sat with her on the hard bench, told her something of them.

"That's Lord Chief Baron Ward. He's known to be a careful and painstaking judge," said Verity.

Wynn nodded. An imposing man in his robes and curly wig, his wide-set eyes had an honesty about them that inspired trust. He was followed by Sir Henry Hatsell and Mr. Justice Turton.

When Mr. Justice Gould took his seat, Verity commented, "Justice Gould once fined a baronet one hundred pounds for contempt of court."

"What did the baronet do?" asked Wynn.

"He kicked the high sheriff and called the judge a liar. Oh, there's Mr. Justice Powell. He's a popular judge. Well-liked and admired for his reputation as a lawyer. He presided at the trial of Jane Wenham, when she was accused of witchcraft. When it was alleged that Miss Wenham could fly, he remarked, 'You may — there is no law against flying.' "

Wynn tried to get a closer look at him. Surely such a man would be on the prisoner's side if the prisoner presented himself well.

Finally came Sir Salathiel Lovell, the recorder who opened the sessions. "Oh him," grunted Verity. "He's too old for his job. They call him Obliviscor of London, he's so forgetful."

Indeed, the man tottered as he walked to his seat, where he seemed to be having difficulty arranging the sleeves of his garment. Wynn had not given much thought to the value of a good recorder. But he would be the man to preserve the words of all these men for posterity. She shivered, hoping that if the outcome were good, the trial might set a positive precedent for men who acted in good faith for the Crown but fell victim to poor luck on these ill-planned privateering ventures.

Then they turned their attention to the crown solicitor, General Sir John Hawles, an eminent man with much political influence, whose hawklike nose protruded from his bony face. Just then he leaned toward his neighbor and drummed skinny fingers on the table before him. There was a murmur in the court as the session began, and Wynn's throat was so dry, she could not swallow.

"Gentlemen of the grand jury, stand together and hear the charge," intoned the skinny clerk in a plain black waistcoat, gray stockings and black shoes with large buckles. The charge was read, explaining the nature of the privateering commission and the crimes inquirable by the grand jury. There were six indictments against the prisoners. The first indictment charged Kidd with the murder of William Moore. On hearing this, Wynn was glad that Sarah had not come to England. Who would want to hear her husband accused of murder in public?

The second indictment was for piracy in regard to the *Quedah Merchant*. The other four indictments were for piracy of the *November*, one Portuguese and two Moorish ships. The Bill of Indictment was read against Captain William Kidd for murder and the other bills against Kidd, Robert Lamley, Nicholas Churchill, James Howe, William Jenkins, Gabriel Loft, Hugh Parrot, Richard Barlicorn, Abel Owens, and Darby Mullins for piracy. The proclamation being made, the prisoners were brought to the bar.

Wynn held her breath, for now she could see Robert as he moved forward with the other prisoners. He held himself proudly, and as he passed William, she saw him lay a reassuring hand on the captain's slumped shoulders. But when he turned, she saw that his face was drawn and he had lost much weight.

"William Kidd, hold up thy hand," said the clerk.

"May it please Your Lordships, I desire you to permit me to have counsel," said Kidd. Wynn had to strain to hear him, his voice was so weak. This was a far cry from the man who had once boomed out orders aboard the *Adventure Galley*.

"What would you have counsel for?" asked the recorder in his warbling voice.

"I beg Your Lordships' patience till I can procure my papers. I had a couple of French passes, which I must make use of in order to show my justification. I gave them to Lord Bellomont in New England."

Wynn's face burned, for she had the passes in her possession. Kidd looked so pitiful, she was tempted to rush forward and hand them to him. However, she did not think that wise. Since she had not been allowed to see Robert, she had not been able to give him the passes, and she did not trust anyone to deliver them. She must put them in Robert's hands herself.

Wynn's heart sank as she watched the court intimidate Kidd. In the dock Robert leaned forward, his face red with rage. Wynn feared his anger might so overcome him that he would insult the court and be punished for contempt. Then her pulse quickened, for the court, not being able to make William plead, moved on to Robert.

"Robert Lamley, hold up thy hand," said the clerk. Wynn's heart contracted as she looked at him. He stood straight and held up his hand, his eyes burning.

After he was sworn in, the clerk asked, "Are you guilty or not guilty?"

Robert's voice boomed out, "Not guilty." In her seat, Wynn took a deep breath.

"How will you be tried?"

"By God and my country."

"God send you good deliverance." Then he repeated the same words to all the other prisoners.

Then William was tried for the murder of William Moore. Wynn already knew this trial was a sham. Discipline for disobedience aboard a ship was commonplace and severe, even in the king's navy, and sailors sometimes died from flogging and other punishments. To say that Kidd actually murdered the poor gunner was atrocious.

"Do you want to leave?" asked Verity.

Wynn shook her head. "No, it's the least I can do for Sarah." She sat grimly on as the trial proceeded.

Again Kidd pleaded for counsel, and finally Justice Powell granted that Dr. Oldish and Mr. Lemmon be counsel for him provided there was any matter of law that he had to plead. There was a pause, during which the counselors came forward. Each wore a powdered wig and brocaded tunic with short sleeves. Lace-frilled shirt sleeves were bound with ribbons above their wrists.

Now that counsel was granted she had to get the French passes to them, thought Wynn. She reached under her cloak and retrieved them. Then she slipped out of the benches in the gallery and went down the stairs.

Entering the courtroom, she looked neither right nor left but focused on Mr. Lemmon's blue brocaded back. Robert was in the dock to her right with the other prisoners, but she dared not look at him. She took advantage of the pause in the proceedings to walk down the aisle and approach the counselor.

"Excuse me, sir," she said.

He turned to look at her and then several men turned to stare at her, aghast that a woman should have slipped in unnoticed. But before anyone could stop her, she handed Mr. Lemmon the passes. "I believe these are the documents your client seeks."

Everyone spoke at once and the clerk called for order, but through the din, the counselor asked her, "Who are you and how did you come by these?"

Robert, aware of what was happening, stood and gazed at Wynn. She saw his dark eyes flash, but still she concentrated her attention on Dr. Oldish and Mr. Lemmon, although her heart was bursting with the desire to rush to her beloved. "I am Mrs. Robert Lamley." A murmur ran through the court.

The two men were examining the passes. "They seem to be genuine," said Dr. Oldish. "They bear the coat of arms of the French East India Company."

Another murmur now arose in the courtroom. Wynn gave a small curtsy and turned back to go up the aisle. She could feel Robert's burning stare penetrating her back, but she bit her lip and kept herself from turning.

All eyes were on her now as she went toward the door at the back of the room. But as she reached the threshold, a guard stepped in front of her.

She stared at the gold frogging on his chest and said in as strong a voice as she could muster, "My seat is in the gallery."

But the guard, having received a signal from the judges, took her arm and marched her forward. Her face burned, and this time she chanced to look at Robert, who was leaning forward, his arms on the dock railing.

The two counselors watched her approach, then nodded to the guard to release her. "Please, madam. Sit here," said Mr. Lemmon, and he indicated a seat near theirs. "We will have some questions for you later."

She swallowed hard and sat, looking down at the floor as the trial continued.

Although the prisoners were questioned about the awful day on which Moore died, for some reason, few questions were asked of Robert. Perhaps, Wynn thought, the counsel for the Crown sensed the first mate's hatred of the court and his loyalty to William Kidd and feared his testimony would be disruptive.

After the sailors had described how Kidd had thrown the bucket at Moore and how Moore had been taken below, Kidd finally had his chance to question a witness, Darby Mullins, able seaman, a stocky little man with large, muscular arms. He had deserted Kidd at Madagascar. As he took the stand, he compressed his lips and looked down at the floor. William rose, supporting himself on the railing before him.

"My Lord," said Kidd. "I would ask this man what William Moore was doing when this thing happened."

No word from Mullins.

"Mr. Mullins, you hear what he says; what was Moore doing?" said Justice Ward.

"He was grinding a chisel," mumbled Mullins.

"What was the occasion that I struck him?" questioned Kidd.

"There was discussion about another ship."

"What was that ship?"

"A Dutch ship," answered Mullins.

"This ship was a league from us," Kidd said. "And some of the men would have taken her, and I would not consent to it, and this Moore said I always hindered them from making their fortunes; was not that the reason I struck him? Was there not a mutiny on board?"

Mullins spoke up, louder now. "No. You chased this Dutchman all the whole night; and they showed their colors, and you put up your colors."

"This is nothing to the point. Was there no mutiny on board?"

"There was no mutiny; all was quiet," persisted Mullins.

Wynn's heart lurched as she watched William become more and more dejected, and finally give up his questioning. The trial dragged on, and Wynn began to feel the oppression of the surroundings. The questions and answers were so twisted that she began to believe that William was, indeed, going to be sacrificed to the politics of the day. Her head swam. If William was about to become a sacrificial offering, would Robert become one as well? Was the first mate as responsible as the captain in the eyes of the law?

Now Robert got up to speak. Though he looked gaunt and pale, his eyes glittered boldly, and his voice was strong.

"Captain Kidd acted in good faith," Robert said, and the court quietened to listen. "It was only his determination and fearlessness that kept the crew from all-out mutiny." As he said it he looked levelly at the judges, who seemed to be listening intently. "This man Moore," he went on, "was agitating the crew and Captain Kidd only wished to put him in line as any captain would who was not afraid to discipline his crew."

Wynn was heartened by his testimony, but when he sat down, the rest of the crew were not in agreement with Robert as to what had happened. She ground her teeth, realizing that these men, like Mullins, just wanted to save their own skins. Only Hugh Parrot, in addition to Robert, seemed to give an honest testimony about the incident with Moore.

Finally Lord Chief Baron Ward said to Kidd, "Have you any more to say for yourself?"

"I have no more to say," responded Kidd, and Wynn could see he was a beaten man. "I had all the provocation in the world given me; I had no design to kill him. I had no malice or spleen against him. It was not designedly done, but in my passion, for which I am heartily sorry."

As Lord Chief Baron Ward summed up the case for the jury, Wynn tried to concentrate on his words. It seemed he was doing a fairly good job, but Wynn couldn't tell what subtleties were being introduced that might affect the jury. He reminded the jurors that the killing of a man was not considered to be a murder unless malice was present.

"Therefore, gentlemen," he concluded, "I must leave it to you; if you believe the king's witnesses, and one of the prisoner's own, that this blow was given by the prisoner, in the manner aforesaid, and are satisfied that it was done without reasonable cause or provocation, then he will be guilty of murder; and if you do believe him guilty of murder, upon this evidence, you must find him so. If not, you must acquit him."

Then the jury left. Wynn stood up to go out and Verity followed her. If they found William guilty, what would she tell Sarah? Questions and random thoughts reeled in her head as she watched the crowd, gathered for the sensational event, chatter about what they'd just seen and heard.

They returned to their seats an hour later as the jury filed in. Their names were called, and the clerk asked if they were agreed as to their verdict, to which they said "yes," in unison. Then the clerk turned to William, standing in the dock.

"William Kidd, hold up thy hand. Look upon the prisoner, gentlemen. Is he guilty of the murder whereof he stands indicted, or not guilty?"

The foreman answered in an imposing voice. "Guilty."

Wynn shrieked then covered her mouth with her hands as Verity held her and the keeper led William out of the courtroom. The court buzzed as the spectators immediately began to give their opinion of the trial. Verity insisted that they return home.

"No, I must stay," whispered Wynn.

"Come home for a while then. They won't begin the second trial for at least an hour."

"I, oh," Wynn clutched at her friend. "How awful."

Truly she had never felt so close to death. The world was bitter and ugly, and she felt she did not want to live in a place where such terrible things could happen. She allowed Verity to lead her away, hardly seeing the streets they passed through on the way to her friend's house. There, she tried to gather her thoughts together as she spooned up the soup Verity served her. It warmed her enough to bring the color back into her pale face.

After a brief rest, she hurried back to the Old Bailey, steeling herself to sit through the second trial — this one for piracy. As before, the justices were on the bench, the jurors in place, and the prisoners at the bar sworn on their oaths. The clerk read:

"You of the jury, look upon these prisoners, and hearken to their cause. They stand indicted by their names and thereunto have severally pleaded not guilty; and for their trial put themselves on God and their country. Your charge is to inquire whether they be guilty of the piracy and robbery whereof they stand indicted, or not guilty."

Some of the prisoners began to plead that they had come in on the king's proclamation and asked for a pardon, but Robert stood stonily silent, and Wynn began to tremble.

Finally the questioning began. When they came to the capture of the *Quedah Merchant* it looked very bad, for the captain of the ship had been an Englishman. As Darby Mullins began to testify, a cold feeling crept down Wynn's spine.

"When we came to Madagascar, there was a ship called the *Mocha Frigate*. Several of the men came up to Captain Kidd and said they had heard he had come to take and hang them. He said it was no such thing, and that he would do them all the good he could. And later Captain Culliford came aboard of Captain Kidd, and Kidd said, 'Before I would do you any harm, I would have my soul fry in hell fire,' and he wished damnation to himself several times if he did."

"That's a lie!" Robert interrupted. Wynn feared the

half-truths and twisted interpretation that was being put on their actions in Madagascar. She remembered William being forced to swear allegiance to Culliford at sword-point when they'd been captured.

"Order, order!" called the justice. "The prisoner will have a chance to question." A murmur spread through the court, and Robert clenched white knuckles on the railing in front of him.

"Mr. Lamley, do you wish to question the witness?"

Wynn sat forward. As was the custom, the prisoner got to do his questioning directly.

"I do." He addressed Darby Mullins, who shrank visibly under Robert's scrutiny. "You were aboard the *Adventure Galley* when we reached Carwar?"

"That's right, sir."

"And up until that time, how many ships had Kidd taken?"

"None, sir."

"And was the captain actively seeking out legal prizes for the Crown?"

"Yes, sir."

"And had he chased any ships while you were on board?"

"Yes."

"And what happened?"

"He let them go."

"Why?" asked Robert.

"Because he found they weren't pirates or French," admitted Mullins.

"So, the captain acted in good faith."

"How can I know why he did anything?" whined Mullins, uncomfortable under Robert's insistent questioning. "He didn't tell me."

But Robert persisted. "Why did you want to leave the ship at Carwar?"

"Because of Captain Kidd. He was goin' on a design of piracy."

"Have you any proof of that?" growled Robert.

"Well, he had Captain Parker and the Portuguese aboard, the ones from the Moorish ketch."

Robert seemed to lose some of his advantage then. There was no denying that Kidd had forced Parker and the linguister aboard the *Adventure Galley*. Still Robert managed to question the man so that his criticisms of Kidd appeared weak as Robert insisted that William was a privateer obviously trying to meet his obligations to his backers and his crew. When Robert finished, he returned to the dock with the other prisoners, his jaw tense.

Still to be heard was the accusation against the first mate. They did not have long to wait.

The counsel for the Crown spoke. "Robert Lamley, you served as first mate under Captain Kidd."

"I did."

"And did you discuss his plans for the voyage with him?"

"I did."

"Were you privy to his innermost thoughts?"

"I believe I was."

"Tell us then what his intentions were when he took goods from Captain Parker's ship."

"It was a Moorish ship, and his own ship, which was a king's ship, needed provisions. So he boarded the Moorish ship to see what they had that would be useful."

Wynn twisted her skirt into a knot as she watched Robert suffer the interrogation, but never did he waver. When he described other incidents of the voyage, he always spoke from the point of view that they were both in the king's service doing the king's duty. She tried to gauge the reactions of the judges, but their serious faces betrayed no expression.

"Was there a mutiny?"

"Yes. The captain continually fought those men who

wanted to turn to piracy as an easy way to make their fortunes. But at all times Captain Kidd honored his commission."

The other prisoners were allowed to question Robert as well, but never once did Robert flinch. Wynn was surprised that he was able to control his temper but perhaps, because William had made a poor showing, Robert knew it was up to him to save them all. The other prisoners were only guilty of following orders, it seemed.

Finally Lord Chief Baron Ward summed up the evidence, and the jury retired. Wynn kept her seat this time, too numb to move. The jury returned, and the clerk called their names. The foreman answered that they were all agreed on their verdict.

"How say you?" intoned the clerk. "Is William Kidd guilty of the piracy whereof he stands indicted, or not guilty?"

"Guilty."

"Is Robert Lamley guilty?"

"Guilty."

Half fainting, Wynn didn't hear the rest of the verdict wherein five of the men were found guilty, and the other four were acquitted.

Now William was on his feet, speaking. She didn't catch the first part, but his voice gathered in volume as he spoke over the buzzing of the crowd. ". . . you'll frame my picture with timbers from my ship and decorate the frame with velvet and gold lace," he said bitterly. "I am buried as a pirate, but I will be remembered as a symbol of unfair times," he pronounced, raising his fist. She barely heard the last words he uttered before the keeper led him away.

When she stood up, trying to see Robert as he, too, was led from the room, she swayed against the back of the bench and was forced to sit down again. Now everyone around her was on their feet, and Wynn clawed her way through the crowd. She shuddered, feeling the cold penetrate to the marrow of her bones. Then she was pushed along with the crowd as they filed out.

Outside, a vicious wind blew her cloak around her and stung her face. She did not even look up when the clock chimed the hour. A fair trial? It was not a fair trial when her husband might be hanged. She returned to Verity's, where she numbly climbed the stairs and lay down in the darkness of her room wishing never to rise again.

Chapter Twenty-six

Wynn's dreams were filled with a ship tossing in a storm. Strong arms held her and she gazed into Robert's eyes, only to find that it wasn't Robert, but a mask of death. She screamed and felt her shoulders being shaken as she climbed up from the depths of unconsciousness.

"Wynn, dear, open your eyes."

Wynn forced her heavy eyelids open and looked up into Verity's concerned face.

"Wynn, thank goodness you're awake. I was worried about you."

"I'm sorry. I'm all right," Wynn said with dry lips.

"Will you take something to eat?"

"I'll come down." While the thought of food was repulsive to her, she also realized that she was being a burden to her hostess and she must make an effort to get up.

"I can bring you a tray."

"No thank you, Verity. I need to be up and about. I cannot impose on you any longer. As soon as the —"

she hesitated "— sentence is meted out, I will leave here." She pushed back the covers and put her feet on the floor. She waited until the room stopped spinning and then stood up.

"Are you sure you can manage?"

"Yes, I'll dress and then come down."

Verity left her, and when she had brushed her hair back from her pale face and dressed, she descended. As she crept along the hallways, holding onto the walls for support, she was reminded of how much colder English houses seemed than houses in the New World. Or was it simply the coldness of her being, now that her lifeblood felt as if it were draining from her?

She traversed what seemed to be an endless distance from upstairs to the large kitchen at the back of the house, where she sat at a table with her back to the hearth while Verity poured her a bowl of broth. It occurred to Wynn that she had not stayed yesterday for the sentencing although she had read it in the faces of the jurors and judges.

"Verity," she said in a voice that gradually gained strength, "I left the court yesterday before the sentences were read. Has there been any news?"

"Yes," said Verity, looking strained.

"It's all right, Verity. I know they found Robert guilty of piracy and William and some of the others guilty as well. They'll hang, won't they?" This last was said with a straightened back as if it were she and not her husband who would face the executioner.

Then Wynn looked down her hands, finding her own sorrow doubled for Sarah's sake. She realized guiltily that she had spared little thought for her friend, so much self-pity did she harbor in her heart. But now she paused to think of Sarah as well. The poor captain. Truly their luck had completely run out.

Verity nodded. "Four others were sentenced to terms of imprisonment." Her voice faltered, and Wynn looked up, bracing herself to confront her fate. If it were possible, she would try to see Robert. Let him know she would always love him.

As they sat there, the sound of a great commotion in the street outside the house intruded on their consciousness. Verity went to the door to see what it was and Wynn followed her.

"They're hanging Captain Culliford today," Verity said. Then she turned, blocking the door from Wynn. "Don't look out," she said.

But Wynn looked past her and saw the cortege led by the admiral's deputy marshal, in an open carriage, bearing on his shoulder the silver oar that symbolized the authority and power of the admiralty. Other officials followed behind him. Finally there came a black-draped tumbrel carrying the condemned man, and she recognized the pirate that had held her captive. He had been tried and found guilty the month before.

It was odd that she felt nothing, not even a sense of revenge, perhaps because tomorrow her husband would meet this same fate. In spite of Verity's objections, she ran out into the street and followed the cortege as it moved over the cobblestones past the Royal Exchange. She elbowed her way forward until she could see Culliford better. He leered at the crowd, making lewd gestures while the crowd, taunting the pirate and screaming for Arabian gold and pieces of eight, milled around the tumbrel. There was even a ballad sung by the raucous crowd:

> "Farwell the raging main,
> I must die, I must die,
> Farwell the raging main,
> I must die."

Now they passed the square keep of the Tower of London and on to the Execution Dock at Wapping on the Thames. Here worn stone steps known as the

Pirates' Staircase led down to the muddy river. Wynn was pressed forward, and as the cart pulled to a halt, she caught Culliford's eye. He looked back at her for a moment, and she thought his lip lifted in a sneer. Then he was yanked to his feet and led down the steps. Beside the scaffold stood the chaplain, who approached the pirate and said something to him.

Then suddenly she wanted to get away. She had not meant to witness this. She turned and tried to push herself back through the crowd, but they hemmed her in. Behind her the chaplain sang a penitential psalm while the crowd chanted, and she was thrown forward, forced to confront the scaffold, where the hangman in his ominous black hood was fitting the noose around Culliford's neck.

Horrified at what was about to happen, Wynn covered her eyes with her hands, fighting the wave of nausea. She stood thus for some moments when an even louder shriek went up from the crowd. Involuntarily she opened her eyes and watched as the hangman pushed Culliford into space. The rope jerked with his weight, and he swung. Hands reached out, pushing and pulling him, and a wizened old man next to Wynn cackled. "A good hangin', it's as good a hangin' as I ever seen."

There the pirate's body would remain as the sun rotted it, the gulls pecked at it, and the tide washed at its feet, for it was the custom to leave bodies thus exposed as a lesson to all evildoers.

Wynn's own throat constricted, and she felt herself begin to slip over the edge of madness as she clawed her way back through the whores, sailors, and old harpies who were still carousing. She gasped as she finally reached the fringes of the crowd and reeled toward a stoop. Leaning over the side of the steps, she retched until she thought she would pass out.

"Excuse me, madam," said a voice behind her. She turned to face a portly gentleman whose face swam before her. "Do you need some help?" he asked. "You are not well."

She shook her head and forced the words out. "No, I'm all right." Then she sank to the steps and he walked on.

She hugged her knees to her chest and buried her wails and sobs in her skirts. She did not know how long she sat there. Finally, when the gray sun faded, she realized it was not safe to be out at that late hour. She pulled herself up and found her way home. As she reached the house, Verity ran down the steps and swept her up.

"My dear girl. I was so worried. Where did you go?" Gently she led Wynn up the steps and into the house.

Verity made Wynn drink some hot tea and rest in the parlor.

"Do you want to talk about it, Wynn, dear?"

Wynn gulped the tasteless tea. "It was awful, I . . ." But when she tried to describe the scene, the words knotted in her throat. She finally shook her head.

"No," she said. "I think I'll go to my room now."

"Of course."

Upstairs she lay on her bed, staring at the ceiling, for how long, she did not know. Hours later she was roused by voices, then footsteps and a rap on her door.

Verity, not waiting for Wynn to answer, burst in.

Wynn sat up. "What is it?"

"Robert's been pardoned," said Verity. "The news just came." Wynn just stared into the woman's face, unable to trust herself to speak.

"Apparently the admiralty decided that Captain Kidd's sentence would be lesson enough. A royal pardon was handed down for Robert."

Wynn tried to absorb this information, her heart bursting with emotion and her eyes filling with tears. "You mean Robert is free?"

"He soon will be if gossip doesn't travel faster than

the deed itself. I sent word as to where you were. He'll come to you, child, as soon as he is able."

"He'll come here?" Then she cried unrestrainedly from relief, the tears flowing down her cheeks and soaking the handkerchief Verity gave her. After the long outburst, she began to mop her face.

"I must get ready," she murmured. "Robert, oh, Robert. I cannot believe it."

Verity ordered the maid to bring her a bath. Wynn took deep breaths to clear her head, then undressed and stepped into the water, impatiently splashing about. She let the maid scrub her and brush her hair. When she was clean, she reached for a fluffy towel to dry herself. After powdering her soft skin, she stepped into fresh linens. Her hands shook as she fastened her petticoats.

Suddenly she froze and listened. Downstairs she heard a door slam and then voices — Verity's and a man's.

"Robert! It's my husband," she said to the maid. "Hurry!"

The maid handed her her dress, but just then boots clumped on the stairs, and the door opened. Wynn was halfway into her dress as Robert stepped into the room, the maid beating a hasty retreat.

"Oh, Robert!" she gasped, as he walked toward her. She let the dress fall in a heap about her feet as his two strong arms, made somewhat thinner by prison life, encircled her. She reached up and put her arms around his neck and buried her face in his shoulder.

"My dearest," he said, kissing her hair. "My brave one. You are safe."

"I?" she cried, looking up at him as tears streamed down her face. "It is you I have been so worried about."

For a few moments they embraced, constantly touching each other's face as if to reassure themselves that they were finally together and safe from harm. She could feel Robert's ribs under his shirt and his eyes looked sunken, but he was well and whole. She held him tightly, still afraid to believe their good fortune.

Finally he lifted her chin and when he looked at her she saw there were tears in his eyes as well. Then he kissed her hungrily and took his time caressing her. When he released her mouth, he whispered, "I'll never let you go again. The sea will no longer claim us, my love. We'll put this all behind us."

"When can we go home, Robert?"

"As soon as we can find passage."

"Oh thank God. How I long to see home again — with you, that is."

He looked at her, a smile beginning to fill his eyes. "You want to return to New York?"

"Oh yes. For that is where I met you."

Then he looked more seriously at her. "Would it not remind you of the tragedy that has befallen our friends?"

She straightened her back. "It will remind us of what we've learned. Our life is there now."

He looked into the distance. "Yes, I would leave England quickly. There is nothing I can do for William now." Wynn knew Robert had his own dark memories to forget, as well.

"What will you do if you do not go to sea?" she asked.

But he smiled down at her, reassuring her that he had put the temptations of sailing behind him. "I will be a wealthy merchant."

She lay her head on his shoulder. "Robert, I don't care about wealth, as long as we are together."

He laughed. "But we shall have both. Let the other devils who are still seduced by the sea bring us riches from all parts of the globe. I shall sit in our country house and let you read to me in front of the fireplace."

She smiled wistfully. It would be a long time until their bitter memories faded, but she drew strength from him. She knew she could never get enough of him, touching him, holding him. If it were possible to put the events of these stormy months to rest, the future could hold riches of another sort for them. She closed her eyes and pictured the peaceful landscape of the farms that lay north of New York. Then she imagined the happy faces of their friends and families meeting them on the quay.

Even Sarah, beautiful Sarah, torn apart by grief as she might be, was still young enough to make a life for herself. Wynn remembered Sarah's determination not to see her husband hanged, and Wynn knew she had made the right decision. She would find solace at home.

Wynn relaxed as Robert began to kiss away her salty tears. She responded to his hands as they moved over her body.

"My husband," she murmured, tingling at his touch. She was still in her petticoat, and Robert lifted her onto the bed. Then he came to her, his eyes and hands caressing her.

"My love," he sighed as he undressed and peeled away her petticoats. Then they lay together, drinking in the feel of each other's flesh. So near a loss had heightened their need and desire for one another. They both indulged in pleasure then, taking comfort in what they had missed for so long.

The *Marianne*'s prow bore through the waves on her approach to New York. Wynn turned to Robert, standing proudly beside her, the ravages of prison life now nearly gone from his face and limbs. As the houses of Manhattan Island came into view, she turned misty eyes toward shore. There her family and his would be waiting. There too, needing comfort, would be Sarah Kidd and her daughter. And there would be friends as well. This was home at last, and as Robert slipped his arms around her shoulders, she knew, looking at the tiny settlement and the tall ships sailing in the bay, that she would never want to leave it again.